# OLD CASTLE SECRETS

## AMANDA DAIRE

Pink Elephant Press

# ALSO BY AMANDA DAIRE

Old Castle Secrets

Old Castle Sparkle

Old Castle Road Trip

Old Castle Rumors

Old Castle Courage

*For my forever mommy-in-law, Cindy Torrey. You showed me what a chosen family could be, and accepted me despite my flaws and even after the marriage ended. I'll always remember and treasure the times we had and the love and affection you showed, and your commitment to working through an issue rather than shutting me out. I hope Heaven is treating you well. We all miss you. xoxo*

# 1

## KHRISTA

Birthdays were for celebrating, so Khrista couldn't let her smile slip. Not today. Not if she intended to maintain the cheerful illusion she so carefully cultivated.

This was not the time to think about her daughter.

To bring herself back to the present and away from the things she swore not to think of during the day, Khrista tuned into the gentle humming coming from her co-teacher as Danielle cleaned up the messy preschool classroom while Khrista handled communicating with parents at dismissal.

Khrista struggled to focus on her four-year-old student, Leah, a new big sister, and the anxious words of Leah's postpartum mother.

Since becoming a preschool teacher in her middle-aged years—ever the late bloomer—Khrista had learned to compartmentalize. Usually. And she should give herself at least a little credit for dodging the emotional bombs that threatened her every day. But after years of remaining upright while fate flung brick after brick at her face, why did a tiny wisp of coppery hair have her buckling at the knees?

Transfixed, Khrista kept her smile glued firmly in place as the newborn's mom lovingly tucked the strand under a hand-knit cap.

Leah leaned over the baby carrier to plant kisses on the infant's precious forehead.

The young mom carried on as if Khrista's mind wasn't luring her away from the bright classroom and toward a bygone era. As if Khrista weren't mentally clutching the end of the balloon string, desperately trying to keep it from drifting off to get tangled in the trees.

"So you think she's adjusting fine?" Tired postpartum eyes connected with Khrista's struggling ones. Khrista smiled brightly, unwilling to let the past creep in when this mom so desperately needed reassurance.

"Leah has been *wonderful* in class. She's been playing in the dramatic play area more and more, showing her nurturing and imaginative side. Today she brought a baby doll over to study at the science table, so I'm pretty sure she'll be teaching her new sister everything she needs to become a world-class scientist." Khrista gestured toward the science corner, where the doll in question sat in the child-sized high chair as if waiting for another opportunity to play and learn.

The relief on the mom's face reminded Khrista what she loved so much about her job. True, now that she was fifty years old, it got harder and harder to lower herself into the tiny preschool chairs—and it was harder still to get back up—but nothing brightened her dreary life more than the innocence of precocious preschoolers.

And though she'd been a failure at parenting, Khrista had become adept at dispensing feedback and advice that other parents could use.

The baby squawked and, thank goodness, the mom hurried her children out the door, muttering that it was feeding time. And heaven forbid the kids should let her speak to an adult for a moment.

As soon as they left the room, Khrista collapsed into the teacher's chair they kept near the sign-in table, burying her face in her hands.

"Hey, you okay?"

Her co-teacher, the ever bouncy Miss Danielle, stopped spraying disinfectant on the table and stood upright, crinkling her otherwise smooth, young forehead in concern.

Danielle rubbed her lower back. Only a few months pregnant, she was already experiencing the aches and pains that came with growing a new life.

"Don't you dare worry about me. I'm supposed to be the one looking out for you."

Danielle pulled up a small purple chair next to Khrista's and rested her elbows on her knees. "You haven't been yourself today. Is there something I can help with?"

"You're a sweetheart for being concerned." Khrista wasn't sure how much she should share with her co-teacher. They'd grown friendly over the last two years of teaching together, but there were some things Khrista didn't share with anyone. "You want the big chair?"

Danielle smiled and shook her head.

"I'm totally fine. But I'm here to listen if you have something to vent about. I love me a good rant."

Maybe letting a bit of the truth leak out would help Khrista unburden herself from the giant weight that hovered over her head, ready to smash the delicate life she tried to build.

She released a pent-up breath, the need to unload gripping her gut and twisting hard.

"Today's my daughter's birthday. She's turning twenty-five, right around your age." Khrista choked on her words. "I just miss her a lot."

Khrista closed her eyes against the tears threatening to spill over her cheeks. She would *not* cry. She didn't deserve the relief tears might bring.

"That must be so tough having her across the country so you can't celebrate with her."

*If she only knew.* But Khrista wasn't about to share the truth of the estrangement with her co-teacher. She would do everything possible to maintain the cheerful facade she'd strived so hard to make real. If she granted front-row seats for people to view her private pain, Khrista would hate herself even more.

So she nodded. She hadn't lied exactly. She just let Danielle continue to believe what she had concluded on her own.

Danielle pouted her lips sympathetically. "Why don't you head out early today? I'll take care of the rest of the cleanup."

Danielle's empathy was almost Khrista's undoing.

Instead of arguing, Khrista nodded.

"I appreciate that, Danielle. I'll come in early to set up and you can spend extra time in bed with your crackers and ginger ale. I swear that's the only thing that helped me cope with the morning sickness when I was pregnant. Oh, and ginger candies. Always keep those in your pocket."

"Good idea—I'll stock up. How is it possible something so tiny can cause this much distress?"

Oh, if she only knew how much distress something she grew inside her could cause. But Khrista wasn't about to break that news to the young mom-to-be. She'd find out for herself as soon as the child grew old enough to realize she was no longer linked physically to her mother.

Then again, maybe Danielle would be a perfect mother and her son or daughter would never want to leave her. Khrista had no idea what a perfect mother looked like, but she knew the reflection of a failed one. She saw one every day in the mirror.

Khrista could usually shove those negative vibes far away from the space she knew as her happy place. Today, her strength wavered.

She stood and reached for her purse on the shelf behind her chair. "Don't worry about putting away all the paints at the easel. They're already covered, and I figured we could let the kiddos have a finger-painting extravaganza to get us through tomorrow's rainy day."

Danielle rocked back and forth from her heels to her toes as if soothing her growing baby. "Sounds good to me! But only if we can add heaps of glitter on top of the paint."

Danielle's mischievous smile warmed the room.

"You're just dying for Adriana's dad to complain to the director again, aren't you?"

"I know I haven't been a teacher long, but I can't believe parents actually complain about their children having too much fun."

"Crazy, right?" Khrista and Danielle often vented to each other about the parents who ignored all the communications they sent out about the importance of getting messy while learning through play. But today Khrista was feeling a bit more sympathetic. "These poor parents have had too many people telling them it's undignified to get messy. I'm glad we can show them it's okay."

Khrista's mind flashed back to that time in kindergarten her mother scolded her for getting her new dress dirty. She rubbed her temple, feeling a headache coming on. Not unusual when she remembered her childhood.

How were so many thoughts—thoughts she tried to avoid as desperately as she avoided spiders and chipmunks—seeping into her conscious state? Normally, the walls were thicker.

"Are you okay, Khrista? You look like you're about to fall over. Maybe I should drive you home."

"No, I'm good. I just—" *It's been a long day of pretending to be okay...* "I don't think I had enough water today. Feeling a bit woozy, but I'll hydrate and get back to normal."

She forced a smile, hoping her stiff cheeks wouldn't crack under the pressure. She'd get through this.

"If you're sure. But I wouldn't mind swinging by your street to drop you off. Honest."

Khrista waved her hand in dismissal. "Truly, do not worry about me. I'm completely fine to drive. See?"

Khrista guzzled her water for show and then wasted no time grabbing her coat from the back of her chair. She dug for her keys in her purse as Danielle asked her what she thought of the agenda for the upcoming staff meeting.

"I haven't seen it yet. Is it posted on the bulletin board?"

Danielle laughed. "You're still not checking emails? Susan is trying to get us to go paperless."

"I never remember. Besides, the only emails I usually get are for trainings I'm not going to and offers for discounts at teacher supply stores." Parents weren't supposed to email teachers directly, as Susan, the director, preferred all communication to go through her first, so Khrista never thought trying to remember how to log into her email was a worthwhile effort.

"Okay, but if you don't read your email, you won't know we're all supposed to write Valentine hearts with what we love about our fellow staff members." Danielle formed her hands into a playful heart shape and fluttered her eyelashes.

Khrista rolled her eyes and told Danielle she would see her in the morning, and did her best not to slip on the ice in the small parking lot on the way to her car.

Her hands shaking, she closed the door and gripped the steering wheel. Her mind spun in directions that would do nothing but slice her open. She needed something. Anything to numb the pain.

But numbing the pain hadn't served her well up to this point. She needed to do better. And right now, as much as Khrista wanted privacy, she shouldn't be alone.

Though Danielle would have been good company, Khrista didn't want to keep her young co-teacher from getting home to her loving husband.

Ignoring the impulse to run and hide in her dark apartment, the one she rented as close to the beach as she could afford on this little island she couldn't bring herself to leave, Khrista forced herself to drive to the tea shop in town. There, she was sure to find the distraction she needed to prevent her from turning down a dark path.

Five years had passed since Khrista had last seen her daughter. Five long, painful years in which she had struggled to forget the horrible things they said to one another. Five years in which she continued to make the mistakes Kaelyn had accused her of all along. Five years in which she promised herself to get her act together so she would deserve the love of her daughter.

Now, on an icy, rainy Wednesday afternoon in February, her

daughter would celebrate another birthday without hearing her mother's wishes for her.

A stable home. Cheerful friendships. A loving relationship.

Healing from the wounds Khrista had given her.

*Twenty-five years old.*

Khrista's age when she had given birth to Kaelyn.

Something about that fact made the pain of missing her daughter more intense than it had been the previous four birthdays she had missed. It didn't make sense, she knew that, but the part of her that begged for a mind-numbing round of Fireball shots didn't register the nonsensical nature of her thoughts.

After parking outside the tea shop, Khrista checked her image in the rearview mirror and attempted to straighten the frizz. Moistening the tip of her index finger, she cleaned the spot of purple paint away from the side of her nose, grateful she had looked in the mirror before entering the tearoom. She inhaled deeply, counted to three and then three more, and exhaled, hoping her brain would slow down with the meditative breathing. She carefully counted the wooden steps that led onto the covered porch of the old Victorian home-turned-tearoom—one, two, three, four—reminding herself that though the last thing she wanted was to be surrounded by people, company was what she needed.

As soon as Khrista pulled open the heavy door to Happil-TEA Ever After Tea Room, she was greeted by a flurry of fluff and energy as a blur of kittens chased one another, scrambling right over her feet.

Therapeutic laughter tumbled out of her as the kittens rolled around and wreaked havoc throughout the shop. Of all the things Khrista loved about this place, the Kit-TEA Comfort Rescue and the rescue cats who resided there in the tearoom until they found their *furever* homes were easily her favorite.

"Pay them no mind. They're learning to settle in. Old Chester will teach them soon enough. So far, they're giving him a wide berth."

Clarice, the sixty-something-year-old owner of the tearoom, brushed a strand of silver hair away from her eye with the back of her hand. Her apron displayed multi-colored teacups, along with the words *"Tea doesn't discriminate"* emblazoned across the chest. She gestured to Khrista, inviting her to follow her to the counter.

"Come on over. I sense you need something warm and comforting."

"Your tea sense is never wrong," Khrista admitted, smiling the brightest smile she could muster. The one she used in the classroom to trick everyone into thinking she was the eternal sparkly, rolled-in-glitter-and-never-sad optimist.

Clarice closed her eyes and waved her hands around in front of her as if summoning a spirit. "The tea tells me you would enjoy a chocolate strawberry blend, topped with frothed almond milk creamer."

Khrista gasped playfully. "The tea is as wise as you are. That sounds heavenly."

Clarice threw her head back and laughed, displaying a neck that didn't betray her age.

Khrista had known Clarice for twenty years—ever since Khrista pulled into the small island town off the coast of southern New Hampshire in a beat-up station wagon brimming with the remnants of her old life, her five-year-old daughter in the back seat. Clarice had been the first to welcome the bedraggled mother, promising that whatever she had been through on her journey to Old Castle, she now belonged to a community that would wrap her in its warmth.

A chosen family.

Clarice had kept that promise. The island was everything Khrista had hoped for—the best place to raise a daughter on her own. A place where the locals would keep her secrets even if they didn't know them and where none of the evil of her past could catch up to her.

This warm, fuzzy protection, coupled with memories of the best times of her life, brought her back to the island five years ago, wishing she had never left. Wishing she had found a way to stay back then.

And though Khrista could barely afford the studio apartment she rented, even with her landlord's generous price break, she would do her best to stay in the town where memories of her daughter animated every corner.

"You seem lost in thought," Clarice commented, passing the steaming cup of tea over the antique countertop. "My ears are always open for listening if you have a worry or two you'd like to share."

Khrista raised the teacup to her nose and inhaled the sweet scent. "How could I have any worries when I'm about to indulge in this heavenly cup of goodness?"

"I hope it hits the spot. And I hope you know I'm here if you need me."

Khrista reached across the counter and placed a hand over Clarice's. "I've always known that. You serve far more than the best tea, and I appreciate it more than you could know."

Clarice's eyes watered slightly, but the unshed tears did nothing to diminish the sparkle in her youthful-if-aging-around-the-corners eyes.

Khrista squeezed her friend's hand lightly before pulling away and cupping the warm mug. She sipped, knowing the temperature would be just right. She moaned as her taste buds welcomed the tantalizing treat.

"This blend may be my new favorite. You've outdone yourself, my friend."

"You say that every time," Clarice teased, pleasure at the praise tinging her laughter.

"Do the new kittens like cuddles? Or should I stick to my favorite ginger, Mr. Ed?" Khrista perused the room, avoiding the faces of the humans in favor of finding the cat whose purrs always settled whatever storm threatened to carry Khrista away. Sure, she had ventured to the tearoom to find companionship, but that didn't mean she had to engage in conversation...

"You know good old Ed is always waiting to warm your lap. He's been hiding since the kittens arrived, but if you go ahead and take your usual spot, he'll greet you in no time." Clarice nodded toward Khrista's preferred table in the side room near the small corner bookshelves and the stone fireplace. With all the interior double doors opened wide and secured with brick doorstops, several of the side rooms could be seen from the counter.

"By the way," Clarice added, "good old Ed isn't averse to the idea of adoption."

Khrista groaned. "If I had the space, I'd welcome all of your adorable furry friends into my home."

Clarice's smile broadened as two kittens jumped onto the counter and raced to the other side, knocking over a pile of event flyers in their wake.

Careful not to spill her tea, Khrista bent to retrieve the papers from the plank wood floor, appreciating the nostalgic creak of the wood as she shifted her feet.

Clarice shook her head and chuckled as the kittens scurried under tables and over feet, causing a ripple of excitement among the tea-sipping, chattering patrons. "We only get one life to live. Might as well fill it with love."

Her words struck Khrista in the heart, and something told her that's where Clarice had intended them to land. Was it any wonder the people in town referred to Clarice and her community of do-gooders as the Love Warriors? She excelled at sniper attacks of nurturing.

Breaking eye contact so Clarice wouldn't stare directly into her soul, Khrista brought the lightly steaming tea to her lips and turned to resume her task of searching for the comforts she craved—her favorite spot and the cat she adored.

Upon turning, however, she nearly choked on her tea. Luckily, the liquid slid down her throat before she embarrassed herself.

Standing directly behind her was a tall, graceful young woman whose copper hair and vivid green eyes reminded Khrista of the day Kaelyn hurried home to tell her all about the "other redhead" she had befriended and how they stood up against the other third graders who picked on them for their unique coloring. Sienna's family had hosted Kaelyn for countless family trips and sleepovers, even though Khrista had been unable to reciprocate. Sienna's mother baked cookies and packed nutritious picnic lunches when the girls went for beach hikes on the weekends.

Sienna had been Kaelyn's best childhood friend. The friend Kaelyn had eventually mourned. Because of Khrista.

Ducking her head, Khrista maneuvered around her, hoping after all these years Sienna wouldn't recognize—or maybe even remember—her.

"Kaelyn's mom—how *are* you? It's been *forever*."

"Oh, goodness. I didn't see you there. How are you, Sienna?" *Please don't want to make small talk. Please be in a hurry to leave.*

*Please don't bring up the past.*

"I *so* wish I had time to catch up with you, but I'm meeting my parents for dinner and just needed to swing by to grab a chai latte so I can stay awake. Jet lag, ugh."

"I won't keep you. You came to the right place for the best chai."

Khrista started toward the bookcase, but Sienna shot a well-manicured hand out to grab her arm.

"I haven't talked to Kaelyn in ages, but I saw her birthday post on Facebook today. You must be so insanely excited to be a soon-to-be grandmom! That post was the cutest. But Kaelyn has always been so creative. Congratulations!"

Bomb dropped, Sienna didn't wait for Khrista to respond. She tapped Khrista on her bony shoulder and went to place her order.

The room swerved, and Khrista's hands trembled violently, sloshing tea onto her sneaker, already stained with tempera paint from her time in the classroom.

*Grandmom.*

Kaelyn was having a baby.

Something lodged in her throat, and breathing became as impossible as fixing her dysfunction. Her vision narrowed until all she could focus on was the exit.

*Run. Get out.*

She thrust her cup onto a vacant table and rushed to the door. Khrista struggled to unlock her car from her key fob as she hastened down the steps.

A quarreling elderly sibling pair blocked her escape at the foot of the stairs.

*Not now, Gerard and Geraldine. Take it elsewhere.*

The aging twins didn't seem troubled by Khrista's presence. Gerard's hunched back stiffened at Geraldine's tone, but he crossed his arms over his plaid jacket and turned toward the street.

Khrista cleared her rapidly closing throat. "Excuse me, please. I can't quite fit around you."

Her nostrils flaring, Geraldine ignored the polite request and planted her hands on her rounded hips. "Gerard is being unreasonable. As usual. He wants a scone and a hot drink but does nothing but complain once we get here. If Clarice is serving blueberry muffins, he wants lemon squares. If she's serving lemon squares, he wants a scone. If she offers a scone, he wants a different kind. You'd think by his age he'd have learned to be grateful for what he gets! I refuse to go in with him acting like this. He's humiliating."

Khrista felt for Geraldine; she really did. But she didn't have the energy or the will to help them hash out their all-too-familiar sibling battles.

"Gerard, Clarice just made a fresh batch of cranberry scones. If I remember correctly, that's your favorite."

Gerard huffed, his exasperated breath forming thick puffs in the cold, late-afternoon air. "She'd be better off marketing them as door stoppers than scones. I will never understand the fuss everyone around here makes over her baked garbage."

Khrista fought the urge to roll her eyes. Clarice had won loads of baking contests, and people made special trips to the island so they could stock up on her treats, often by the dozen. The only complaint Khrista had ever heard was that Clarice didn't offer online ordering.

Besides Gerard's constant complaints, of course.

But Khrista had been around long enough to remember when Gerard had served as chairman of the Board of Selectman and had insisted on Clarice providing the refreshments for all meetings.

Geraldine threw her hands up in the air in exasperation. "Then why did you make me bring you here? I was settled in for the evening with my cocoa and–"

Khrista interrupted Geraldine's less-than-helpful tirade.

"You probably need some caffeine in your system to chase away your crankies." Khrista hoped her jovial tone would lighten the mood so they could move on.

She attempted to step around them, terrified the next person to walk out the door would be Sienna. The need to escape had never been stronger. She had to get out of there. She couldn't break in public.

Gerard moved in front of her, his determination overpowering Khrista's fatigue. She was seconds away from crumbling, and she'd rather not turn to dust so publicly.

He shook a gnarled finger inches from her face. "Don't talk down to me like one of your little children. I'm a grown man and demand respect."

"I don't talk down to anyone, Gerard. Not you and not my preschoolers. If you'll excuse me..."

Craning her neck to look past him, she frantically clicked her fob once again.

Seizing Gerard's arm, Geraldine intervened. "Let her by, Gerard. You've been rude enough."

Gerard waved an angry hand in the air but stepped aside enough for her to pass. Khrista took advantage of the momentary act of consideration and bolted toward her waiting sedan.

The lock took mercy on her and granted her admission to her vehicle. She slammed the door behind her, shielding herself from the outside world and the news she had least expected to hear.

She was going to be a grandmother.

In name only, of course, and only by virtue of genetics.

Tears wouldn't come—they never did for her. The only liquid relief in her life currently taunted her from the glove compartment.

*Don't do it. Be strong.*

But she wasn't strong. Not today. Not now.

Khrista reached over and helped herself to the emergency nips of alcohol she kept in the glove compartment, wishing she had taken the tea to go so she'd have a mixer. She placed one small bottle between her thighs and gripped the other like a lifeline.

Gerard and Geraldine had disappeared into the tearoom, so Khrista let the silence and solitude wash over her like a gentle wave.

She turned the key in the ignition and cracked the window, needing to hear the roar of the ocean behind the tearoom. She closed her eyes and inhaled deeply, breathing in the cold, salty air.

The click of the cap unscrewing satisfied something deep within, and the burning liquid as it slid down her throat comforted her like the bedtime stories she should have told.

Checking to be sure no one was around to see her, Khrista leaned forward and slipped the empty bottle under her seat, then clutched the other in her hand as she shifted into gear. The first nip had been medicinal. The second would be careless.

She'd wait until she returned home. And then all bets were off.

*Grandmom.*

What would she want to be called?

Why torture herself with these painful questions when they'd never matter, anyway?

A few minutes later, she pulled into the parking lot of her small, two-story apartment building, praying she wouldn't run into Rafael, the widowed owner of the building and a sort of father figure to her since she had first washed up in Old Castle. Khrista didn't see his blue pickup parked in his usual spot by the garage, so she quickly gathered her things and hustled into the building, her palm itching to twist open the small bottle she held so dearly.

Khrista dropped her purse and tote bag on the floor directly inside her door, the thud as they landed nearly identical to the sound of her heart pounding in her ears. She leaned against her closed door and downed the nip of vodka with her eyes closed.

As if she could pretend she wasn't doing what she shouldn't be doing.

Her limbs relaxed in that liquored sort of way she was all too familiar with, and Khrista found the strength to slink further into her apartment, shedding the day behind her as she slithered to the bar. She had wanted to make her liquor collection look more sophisticated than having it piled up on the tiny countertop, so finding a tiny kitchen island discarded on a sidewalk in front of a house a block away delighted her. One person's trash quickly became Khrista's minibar.

After fetching a highball glass from the cabinet beneath the island countertop, she poured the ingredients to mix herself a Tidal Wave, a drink that conjured images of lounging on the beach rather than surviving an emotional tsunami. She poured the last of her rum, cursing herself for forgetting to drive off-island into Portsmouth to stock up when she knew she was running low, and added extra gin to compensate for the absence.

Clutching the drink, she hastily grabbed the bottle of peach schnapps with her other hand. This was going to be one of those nights. Khrista dragged herself to her sofa, used one foot to swipe the pile of laundry to the floor, and planted herself onto the cushion.

Normally a drink or two or three could satisfy her need.

There was nothing normal about today.

*Grandmom.*

Would Kaelyn's baby have the same hair as her momma? Would it be as shiny as a newly minted penny? Who was the father? Would he contribute the same coloring? Or would he gift the child with black hair to contrast with Kaelyn's?

The questions flowing through her mind turned her sipping into gulping, and right when Khrista started drinking directly from the bottle of schnapps, she had the brilliant idea to break her own rule about forgetting the past.

Buzzed laughter erupted as she stumbled back to her purse by the door and bent over to retrieve her phone. She stopped at her bar on the way back to the sofa, snatching the vodka and cradling the bottle in her arms maternally.

This was justified. Anyone would want to drink away the memories if they had a day like the one she had.

Khrista settled back onto the couch and checked her phone.

Multiple texts from Matt, her sort-of boyfriend, lit up her screen. She squinted to see clearly. Since turning fifty a few weeks ago, her eyesight had taken a turn for the worse. She hadn't surrendered to the idea that she needed reading glasses, but as the blurred words swam in front of her and her eyes ached, she thought she should reconsider.

"Hey, babe. Hope you're okay. I know it's K's birthday and you'll probably be sad again since you can't spend the day with her. Next year I hope you'll take me up on my offer to fly you out there (or fly her here if she wants.) Want company? Been trying to reach you, but you must be busy. Xo"

How to respond to a man she'd been lying to about the state of her relationship with her daughter?

Matt was a family man. His adult daughters ruled his world. He'd never understand that she had alienated hers. She had family secrets while he had family brunches. When his girls had problems, they went to their dad for help. And though Khrista had avoided meeting them for all these years, making sure she had excuses anytime they visited the island, Matt's stories of them made her feel as if she had known them all along.

Heck, from the moment she had met him when he had given the diversity training at a staff meeting at her school, he had exuded family man charm. When Khrista thanked him for sharing his experiences as a Black man who had lived in various small towns, she had easily slipped into the make-believe role of a loving mother whose only problem with her daughter was a made-up three thousand mile distance. He had made her feel so normal. So wanted. He had looked at her like she was worth something.

She had so desperately wanted to be worth something.

So Khrista lied.

And then, as things grew more serious between them, the lies became more complex.

She hadn't meant for it to happen. She hadn't known they'd go on a first date, let alone three years' worth of dates.

Keeping him at arm's length became harder and harder every day, but she wasn't ready for Matt to uncover the truth, so she kept her mouth closed and the distance between them open.

He'd leave her once he knew who and what she really was.

It was selfish to string him along, but Matt was the only true joy she had in life.

She was selfish. Hadn't Kaelyn pointed that out to her?

She didn't respond to his texts—didn't even read the earlier ones. What could she say when her world had her by the throat?

Her tired eyelids drooped, and her bottle ran dry. Had she been about to search for something online?

Oh yes, her daughter's social media post. Khrista had never searched for Kaelyn on social media before, respecting her daughter's screamed commands.

*"Don't ever try to find me. I never want to see you or hear from you again!"*

Slammed doors and red-faced commands didn't lie.

But mothers did.

When they didn't know how to fix what they broke.

The consumed alcohol made her unsteady on her feet, but fatigue had settled in and Khrista needed her bed. She could look for her daughter on her phone once she was settled in for the night. No use falling asleep on the couch again and waking up to a stiff neck. Fifty wasn't as forgiving as thirty, and couch-sleeping wasn't what it used to be.

One more drink. To ease the pain.

Khrista struggled to open the bottle. Couldn't see the label to know what she was opening, but whatever it was would be the liquid bandage for her broken soul. She was sure of it.

Her hand cramped as she tried to twist the lid. The room bobbed. She laughed a little.

She was such a fraud. If the parents of her preschoolers could see her now, they'd be shocked. The rumors would fly. Community members would rush to fix her. To uncover the truth. They'd tell her life was too short to allow an estrangement of this magnitude.

"Blast you!" Khrista threw the bottle, immediately regretting her fit of rage when the glass shattered all over her wall.

She'd clean it up tomorrow. Along with the rest of the mess in her apartment.

Bed was calling.

Stumbling, Khrista tripped on the rug that separated her bedroom space from her living room space. She slammed her head hard on the corner of the bureau on her way down.

Blood welled at her temple, but she was too tired to brush it away. Instead, she remained there on her floor, bleeding onto the pile of magazines she had meant to recycle.

Khrista closed her eyes, pretty sure she should call for help, but too numb to bother.

# KAELYN

**K**aelyn leaned back and rested her head on her husband's solid but comfy chest as they stood together in the large, sparkling white kitchen of their new home. No matter how frail the foundation of her world sometimes felt, he was always there to remind her that her new life was built on solid ground.

With his arms wrapped around her soon-to-be-expanding waist, he cradled both her and their baby-to-be with all the love and care she had learned to expect from him.

"Every one of my wishes has come true, and it's all because of you." His murmured English-accented words in her ear sent chills over her shoulders, causing her to squeeze the arms that held her so dearly.

"I could say the same for you, husband."

Oliver moaned into her ear. "Why are you so perfect?"

She turned into him, eagerly accepting his kisses and pressing into his passion.

Doubts crept into her mind, though the rational part of her knew they made no sense. Still, she had learned after her childhood of trauma that if she didn't voice her concerns, they would eat her up and destroy any relationships she cherished along the way.

"Are you sure you're okay with this, Oliver? We hadn't really talked about when—"

His interrupting kiss was rougher than normal, igniting her desire and reminding her that nothing could impede this love of theirs.

Not the past. Not the present. The future was all theirs.

He pulled away, his eyes seeking hers, almost daring her not to see the truth in the blue swirly depths.

"Finding out we're pregnant was the second best thing I've ever heard. A close second to when you agreed to marry me."

Fighting tears—she knew she didn't deserve this man, but hoped he'd never figure it out—Kaelyn wrapped her arms around his trim waist, resting her head over her favorite place, where his heart thumped the most beautiful of all love stories.

Oliver kissed the top of her head, lingering there, smelling her freshly shampooed hair.

"That we found out on your birthday and on our first night in our dream home..." His voice cracked and he hugged her tighter to him. "You can't tell me fate hasn't played a part in this life we're building."

She pulled back slightly, desperate to see his eyes again. She saw herself reflected in his emotional depths, and she was shocked at the beauty she saw there.

Not that she herself was beautiful. No, she had never seen herself that way, though Oliver told her every day that her cursed red hair and her face full of freckled flaws was enchanting and adorable. Kaelyn didn't agree but had learned to accept that he saw her that way.

Pregnancy hormones, or perhaps it was simply his love, had her feeling more beautiful today than any other day in her life.

And this life? The *most* beautiful. More than she had ever imagined for herself.

Kaelyn placed a hand on his cheek, loving the scruff he hadn't yet shaved rasping against her palm. "I'm so glad we did the test together. I didn't know how to feel, but watching the hopeful joy on your face reassured me that everything was okay, even if we were straying from our planned timeline."

"I would have been upset if you did the test without me. Our relationship is strong because we don't keep things from one another."

Kaelyn forced her body to remain relaxed, though every part of her threatened to tighten. She had always been honest with Oliver, and yet there were some things she tried not to think about and so had never shared.

Oliver kissed the top of her head. "My father was a great man and I think my parents had a good marriage, but he kept secrets from my mum too often. Never anything major, but enough to erode my mother's trust in him. We'll never be like that."

She fought the nausea rising in her gut. She smiled up at him, hoping he wouldn't notice the discomfort she tried to hide.

"I think we can agree this way will be better than anything we could have dreamed or planned." Oliver grasped her hands between his bigger ones and lifted them to his lips, lovingly dropping a tiny kiss on each knuckle. "No matter what happens in this life, it will be better because we're together."

She believed him. She believed *in* him. Just as he believed in her, despite anything she may have believed about herself.

This house. This life. This baby.

Perfection.

All was right in her world, and she had no need to worry about a thing.

"I love you, Oliver."

"And I love you." He bent down to kiss her belly. "And you, baby Fox."

He cleared his throat and straightened his spine, his expression turning from mushy love to fierce determination.

"We should probably try to get some tasks completed before lunch. Go put your feet up and work on growing that baby for us."

Her giggle surprised her. Kaelyn wasn't one for giggling or being silly in general, but he coaxed out strange aspects of her personality she hadn't known existed, even after four years together.

"I don't think I need to do much to grow the baby at this point.

He's the size of a seed, if that." She didn't really know but thought she heard something like that before.

"Oh, assuming it's a boy, are we? I hate to break it to you, my love, but you are wrong." Oliver touched her still flat belly. "This will be a little girl, with your hair, your eyes, your joyous laughter, and eventually, if we're lucky, I'll forget to put sunscreen on her so she can develop your adorable freckles."

He brought his index finger up to tap the freckles around her cheeks and nose. She wrinkled her nose in response. She had never been a fan of her freckles, but Oliver made her feel as though they were the most unique artistry on a canvas that refused to be bland.

Though it seemed like she was still honeymooning with her loving husband, Kaelyn did want to accomplish something on the days she had taken off work. They had a new home to settle into, unpacking to do, and, later, a beach to explore.

She had thought a week ago that buying this home right near the ocean—they couldn't yet afford beachfront property, but from the upstairs bedroom window they could almost see the shore across the street—was the cherry on top of a glorious life sundae, but finding out she was carrying his child added heaps of cherries on top. And full-fat, real dairy whipped cream.

And sprinkles. Loads of them.

This was her chance. Her chance to prove she could break the cycle. To put an end to the pain her mother's parenting—if you could call it that—had inflicted on her.

"If you're sure you don't need me in here, I'll sort our clothes and get the bureaus and closets organized."

Oliver kissed the tip of her nose, then each of her cheeks, and finally landed upon her waiting lips.

"Call me if you need anything. I wouldn't mind coming to the bedroom to assist you."

"Mmm," she moaned and reached up to yank his head down to hers for a deeper kiss. "That can be our reward."

He squeezed her, and she laughed, pulling away to get to work. The smile wouldn't leave her face, and she paused to watch him retrieve his tools from the makeshift tool bench on the other side of the kitchen. He had never been overly handy, but watching him wield that hammer made something deep in her belly dance.

He groaned at her, the flush across his cheeks betraying his matching thoughts. "Stop looking at me like that or we'll get nothing done."

Kaelyn sucked her lower lip into her mouth and grinned, winking saucily before turning away.

Before she made it to the bottom of the stairs, a wave of nostalgia slammed into her chest, warming her and accelerating her blood flow.

She spun toward him and announced, "I'm glad I blew off that frat party senior year and decided to hang out with the geeky computer English dude down the hall instead."

Without missing a beat, Oliver responded, his voice echoing off the empty walls. "And I'm glad I was so drawn to that almost-emo sad girl who flipped my world around completely."

He whistled, and she took the stairs two at a time, floating on a cloud of love all the way to the bedroom.

It was true. She had been sad. He had been geeky. She wasn't sad anymore. What was there to be sad about?

He was still a bit geeky but in all the best, hottest ways. Oliver took care of her, and she took care of him.

Kaelyn never had a male role model in her home, not really, but her baby would. Between her mother hiding her from her father and then him dying when Kaelyn was still young, followed by a mother too dysfunctional to get into another relationship, Kaelyn had gone without.

And now she was the kind of person who found joy folding her husband's boxer briefs and lining them up neatly next to hers in a drawer. Sure, she could give him his own underwear drawer, but for now, at least, she wanted their intimate garments to remain together. Just like in that first teensy apartment when she and Oliver had moved off campus to live together, gambling that this magical thing that sparked between them could carry them through the getting-to-know-you-more period and into a lifetime of happiness.

They hadn't been wrong.

She sat on the edge of the bed and cupped her belly, already loving the fresh addition to their family.

She wouldn't think of the past.

That was a sure way to ruin the present.

Kaelyn busied herself with unpacking the framed photos she wanted placed on all the surfaces of their room, too uncomfortable to sit with the silence. Silence was where darkness lurked, and she wouldn't allow any stress to creep into her life and to infect the environment in which her baby needed to thrive.

Hours later, when the room was orderly and peaceful with everything in its place, she followed the sounds of a hammer banging and found her husband hanging family portraits in the spacious foyer.

She circled her arms around his waist from behind, and he paused in his banging to squeeze her arms with his free hand.

"I like when you're all sweaty." She kissed his back, the wet heat penetrating his t-shirt. "You ready to take a break for lunch? I don't know if it's too soon to claim pregnancy cravings, but I'm dying to try that Indian place down the street."

"Anything for you, love."

Though his native English accent had faded a bit, the way he pronounced his endearments still hit her hard.

"I know this isn't your favorite subject." He lowered the hammer and turned toward her. "Do you want to print off some of your family portraits? I know you don't have any physical copies with you, but I want our lives equally represented in our home, and I have so many."

The youngest of five brothers, Oliver valued family in a way that made her admire him even more.

She shook her head.

"You know I don't. But I don't feel an imbalance at all. Your family is my family."

"My mum sure thinks so," he teased. "I swear that's why she left England to move here. She claims it was because she couldn't be away from her youngest son, but I believe it's all a thinly veiled lie and she simply couldn't resist you. Can't say I blame her, though."

Her smile spread across her cheeks. She adored his mom, and while she always heard horror stories about newly married couples and mothers-in-law, Kaelyn had felt like their little circle had warmed significantly when Ruby settled so close to their spot on the California coast. Widowed shortly after Oliver moved to the states for university, Ruby had needed a change, which she had found in moving across the pond. Her other children had already married and spread out around England, and she claimed none of the spouses made her feel as welcome as Kaelyn had.

"The only family I have," she reminded him, "is the family we're building together."

He pulled her to him, caressing her hair and squeezing her shoulder.

"Are you certain? They don't have to be in your life presently for you to honor their place in your past."

Every muscle in her body tightened.

"There's nobody. My mother is dead to me, and she made sure I had no father or grandparents. Luckily, there are no siblings because I wouldn't wish her on anybody."

"Never know," he teased. "Those DNA results might surprise you with a half-sibling or something."

She jerked away and made a face. "Ha. Ha. You're not funny."

He grabbed her fleeing wrist and pulled her back.

"Apologies, love. I didn't mean to upset you. Forgive me?" He held his forehead against hers, helping her to steady her breathing.

"There's nothing to forgive, Oliver. You're nothing but considerate." She sighed. "I know you can't understand the hatred I have for my mother, but that's because you were gifted with the perfect parents."

If there was one thing that annoyed her, it was his constant desire to make her think positively about her mother.

She couldn't blame him for not understanding. She was the one who didn't want to talk about it. How could she? Thoughts of her mother and the life Kaelyn had escaped brought her right back to those dark feelings. Including that part of her life in her present, wonderful life with Oliver would be detrimental.

He made a goofy face and wiped away a drop of sweat that dripped from his temple. "You wouldn't think that if you grew up with them, but in retrospect, I don't have a lot to complain about. Hey, do I have time for a shower before we head out, or are you completely famished?"

"We have time for a shower." She grabbed his hand and led him up the stairs, gratitude and love bubbling over into intense desire for the man she was lucky enough to marry.

Nothing would burst this bubble.

Not even the ghosts of the past.

**3**

---

# DAISY

Daisy thought she'd feel more hollow, more alone after the sudden death of her husband of fifty-three years. Instead, standing in the closet she had shared with the devil himself, she felt relief.

Lonely had been a pair of pointed high heels she had metaphorically balanced on every single day of her marriage, never quite growing accustomed to the pinching of toes and never capable of slipping into well-worn, comfortable slippers. Lonely had been half-eaten dinners and burned food stuck to the bottom of pans, thanks to a man with anger issues who lived to distract her from whatever task she attempted.

Lonely had been losing her daughter.

She had lost Khrista several times, but the last time it had been final. And Khrista had taken Daisy's beloved granddaughter with her.

Twenty years of loss. Twenty years to reflect on the poor decisions she had made.

Twenty years to hate her husband more.

But Daisy could never have left him. How could she have? She had no education, no job. Her parents had taught her the value of putting her husband first, no matter how ill his temper. She had sworn an oath before God and her family, and by God, she upheld it until the day that menace keeled over in his armchair.

Five hours.

That's how long Daisy waited to call an ambulance. She knew he was dead; she wasn't heartless enough to not check his pulse. But she couldn't bring herself to make the call. Daisy hadn't been ready to admit she'd soon be free.

Everyone assumed her delayed response had been shock.

She supposed they were right. They'd never know the underlying cause of the shock, however.

Daisy had often read about women having trouble clearing out the closets of their late spouses, sniffing sweaters and crying into handfuls of ties.

She'd never be one of those women.

Ten garbage bags.

That's how many it took to hold all the clothing she tossed from his side of the closet.

She'd call a local charity to pick it all up as soon as possible.

Fifty-three years of putting away his stuff had been enough. It was time to simplify, and that meant getting rid of everything but the essentials. And nothing that belonged to him was essential to her.

Once upon a time, she had thought Harold was her savior. He swept into town in his military uniform, charming her and her friends with his sweet smile and his romantic, if pushy, ways. Daisy couldn't believe her luck when he picked her—*her!*—to be his sweetheart. She lost friends over it because she hadn't been the first to have a crush on him and they couldn't handle her good fortune. But when Harold picked her, she knew it was meant to be. He'd rescue her from her abusive, overbearing parents and she'd be given a shot at freedom.

A shot Daisy had never dreamed she'd get.

At seventeen, she had been incredibly naïve.

It had taken three months for her to realize she had traded one prison for another, and one man's harsh discipline for another's hard temper.

But she stayed.

For all those years, through all the pain, she had stayed.

Maybe at some point, Daisy had thought she could change him. If she loved him enough, if she served him enough, if she gave him children.

None of it worked. She had loved him. She thought so, anyway. She certainly served him. And she had done her best to give him children, though only one survived to adulthood. Miscarriage after miscarriage, and two stillborns later, she finally birthed a living, breathing, healthy child after three years of trying.

It still hadn't been enough.

And rather than Daisy changing Harold, the opposite had occurred.

He had changed her.

Pain gripped her heart as she thought of all the mistakes she had made with her daughter.

Daisy had been in so much pain.

It was no excuse. She knew that now. But she had carried such anger and regret that her life had never been her own. There were days when she didn't want to live, let alone raise a spirited, wild child who defied every rule and refused to believe that parents had any say over how she lived her life.

Harold had been too harsh. Daisy tried to mitigate his anger, but going soft on Khrista only made her act out more.

Daisy shook her head to clear away the memories that threatened to creep in. She tied up the last trash bag she had filled, and when she couldn't lift it, she left it against the wall in her room, on his side of the bed. Maybe she could hire a neighborhood boy to come in and move the bags out to the driveway.

This would have been a good time to have friends. Maybe they'd have grandchildren to offer up for assistance.

Alas, she had no one. Daisy had given up on friends after all the years of Harold humiliating her in front of them.

Anger coursed through her and she wished Harold were here so she could whack him one. He deserved it. But she'd never had the nerve to hurt him back the way he hurt her.

Daisy reached into the depths of the closet and drew out an old t-shirt Harold had saved from a rock concert he attended with his buddy back when they were younger. She hadn't seen the awful garment in ages, but the memories it held stung as if he had just flaunted the blasted shirt at that moment.

Contradicting her own thoughts, she pulled the ratty thing to her face, scrunching her nose at the scent of his cologne and body odor mixed with the stale fragrance of something forgotten in a closet too long.

Memories of the time when he left her and their daughter alone at the house with no food, no running water, and no transportation, let alone money, to go on a road trip with an old school pal burned into a brain that tried to forget.

Except she couldn't forget the hunger. The betrayal.

That he hadn't returned until after Khrista's tenth birthday.

Daisy hadn't been able to give her daughter so much as a cake. No gifts. Nothing but a peanut butter sandwich on the last of the stale bread.

She'd never forget the hurt on her daughter's face when she realized her birthday would be, once again, nothing special.

Daisy had always wished she could be one of those mothers who made the best of any situation, but she had never learned how to dig her way out of the disappointment and sadness she so often fell into.

Now that she was approaching seventy years old, the evidence of her failed parenting attempt haunted her dreams every time she closed her eyes.

Khrista had made sure she expressed what a failure Daisy had been. Daisy didn't blame Khrista. Not anymore.

At least her daughter had been a better mother once she had her baby. A sweet, kind mother to her daughter—Daisy's precious grandbaby. Certainly, Khrista had learned from Daisy's mistakes and brought Kaelyn up in a world of rainbows and unicorns and balloons and ice cream sundaes. And birthday cakes.

She most certainly never would have messed up something as important to a child as a birthday.

Daisy pushed her face into the bunched-up shirt once again. The disgusting shirt he had flaunted to upset her whenever he could—until she had buried it in the back of the closet and pretended not to know where it disappeared to. He hadn't liked that she stood up to him when he got home from that abandonment tour, and he made sure she couldn't leave the bedroom for days.

Barely able to breathe, Daisy released a scream she had held for over fifty years. Fifty-three long, painful, hateful years.

The scream penetrated the threads of the shirt, neutralizing its poison. Or feeding it.

Whatever it did, she couldn't deny the relief releasing the anger brought.

Fifty-three years of a wasted life. Of wasted opportunities. Of wasted space on the planet.

Harold had stolen those years from her. He had promised love and protection and a happy family and had given her rags to clean up and a life to regret.

When her throat grew raw from the years of pent-up rage flying out of her, she threw the shirt on the floor and pivoted away from the closet.

But the shirt called to her like a beacon of hatred, drawing her in.

Daisy groaned as adrenaline propelled her forward, easing her aching back into a bend deep enough to lift the dratted garment from the floor.

Her shoulders trembled when she returned to her upright position, and her hip clicked as it had been doing lately. Suddenly more calm than she had been in decades, Daisy strode to the kitchen, cradling the shirt in her arms as if it were a precious remnant of a life well-lived.

She folded it neatly and placed it on the yellowed counter, counting the holes she could see around the collar and imagining her husband's smiling face as he donned it despite her objections. Oh, how gleeful he had been. How proud.

How happy.

She opened the drawer beneath the shirt and withdrew her pair of kitchen scissors.

Daisy picked up the shirt, smiling down at it for the first time in its pathetic, cotton-blend life.

"It ends here, Harold."

She snipped a hole in the shirt right above the spot where her husband's heart once beat.

Laughter bubbled up inside her, and for the first time in a very long time, she felt free.

Daisy snipped and laughed and laughed and snipped. She had turned into a crazy woman, but Harold had been the one to push her over the edge. Even from the afterlife.

When the shirt lay in tattered pieces that resembled her broken heart, Daisy whispered into the silence, "It all ends here."

Satisfied she had properly exorcized Harold's ghost, she summoned what remained of her energy and dragged the bags out to the curb. There was no neighborhood boy to ask for help. There was no support system.

There was only her and her pathetic excuse for a life.

And the newly hatched realization that she was finally free to find her daughter and mend what she had broken.

**4**

---

# KHRISTA

Her head throbbed, and when Khrista tried to open her eyes, the light streaming into them may as well have been an ice pick being driven into her optic nerves.

The strong arms holding her were her only solace. She could simply lean back into the warmth, close her eyes, and let go...

Those same strong arms that had brought her comfort began to shake her.

"Khrista. Stay awake. Jeepers creepers—I've just got the blood to stop gushing from your head. If you don't work with me here, I'll have to take you to the hospital."

No, she couldn't go to the hospital. Then everyone would know.

She forced her heavy lids upward and gazed into the concerned eyes of the man she least wanted to see at that moment.

"Matt." Her words barely reverberated from her desert-dry mouth. Her sandpaper tongue tried to bring life to her cotton ball lips, but despite all the liquid she had consumed, there wasn't a drop of moisture to be found. "What are you doing here?"

Her words slurred, but she wasn't drunk enough to hide the shame. Having him find her, passed out and with a head wound, on the floor of her sloppy apartment... This was the stuff of nightmares.

Matt sighed. "A hunch, I guess. I knew you'd be having a rough day, and when you didn't answer any of my texts, I got concerned. Good thing, since I found you like this."

Sternness mixed with worry etched his face. She wanted to reassure him she was okay, that this wasn't the first time she had messed up like this. She wanted to send him away, to pretend he hadn't had this glimpse behind her curtains of madness. She wanted to smile and sing a cheerful song and live the life she had built outside of these walls.

She couldn't do any of that. So Khrista closed her eyes.

He shook her again, harsher this time.

"That's it. We're going to the hospital."

He started to lift her, but fear cleared the swirly fog out of her mind. Not entirely, but enough to motivate her body to bear down and refuse to be lifted.

"That's more like it," he said. "Give me some fight, woman."

She turned away from him, but he continued to hold her.

"Help me get you to the sofa, okay?"

She nodded, grateful for the dryness so no tears would force their way past her lowered inhibitions.

How long had she been on the floor? The only light in the apartment came from the overhead bulbs, so it was still night. Her eyes wouldn't focus for her to see the clock.

Matt held her upright as she stumbled across the room. He adjusted the decorative pillows around her, and he was polite enough not to comment on the unkempt state of her apartment.

A moment later, he brought her a big glass of ice water, which she downed gratefully. Khrista recoiled at the crackers he held out for her, but when he refused to relent in his insistence, she took those, too.

"How'd you get in?" Had she left the door unlocked? That was so unlike her, but then again, she had been an emotional disaster.

"I called Rafael. He was concerned when he heard my concern, so he let me in. When I saw you on the floor, I ushered him away. Figured you wouldn't want two of us hovering, and with the stench of the alcohol in the air, I had a feeling what had happened."

"Oh." Khrista couldn't think of anything else to say. Her facade was shattered, her carefully constructed image forever tainted. He'd take care of her for the moment—his sense of responsibility wouldn't allow him not to—but he wouldn't want her in the days to come.

She couldn't blame him for that.

At least she could be grateful he had sent Rafael away.

Rafael had known Khrista since she first pulled into town twenty years ago with nothing more than a plan to start a safe new life with her daughter in a place where nobody knew her. The name of the town on the map had drawn her in, and the idea of living on a cozy island not too far from the mainland enticed her, triggering feelings of safety and conjuring illusions of *home.*

And since Kaelyn's father had died of an overdose and would no longer be a threat, their days of bouncing from one shelter to another could finally end. She'd do whatever it took to give her daughter the stable life she deserved.

Rafael had recognized her unspoken desperation and offered her a job at his restaurant before she could even say she needed one.

He had become very much a father figure to her, taking her under his wing and always welcoming Kaelyn in the restaurant whenever school was out or Khrista lacked childcare. Kaelyn loved helping to set the tables, and her favorite chore had been delivering the salt, pepper, and ketchup containers to the back counter for refilling. She had felt important and part of the restaurant family.

When Khrista returned to Old Castle after losing Kaelyn, desperately needing to be close to the memories where she and her daughter had been happy, Rafael offered a deep discount on the little apartment in his building near the sea, right down the street from the tiny cottage where she had raised Kaelyn until the increasing costs of living on the island had driven them north. Everywhere she looked, she could see her freckled, free-spirited redhead climbing rocks toward the sandy shores, scaling trees in the neighbor's yard, or riding her bike up and down the dead-end road.

The memories both cut her and soothed her.

She needed them.

Khrista would be forever grateful for everything Rafael had ever done for her. If not for his generosity, she would never have been able to afford to live on the small island again.

And though she had never been honest with the widower about what had happened with Kaelyn during their time away, sometimes the look on his face suggested he knew more than he let on. But she appreciated that he never asked and never demanded answers.

Matt brushed her hair away from her face.

"You've had a tough time lately, Khrista. We all fall now and then. I don't blame you for wanting to get sloshed."

His beautiful, compassionate, full-faced, gleaming-teeth smile sought to bring her back to the world of the living. She closed her eyes.

He gently shook her shoulder. "I was a wreck when my girls went off to college. I'm lucky enough they moved close to home after school and settled within driving distance, but I imagine I'd have trouble on their birthdays and holidays if I didn't get to see them."

Matt took her glass to refill it, and when he returned, he carried a vase of flowers in the other hand.

"These were outside your door. Looks like your daughter continued her tradition of sending you flowers on her birthday."

Matt spoke the words with an uplifting conviction she associated with him. His optimism was often stronger than her self-doubt, but now was not one of those times.

Right now she was scraping along the rough bottom of a swimming pool, the skin on her knees tearing open and her lungs gasping for breath. The light was shining through the water's surface, but she couldn't get herself off the bottom and she most certainly could not swim to the top to free herself from the agony she had imposed upon herself. Her self-hatred kept her weighted down and drowning.

Matt smiled brightly, gazing into her eyes the way a parent would a sick child.

"Here. Look at this beautiful bouquet. She knows all of your favorite flowers, and once again she didn't fail to include them in your birthing day surprise." He chuckled, the round Dad-bod belly she loved so much rumbling with laughter. "I suppose it's not a surprise if it comes every year, but you get my drift, right?"

Khrista closed her eyes so tight she thought her eyelids might shatter. She wanted to scream to him, "*I sent them myself! The only surprise would be if my daughter even thought of me at all.*"

But she didn't. She held on to her secret despite her drunken state. To maintain her lie for another day.

Daggers dug into her belly, and her world tilted. She hated lying to this man who took care of her in ways nobody ever had. He showed her every day that a man could honor a woman and not hurt her.

But he *did* hurt her. Not by anything he did, but by effortlessly flaunting his perfection in the face of her negligence.

Matt scooped her into his arms once again, and she allowed herself to take the comfort he so freely offered as he sat beside her on the couch. He brushed her bloody, sticky hair away from her face gently, his large fingers dancing over her skin like she was a delicate porcelain doll.

She didn't deserve him. She knew it. But she wasn't strong enough to walk away.

"It's okay." He kissed her forehead. "I don't blame you for seeking refuge in a bottle tonight. I can't imagine going so long without seeing my beloved children. Even now that they're grown."

But Matt didn't understand. There was no way he could. He would never do anything to compromise the relationship he had with his children. He put them first. Like a parent should. He was kind and gentle and giving and fair. He was even-tempered, and he understood the intricacies of child development without ever having to take a class.

Unlike her.

Khrista had been a disgrace to the parenting community. She never would have been a mommy blogger. And she had waited far too long to educate herself on the proper ways of listening to and rearing children.

She tried to sit upright, desperation to be in her own space clawing at her.

"I wouldn't move so fast if I were you. You don't want to get sick."

Khrista mumbled something, but she didn't know what she tried to say. He smiled that healing smile. Once again, he uttered promises —promises she knew he wanted to keep. He tried to get her to promise that next year, or the next holiday, she would allow him to purchase the flight for her to go see her daughter, even though she had declined his offer every time he had made it. Enough time had passed, he said, and there was no reason they should wait another year to see each other.

But that was the problem.

It wasn't simply that Khrista lived on a preschool teacher's salary. Sure, she had let him believe that accounted for the lack of travel. And though he had offered time and time again to fly her daughter to the East Coast or to fly Khrista to the West Coast, what he didn't realize was that she had no idea where her daughter was, and she wouldn't be welcomed even if she did.

Struggling to suppress the nausea, Khrista stumbled to the bathroom and splashed water over her face.

Matt was right. She needed to see her daughter, and no excuses were strong enough to make it okay that it had already been five years. She could not allow another five years to pass.

She gazed at her sorry excuse for a reflection, gingerly tapping the bandage Matt had placed on her cut forehead.

When had she become this person?

Cheerful and kind in public and drunk and disorderly in private.

She needed to be the person she forced herself to be in public. If she could do it some of the time, she could do it all of the time.

To accomplish that, she had to give up the drinking.

She *would* quit drinking.

This wasn't the first time she had decided to quit drinking. The vow was one she often pledged to herself in the mirror after a tough night.

But she had never believed it before.

Maybe it was the drunken haze telling her lies and making her more optimistic, but she was ready to commit once again.

To improving her life.

To quitting the alcohol.

To leaving behind all the excuses she made day after day.

And to doing her very best to live a life she could be proud of. One her community members already thought she lived... the one Khrista had created from her imagination.

She needed to stop being a fraud.

She wasn't ready to tell Matt the truth, but she was ready to take herself seriously and stop living this life.

And then, and only then, once she had managed to quit the bad habits, Khrista would be the mother her daughter had always deserved and wanted. And maybe then, if she was lucky, her daughter would see she meant more to Khrista than their history suggested.

The next morning, Khrista found a sweet note from Matt propped up on the table alongside a toasted bagel with cream cheese and a cup of iced coffee he must have made himself. She held the note to her chest, absorbing the kindness from the gesture. Her throat tightened and her eyes stung.

She halted in the middle of her living room, gazing around the space which was considerably tidier than it had been yesterday, courtesy of Matt. Khrista had never been the neatest, most organized person in the world, and Matt always joked about being Type A. Normally she'd burn with embarrassment about him not only seeing her disarray but also cleaning it up. However, today was a new day and her life was headed in a new direction. She'd probably never ask for help, but if someone close to her took it upon themselves to perform an act of service, why let it upset her?

He had now officially seen the worst side of her.

She had to make sure that was a one-time deal.

Khrista paused in front of her bar, oh so cleverly disguised as extra kitchen storage, on her way back to her room. Her mouth went dry, and the temptation to pour a glass to numb the pain of the humiliation she had endured last night—the humiliation she had reaped upon herself, that is—hit hard. The sunny disposition of moments ago fled behind the clouds of liquid courage. Clouds that always seemed to promise salvation, yet never delivered for more than the time her brain spent numbed.

She turned away before she could make that mistake again. Khrista remembered enough about the previous night to know she had made herself a vow right before she retched in the sink.

She had never cleaned up her act for herself. She hadn't been able to do it for the fantastic man who would, rightfully so, break things off if he knew the whole truth. She hadn't even managed it for her daughter, the young child who looked at her through confused eyes that once adored her, or for the adult daughter who needed her gentle guidance and got Khrista's neglect instead.

Khrista hadn't been able to accomplish her goal for all the best reasons, but now she had another compelling reason.

A grandbaby.

A chance to undo all the horrible things she had done. A chance to undo all the horrible things she had been through. A chance to make things right in her daughter's eyes. To show she knew now how to be a better person. How to treat a child. And how to overcome the victimhood she had clutched so tightly to her identity for so long.

Khrista gathered the last of her bottles in her arms and lugged them to the sink. After placing the bottles on the small counter space, she twisted the cap off the Fireball, her daily go-to, and poured it down the drain, one agonizing drop at a time. The spicy scent hit her hard, and she stopped pouring.

Hands trembling, she screwed the cap back on the bottle and paused.

She couldn't do it. She wasn't ready. She could be strong, even with the contents of the bottles remaining in their vessels. But part of her needed to know the alcohol was there if she needed it.

Khrista carried her collection into her bedroom area. She went into her tiny closet, removed a box from the shelf, and lined the bottles up like little soldiers against the wall. She saluted them, told them they had been good adversaries. They had put up a good fight to keep her on their side.

"I'm leaving enemy territory, my friends." Khrista paused and stared at the labels of each and every bottle, memorizing their design and the smooth necks. "Though part of me enjoyed my time with you, from here on out I will use all of my power and might to fight you."

Before the bottles could mock her or taunt her or seduce or invite her, she placed the box she had removed to make room for the liquor back on the shelf in front of them and did her best to forget they existed.

If she couldn't find the strength to dump the toxins down the drain, maybe Khrista could convince herself that her power came from knowing they were there and actively choosing not to take them out of retirement.

Her shower washed the night away, and although she winced when the shampoo and the hot water hit her foolish cut from last night, she smiled anyway. Today was a new day, and she would succeed.

Khrista got to work early, as she had promised Danielle, and congratulated herself for her track record of reliability at work and of carrying on throughout every day. She had become adept at nurturing each child who entered her classroom just as she should have nurtured herself, and most certainly how she should have nurtured her daughter.

If she was to heal, Khrista would have to stop self-sabotaging and accept that she could not change the past. Instead, she would have to work hard on changing the present and the future.

When the day ended with hugs and goodbyes from her adorable students, Khrista hurried off to Happil-TEA Ever After Tea Room and surrounded herself with the people who would unknowingly drag her out of the abyss and into the light. Although she kept to herself, tucked into the corner with Mr. Ed purring on her lap, the ambiance of the surrounding chatter comforted her.

She'd work her way up to being social. Maybe she'd join one of the many clubs Clarice organized at the tearoom. Maybe she'd check with her long-time best friend, Elanna, to see if she could make time in her busy schedule to have tea with Khrista. Maybe she'd step out of her self-imposed exile and blend in with the community better.

But for now, she'd do what she could and forgive herself for not doing more.

She stroked Mr. Ed's neck and sipped the tropical green tea blend Clarice had offered.

And she only thought of her soldiers every other minute.

# KAELYN

They say when a woman is pregnant, she suddenly sees pregnant women everywhere. Something about the psychology of being more tuned in to people who are in similar stages of life. This phenomenon wasn't restricted only to pregnancy—buy a blue car, suddenly all you see are blue cars everywhere, especially when you're trying to locate your own in the Target parking lot. Have a baby, and suddenly every person you see is pushing a stroller or placing a child into a car seat.

Not Kaelyn, though. Everywhere Kaelyn looked, she saw disaster.

As her husband drove her to their first ultrasound appointment, he practically buzzed with excitement. She wished she could, too. Instead, Kaelyn looked out her window and saw evidence of a recent wildfire charring trees that once stood so proudly. She saw homes with broken-down vehicles propped up on blocks in driveways. She saw dilapidated buildings that housed broken families and lost dreams.

Sure, these instances were isolated and rare on the drive to the hospital from her swanky neighborhood, and she could admit that to herself when Kaelyn stopped to analyze her emotions. Even so, those disasters dominated the landscape of her mind.

Everything good fell apart eventually.

Always in tune with her feelings, even when she wished he wouldn't be, Oliver reached out his hand and gripped her bare knee. The sensation of his rough fingers on her freshly shaved skin sent chills throughout her body, but mostly his gentle and comforting touch quieted her mind momentarily. If only she could bottle him up —his very essence—and take him like Xanax.

"Hey, love, you seem distant today. Is everything all right?"

She continued gazing out the window, not wanting to alarm him, but not sure how to express that everything could not be okay when so much of the world was falling to decay around them. He would laugh at her if he heard her thoughts and tell her that one nearly condemned property in an area of million-dollar homes did not mean something would go wrong with their baby.

She knew he would offer this assurance, and she knew she should believe him.

Instead of letting him into her thoughts as she normally did, Kaelyn muttered that she was okay. She hoped he would drop it and continue buzzing about the upcoming ultrasound. She needed his excitement. Needed his positive energy.

"Be honest with me, love. Are you having doubts about the baby?"

She gasped. "Of course not!"

Her sharpness made him jump, his shoulders rising in reaction to the startling noise that had emanated from deep within her body and cascaded out of her mouth in a roar.

She softened her tone and tried to smile. "This is the happiest accident ever."

They had wanted kids together; they just hadn't talked about when. She had missed a few birth control pills when things were crazy at work, but she hadn't thought it would be a problem.

Her hand moved to her belly.

It wasn't a problem. She was delighted. Nothing could keep her from feeling happy about this new life blossoming inside her. This baby may not have been planned, but he was far from an accident.

"It's okay if you're having worries or concerns. People go through all sorts of emotions when they find out their lives are going to change."

"Are *you* having doubts?" She didn't want to believe it could be true, but maybe Oliver's questions were a way for him to open the door to admitting he thought going through with this pregnancy was a mistake.

As much as she loved him and practically worshiped him and his goodness, she would leave him if it meant saving her baby.

"My turn to say, 'Of course not.' I've never been happier. But if the daggers you're flinging at me are any indication, I fear suddenly that my place in this family may be in jeopardy and you may kill me in my sleep if you sense I could have doubts."

He laughed and squeezed her knee, and she so badly wanted to laugh as well.

A small chuckle may have wiggled its way from her throat, but if she actually did laugh, it was a product of being on social autopilot and not a reflection of joy or good humor.

Where was the joy and good humor she normally had?

She was happy, darn it! She had everything. *Everything.*

And yet...

Kaelyn resumed staring out the window and tried hard to zero in on the beautiful California coastal landscape. Still, all she saw were rotting swing sets in backyards and lost dog posters fading away on phone poles.

She turned the radio up, pretending she loved the song. Kaelyn could no longer hold back the tears and didn't want to give her husband any reason to worry. Silent tears streamed down her face, and she did her best not to sniffle.

Oliver lowered the volume, and unluckily for her, they hit a red light and he could look at her. She could never hide anything from him, but especially not if he could see her face.

"Love, you're crying. Talk to me. I need to know what's wrong so we can work together to fix it."

She had worried him. She never wanted to worry him. She wanted to give him the same level of joy he gave her.

"It's stupid. Hormones. I think."

"Tell me what it is you're thinking about. I can't promise to fix it, but let's experience it together."

As usual, his warm concern settled her raw nerves like a salve to burned skin.

"I can't explain it all. I just feel like... I don't know." Revelations swamped her mind, and her unraveling emotions forced a direct confrontation between her conscious mind and feelings she never wanted to feel, let alone verbalize. Yet something prevented Kaelyn from keeping those emotions buried where they belonged. "I guess being pregnant and going to hear the heartbeat for the first time is making me wish things could have been different with my mother."

"Oh, love."

"It's okay, really. I made peace with my mother not being in my life. I made peace with that the day I left for good. And I've made peace with it every day since." She drew in a breath, shocked at how the ragged edges of a breath that should have brought relief instead sliced her insides, leaving her bare. "It's not even *her* I miss, I don't think. I think it's just that this is a time when most daughters want to share the news with their mothers, get advice on all the little and big things, buy those cute little 'If Mom Says No Call Grandma' onesies."

Her throat closed off, rendering her voiceless, and she sobbed. The sobs wracked her body and shook her to the depths of her soul. Kaelyn had never imagined feeling this way again, but in giving voice to her worries, sadness, and fears, she had brought herself back to those early days of learning to live without even a figurehead of a mom.

Oliver veered off into a parking lot and slammed the car into park. The seatbelt strangled him as he reached across the vehicle to hold her hands. She sobbed harder, unable to imagine her world without the love this man so willingly gave and knowing she would do everything to hold on to him.

"I'm okay, Oliver. We have to keep driving so we're not late."

"They will wait." He unclipped his seatbelt and tossed her purse off the middle console into the back seat. He awkwardly draped his arms around her and pulled her head to his shoulder. Her seatbelt cut into her hip, but she didn't tell him.

She fought annoyance at his insistence on stopping. They couldn't be late.

"I don't like you feeling this way, Kaelyn. There's so much going on in our lives, and most of it is good. Well, all of it is good from my point of view. And from yours," he rushed to add. "I'm beside myself when you're upset. I never see you this way, but if this is how you're feeling, I want to know. We'll get through it together. God, I sound like a blubbering fool."

She laughed and buried her face in his shoulder, smearing tears and mascara over his blue button-down shirt. "They're gonna take one look at us and think we're insane."

"I'm sure they've seen worse. Besides, I've always liked your raccoon-eyed emo look."

Kaelyn playfully pinched his arm, and he feigned hurt. His antics made her smile, and she fumbled into the glove compartment for a tissue.

"We've got to go, Oliver."

He ignored her. She seethed a little, but didn't want to fight about their different approaches to time management when they were going into an appointment they'd remember the rest of their lives.

The memory had to be perfect.

So she held her breath and waited.

"I know this is an unpopular opinion and you won't like it—"

"Then maybe this is one opinion you shouldn't share with me," she teased.

"I probably shouldn't, because it's not my place to tell you what to do." He ran his hand up and down her arm from her shoulder to her elbow and then squeezed her elbow in reassurance.

She huffed playfully before blowing her nose loudly and indelicately into her tissue.

"Well, you know since you've led with *that* I'm gonna need to hear what you have to say."

Kaelyn flipped the visor down and studied her mascara-smeared face, grimacing at her reflection. He wasn't wrong about her raccoon-eyed look. Add the red splotches on her freckled face, and she became the illustrated dictionary definition of a complete walking disaster. She should just keep the look. It certainly fit.

She peered at him out of the corner of her eye.

"I think I know what you're thinking, though."

He smiled and tucked her fiery, unruly hair behind her ear. "If the estrangement between you and your mother is hurting you so badly, perhaps it's time to reach out."

She groaned. "Can you please drive?"

"It makes sense. It's been how long? Four years?"

"Five."

"Five years. You were practically a child when you left. You're more mature now, and you're in a completely different place in life. You're not reliant on her for anything. She has no power over you."

"She never did." Kaelyn hated that she still, after all these years, sounded defensive. But she avoided talking about her mother for many reasons.

"You are the strongest woman I have ever known." His voice thick, he continued, "I'm not saying you should let her off the hook for anything that transpired. I know you haven't wanted to talk about it in all these years, but you talk in your sleep sometimes."

She stiffened. He had never told her that before.

When Kaelyn was a little girl and used to stay at her best friend's house, Sienna would tease her about talking almost nonstop when she was sleeping. She always lamented that no matter how hard she tried to unveil Kaelyn's secrets—her deepest, darkest secrets—the speech always came out as gobbledygook. Sienna joked that Kaelyn was the supreme ruler of a far-off land with its own language, and she didn't come from her mother at all. At first, that joke had hurt Kaelyn because she loved her mother and couldn't understand why some of the other parents whispered about her at the playground and why Sienna sometimes made jokes about Kaelyn not belonging.

She had grown up thinking everyone in Old Castle liked her mom.

People were pretty nice to her at the restaurant she worked at, and Rafael acted like a grandfather to Kaelyn. Other people acted like family, too, like Clarice and Elanna and others. So overhearing some of the parents at the school talk about Khrista messing things up and not being a good mother confused Kaelyn and made her tighten her hold on the secrets of what life really looked like behind the doors of their tiny cottage.

That loyalty died when her mother crossed lines even Kaelyn hadn't believed she could cross.

Had Kaelyn inadvertently given away her secrets while she slept alongside Oliver? Had she revealed any of the truth she so desperately wanted to hide from this man who thought she only withheld minor details? She didn't want to have this conversation anymore.

"We need to go, Oliver. Seriously. They'll cancel the appointment if we're not there on time, and then we'll both need to take time off work again to reschedule. This is silly. I don't know why I got so upset. I think it's just nerves. Now can you *drive?*"

"Will you think about what I'm saying? I would be there with you every step of the way."

"I know you would be, Oliver. And believe me, there's no one else I'd want by my side. You give me strength, you help me find my strength, and you can believe me when I tell you you're the only family I need."

She quirked a smile, and he smiled in return before poking the little crease on the side of her cheek he always loved so much.

"There's no point reaching out anyway because nothing would have changed," Kaelyn went on. "My mother has never been one to accept responsibility or admit she did anything wrong, even when it's blasting her in the face. I left that toxic life for a reason."

"How toxic could a relationship with her be when you're three thousand miles away and becoming a mother yourself?"

She meant to laugh, but it came out as a guttural threat. A threat to her existential existence.

She had always been Sisyphus pushing that large boulder up the hill in her relationship with her mother, and her mother eventually turned into the very boulder Kaelyn tried to keep on the up and up. The boulder who steamrolled Kaelyn on the way down.

The only way to improve her life had been to flee. And it was no coincidence she wound up on the opposite coast. Transferring from the college she had initially attended in Boston to the one in Oregon had been the best decision she had made. Even though she had worked overtime building websites for small businesses to save up money for the cross-country trek and had nearly failed school in the process, she had managed to pull her grades together enough to continue qualifying for the grants she had been entitled to.

Kaelyn sighed to punctuate her laughter. "You'd be surprised. Luckily for you, I love you enough for you to never have to find out."

"And I love you, my little tumblebear." He poked her nose, and she swatted his hand away. "In all seriousness, though, you're entitled to change your mind whenever you want to. And I will support you no matter what you decide you want to do. You and this baby are my life. Whatever makes you happier is what I will commit my efforts to."

Her tears streamed again, but this time they were tears of happiness.

SHIVERS RAN through Kaelyn as she sat on the end of the paper-lined examination table in the ultrasound room. The room was chilly, but so was her heart.

She had tried to answer all the questions as accurately as possible, but some of them were unexpected and tripped her up. She hadn't considered that they'd ask about previous pregnancies and such.

Would they know she had lied?

Oliver hadn't seemed suspicious when she hedged a bit. He simply rubbed her back and encouraged her to take a deep breath. He knew her emotions were all over the place and likely attributed her hesitation to hormonal fluctuations. He had always been sensitive to stuff like that, which would make him the best pregnancy partner. He had never shied away from purchasing tampons when she needed them or giving her extra back rubs when the cramps kicked in. He knew to ask if she needed chips (or "crisps," as he called them) with her ice cream, or if she needed a giant mug of ginger tea.

And right now, he somehow sensed she needed his touch to keep her grounded to the moment.

The technician re-entered the room and instructed Kaelyn to lie back. The crinkly paper echoed in her ears as she shifted into position.

The joy on Oliver's face was *everything*. He looked like a kid being offered a sundae with candy topping for breakfast, and knowing she and their baby were the candy made the world shift back into the proper orbit.

He continued to massage her shoulder as the ultrasound technician lifted the gown to reveal her belly. Kaelyn jumped a bit when the cold jelly squirted onto her abdomen, and she tried to focus on the screen as the technician moved the wand all around, searching her womb to make sure everything seemed the way it should at this early stage.

*Don't think about it. Don't think about it. Do. Not. Think.*

Oliver became downright giddy when the technician stopped and alerted them to the spot where their little bean's heart pumped.

"Everything is looking great! Your doctor will be in touch to go over the results of the ultrasound, but I can tell you to enjoy this first pregnancy. It will be your most memorable one." The technician handed a towel to Kaelyn so she could wipe the goop off her belly. "Oh, there's a bathroom right over there. For most women, emptying the bladder after the ultrasound is second in pleasure only to hearing the heartbeat."

The technician smiled over her shoulder as she said goodbye and left the room.

And though Kaelyn tried to wrap Oliver's happiness, excitement, and pride around her like a comforting quilt, all she could think about was keeping him from discovering she was a fraud.

The pain of having been here before, in much different circumstances, resonated deep inside her soul and nestled in like a painful intruder that broke in not just to steal things, but also to plant bombs all around the house, hidden in every corner, leaving no real clues about where the trip wires could be.

Oliver looked at her with such trust. He shared everything with her. Expected her to do the same. And she trusted him implicitly.

She needed to tell him about her previous miscarriage and the circumstances surrounding the sad event. Though she had kept the shame of that moment secured in a secret chamber of her heart, Kaelyn couldn't stop thinking about how Oliver deserved access to every inch of the organ.

But how? When he already thought he knew everything?

He had, in the past, explicitly asked her about previous relationships. She had been given so many opportunities to open up and confide in him, and yet she had frozen each and every time. Knowing Oliver as she did, he'd more than likely be supportive and comforting.

And yet there was that tiny part of her that wondered if he'd view her differently. If he'd trust her a little less. If he'd question whether she was as perfect as he always said she was.

She always thought she could leave the past behind in New Hampshire, but every day pushed her further afield.

Kaelyn only hoped she could manage the stress better now than she had in the past.

**6**

───────

# DAISY

The room was awash in bright lights, and beeping echoed through every pore in her body. She tried to call out to Harold. Something was wrong.

Her eyes wouldn't fully open.

Her chest felt funny, like the skin was being pulled too tight.

Her mouth was so dry, it was as if she hadn't consumed water in weeks.

"Hello, dear. You're awake!"

Daisy took in the scene through squinted eyes. A nurse. Or a child dressed up as one, anyway. She looked no older than a young girl. Then again, most of the women on the stories Daisy liked to watch on the TV looked younger and younger as Daisy got older and older.

Daisy remembered watching a daytime talk show where a bunch of women in different age groups joked about how as they got older their doctors got younger until they started seeing doctors and other healthcare professionals who seemed as if they were fresh from the sandbox.

The audience had laughed. And Daisy wondered what it would be like to have friends to joke with, to help each other navigate the hurdles of life with humor.

Her voice rasped out against the sandpaper of her throat and tongue.

"Who are you?"

Daisy hadn't meant to sound harsh, but if she wasn't mistaken, she was now in a hospital.

The last thing she remembered was struggling to drag a giant trash bag full of Harold's things out to the curb. Nausea had overwhelmed her, but she remembered nothing afterward.

"Why am I in a hospital?"

"Oh, honey, you came in last night. I'm not sure of the details because I wasn't on, but a Good Samaritan found you collapsed at the end of your driveway. The heroism of your rescuer is the talk of the hospital. You had a heart attack—a minor one!"

A minor heart attack? The woman acted like she had nicked herself shaving and not suffered from something that could have killed her.

Did it kill her?

Daisy lifted her shaking hand to her chest. "But I'm alive?"

The child nurse laughed, and if Daisy was a nicer person or in a better mood, she may have found it enchanting. She hadn't been around young people for some time.

"You sure are, honey. Trust me when I tell you this place is not heaven."

If the child called her a condescending endearment one more time, Daisy wouldn't be responsible for whatever came out of her own mouth.

"But my husband is still dead?"

The nurse flipped through a chart and pulled her stool over to the bedside. With empathy making her face droop slightly, she extended her hand and placed it on top of Daisy's hand—the one not hooked up to the IV.

"It says here you're widowed, Daisy. I'm so sorry. Was it recent?"

Daisy felt like the skin at the sides of her mouth would crack as her lips drew up in a smile. She hadn't died. He had. She still had a chance to live a life. She still had a chance to do it all over again.

"Am I dying?"

"I'll let the doctor fill you in on your condition, but you did very well in your surgery, and your numbers are looking phenomenal now. You'll have to make some modifications to your lifestyle, but you won't be dying today. Not on my watch."

The nurse brought a wet washcloth to Daisy's face, and Daisy forgave her for being young and kind and beautiful and wrinkle-free as she moistened Daisy's parched lips.

"Water?" the angel offered.

"Please." Daisy's croak was embarrassing, but she didn't mind begging to have her thirst quenched.

After the nurse departed, Daisy's mind whirled.

She had so much to do.

She had so much of a life to live.

She had so many things that remained unsaid and needed to find a voice.

So many wrongs to correct.

So much joy she hadn't yet experienced.

And it wasn't too late.

Praise the heavens, *it wasn't too late.*

WHEN THE HOSPITAL discharged her and discovered they'd be sending her home alone with what they referred to as "no natural supports," they connected her with a visiting nurse and a social worker who would come into the home and help her get settled. Nothing like the whole medical world knowing she had no family to look after her.

Merigold, the social worker, had been instrumental in setting Daisy up with a social network. She got her one of those new phones they always showed on the television commercials. The social worker called it a smartphone, but Daisy thought it was pretty stupid most of the time. It never seemed to do what Daisy wanted it to do.

Merigold had also set up a transportation system to bring Daisy to the local senior center on Mondays, Wednesdays, and Fridays, and Daisy hadn't been able to hide her uneasiness.

"You've been pretty sheltered here, haven't you, Daisy?" Merigold had asked, and the question sounded a little too pitying for Daisy's tastes.

Daisy had pretended not to hear because it was easier than trying to explain.

After the first day of going to the senior center, Daisy had realized her clothing was all wrong. Everyone welcomed her into the group, but she knew she stuck out with her old fashion. One of the biddies asked if she had gone retro and that's why her clothing looked like she walked out of a 1990s clothing ad. Daisy avoided making eye contact with that jerk again, but she supposed the lady had a point about Daisy's wardrobe.

She hadn't purchased a single new item of clothing in a good twenty years, and though she hadn't cared much when she rarely left the house, she certainly cared now.

She asked Merigold to help her pick up some new items of clothing from the store.

"I can do you one better," Merigold had said. And then she showed Daisy how to shop right from her phone.

"This certainly opens up a new world for me!" she'd marveled.

"Just remember to go easy. Don't shop in the middle of the night —trust me. And remember that it's real money you're spending, so keep your budget in mind."

"Oh, I've been keeping the budget in mind for years. Time to have some fun. Do you like these floral patterns or the stripes better?"

"Definitely the floral." Merigold clicked on something and a bunch of different color options popped up. "If I were you, I'd get one of each."

Daisy took her advice, and now she carried herself into the senior center with more confidence than she had had in too many decades to count.

The first couple of days had been nerve-wracking, but Daisy looked forward to her days at the senior center. Though she preferred her own cooking, she did appreciate the opportunity to eat a hot, prepared meal with a group of other seniors. They had been welcoming for the most part, and though she hadn't wanted to join in the board game sessions, she had enjoyed watching television with a small group of women.

But today she was on a mission.

Daisy raised her hand to gesture for one of the young girls at the senior center to come over and help her with an email. Belle, if Daisy's eyes were registering right as she squinted to read her name tag.

This technological stuff was coming pretty naturally to her, considering she'd never touched anything but a word processor in her lifetime.

Belle returned to the computer area of the large room and directed her full attention toward Daisy at last, pulling Daisy back to the task at hand. "Yes, Daisy dear. What can I help you with?"

"First, you can tell me why all you young girls are always calling people 'dear' and 'honey' and 'sweetheart.' I know you mean well, but it makes me feel like a child."

Belle's cheeks reddened, and she looked down at the keyboard.

Daisy cursed herself for her bad manners.

"I'm sorry, Belle. I didn't mean it."

"No, it's okay. You're right, we don't tend to think of how those endearments might make someone feel. But I suppose it's a little like you referring to us as young girls when no one here is under the age of thirty-five." Belle winked and Daisy got the hint.

"I guess we all have a lot to learn." Daisy grinned and gestured to the computer. "I heard some of the other ladies talking and they said something about being able to find people's email addresses on the computer. Can you help me do that?"

Belle put a hand on her hip and cocked her head to the side, studying the screen. "Sometimes it's possible to find addresses, phone numbers, and things like that. Email addresses are a little trickier. But we can try."

Daisy straightened her shoulders the slightest bit. If she could find her daughter's email address, then maybe Khrista would be impressed enough to believe that Daisy had changed. Maybe then she would give her another chance.

"Who is it you want to find? An old boyfriend?" Belle's teasing voice sent a shiver down Daisy's back.

"Goodness gracious, no. I never had another beau, and I'm certainly too old for that now." And why would she want to imprison herself again when she finally had the chance to live free?

So often, people assumed that a fifty-year marriage meant happiness and love.

She didn't have the energy to dissuade them of their fantastical notions.

Belle crossed her arms over her chest. "Nonsense. There's an entire market out there where people are trying to set up older couples. You're not dead, you know what I mean?"

"I may be very much alive, but that part of me is most certainly dead."

"Well, if you change your mind…"

"I won't."

Belle leaned over the computer desk, her long necklace dangling as she studied the screen.

"Okay, so who are we searching for?"

"My daughter."

Belle stood upright.

"You don't already have her email address?"

"No."

"Can you call her and ask?"

"No."

Belle studied Daisy's face as if she were waiting for an explanation. Daisy was not ready to oblige.

"Oh, right. Why would you have her email address?" Belle chewed her lip as she tried to backtrack out of the dangerous territory she had inadvertently wandered into. "Since you're just learning the computer and everything. Okay, let me type in her name and age."

Belle's perfume—a mix of something sweet and something a touch spicy—wafted into Daisy's nostrils as Belle leaned over her to type on the keyboard, leaving her unasked questions lingering in the air.

"See, you just go to this search bar and enter the name and any other information you have. Since her name is fairly common, we need to narrow down the search a bit. Where does she live? City? State?"

"I don't know." Tears pooled in the rims of Daisy's eyes. She wasn't much of a crier, but not knowing where her daughter had been for twenty years had taken a toll. "I think she may be in New Hampshire. Or might have been in New Hampshire at some point in her life. She used to talk about escaping there."

"Hmm, let's see here." Belle leaned forward to inspect the screen. "There's a Khrista O'Donnell in Arizona."

"No, she never liked the desert."

"There's one in Washington. What's her middle name? There are a few different initials here. Oh, that one is too old to be your daughter."

Daisy gave her more information—Khrista's middle name, her birthdate, where she graduated from. Anything she could think of to help narrow the search.

"Oh, wait. It looks like we have a Khrista O'Donnell in Old Castle, New Hampshire. Old Castle... isn't that near Portsmouth? I read about that place—I think it was that place, anyway—on a travel blog about the top ten quaint towns to visit in New England. My husband and I were looking for a cute place to visit on our anniversary a few years back. We ended up going to Maine, but Old Castle was a close second, if I remember correctly."

"Old Castle."

Daisy's mind drifted to all the stories and fairytales she had stopped reading and telling her daughter when Khrista had grown old enough to read them on her own. Oh, how Daisy missed those times when they could put their differences aside and wave the white flag to call a ceasefire on their battle of wills. Khrista's curly hair would brush Daisy's chin as they snuggled up before bed, the warmth of her daughter's breath against her skin soothing all wounds.

How wonderful it had been when it was the two of them, safe in a cocoon as they escaped into the pages of a storybook.

Until Harold would demand Daisy's attention.

"I've never heard of Old Castle, but it sure sounds like a place she would want to escape to." Daisy clicked her fingernails on the desk next to the keyboard. "Is there an email address there?"

"Actually, there is. I can't promise it will be a current one, but we can certainly try it if you'd like to." Belle did something on the computer that she called copying and pasting, but Daisy thought it was a dumb thing to call it when there was obviously no glue . She opened up another window and helped Daisy create an email account of her own.

"So you type in this box, and when you're done, you can move the mouse right over here and click 'send.' Easy peasy."

"And how long does it take to get to the person?"

Daisy hated feeling so naïve, especially since she had once been one of the smartest girls in her class. That's what her teachers had said, anyway. Harold strongly disagreed, telling her the male advisor who encouraged her to further her education was trying to get under her skirt. Harold insisted she'd be better served by taking care of their house than by pretending she was smart.

She would not think of him. She had given up enough of her life to that man. No more.

"It depends," Belle said. "It goes pretty instantly, but people don't always check their email right away. And these days, everyone is so used to being able to respond quickly with a text or an instant message that sometimes emails languish in inboxes for a while before they get seen or responded to."

"Okay, I've got it." Daisy didn't entirely, but she was ready to have Belle move along so she could work on the note to her daughter. "And how will I know if she writes back?"

Belle helped her set up the email on Daisy's new smartphone.

She showed her how to access the inbox and encouraged her to try it while Belle observed.

"You're a natural!" Belle exclaimed. "Let me know if you need anything else. I'm going to make some tea. You want a cup?"

Daisy nodded and requested two sugars. After fifty years of Harold restricting her use of sugar, she was finding herself going a little crazy with it these days, and some of her new clothing was already getting a bit tight. But she didn't want to deny herself, and she wouldn't.

Life was too short for that, and at her age, Daisy was more aware of her limited time and less concerned with a few extra pounds around the middle.

She poised her fingers over the keyboard, appreciating how much easier it was to type on this than it had been on the typewriters in her high school typing class.

Daisy hadn't thought through what she would write to Khrista, so she let it all pour out in a stream of emotion.

*Dear Khrista,*

*I'm sure you weren't expecting to hear from me. It's your mother, Daisy. You're probably shocked I'm on a computer and sending this email, but some of the girls—backspace—young women at my local senior center have been helping me. They don't know why I'm so eager to learn about email, and that is my secret to keep.*

*I owe you so much, Khrista. If I could redo everything, I would. I would spend more time chasing fireflies with you. I would read more fairytales to you—the happy ones, not the ones where they cut their toes off to fit into shoes that weren't made for them. I would have swept you up in my arms and together we would have left your father a long time ago, and I would have made you my priority.*

*If I could do it all again...*

*It took me a long time to realize I was at fault, and it took me a long time to understand you were right to take Kaelyn away. I wasn't able to protect you, and I'm sure you thought I wouldn't protect Kaelyn, either. I'd like to think your instincts were wrong, but history has shown my judgment was poor and my strength nonexistent.*

*You owe me nothing. I owe you everything.*

*Things are different now. I'm free. You were smart enough to find freedom earlier on, and I'm happy about that. I hope in your life after escaping us you never had a day of struggle, and I'm sure you've settled in with a nice man who treats you well, have probably built your dream home on a big lot of land, and are running a rescue for all the stray cats you used to try to save. I imagine Kaelyn is a big sister to a whole lot of little rugrats with your eyes and your laughter and your wild curls tumbling around their shoulders as they race around under the rays of the sun. I'm sure you've taken the opportunity to undo all the harm I've done and to end the generational curse.*

*I'm sad I never got to meet them, but I must admit I find comfort in these imaginings of your happy life. The life I'm sure you're living, where all of your dreams are a reality and no one holds you back from accomplishing all you were put on this Earth to accomplish.*

*I know your absence from my life is all my fault.*

*I didn't know it then. But I know it as surely as I know that your toddler smiles were all that got me through some days.*

*Khrista, please forgive me. I love you. I have always loved you, even when I didn't know how to show it.*

*You are my world.*

*I know it's hard to believe, but you have been my world since the moment I first knew you were growing inside me. When I first felt you kick, I knew I would do nothing more important in my life than give birth to you. When I held you to my breast, and you hungrily lapped up all the milk you could, my heart grew so big I didn't think it would fit in my chest. When you started growing more independent, I tried to understand you needed to grow away from me. I failed in that understanding. And I failed to understand you could be an individual and you would know better than I how to live your life.*

*I was wrong. I don't expect you to forgive me, but I hope you do. I hope you have missed me even a small amount. Because I have spent years longing for you, wishing for you, and praying for you.*

*If I could do anything differently, I would turn back time and kick your father out of the house the first time he turned cruel. The first time he raised his hand to you or to me.*

*Anyhow, I know this is all out of the blue, and probably ruining your day. I'm sorry if that's the case, but if you want to reach me, you can send me an email back, or I even have a cellular phone now. Here's my number.*

*Love,*

*Mom.*

*P.S. In case it wasn't clear. Your father is dead. Finally. We are both free.*

DAISY DABBED a tissue over the tears that had poured down her cheeks and nestled into the wrinkles at her neck. She had never before opened her heart to those feelings, and now that she had allowed herself to acknowledge the truth of her past, Daisy couldn't keep the emotions confined to all the neat boxes she had previously locked them in.

She reread her message, her cheeks burning her raw from the inside out. No way could she send that. It was too open. Too honest. Too heavy with guilt and expectation.

Before she could reconsider, Daisy hit backspace, deleting all the words faster than she had written them until the blank screen mocked her with every blink of the flashing cursor.

If only deleting a life of bad choices were as easy as deleting words from the heart.

With the screen cleared, she typed again. This time, she kept it simple.

*Your father is dead. We are free. And though I can't change anything I've done to hurt you, I hope this letter finds you well.*

.   .   .

Before she could second-guess her decision, she hit send, quite sure there was no way to undo an email once it was sent.

7

——————

# KHRISTA

Khrista scanned the group of women gathered around the tearoom, all tuned in as Elanna, Khrista's best friend and the only one Khrista had ever opened up to even slightly, passed out assignments for the fundraiser they were organizing for the rescue. While many of the faces were familiar, they were mainly parents Elanna knew from the school and had roped into attending and not people Khrista knew well.

The idea for the fundraiser was born only hours ago when Clarice casually mentioned during their Saturday morning social tea time that one of the new kittens was born with a genetic defect and would be difficult to re-home because of the cost of ongoing care. Elanna did what she so often did—leaped for the opportunity to help.

Everyone in town loved the tearoom for many reasons, but one thing always mentioned in reviews was the ability to visit with and potentially adopt the cats. The rescued cats never seemed to mind all the love and socialization so often heaped upon them as they awaited their fur-ever homes.

"Khrista, maybe your students could help create posters to hang in storefronts downtown?"

Khrista hedged, not wanting to seem unwilling to help, but not sure she could be trusted to fully engage when she was so new to this social engagement.

"I teach threes and fours, so most of their art is more the finger-paint variety. They're not developmentally capable of creating images yet, and most of them can't write much. But what do you think about an art show/auction? I can give all the kids canvases and they can go crazy with the colors and glitter, and then we could set them up in the town square and community members could bid on them or buy them outright, whatever everyone thinks would be the most fun."

The ladies and the two gentlemen who joined the committee nodded and murmured praise for the idea.

"Brilliant." Elanna waved her always perfectly manicured fingers toward Mary, the group's volunteer secretary.

Mary, a near-retirement public school teacher, jotted down the ideas as the brainstorming continued.

Excitement welled in Khrista at the opportunity to get out of her own headspace and to do good for the town and, especially, the kitties.

Always an animal lover, she had stopped taking in new pets after her last beloved feline had crossed the rainbow bridge. Khrista missed the companionship, but she had spent years as a borderline hoarder—hoarding all sorts of things, including pets. At one point she'd had ten cats, three parakeets, five guinea pigs, an assortment of hamsters and gerbils, and two dogs. It wasn't easy to house that many pets, and even harder to afford them. Yet she had struggled to learn to say no when she became the go-to dumping ground for anyone who needed to re-home their animals.

The house she and Kaelyn had lived in had been a small one, and Kaelyn had always been too embarrassed to invite her friends over.

Khrista had thought Kaelyn was being ridiculous—what kids didn't love pets?

It wasn't until after Kaelyn left for college and refused to bring her luggage in when she'd come home on holidays for fear of the smell invading her clothing that Khrista had to admit she might have a problem.

She had stopped accepting all the re-homing invitations people frequently sent her way. Khrista continued to care for her pets until their time ended naturally. And she spent her free time in the tearoom enjoying the cats who, like her, had been cast away for one reason or another.

Stroking Mr. Ed's long ginger fur as he snuggled into her lap, Khrista knew she had a lot to be grateful for.

And she also had a lot to make up for.

She had wanted to change forever. Now was the time. She had never felt more sure. More ready.

Would she be strong enough? Smart enough? Committed enough?

Khrista pushed the annoying, intrusive thoughts of self-doubt into the corners of her mind with the cobwebs that gathered there. She'd grow her confidence into a large, furry spider and let it feast on the annoying-as-black-flies-at-dusk negativity.

She had made it a full day without drinking even the maintenance drinks she had allowed herself through the years, and she didn't want to curse that by questioning herself. Her hands had trembled a little and she had only thought about the bottles in her closet about fifteen times.

The important part, however, was that she had not gone near them.

Khrista planned to work hard to reconnect with her community. Clarice would welcome her to the tearoom every day, just as she welcomed all of Old Castle's residents and visitors alike, and that would be Khrista's saving grace. Her plan for self-preservation included starting the day with a healthy breakfast, maintaining her sunny public disposition at work, staying at Happil-TEA Ever After until closing (unless she had other concrete plans that kept her mind occupied), and then walking on the beach before heading home and settling in with a relaxing cup of Clarice's special bedtime tea blend, which she had appropriately named, Slip Into Something Dreamy.

On occasion, Khrista had considered searching for Kaelyn online. Would the post with her pregnancy announcement be public? Would Khrista be brave enough to reach out to say hello? To beg for her daughter to find her way home?

So far, she had resisted the urge. Searching would almost certainly send her back into the comforting curves of her favorite bottles, and right now she was too much on the precipice of change to take the chance.

Khrista had never held such a firm conviction to do better, and she couldn't mess it up. Again.

But the urge to contact her was strong.

Maybe she could reach out to her daughter.

But could she handle the potential rejection?

She had to get herself under control before testing the waters.

Throwing herself into the various projects kept her busy, and though Khrista had tried this before and still ended up drinking when she was alone at home, this time would be different. This time, she had the strongest motivation to change.

Elanna's confident voice pulled Khrista out of her head and back into the meeting that was meant to distract her from venturing into the depths of those very thoughts.

"So Khrista, is two weeks enough lead time for you to get those canvasses to me?"

"Absolutely. I'll swing by the craft store and pick them up this weekend, and I'm sure Danielle won't mind if I shuffle our lesson plans around a bit this week."

"Perfect."

They finished up the meeting and about half of the group said their goodbyes and left the tearoom while the rest stayed chatting.

Everything felt right. Normal. As if this public persona of hers was her true self.

And then Mary unknowingly put a pin in Khrista's bubble of momentary happiness.

"It's so good to see you for longer than a quick hello," she said. "I've been meaning to tell you, I absolutely loved the post Kaelyn put up announcing her pregnancy. You must be beside yourself. I always knew Kaelyn had an artistic eye, but the little booties propped up next to the keys to her new home—the artistry of how she pulled the whole thing together truly touched me. I wrote to her to ask if I could use it for my art students. She's one of the students I'm glad I can follow even long after she's departed my classroom. I don't see her posting often on Facebook, but when she does she certainly takes my breath away."

Luckily, Mary was more interested in hearing her own voice than in Khrista's response, so Khrista hung on to every word she uttered, hoping for another hint into her daughter's life. She reminded herself to smile and nod when inside her heart throbbed and her organs felt too big for her body.

"Will you go out to see her during the pregnancy or wait for the birth? Oh, who am I kidding? I'm sure you'll do both. She might even want you to stay a few weeks to help her get settled after the baby arrives if you can get the time off work. People do that these days, especially with families separated across the country. My friend..."

Absently, Khrista nodded again, no longer registering the words coming out of Mary's mouth. She could only hear dramatic shifts in cadence. Lost in thought, she was grateful when Mary shifted to talking about her volunteer schedule and her husband's impending retirement plans.

The knowledge that these people were privy to information Khrista so badly wanted access to pained her in ways little else could. It tore at her guts and twisted deep inside her chest. Holding herself together in a public place—the place she could normally escape from her inner torment—grew harder and harder as the minutes ticked on.

When Lucia approached to ask Mary about her husband's health, Khrista took advantage of the distraction. She interrupted Elanna's conversation, gave her a quick kiss on the cheek, and told her she was going for a run on the beach before it got too dark.

She ran, but not to the beach.

She ran to her car, and then raced home and grabbed her bottle of Fireball, one she had found stashed away in her cereal cupboard and immediately placed with the rest of her soldiers. Khrista clutched it tight to her chest and allowed herself to feel the energy of the liquid promising to flow through her veins.

She wouldn't open it. She couldn't. It hadn't even been two full days since she had vowed to change.

She carried the bottle into her living room and placed it on the coffee table in front of her couch.

Khrista stared at the bottle as it would start performing for her. As if it truly were a living, breathing adversary.

Who was she kidding? It was.

She had never been one to win battles, no matter how hard she fought, but she had never had a grandbaby before, either.

Instead of the alcohol, Khrista treated herself to some raw cookie dough and a cup of freshly brewed loose leaf tea she had brought home from the tearoom. The chamomile and lavender worked hard to help settle her nerves, and she visualized healthy thoughts. She wrapped herself in a cozy blanket on the couch and flipped mindlessly through her phone.

She read the news.

She caught up on celebrity antics.

She perused the preschool teacher blogs for fresh ideas for her classroom.

And then she found herself on Facebook.

Khrista couldn't stop herself anymore. It wasn't fair that all these other people saw her daughter announcing her pregnancy, and she was being kept from it.

She quickly typed her daughter's name into the search bar.

No results found.

Variations on the spelling popped up, with other faces suggested to her instead of the one Kaelyn she actually wanted to see.

She searched again, trying Kaelyn's middle name instead of her last name as she had seen other young women do, and then begrudgingly entering the last name of the jerk Kaelyn had been dating when the estrangement began.

Nothing.

Why had no one mentioned anything to her about her daughter's social media presence before this pregnancy? Why hadn't they shared other details–was she married? Surely she would have posted photos of a wedding. Why had no one asked her why she, the mother of the bride, wasn't in any of the photos?

Khrista didn't need to examine her questions too closely to know the answers. The people who had known her the longest protected her. Though the only one who knew everything firsthand was Elanna, there was little doubt that news had traveled around the island. Old Castle was a small community, and while many people would spread rumors, just as many would wrap a protective bubble around Khrista.

Or maybe she was delusional.

Maybe she had spent too much time lost in a buzz and avoiding all mention of her daughter and that's why she hadn't heard anything.

Khrista called Elanna to ask her. She'd know. She'd be honest.

Elanna picked up on the first ring. "Hey hon. I can't talk long because I'm about to pick up dinner for the kids. What's up?"

Khrista let her questions tumble out, impressed with herself at how calm she remained.

Elanna answered without hesitation. "That's easy. Tons of people here didn't know Kaelyn since you moved back after your big fight. As far as I know, her Facebook was deactivated until very recently. I didn't even know she had one until I heard the same rumors you heard, and when she accepted my friend request a few days ago, I scrolled back and didn't see any information other than the pregnancy announcement. It says she's married, but she didn't tag the guy."

Married. Her daughter was married. And pregnant.

A ripple of joy for the life her daughter built nearly toppled over the sadness at Khrista's absence in that life.

Biting back emotion, Khrista had to ask, "Can you tell me the name her Facebook account displays? I'm trying to find her."

"Oh, honey, that's great! Ah, I can't tell you how relieved I am to hear that you're taking that important step."

"Don't get too excited," Khrista cautioned. "I'm not contacting her. I just wanted to see what everyone's talking about."

Elanna's silence tarnished the conversation and filled Khrista with regret. She shouldn't have called. She shouldn't have asked. She shouldn't have wondered.

"Hold on one second, let me just check her profile real quick. I've got you on speaker, so don't say anything too wild." Elanna mumbled as she tapped on the screen. "Okay, here it is. Kaelyn Fox."

Khrista thanked her friend and ended the call, her fingers shaking as she eagerly entered the information into the search bar.

Nothing came up.

Khrista bit back a scream, but refusing to release the volatile emotion led to a pounding head and an aching jaw.

Her daughter must've blocked her from finding her on social media.

How cruel.

How deliberate.

Kaelyn wasn't simply angry with her mother and didn't just feel she was better off maintaining a distance from her. This was a deliberate, hateful act.

Kaelyn hated her mother. What she had screamed at Khrista that day hadn't been the angry impulses of a young adult trying to find herself.

Not merely hormonal imbalances.

It had been pure, unadulterated *hate*.

And there was nothing Khrista could do to change it.

How could she when she'd never have a way to contact her? Not even if she battled the demons that had led her down this dead-end road.

She grabbed the bottle and twisted the cap off, then brought it to her lips, relishing the burn as it traveled down her throat and helped her find peace again.

The peace wouldn't last, but it was better than having to feel the pain so intensely.

Twenty minutes and a quarter of a bottle later, a text arrived from Matt. He wanted to know if she was available for a last-minute dinner with his children.

Khrista laughed to herself as she tried to formulate a response.

"Sorry, I'm not fit to be around people because I'm a drunk, and even though I could have killed myself the other night, here I am, hitting the bottle again."

Or maybe, "I would love the company, but I've avoided meeting your kids for almost three years already, so why push things now?"

Or perhaps more subtly, "I can't because I'm a broken human who can't be around happy families because I drove my own daughter away and lie to everyone close to me to cover up my failures and anguish."

Instead, she settled on the tried and true, "That sounds like so much fun! Thank you for thinking of me, but I've been fighting a migraine all day and need to stay in a dark room with a wet washcloth on my head. Please send my regards, and I hope we can do it soon."

As soon as she sent the text, Khrista turned the phone off. Less guilt that way.

Not that Matt would try to make her feel guilty. No, he was forever supportive. But she'd hear the undertones of disappointment in his voice, and she didn't want another excuse to medicate herself with the bottle.

She took one more swig before tightly capping the bottle, stumbling into the doorframe, and placing the enemy back with its fellow soldiers on the shelf in her closet.

Khrista slipped into exercise clothes and her running shoes, enjoying the way the room seemed to spin ever-so-gently as she bent over and attempted to straighten up again.

One drink was okay, right?

She had stopped before getting drunk. She could still function. Khrista would stick with her plan to run on the beach.

And she would pretend she hadn't already broken her promise to herself.

THE NEXT MORNING, Khrista awakened with a sunnier disposition. The run on the beach had done wonders for her spirit, energizing her so much that she had cleaned her entire living room, put away laundry that had languished near her couch for weeks, vacuumed, tossed out old, expired condiment bottles from her fridge, and scrubbed down her kitchenette counters before the endorphin high tapered off. Khrista had some trouble falling asleep, but once she did, she slept through the night.

She hopped out of bed the next morning. The freshness of a Sunday morning invigorated her, but more often than not, she had squandered the weekends away by giving in to her temptations to numb and hide. Though Matt often tried to make plans to see her on the weekends, she had earned a Master's degree in avoidance and excuse making.

Much easier to keep him at arm's length so she could maintain her lies.

That was the past.

Her only plans for the day were dropping by the tearoom for her daily dose of caffeine and hitting the craft shop in Portsmouth for the canvases she had promised Elanna. And though she normally stocked up on her little bottles of alcohol while off-island so she wouldn't be spotted, she would detour around any of the streets with liquor stores while in the city.

She took an extra-long shower, put some care into choosing nicer clothing than her usual leggings and oversized tee, and even put on a little makeup, which Khrista hadn't done in forever.

She felt like a new woman with new goals and something resembling motivation. And though it appeared she had lost some weight on her already too-thin frame since she had last worn these jeans and the scoop-necked blouse, she felt more like a human.

When Khrista arrived at the tearoom, she immediately noticed a small group of women, most of them older than her, gathered in a circle of chairs by the stone fireplace near where Khrista usually liked to sit.

The clickety-clacking of their knitting needles drew her in, which was hilarious because she didn't have a crafting bone in her body beyond the kinds of crafts her preschoolers could handle. Yet Khrista suddenly had the urge to create something.

*A baby blanket.*

She asked Clarice if the knitting club was accepting new members.

"They always are. Why don't you go on over and speak to them?"

Khrista blushed. Why did she suddenly feel as shy as one of her students on the first day of school?

"Khrista, this is your home. Surely you know some of those women?"

Khrista shrugged. Maybe she had, once upon a time. But between moving away ten years ago and then maintaining her personal bubble for the past five years since she returned, she couldn't place any of the faces.

Clarice *tsked* and grabbed Khrista by the elbow, marching her through the pegged-open double doors and over to the circle of rocking chairs.

"Hello Knot-TEA Knitters. This is my wonderful friend and longtime tea aficionado, Khrista–though I'm sure many of you know her, or of her, at least. She teaches preschool over at Old Castle Early Childhood Center. She'll tell you she has no ability to knit, but she'd like to try. You don't mind if we pull up an extra chair, do you?"

One woman, whose bright smile immediately took ten years off her appearance, said, "We'd be delighted to have you. I have an extra set of beginner's needles here and some yarn I'd be happy to share."

"Thank you so much." Warmth bloomed inside Khrista's chest as the women made space for her to join the circle and eagerly handed her things from their own knitting bags.

She loved this town because she was always made to feel so welcome. When she allowed herself, anyway.

But there was another reason for the expansion of her heart.

She had no control over Kaelyn's feelings, and she had no say over whether her daughter allowed a relationship with her grandbaby.

But Khrista could make the baby a blanket.

"I'll be going to the craft store later today. I can pick up my own supplies then, but I would love to borrow these for now, if you really don't mind."

The women went around the circle, introducing themselves and showing their projects. Isabelle, whom Khrista recognized from the library, held up a tiny baby bootie, which she was making for her fifth grandchild. Carmen showed off an almost complete afghan for a just-married daughter. Adelaide was making scarves for the homeless, Irma was trying her hand at making socks, and Ellie went on a rampage about how she had to tear out the second arm of the sweater she was knitting *again* because she couldn't get it just right.

Winnie, the woman who had first welcomed her, asked, "Do you have an idea of what you'd like to make?"

Without hesitation, Khrista's response flowed out. "I thought I could try a baby blanket. Just something basic."

"How precious. Do you have a baby coming soon into your family?"

Khrista stiffened. Maybe this was a bad idea. She hadn't thought through the lies she would tell or the stories she would weave.

So Khrista did what she had learned to do so many times in the past. She changed the subject.

"Those are the most beautiful colors I have ever seen," Khrista exclaimed, reaching across to touch Adelaide's scarf. The chunky yarn in bright pinks and oranges proved too tempting to resist. The softness didn't disappoint. "Truly lovely."

If Winnie noticed the deflection, she didn't draw attention to it.

"Well, come on over. Let's get you going."

Winnie started the yarn and needles and took a moment to teach Khrista a basic stitch. Khrista amazed herself with how quickly she grew to love the clacking of the needles and the sense of accomplishment as she created a chain. When she got to the end of the line and Winnie told her to stop, she struggled to learn how to double back with the second row.

The women all laughed and shared stories of their early struggles. Khrista howled in laughter when they coyly added that they were children when they had those struggles.

When Khrista snorted, the rest of the ladies broke into raucous laughter, sending the cats who had been resting in front of the fire out of the room.

Irma came to her rescue and shared how she had only learned to knit about five years ago, after the death of her husband, and that though it had taken some time to catch on, she now felt quite proficient.

By the end of the hour, Khrista had three lines that loosely resembled a blanket-to-be and a heart full of joy at feeling like part of a close-knit group.

She would pour all of her unbridled love and hope into this creation for a baby she may never know, but would love just the same.

On her way out of the tearoom, she lingered by the back room where Clarice was organizing her new shipment of tea.

"Winnie mentioned you were looking for someone to provide transportation for a member who doesn't drive so she can come to the tearoom for some social engagement." Khrista took the box from Clarice's hands and carried it into her tea sorting area where she sold tea by the ounce from bulk tins for people who wanted to take it home or create their own blends. "I'd be happy to pick her up."

Clarice pressed a hand to her stomach. "That would be wonderful. We have a homebound senior who's very lonely. Her husband died about a year ago and she hasn't been willing or able to come in since. We're starting up an elderly social circle for our older community members. On NPR they were talking the other day about how loneliness is such a problem for the elderly. I hate to think of that happening here in our little community where we pride ourselves on taking care of each other."

"I may not be elderly quite yet, although my knees might tell you otherwise, but I've always benefited from that community spirit here in Old Castle. You took me in on two separate occasions when I was at my lowest, and if I can give back even in this smallest way, I'd feel so good about that."

"That's just what we do here, darling. You know we are one big family here. And like it or not, we're going to keep loving each other no matter what." Clarice placed a hand on Khrista's shoulder and squeezed gently before turning back to her work. "Let me write down her address. Maybe you can bring her on Wednesday evening for the social circle. We're having a make-your-own-tea-blend event, and maybe even a paint-your-own-teacup party for the group. Although I might hold off and do that next week. Or maybe we should do the teacup first and the tea blend second."

Clarice tossed her hands in the air, her bracelets jingling.

"This is just me thinking out loud. I'll phone Bess and let her know you're coming. She's ambulatory so she can get herself down the stairs. You'll just need to pull up to the door and beep and she'll come down."

"I look forward to meeting her." Khrista opened one of the tins of tea and inhaled the sweet peach scent. "One question, though. Do I get to stay for the blending party?"

Clarice tossed her head back in laughter. "Of course you do. I wouldn't have it any other way."

After running to Portsmouth to stock up on canvases—and spending a mini fortune on yarn and knitting needles—Khrista went home and manically cleaned all the windows in her apartment, finding a new sense of joy in the cleansing of all the things she had neglected for so long.

She bagged up a bunch of clothing from her closet to donate and then felt inspired enough to clear out some of her kitchen cabinets as well. Once she had a trunk full of things, she brought them down the street to a donation drop-box. A thought occurred to her as she drove, motivating her to pull over and, on her smartphone, log into her bank account.

Khrista made little money and always struggled to pay her bills, but she needed to do something proactive. She would make a blanket and she would start a savings account for the baby.

With a few clicks, she opened an online savings account with a decent yield. Khrista set up a transfer on her account for twenty-five dollars weekly and vowed to pick up more hours at work if she could or, even better, she would put the money she normally spent on alcohol into the account and would feel satisfied watching the amount grow, knowing she was doing something more positive with it.

When she got home that night, she answered Matt's texts from the night before.

"Hey, Matt, so sorry I've been strange this week. A lot going on that I'd love to catch you up on. Are you free for dinner tonight?"

Matt responded almost immediately, telling her he understood and hoped she was okay, and he could be by in thirty minutes to pick her up.

Khrista waited downstairs as she usually did when he was coming to get her, and watched him pull up with gratitude in her heart.

Pride, too.

Despite all of her flaws, she had found a good man who seemed to care about her more than she could have hoped for, plus she made it through the entire day without turning to the bottle. Not even for one sip. She had barely thought of her nemesis.

For the first time in many, many years, things were looking up.

# 8

## KAELYN

Wrapping her mind around her work grew more and more difficult as the week passed. Kaelyn sipped her iced latte from the specialty tearoom en route from home to work, relishing the spicy decaf chai and the creaminess of the oat milk. The first thing she had done after they put an offer in on the house had been to seek out a tearoom that would remind her of one of the things she missed the most about her old hometown. True, this place didn't quite compare to Clarice's, but it helped her feel a little closer to the parts of her childhood she had enjoyed.

She was collaborating on a big project with her team and they had a meeting scheduled for the following day. Though Kaelyn should have been at least seventy-five percent done with her portion, her progress bar hovered closer to the thirty-five percent mark.

Graphic design was her passion, and she loved manipulating art and using her creativity. Bringing someone's vision to life, or, more typically, convincing them that her idea had been their vision all along, fulfilled her in ways she had been excited to discover in college.

But right now, all of Kaelyn's thoughts seemed to be stuck in her uterus.

Yet another wave of nausea washed over her. She nearly spilled her tea in her rush to put it down and hurry off to the restroom yet again. Kaelyn sensed the sympathetic gazes on her as she hastened past her office mates. When she returned to her desk after a bout of the ineptly named morning sickness (considering it stuck with her all day and all night), there was usually a little gift of a peppermint candy, a fresh cup of water, or a piece of dark chocolate waiting for her. Sometimes there would be a little note telling her she was doing great.

Everything Kaelyn had read suggested morning sickness was a good sign the pregnancy was progressing normally.

She held onto that hope.

Once back at her desk, she thanked her understanding coworkers–many of them parents themselves–for the pile of ginger candy and saltines they had left. They were too thoughtful. And obviously having fun with this.

Her mind had transformed into a hamster running on a wheel—constantly moving but getting nowhere. Kaelyn wondered if she would have another idea for the rest of the week. Or the month. Heck, would she ever have her brain back again? She had heard of "mommy brain," but she hadn't imagined it would set in so soon. The baby wasn't even kicking yet.

Distracted beyond belief, Kaelyn went through the mindless tasks of checking her social media and her email. She had turned off notifications days ago to minimize distractions, but now she *craved* a distraction.

She answered messages until she came to one that had her perplexed.

Kaelyn and Oliver had purchased DNA ancestry testing kits for each other for Christmas. They thought it would be cool to see how their genetics compared.

She had received her results back, but hadn't had much of a chance to explore it.

Now she had a message saying she had a new close connection.

Typically, when she received those messages, she was disappointed to find it was some distant cousin, like a fourth or fifth cousin who barely counted as a relation. Kaelyn didn't know what she hoped for, and maybe she didn't hope for anything. But there was a pit in her stomach each time she clicked onto the site.

This time, the bottom of her stomach dropped. She had always wondered about that cliché, but even though she was sitting, she felt that exact feeling.

She had matched with a grandmother.

Would it be a paternal grandmother? Or the maternal grandmother her mother had taken her away from?

Although her father had died long ago, Kaelyn had always hoped that she could connect to her father's relatives. Maybe his parents were still alive, or he'd had other children after her mother left him. She might not feel so alone in the world if she had half-siblings. Maybe she'd get the chance to connect with people who were more like her than her mother had been.

Would her mother have told her if her father had sired more children after she left him? Would she have known?

Kaelyn didn't want to think about the loneliness of growing up fatherless, but the thoughts festered. She had vague recollections of her father pushing her on a swing. She remembered a big fight. And then, just absence.

Were any of the things her mother told her about her father true? That he had been abusive? That they had moved from shelter to shelter, hiding from him, until Khrista got news of his death and felt safe enough to settle down with Kaelyn in one place, in Old Castle?

Her phone rang, and Kaelyn picked it up on the second ring. That call led to a flurry of activity that kept her busy for the rest of the day. Fifteen minutes before it was time to head out, she checked the DNA site once again.

She clicked on the connection and read the name.

*Daisy O'Donnell.*

Her mother's mother.

Kaelyn had few memories of her time with her grandparents, but she remembered the overall feeling of being adored. Her grandmother would make her special garlic cheese biscuits and let Kaelyn help roll them into little balls. Her grandfather would leave the room so Kaelyn could watch cartoons on their one small TV. She was never allowed to sit in his chair, but that hadn't bothered her. She had avoided it like hot lava.

Her last memory of them was hazy. She had been around five years old and visiting for the weekend, but her mother had been cranky the whole time. She remembered waking up from a nap in the room they shared and hearing lots of yelling and anger downstairs. Scared, she had buried her head under a blanket.

Something about the anger frightened her. She didn't know what to do. Was Mama okay? She sounded so mad. But Mama had always told her if she heard fighting to stay away. Kaelyn hugged her toy panda close to her chest and tried not to cry. Her mommy would take care of things.

After singing Twinkle Twinkle Little Star to her panda *twelve* times, her mom came to her room, and Kaelyn never forgot her mom's teary, puffy face as she scooped her daughter up in her arms and, without explanation, carried her away. She left half of Kaelyn's clothing behind—she was in such a rush. Kaelyn couldn't see her grandmother's face as she searched her memory banks, but she recalled spindly arms reaching out for Kaelyn and her mother forcefully yelling, "No!"

Her yell had hurt Kaelyn's ears.

Her mother buckled her into her booster seat and drove away, ignoring Kaelyn's pleas for information. Her mother sobbed the entire way, driving through the night and into the next day. Kaelyn had a vague memory of waking up in the middle of the night and being scared again because the car had stopped and her mom was weeping with her head on the wheel.

"Mama?"

No response.

"Mama." Kaelyn had grown more concerned. What if there were bad guys outside the windows? It was too dark to see, with only a little bit of light streaming in. What if they tried to get her?

"Mama!" Kaelyn's little voice went from shaky to urgent as she pleaded for her mom to wake up.

She tried to unbuckle herself from her seat, but her hands were shaking and cold and she couldn't press the button.

"Mama! Mama! Wake up! I'm scared!"

Her mother's head jerked up. "What's the matter?"

Kaelyn burst into tears, her whole body shaking and vomit burning in the back of her throat. She didn't throw up, but she wanted to.

"Kaelyn, is there something wrong?"

"I forgot my teddy bear book at Grammy's house."

"You woke me up for that? Darn it, Kaelyn." Mama banged her hand against the steering wheel. Her voice hurt Kaelyn's ears. "I need to sleep so I can drive safely. Go back to sleep. I'll get you another stupid book."

Kaelyn didn't know why her mom was talking to her like that. She sometimes yelled if Kaelyn didn't listen right away or if they were running late and Kaelyn wouldn't get her shoes on, but she had never been mean to her before.

Kaelyn's heart shattered.

"You're mean. I hate you!" And then Kaelyn buried her face in her hands and sobbed as if the world had ended.

Because for her, it had.

That was the night when she had started to lose faith in her mother's ability to protect her and when the bad guys outside the window turned out to be her mom on the inside of the car. The night when the fragile bond of trust had begun to crackle.

Although her mother apologized for snapping at her and for forgetting her favorite book, their relationship had never been the same. Especially when days turned into weeks and the seasons changed without seeing her father or grandparents again. Her mother pulled away from her in ways Kaelyn hadn't understood at the time. She only remembered feeling alone and scared and cold and uncared for.

Kaelyn's mother had developed a habit of isolating her from

everyone she knew and loved. Her father. Her grandparents. And ultimately, her.

KAELYN SET her laptop aside on the plush leather couch when Oliver opened the front door.

"You're late."

She met him halfway and wrapped her arms around his neck. He kissed her in tiny little butterfly kisses all around her face, making her giggle as his adoration washed away the stress of the day.

"You're a magician." Kaelyn melted into his comforting body, resting her head on his shoulder.

"I hope you remember those words and try not to be mad at me."

"Why would I be mad at you? Did you do something?"

He lowered his head bashfully. "Okay, yes, I did. But I couldn't resist."

The adorable, boyish look on his face prevented her mind from spinning to any level of suspicion. Not that she would ever suspect him of anything but perfection, anyway.

Her friends hated that when they got together and they inevitably started bashing their partners, Kaelyn never had anything bad to say about him. He loaded the dishwasher perfectly, he never left his socks around on the floor, and he treated her like an equal. He accepted her faults, claimed she didn't have any, and, even on the rare occasion when he was in a bad mood, he greeted every day with reverence and made sure to turn his mood around until he infected the both of them with severe cases of the cheeries.

Okay, so sometimes the positivity could be a bit...much.

Sometimes she wanted to scream at him that he annoyed her with his constant upbeat attitude when she wanted to vent and complain.

There were times when she felt like a horrible person because she could get moody from time to time and not want to be fixed.

But still, she couldn't ask for better. Kaelyn trusted him more than she trusted herself.

"You'd better start 'splainin', mister."

Oliver brought his hand from behind his back, and she realized he'd been hiding something back there. She recognized the logo on the bag as a specialty boutique on Rodeo Drive–one she had done graphics work for in the past.

He pulled the item out of the bag and she gasped, clapping her hands together in delight.

"I know I should have waited for you to shop with me for the first baby item, but I was driving by and saw this in the window and I couldn't help myself. Please don't ask me how much I spent on it, because I don't want to have to lie to you, but I also don't want to admit how foolish I was."

She laughed and shook her head.

"Whatever you paid was not enough. That is the most adorable sweater I have ever seen. How is it so small?"

She took the tiny creation from his hands and marveled over the workmanship.

"It's so soft. I cannot *wait* to see our baby in this."

He exhaled dramatically. "You're not mad?"

She rolled her eyes and grinned.

"As if I could ever be mad at you."

"Oh, I remember a time when I used a metal spoon on your nonstick frying pan and scratched it all up. Pretty sure you refused to speak to me for a week."

"I didn't speak to you for like an hour, Mr. Dramatic. Besides, that nonstick pan set cost a mini fortune. I saved up for it *forever*, and it was one of the first domesticy things I bought myself."

"I know." Oliver cupped his hands, one of them still holding the boutique gift bag, on her waist, and tugged her hips to his. "I'm so glad I brought you to the side of cast iron and stainless steel."

He rubbed his nose on hers, and Kaelyn yanked on his neck to bring his lips down for a kiss.

"I'm so glad you brought me to any side that involves you."

"I like the effect hormones are having on you." He moaned against her mouth, and, in a sudden thrust, pressed her body to the wall. As his hand went for the hem of her shirt, she put a palm over his to still him.

"The hormones are great at times, but right now I can't give them free rein. I have work to do."

"Who needs a job, anyway?"

"Maybe you can direct that question to the mortgage company. Pretty sure they liked that we had income." Kaelyn giggled as he buried his scruffy face against the delicate skin of her neck.

"Are you sure I can't entice you for a minute or two?"

"Oh, well, when you put it that way, it just gets me so excited. A whole minute or two of your time? What ever would I do with that amount of pleasure?"

"It wouldn't be my fault if you're responsible for making me come undone so quickly."

He kissed her long and hard, and Kaelyn cursed herself for not being more productive at work during the day. She'd so much rather spend time wrapped in her husband's loving embrace instead of fighting brain fog in front of a screen.

He had the most amazing ability to make her forget stressful things.

And for the baby's sake, she needed to limit her stress levels. Oliver pulled away the slightest bit, his hooded eyes looking tormented for a moment, before his familiar smile lit up his face once more.

"Well, since you're so good at resisting me today, I guess I can change the subject. Do you have a block of time this weekend to go over ideas for the nursery?"

She ducked under his arm and moved back toward the couch.

"Too abrupt of a topic change?"

Hiding her annoyance took an inordinate amount of effort.

"Not at all," she lied. "I'd love to discuss ideas. I just have *so* much work I have to do. The baby makes me throw up so often during the day that it's been impossible to get anything done at work."

"I'm sorry, love. I wish I could take on some of the suffering in your place."

"I wish you could, too," she teased. "This growing baby business isn't nearly as angelic as they make it seem on the commercials."

"That's why it's important to get with the 21st-century and not watch commercials," he teased back, knowing full well she had to study them as part of her job.

Oliver leaned over and kissed her lips, chastely this time, and then excused himself to take a shower. He paused and turned to face her again.

"Not to heap tasks on, but we've got to start touring daycares sooner than later. Apparently there are waitlists."

Every time he mentioned daycare her gut throbbed. Why was the idea of leaving her baby with strangers so unappealing?

He must have noticed the disgust on her face. "Mother has offered to mind the baby if we prefer."

Perhaps a better option, but her heart still ached at the idea of someone else being there for her baby's smiles and laughter. Someone else soothing her baby's cries.

She needed to get over that because they needed both of their incomes to live where they lived. And she loved her job.

"Can we talk about it later?" She gestured to her computer to remind him that she had work.

While he was in the shower, she took the time to check her socials and her email. She needed to shift her mind away from the pain of not being with her baby every single second.

As soon as she opened her inbox, she was greeted by another message from the DNA site.

She opened the email, and every part of her body shook.

She had tried so hard to push this latest development to the back of her mind. She didn't have time to think about a long lost grandmother, especially if there was a chance she had also reached out to Khrista.

And yet...

She couldn't resist the urge to open the stupid message.

The email alerted her to a new message in her inbox on the ancestry site from a Daisy O'Donnell.

Her stomach tightened, and she thought she would throw up for the eight millionth time that day. Kaelyn closed her eyes, took a deep breath, and waited until the wave of nausea passed. Then, knowing Oliver would be out of the shower in a few minutes and not wanting him to see her reaction right away, because she knew he'd be overly enthusiastic and try to push her into something she wasn't sure she'd want to do, she hurriedly opened a new tab on her browser, logged in, and read the message in her inbox.

*Dearest Kaelyn,*

*I am your grandmother, as you can see from the DNA match. I know you don't know me and probably don't remember me, because the last time I saw you, you were only a tiny girl.*

*I know your mother made decisions she felt she needed to make, but I'm hoping now that you're an adult and I'm free of so many of the things that made my life a threat to you, I'm hoping we can reconnect.*

*I don't know how your mother will feel about this, but you're an adult and I hope she'll find it in her heart to be okay with this.*

*Over a month ago, I tried to reach out to my daughter. When she didn't respond, a friend suggested I try this ancestry kit in hopes that she would have also taken it and we could be linked. While I haven't seen her on here, I am delighted to have matched with you. I've never believed in fate or luck, but if I hear back from you I will become a believer.*

*I'm a seventy-year-old woman and I've missed you for my whole life, even before you existed.*

*If you don't feel comfortable reaching out to me, or if your mother would rather you didn't, I understand. You don't owe me anything, and neither does she.*

*But more than anything, I hope you'll want to message me back. I don't know where this communication will lead, but I hope it leads me back into your heart. Because you have never left mine.*

*Love,*

*Grandma Daisy*

KAELYN SLAMMED her laptop closed as Oliver emerged from the bathroom. She swiped away at the tears that fell over her cheeks, hoping he didn't see.

Oliver had always been ridiculously observant, but she hoped she had moved fast enough to hide her reaction from him.

Why? She couldn't say.

All she knew was she wasn't ready to share this tiny slice of... hope? Confusion? Fear?

Whatever it was, she wanted the time and space to sort out her feelings without her own personal Mr. Fix It influencing her decisions.

He went straight into the kitchen, his short brown hair dripping and a towel wrapped around his waist, and she could hear him filling a glass with water from the fridge. He had probably left a puddle of water outside the tub again.

He called out over his shoulder to her.

"Hey, babe. Did you remember to take your prenatal?"

"Yeah."

She picked up her closed laptop and her folder of notes. "I'm gonna set up shop in the guest room to work for now. I brought home subs for dinner, but I'm not hungry yet. Go ahead and eat without me and I'll see you when I come to bed."

Kaelyn didn't wait for his response. If he noticed she was upset and asked her why she was being so abrupt and dismissive, she'd break down. She didn't have time to break down. So she hurried up to the spare room and shot off a response to her grandmother.

She tried to focus on work, but her eyes blurred every time she turned to that screen.

Her grandmother was awaiting a response.

*Her grandmother.*

Kaelyn had never been impulsive. Rash, perhaps. Temperamental, absolutely. But she carefully planned all of her moves, and she typically loved to consult with Oliver on decisions now that they were life partners.

Her heart had different ideas for this grandmother situation.

Excitement welled in her belly and rose into her fluttering heart.

What would it hurt to respond?

Not like they were going to see each other or anything. Maybe the whole communication thing would fizzle right away. They didn't know each other. Why get Oliver's hopes up that she'd suddenly have a biological family? He wanted that for her, but she didn't want to be pushed. Or pressured. Or influenced.

As much as she loved sharing her life with Oliver, she wanted this one thing to be hers and hers alone. For the time being.

She'd tell him once she knew how it would play out.

She should get it over with. Send a message so she could focus on work. That's all this was. Just a mind-clearing mission.

Not her getting her hopes up.

She opened the message again and, before thinking it through, she typed.

*Dear Grandma,*

*Thank you so much for contacting me. I wouldn't have known where to start looking for you. I didn't remember the name of the town or even the state where you live, so I'm so excited you found me through this DNA thing. I'm so glad this new stuff exists so we can make this connection.*

*I remember some fun times we used to have, and I have never forgiven my mother for taking me away from you the way she did.*

*Don't worry about how she might feel or what she might think about our reconnection. She's out of my life, and, as you said, I'm an adult and can make my own decisions. Her days of ruling over me and making decisions about who's allowed in my life are over.*

*I hope you and Grandpa are well. Thank you for the kind words.*

*I may not remember what you look like, but you never left my heart either.*

*Love,*

*Kaelyn*

SHE ADDED her contact information to the bottom of the message and sent it before she could think twice, and then she did her very best to get the work done that her team was counting on her to do.

A small voice inside tried to guilt her for keeping this from Oliver, knowing how excited he'd be. She'd tell him when the time was right. She couldn't bring herself to discuss it openly and have to analyze all the feelings this communication stirred up.

She didn't climb into bed until almost three in the morning, but when she did, Oliver wrapped his arms around her and pulled her in tight the second her body hit the sheets. Maybe there was a chance the world would right itself again. She fell asleep instantly.

Over the next few days, Kaelyn and her grandmother sent messages back and forth, first over the DNA messaging system and then they moved into texting. Her grandmother said it was the first time she had really texted, but after a few attempts and some coaching, she had grown quite proficient. She had even learned to use a few emojis, though Kaelyn had had a good laugh when her grandmother bragged about the giant eggplants she had bought at the farmer's market and sent the corresponding emojis.

Kaelyn wasn't about to explain that one to her.

On the fourth day of their correspondence, her grandma asked if she could fly out to see Kaelyn.

Without hesitation, Kaelyn said yes. She told her all about her new home, the guest room her grandmother could stay in, and how wonderful it would be to see her again. They made plans to walk the beach—her grandmother said she hadn't seen the ocean since her daughter had been a young girl—and to see the Hollywood sign if they had time.

Getting enough time off to travel to her grandmother would have been a challenge for Kaelyn, especially with maternity leave coming up in the not-so-distant future, so how awesome that her grandmother, who said she had never even been on an airplane before, was willing to come and see her?

How bad could this woman have been when she was being so kind and so giving and accommodating? And she didn't even know Kaelyn. Not really.

She was willing to come and stay in a home with a man she had never met and a granddaughter she hadn't interacted with in twenty years.

Kaelyn hoped she could make up for her mother's shortcomings.

Kaelyn had been sad to find out her grandfather had died, but she remembered little about him anyway, and strangely, her grandmother sounded pretty okay with his passing.

That was a story Kaelyn needed to uncover, but it would probably be best over tea in her sunroom rather than texting.

Kaelyn sent a quick selfie to Oliver as a prelude to their planned date night, just like they had always done. She put a little extra effort into a more seductive pose to make up for her purposeful avoidance of him over the last several days. She wanted to open up to him about her grandmother, but the more time that passed, the longer she knew the conversation would have to be. And he suspected something. His quizzical looks hadn't escaped her notice, but she'd blamed the big work project for her distraction.

Why was she so scared to talk to him about this?

She looked forward to their date. A chance to reconnect after a crazy week.

A movie in addition to dinner would have been fun, but with her level of exhaustion, Kaelyn wouldn't make it past the previews, let alone through an entire film.

Oliver was cool with that because he preferred to snuggle up with her in their bed while watching a movie, anyway.

Besides, he made better popcorn.

They met at home so they could drive together, but their conversation consisted of small talk, work talk, and intermittent silence. Even so, he kept a hand on her knee as he drove, anchoring her to the present.

The need to talk to him about the deeper stuff plagued her. So much so that her already-too-frequent need to pee increased along with her thumping heart.

Oliver sensed something was off with her. He didn't have to tell her for her to know—they had the kind of connection where they almost eerily sensed so much about each other. She'd been keeping quiet about her grandmother long enough to grow uncomfortable with her lack of sharing. He'd given her the space he must have sensed she needed.

She had to broach the subject over dinner.

Before they entered the restaurant, the urge to spill her secrets rose in her throat with the same urgency as her bouts of morning sickness.

She paused on the sidewalk outside the restaurant's glass doors. Oliver dropped his hand from the handle and turned toward her, his eyes darkening with concern.

Why was she being so weird? She had never hesitated to tell him anything before.

Almost never.

Before she could think, Kaelyn blurted out a stream of words she hoped made more sense to him than to her, since the thudding of her heart drowned out all other sounds, making her voice sound far away.

"Please don't be mad. I haven't meant to keep this from you, but it's been all so new and crazy and we haven't really had a chance to talk that much about anything except baby stuff, and, well, I wanted to make sure it was an actual thing before I said anything about it, and I wasn't really sure how I even felt about it so I wanted to sort of process everything before bringing it to you and—"

"Kaelyn, love."

He gripped her shoulders and steered her fully toward him, demanding eye contact, which she begrudgingly gave. She chewed her lip and twisted her ankle around as they stood.

"What are you talking about? I don't mean to be rude, but would you please spit it out? My anxiety is increasing with every word in this run-on sentence of yours."

Kaelyn laughed nervously, wondering if she had remembered to put deodorant on because her armpits suddenly felt damp.

"My grandmother—my mother's mother—contacted me recently."

He frowned slightly and scratched his cheek.

"I know," she continued. "It's so weird. She found me on the DNA site and we've been chatting for the last few days."

"The last few days? Why didn't you mention it?"

"I didn't mean to keep it from you. Okay, I guess I did. I needed to sit with the idea of being in touch with someone from my past before I could invite your thoughts on it. I'm sorry I kept it from you."

He lifted her sweaty hands, giving them a squeeze before bringing her knuckles to his lips. "You don't need to be sorry. This is delightful news."

"I think it is. I guess I didn't realize how strange I was feeling going through life with no family. Other than you, of course. Which, believe me, is way more than enough. If I could only choose one person, it would be you."

"But the beautiful thing is, you don't have to choose."

"I sort of invited her to come and stay with us for a little bit. I hope that's okay with you."

He smiled, but there was tension in his cheeks.

"Of course, you can have any guests you'd like."

Kaelyn studied his face. What was wrong? Was he actually upset that she hadn't told him sooner? Did he prefer to be part of the decision to have her visit?

"Oliver, why aren't you looking at me? I have to admit, I thought you'd be jumping out of your skin in excitement."

His gaze met her eyes, and she was reassured by the warmth there, if a bit chilled by the absence of joy.

"I'm thrilled you've reunited with your grandmother, and I can't wait to meet her. I just worry that it was so easy for you to hide something so big from me."

This was not the reaction she had expected, and knowledge of all the other things she hid crept into her conscience.

He squeezed her hands gently and stepped closer, his warmth radiating to her body.

"Just promise me there's nothing else you're keeping from me. I want you to know you can tell me anything."

A tiny fluttering in her belly gave her the out she needed. She startled and gripped her belly, her eyes widening in shock.

"Oliver, I think I felt the baby move."

And with that distraction, she cemented her lies into the past, knowing if they ever found their way into the light again, Oliver would have reason to lose faith in her.

9

---

# DAISY

Daisy's realtor, the daughter-in-law of one of her new friends at the senior center, marveled at how quickly Daisy's home had sold. Daisy couldn't believe it herself—only two days on the market and she hadn't done anything to update the place other than a good cleaning. The realtor marveled more that Daisy had managed, at her age, to clear it out and be ready to move before the end of the week.

Merigold, the social worker who had become a close friend even though she was nearly forty years younger than Daisy, had taught Daisy how to sell her items online right from her phone. She set her up with the Facebook and showed her the online yard sale groups and what she called "the marketplace." Daisy had given away or sold almost every item, and the things she wasn't able to sell right away, she stacked up in the driveway for a nonprofit organization to pick up to distribute among their thrift stores.

Overall, Daisy felt positive about the change.

So long as she kept focused on the tasks at hand and not on the fact that weeks–almost months–had passed with no response from Khrista.

Had the email address been wrong? Or did Khrista delete it along with Daisy's hopes of a reunification?

Her senior center friends—she still couldn't quite believe she had friends!—tried talking her away from the edge. They thought the precipice she stood on was a dangerous one. That she would give away all of her material goods, sell the home she had spent a lifetime taking care of, and endanger herself flying across the country alone when she had never stepped foot in an airport. Though it had been their idea for her to send her vial of saliva into that DNA site in hopes that either Khrista or Kaelyn would have done the same and they could connect that way, they were shocked when she *did* make the connection and took the next logical step.

At the senior breakfast, Patricia was the first to break the silence when Daisy excitedly told them her plans. She pushed herself forward in the dining room chair, clutching the rounded edges of the table to steady herself.

"Call or text, sure. But sell off all your belongings, including your home, and fly across the country to stay with a person you don't really know?" Patricia took off her glasses and placed them on the table next to her fruit plate. "Let us help you. I'm sure we can get you out of the real estate deal."

Daisy shook her head and smiled. "I don't want out. This is the most sure I've been about anything in my life."

Karen let out a sigh and tossed her danish on her plate. "This is the sort of thing young kids do, Daisy, not women our age."

They all seemed to be in agreement, each heaping their objection onto the others.

"Traveling has really changed, you know. It's not easy navigating those airports and security and..."

"Things just aren't safe for older women traveling alone. You could get mugged or assaulted or..."

"Oh, nonsense." Her bravest friend, Margaret, waved a hand in the air and crinkled her face in disgust as they all tried to dissuade Daisy.

Margaret had been the one Daisy most envied when she first met her at the senior center. She dressed in a way that was far more youthful than the lines around her eyes suggested, and she carried herself with more confidence than any other woman she had ever known.

As they sipped tea together at the center, Margaret seemed thrilled to have Daisy's rapt attention as she shared details of her around-the-world adventures. She told of how she hitchhiked across Europe when she was in her forties, and she swore she would do it again sometime soon. She made Daisy drool with stories of cooking classes in Italy, of devouring strange and unusual—and mind-blowingly delicious—dishes in Zanzibar, and even trying haggis in Scotland.

Daisy had always wanted to travel, but she had never imagined she actually would.

But now was her chance.

"Margaret, I hate to trouble you, but would you be willing to help me make a list of things I'll need for when I travel? Merigold showed me how to use that TV tube on my phone to watch videos about going through airline security and such, but I know there's a lot I don't know, and I hoped for advice from you."

"Oh, sugar. A list is no fun. I'll take you shopping and we'll get you everything you need."

Daisy hadn't been able to turn her down, not that she would have wanted to. The last time she had shopped with friends, she had been a young girl of sixteen or seventeen. Before marriage.

Before isolation.

Before imprisonment.

Margaret picked Daisy up in her fancy BMW. She called it her "I didn't get married and have children" car.

Daisy thought it a bit flashy for someone of their years, but who was she to judge? She didn't even have a license.

They started the day at a luggage score after Daisy confessed she gave away her old 1970s hardback luggage when she used it to pack some things that she donated. Margaret insisted she have a suitcase with four wheels that could rotate from any direction.

"Trust me, Daisy. When you're working your way through the airport, you'll be glad your suitcase will be able to walk alongside you."

"And this is why I asked the expert."

Margaret seemed to enjoy being called the expert, and Daisy was happy to fuel her ego. She'd been instrumental in helping Daisy find the courage to leave her comfortable bubble and explore the lost parts of herself.

"I'm glad you didn't listen to those biddies. You have to be brave in life, otherwise, what's the point?"

That baggage felt a bit too heavy even for a luggage store, but Daisy nodded in agreement. "I wasn't feeling too brave when I sent that message to my granddaughter. Kaelyn's her name."

"You've mentioned that a time or two," Margaret teased. "And don't think I've missed the way your voice livens up when you say her name."

Daisy didn't try to hide the smile as she caressed a leather suitcase, enjoying the smoothness of the material and the joy of anticipation.

"You think I did the right thing in reaching out? I've had nightmares about my daughter getting more angry when she finds out I bypassed her and contacted Kaelyn. I didn't think it through before sending the message, but now all I can think of is what could go wrong."

"Maybe it's time to replace those thoughts with what could go *right*." Margaret turned away from the set of flamingo pink luggage she had been eyeing and gave her full attention to Daisy. "Look, you tried to reach your daughter, yes? She hasn't responded for whatever reason. You don't have all the time in the world to wait. So you tried your granddaughter and got what you wanted. Maybe this contact will be the bridge that leads you back to your daughter."

"And if the bridge is washed out?"

Margaret shrugged and turned toward another luggage display. "Then at least you tried. And at least you'll have your granddaughter."

After finding a set of luggage they agreed would be perfect, they stopped for lunch at a little Italian place Daisy normally wouldn't have glanced twice at because it looked far too fancy for her. Margaret's matter-of-fact words reassured her and took the edge off the anxiety. Her heart and stomach still flip-flopped, but Margaret was right. At least Daisy would have Kaelyn.

That was a chance worth fighting for.

And it wasn't like things could get worse between Daisy and Khrista.

She held her breath at that thought. She didn't like it one bit.

"Hey, yoohoo." Margaret waved her hand in front of Daisy's face as the waiter placed the basket of bread and butter on the table in front of them. "If I learned one thing as a solo traveler, it's that worry doesn't solve any problems. But you know what does? Focusing on the good things on the plate in front of you."

Daisy appreciated Margaret's sage words of wisdom, and did her best to follow her guidance.

The bread was divine, and the handmade gnocchi even better. Daisy vowed that if this trip to California went well and if she survived to plan a future trip, she'd go straight to Italy and eat her way through every pasta dish she could find in that beautiful country.

She mentioned her plan to Margaret as she sopped sauce up with the last piece of bread, and Margaret made her promise she would invite her on that trip.

The idea of having a traveling companion brought the lightness of a dandelion's wisps to her insides.

After lunch, when Daisy felt far too full to move, they stopped at a tea shop and ordered a digestive blend made with peppermint and ginger. Margaret swore by this as a solution for clearing the belly so they could continue shopping, and Daisy had to admit that after drinking a cup she had more of a spring to her step.

She was beside herself with excitement over hitting the next set of stores with Margaret, even though her feet ached and her ankles had begun to strain against her compression stockings. She couldn't believe Margaret was so willing to spend this whole day with her. Maybe they were both a little lonely.

Daisy had overheard a few of the women at the senior center gossiping about Margaret, saying she was stuck up and thought too much of herself because of her "worldly" adventures. They said that every time anyone talked about anything, Margaret had a story to tell about some far-off country and adventures she had there. Some of them wondered if her stories were even true.

Daisy felt the stories were all authentic. And she appreciated the passion in Margaret's eyes when Daisy asked questions about her adventures. Daisy was always genuinely excited to hear them, and she sensed Margaret's appreciation.

Margaret dragged Daisy through several stores at an outlet mall nearby, two towns away. Daisy had always wanted to go there ever since it opened up, but that had been about seventeen years ago and she had never made it. Harold didn't like to venture outside of the town boundaries if he could help it, and his wife's desires sure didn't spark any inspiration. He always said they had everything they needed in their little town, other than the warehouse store where they'd go once every other month to stock up on some things he liked, like the type of butter he insisted on and the giant bags of flour he demanded they purchase, even though she preferred a different kind.

He wasn't the one to do the cooking or baking, but he sure had his opinions.

Margaret introduced Daisy to a myriad of new things. A travel pillow to wrap around her neck so she could nap during the flight. A little bag with several compartments that would easily slide under the seat in front of her on the plane, so she could keep the essentials with her for the entire flight.

Margaret tossed multiple things into the basket. Sanitizing wipes, a silk eye mask to help her sleep en route, mints, anti-nausea medication, and a little hammock that was supposed to be attached to the food tray and dangled down so one could put their feet in it. Daisy wasn't so sure about any of these things, but she wasn't about to say no to Margaret's wisdom. If Margaret thought she needed them, Daisy was sure she was right.

Instead of grabbing dinner while they were out at the mall—they were still too full to cram another meal in—Margaret talked Daisy into stopping at a little old-fashioned ice cream place.

Ice cream for dinner!

Daisy couldn't believe how quickly she agreed to the plan, and she also couldn't believe how giddy she felt at the idea of it.

They had ordered a make-your-own-sundae buffet which now adorned the table with all sorts of outrageous treats Daisy never would have had while Harold was alive. He thought it important for her to maintain a trim figure, even as his waist expanded over the years. Daisy wasn't sure when the last time Harold had been able to see his shoes when they were on his feet, but he never hesitated to call her fat and tell her she was getting too wiggly, and not in the right places.

Margaret encouraged her to indulge in all the whipped cream, hot fudge, caramel, and extra sprinkles she could fit in her bowl.

Sure her eyes were bright as a kid's on a bountiful Christmas morning, Daisy heaped an extra-large spoonful of marshmallow topping on top of all the other confections for good measure.

"This one is for Harold."

Margaret raised an eyebrow.

"You go, girl. I assume Harold is your husband?"

Daisy nodded as she closed her lips around a giant spoonful of deliciousness. After swallowing, she responded.

"*Was* my husband. Unfortunately."

She couldn't believe she had said it out loud. What kind of woman was she to disgrace her husband of fifty-three years so brazenly?

"Oh, do tell." Margaret joined her in taking an extra-large bite of ice cream and moaning with her eyes closed as it hit her taste buds.

"I don't want to talk about him. You never married?"

"Heck no. Too many men out there to settle on one. Besides, I was never the kind to want to pick up after another adult human. Or child human for that matter."

"Did you choose not to have children? Or did it just sort of happen that way?"

"Oh, it was a choice. As soon as I learned there were ways to avoid that particular lifestyle, I was all in. Don't get me wrong, I love children. Well, I like children okay, from a distance."

Margaret laughed and took another bite. She didn't wait to swallow before speaking again around the ice cream in her mouth.

"I'm a wonderful auntie. I sent care packages from around the world, and I put aside money for each of the kids, so when they turned eighteen they got a pretty nice contribution/graduation gift from their crazy aunt Margaret. That was good enough for me."

"You're so brave. I didn't even know it was an option not to get married and have children."

"Would you have done it differently?" Margaret asked, washing her ice cream down with a long sip of her lemon iced tea.

Daisy hesitated. "I know the correct thing is to say of course I wouldn't have changed a thing. But I don't know. Things never really went the way I thought they would. Happily-ever-after never really came my way."

"Didn't you say you were married fifty-something years? Surely there must've been something happy in it to keep you there for that long."

"Happy?" Daisy swirled her spoon around her ice cream, mixing the toppings into one giant ball of luscious delight. "I never thought the point was to be happy. That's a lie. I thought that at first, but Harold quickly taught me otherwise. And then I thought if I could just have a large family full of children I would be happy then. That didn't happen either."

"Did you only have the one daughter?"

"Yes." Daisy continued to stare into her bowl, watching the swirls form in the puddle of melting ice cream. "Just Khrista. But we didn't only lose touch because of her father."

The sanitized snippets Daisy had shared to justify the estrangement melted away with the contents of her bowl. She couldn't stop the honesty from pouring out of her while she held Margaret's rapt attention. "The last time I saw her, she said I was dead to her."

Margaret slammed her hand on the table. "See? That's what I'm talking about. You can't even trust your own offspring."

"It's not her fault–I didn't know that then, but looking back, I drove her away. I intervened when I shouldn't have, getting involved in the messy relationship she had with Kaelyn's father. I thought I was doing the right thing, but now..." She'd never forget the look of betrayal on her daughter's swelling face, or the hurt behind the black eye. "Anyhow, before Khrista was conceived, I tried getting pregnant for a long time. I thought for sure if I could give Harold children, he'd find more value in me as a wife. I didn't have too much trouble getting pregnant, but staying pregnant was a different story. I lost count of how many miscarriages I had, and I even had to give birth to two already dead babies. That messes with a woman, as I'm sure you can imagine."

Margaret nodded. "I can imagine."

"Eventually, one of my pregnancies stuck. I made it all the way to the day after my due date. But as I held that darling baby in my arms, the tension in the room grew. I was bleeding too much. I vaguely remember them taking the baby from my arms, and then when I awoke, I no longer had a womb. All my dreams of having a large family vanished. And I didn't get any say in it."

Margaret reached to the center of the table and scooped up a bunch of candies and dropped them onto Daisy's pile of ice cream.

"You deserve extra. That must have been absolutely devastating. Though I've never wanted children of my own, I can only imagine how terrible it must have felt for you to lose the option when it's all you really wanted."

Tears swam in Daisy's eyes. It was foolish to cry over something that happened fifty years ago.

But having somebody to confide in, somebody who seemed to understand, someone who validated her emotions and feelings for the first time in her life felt, well, *good.*

"It was a crazy time. There I was, in my very early twenties, going through menopause when I should have been delighting in my newborn. To be honest, I think I'm just now realizing I resented Khrista for it. That sounds horrible—she was only an infant, and it's not like it was her fault. But that's exactly what happened. I resented my infant. And whenever anything went wrong in her childhood, all I could think about were the babies that died inside me and the babies I would never have, and then I would get so angry because the one I did have didn't even seem to like me."

Daisy laughed, though she didn't know why, since it wasn't funny at all. What kind of mother resented her child for something she had absolutely nothing to do with? It was ludicrous.

Margaret shoved her empty ice cream bowl away from her and pointed her index finger in Daisy's direction. "I think we need to move this ice cream date to the bar. This conversation calls for margarita night."

Daisy smiled through her tears.

"Margaret, you may be the wisest woman I've ever known."

"You betcha, sugar. I learned a long time ago how to drown out sorrow and how to live for the moment."

Of all the things Margaret could teach her, Daisy desperately hoped this would be the lesson to stick with her.

**10**

---

# KHRISTA

In her excitement to serve her community by transporting Bess to the tearoom for the tea blending event, Khrista arrived at Bess's home about fifteen minutes too early. She checked the address to make sure she was at the correct place, then drove away from the house so she wouldn't make Bess feel rushed by waiting outside in her driveway.

Khrista pulled over by a rocky beach near Bess's home. One of the many advantages to living on a small island was that an ocean view was never hard to find. Even though Old Castle connected to land by virtue of a not-too-long bridge, it still felt pretty remote.

She shifted her car into park and scrolled around on her phone to kill some time. She played a quick game of solitaire and reflected on how busy she had been all week. Fatigue had hit hard, so she had fallen asleep early every night, whereas before her new lifestyle change, she had spent many nights nurturing the few drinks she'd allow herself on work nights–spread out so she wouldn't get wasted and have to deal with a hangover the next morning–and playing games on her phone and hating herself with every minute of quiet that ticked by.

Khrista hadn't been completely clean and sober lately like she had hoped, but she had restricted her drinking to only one drink each night. Just enough to take the edge off, but not enough to send her into oblivion. Not even on the weekends.

For her, that felt a lot like success. She could do this.

When the time for her arrival rolled around, she pulled back up in front of Bess's cottage home. Bess's cottage reminded Khrista of the one she had shared with Kaelyn back when they first moved to the island. She had been devastated when the owner of the cottage had raised the rent so high she had no choice but to vacate it.

She had struggled to find a way to make it work back then, but by that time the cost of living on the island had exploded. There were few vacancies, and the apartments that were available were way out of her price range. Though Rafael did his best to give her as many hours as she could work at the restaurant, she hadn't had the energy or drive to work all of her waking hours. Especially with a growing daughter who had a lot of needs. Though she had found a lot of support in the community, she still had her pride. And the last thing she wanted was for anyone to know the depth of her struggles.

When Kaelyn went off to camp for the summer, Khrista knew she needed a place to bring her home to at the end of the season.

And though giving her daughter the stability of a roof over her head meant moving off the island, it had been the best she could do.

Kaelyn didn't agree. Or appreciate the move.

Khrista blinked and turned her attention back to the moment, realizing she had been sitting outside the house like a creeper. She beeped as instructed and waited.

Three minutes passed, and Bess didn't come out.

Five minutes.

Ten minutes.

If they didn't go soon, they would miss the social event, which was the whole point of Khrista picking Bess up. The tea blending would begin at seven on the dot, and they wouldn't be there for the instructions.

Khrista beeped again, and when there was still no response, she called the phone number Clarice had given her.

No answer.

Worry gnawed at Khrista's gut. Not thinking twice, she left her car running while she jogged up the steps to the door. She knocked, but there was no response. Khrista twisted the doorknob and found it unlocked. She slowly pushed the door open and called out Bess's name. Still no answer.

The door would only open wide enough for Khrista to slip in. An overwhelming stench of cat urine greeted her, slamming into her nostrils and making her wince at the power of the nauseating, yet familiar, smell.

There was nowhere to walk without stepping on random objects. Garbage, clothing, miscellaneous papers. Khrista had heard of homes like this, and she had feared her house would become like it, but she had never actually seen it for herself. She called out Bess's name again and walked through the mess and into a living room, where boxes piled up nearly to the ceiling. Cats sat on seemingly every surface, watching her with their trademarked curiosity.

Khrista jumped when a door off the living room opened, opening less than halfway because of the clutter on the floor behind it.

A woman emerged and gasped when she saw Khrista standing there. Khrista clutched her chest in shock at her sudden appearance and relief at finding a living soul.

"I'm so sorry to scare you. I'm Khrista, I'm here to pick you up to take you to Happil-TEA Ever After. For the tea blending event? I tried calling you and I beeped my horn, but then I got worried because you weren't responding."

A cat *meowed* as if telling her off.

She didn't belong there, and bile rose in her throat when she realized her terrible breach in etiquette.

Bess pressed her hand to her chest as if trying to steady her breathing. "I was having some trouble in the bathroom. Why did you let yourself in like that?"

The woman's anger pierced a hole straight through Khrista's chest. Khrista's cheeks burned. She had been humiliated before, but this faux pas was unforgivable.

"I was worried. I'm so sorry—I'll wait outside."

"The only reason I agreed to this was because Clarice said you'd pull up and wait outside. This is outrageous." Bess made her way through the room, climbing over piles of things, a haze of fury marking every step.

Where was the reset button on this day?

"Please don't be mad at Clarice. I shouldn't have come in. She told me to wait outside."

Khrista turned to leave, hating herself for screwing up this task she had so desperately wanted to excel at. If she couldn't even manage to deliver someone safely to the tearoom, what hope was there for her to be a contributing member of the community?

"All of you people are so judgmental. Don't think I can't see the look on your face."

"I-I-I'm very sorry. The door was unlocked, and I was afraid something was wrong. I swear I'm not judging. I'm not exactly a neat freak myself."

"I asked for a ride, not an intervention." Bess's round face reddened deeply, and she pursed her lips, refusing to make eye contact. "I can't keep up with things the way I used to."

"It's okay. Really. I'm not one to judge anyone else."

"It hasn't always been like this." Bess, dressed in elastic waistband pants and a blouse that was a little too tight on her round figure, pushed a cat off the end of the sofa. She sat and buried her face in her hands.

Khrista moved quickly, as quickly as she could without falling and while making sure she didn't step on something breakable. She made it to the couch and moved a small stack of newspapers so she could sit beside Bess. Cat fur poofed into the air around her as she sat. She fought the urge to sneeze.

"We can pretend this never happened. Are you ready to go? I'm really excited to make my own blend of tea. Are you?"

"I don't know if I can go now." Emotion cracked Bess's voice and the flush on her face spread to her neck. "I'm better off never leaving the house."

"Nonsense."

Khrista summoned all her positivity. Bess needed the injection of happy vibes to give herself the courage to step out of her comfort zone and toward improving her quality of life.

"You'll feel so much better once you get out of the house for a little while and visit with some friends, have a nice cup of tea. Make your own tea blends to bring home. We can forget all about this rocky start of ours. I promise I'll never bring it up."

Bess's hands shook as she fiddled with the corner of a stained throw pillow.

"I don't know how I let it get this bad. I started taking in more and more cats because I was so lonely. My husband died and my kids don't come around like they used to. I've always been a bit of a collector, but now it's gotten out of control. I know people would think I don't know that, but I do. I can see it."

"Well, my new friend. I'm happy to tell you I've been going through some crazy stuff in my life, too. You're not alone." Khrista kept her gaze trained on Bess, not wanting to take in the scene and allow herself to be distracted by thoughts of what her life could become if she didn't turn things around. She tapped her hands on her lap and brightened her tone. "I happen to be looking for ways to keep myself busy so I don't self-destruct. I'm telling you the truth when I say I'm not at all a neat freak and I have no organizational skills whatsoever, but I'm able-bodied and I'd be more than happy to come over and pick things up and help you figure out a way to get a bit organized."

Bess continued fiddling with the hem of her sleeve and refused to look at Khrista.

"It won't look like one of those makeover shows, but I think you'd be happier with it. As a matter of fact, I just did something similar in my own apartment. It was getting out of control and I took a few days and cleaned it up and put things away and I feel so much better at the end of the day when I come home."

"I could never ask that of you."

"That's great, because you didn't ask. I offered. In fact, I insist. I need a project to fill my time and you need help. That's what we do here in this town, right?"

Khrista nudged Bess with her elbow.

"Trust me, I'm not one to want to accept help either. But Clarice is always reminding me that neighbors help neighbors. And this is a small island with only one town and a population of eight hundred, last I checked. If we can't stick together and help each other out, there's no hope for this world."

Khrista wrapped an arm around Bess as she would one of her students if they were having a bad day.

"Please let me believe there's hope for this world. I swear, if you let me help you, you'll actually be helping me."

A black cat with a white chest and paws jumped onto Khrista's lap and rubbed against her chin, demanding attention.

"Oh my goodness, and I have to tell you, I'm so jealous of your cats. I got to the point once where I had too many cats, so I haven't allowed myself to get any new ones after the last died off. If I could come here and spend time with your pets, I'd be so happy."

"Okay, okay. You don't have to keep selling it."

Bess leaned forward and grabbed a tissue from a box under a pile of papers on the coffee table. Pretty amazing that she knew how to find the box of tissues without moving anything.

"I hope you're serious about not telling anyone. I get enough of their concern without them knowing the state of my home."

"I give you my word."

Khrista had never considered herself much of an honorable person, but she would never betray this woman's confidence. Not unless she needed to for safety reasons.

Bess cheered up significantly on the drive to the tea shop. They chatted about her cats and all of their unique feline personalities. She had sixteen of them, but hadn't taken in any new ones in over a month. Khrista was probably one of the few people Bess would encounter who could understand just how much of a feat that was.

She said changing their boxes was getting difficult, and she had a few old ones who didn't always use the litter box. Bess grew frustrated with having to clean up everything and dodging piles throughout the house.

"It's still embarrassing, but I have to admit, it feels good to have someone to confide in about this. I've felt so overwhelmed over the whole thing. I haven't even been going for my doctor's appointments because I'm worried they'll smell something on me after one of the neighbors asked me about the smell when we were chatting by the mailbox one morning. I don't want them thinking they need to send someone to my house to check on me. You know, like elder services or something." Bess's mouth dropped open. "Oh, dear. Do I smell now? I took these clothes out of a bag in my closet, but what if the cat peed on them and I didn't know?"

"You smell fine, Bess. I'd let you know if there was a problem."

Bess didn't respond, but Khrista hoped her reassurance helped Bess relax enough that she could enjoy the evening.

They were greeted with enthusiasm when they entered the tearoom. Clarice walked them through the setup while the other attendees were fast at work. She had a variety of teas laid out on a buffet-style table—black, green, white, rooibos, guayusa. She encouraged them to choose from those teas for a base, and then to add some of the special things from the other table.

On the other table, she had lined up an extensive selection of flowers, fruits, and flavors, such as dried peaches, blueberries, strawberries, chocolate chips, jasmine and hibiscus flowers, and much more.

A heavenly fragrance hung in the air, and there were many laughs to go around as the attendees experimented with flavor profiles. At the end of the night, they each went home with several small tins of their own creations. In addition to the ones they had created individually, Clarice encouraged them to exchange samples of one another's blends.

Khrista couldn't wait to dig into hers. She hadn't been able to resist making an apple cinnamon blend that set her right at ease, reminding her of the comforts of fall. And the chocolate mint smelled like Christmas in a cup. The blueberry white tea? Scandalous moments on the beach.

And though her imagination carried her toward the memory of her favorite way to top off a cup of tea, she recited her promise to herself.

She would not add alcohol.

Even as she thought the words, she knew she lied.

Maybe she wouldn't add more than a dash of alcohol.

Much better.

Better to make a plan she could actually stick to. A plan she could believe in had to be better than a plan that was impossible to follow through on.

Dropping Bess off with a hug and a promise to follow up with her in a few days, Khrista felt inspired to go home and fix herself a cup of tea, to which she did *not* add alcohol, and to declutter some things she hadn't yet decluttered in her apartment.

Scary to think how similar to Bess she had once been—not to the extreme point poor Bess had reached, but her house had been pretty hopeless when Kaelyn still lived at home.

And she had slipped down that slippery slope more recently, too. Having Matt unexpectedly stop by the other night had reminded her of how humiliating it was for people to see that lifestyle. The humiliation fueled her with the adrenaline she needed to clean up her act.

Khrista knew from experience it wasn't always that simple.

But tonight she had an abundance of energy and knew she needed to keep herself busy.

She started with her makeup box, only keeping the items she actually used. So many things had expired years ago, and Khrista didn't even remember a time when she used more than mascara and lip gloss.

With that task completed, she was too tired to do anything physical. So she sat on her couch and started clearing out her email inbox.

After a missed CPR training because she hadn't read the email, Khrista had confessed to Danielle that she couldn't remember how to log in.

Danielle had been shocked. Or pretended to be. "You just leave emails unread in your inbox? I mean, I don't check mine constantly like my parents do, but how can you stand to have them building up like that? Ugh, the clutter!"

"You think that's bad? I don't even know how to get into my personal email anymore. I got locked out months ago and gave up trying."

"Khrista! Give me your phone. I'm getting you into your account."

Danielle cracked in with just a few taps and verifications. Her mouth dropped open when she saw the amount of unread emails in Khrista's inbox.

"Over twenty thousand! You're in big trouble if they start charging for storage, which a lot of the free email providers are doing now. Oh my goodness, I'm going to have nightmares about this." Danielle rubbed her pregnant belly and shook her head. "Don't you wonder what you're missing?"

Khrista laughed at the reaction. "I promise I'll delete the junk. But it's not like I get important correspondence in my email. Just coupons and offers to buy my timeshare when I've never even owned a timeshare."

Now was as good a time as any to delete the junk and alleviate Danielle's anxiety about all the notifications. Khrista smiled at the memory of Danielle's reaction.

When she was on the tenth page of her inbox, one email jumped out at her.

Like a ghost haunting her from the other side, the name in the "from" box startled her. Icy shards lodged at the base of her brain, threatening everything.

*Daisy O'Donnell.*

She hadn't seen that name for so long that it seemed like a foreign language that had gone extinct.

She didn't want to open it.

She *really* didn't want to.

And yet, without being fully aware of what she was doing, her finger tapped on the notification and displayed the brief message.

Khrista read the message, grateful she remained numb.

She turned off her phone, went to her bedroom, and took a bottle out of the closet.

"Come to me, my little soldier."

She took a swig, swirling the liquid around her tongue. Relishing the burn. When she swallowed, her nerves flickered to life, which was the opposite effect she sought.

A scream grew up from her toes to her knees to her waist and into her throat. Khrista wanted to take another sip, but her throat closed and her lips refused to open.

The scream lingered there with no way to escape.

Yet the anger continued to grow. Her temperature would have shattered the thermometer. Her blood pressure should have given her a stroke.

The amount of fire building within her could blow the roof off if she released the flames.

Khrista lifted the arm that held the liquor bottle and threw it with all her might against her bedroom wall.

"I will not be like *him!*"

Her father had been a raging alcoholic. She didn't want to emulate him for one second longer. Why hadn't she ever considered this before?

He was dead.

She would not honor him by giving in to his bad habit.

The one thing he had given her. His alcoholism.

She would be better than that.

Khrista gathered up all the bottles, and as she had weeks before, she carried them to the sink.

This time, she didn't hesitate. She dumped the contents of every bottle down the sink, swearing they would never have power over her again.

The smell of the combined liquors, which usually excited her and calmed her at the same time, made her want to vomit.

Khrista could almost smell his unwashed body after days of him sitting in his chair, rotting with his cigar and his liquor.

Why had she ever taken up the habit?

Oh yeah, because she was just as bad as he was.

But no more.

He was dead.

She washed the alcohol down the drain and took the bottles downstairs to the recycling bin. Khrista slammed them into the blue barrel, not even caring if any neighbors noticed her out there.

She had to be honest with herself, and if that meant being honest with her community members as well, then so be it.

Khrista returned to her apartment long enough to grab her phone and her keys and her jacket, and then she practically ran to her car and drove to Matt's place.

When he answered the door, she walked right into his arms, relishing the feel of his comforting embrace. His soft edges soothed her sharp ones. He was everything she wasn't, and though Khrista typically tried to keep a bit of emotional distance, she needed him now.

He wrapped his arms tightly around her and closed the door, muttering sweet words of reassurance as she clung to him.

Even though Matt had no idea what had driven her to stop by, unannounced, and to lay all her misery at his feet, he stepped into the role he so often played—the reasonable, kind, reassuring partner.

After a few minutes of standing in the arched entryway with his arms around her, he asked if she wanted to come in and sit down.

"My father is dead."

"Your father?" Matt's eyebrows drew together, and she wanted to trace the lines between them.

"We weren't close."

That was an understatement.

He nodded. He understood without explanation.

"It can be hard to lose a parent even if you're not close," he said.

"Yeah."

Khrista had no other words than that. How could she explain that she needed comfort and wanted to celebrate at the same time? That her father's death set her free? That the true source of her pain was self-inflicted and had to do with her own poor parenting?

That she had been lying to his kind face for three years.

So instead, Khrista would simply stand there in his entryway while he hugged her tightly and continue to pretend she was the person he thought she was.

Matt kissed the top of her head, his warm breath helping her to thaw.

"I know it's not something you like to talk about, but I've always sensed there was something from your past you've been withholding. I'm thinking it has something to do with your father."

She stiffened, but didn't pull away.

"Sometimes when I move a certain way, you flinch. It's quick and I don't know if you notice it, but I do. I've waited for you to open up, and I will continue to wait, but I hope you know you can trust me."

She trusted him. As much as she could trust a man. More than she ever thought she'd trust.

But she didn't trust herself. And that was the hardest confession to make.

Khrista rested her head against his thick chest, lulled into a false sense of security by the *thump-thump-thump* of his heart beneath her ear.

**11**

---

# KAELYN

Kaelyn chewed on the side of her fingernail as she waited in her car at the airport.

Would she recognize her grandmother? Would she randomly approach some seventy-year-old woman and frighten her with her enthusiasm, only to find out it was the wrong senior citizen?

She should have asked clarifying questions.

She should have asked what her grandmother would be wearing. Or the style of her hair.

Something to prove this woman she hadn't seen in over twenty years was her blood relative.

Eagerly anticipating an interaction with a blood relative had her feeling a bit on the wonky side. Kaelyn had thought all bloodlines had been severed when she cut the cord that bound her to her mother. She hadn't considered that her grandmother would find her when she needed it most.

Her legs jittered and warmth coursed through her body as if she had consumed an entire carafe of cold brew coffee, despite having been on a decaf binge since turning the pregnancy stick pink. She should have accepted Oliver's offer to go to the airport with her instead of his usual Saturday morning visit with his mother, followed by a run with his buddy. He'd help with the anxiety.

But she was a big girl and could do this on her own.

As often happened lately, Kaelyn's hand flew to her belly. She could feel her body changing as her baby grew. Kaelyn's breasts grew heavier each day, and she noticed a softening around her waist. She had just started to show, but most people still couldn't tell.

Oliver could. Every opportunity he had, he ran his hand over the curve of her belly, as if sculpting her out of clay.

Though Kaelyn had been certain she had felt the baby move days ago in front of the restaurant–tiny fish kiss bubbles in her belly–she quickly dismissed the sensation as wishful thinking.

Mommy blogs said that early quivery feeling was often gas.

But Kaelyn could envision her baby swaying in the amniotic fluid like a resilient dandelion bending in the breeze.

She didn't want to rush things, but the excitement for what would come sometimes overwhelmed her.

Groups of older women crossed at the crosswalks, dragging their wheeled suitcases behind them. She searched the crowd, but all of those women seemed to know one another.

She really hoped her grandmother would remember to text her when she was on her way out.

As the thought entered her mind, her phone buzzed with an incoming text.

"Did you get Grandma yet?"

She sighed in irritation. Oliver was checking in, but Kaelyn had been so excited about the prospect of it being her grandmother that she nearly cursed when she saw his name on her screen.

She sent a quick "not yet" and then felt bad for being abrupt, so she sent a kissy face emoji.

Killing time as she sat with the car running in the waiting lot, Kaelyn clicked open her Facebook app, posted a quick status about the baby being the size of an avocado and being able to make a fist and suck his thumb, and just as she tapped the post button, another text popped up.

Her grandmother.

Thank goodness.

"I'm on the upper level outside the terminal, and I cannot wait to see my baby girl!"

After battling traffic and drivers who appeared to have never operated a vehicle before, Kaelyn pulled up to the designated doorway. She knew her grandmother as soon as she saw her.

Not by her looks, but there was some kind of connection that hit her straight in the heart.

Kaelyn put her hazards on, opened the door, and ran over to hug the woman whose smile matched her own.

"Oh darling, I never dreamed I'd be here in this place, with you, and I have never been happier."

"Same!" Kaelyn gave her another firm squeeze, careful not to squeeze too hard because her grandmother's shoulders felt small, dainty, and breakable beneath her enthusiasm.

Her grandmother was built like Kaelyn's mother—slim, narrow, petite. Kaelyn had always been wider than her mother, making her feel fat when she could no longer fit into her mom's clothes in middle school. Not that she wanted to wear them anyway, but she had always thought it funny that they could share the occasional sweater. She had learned over the years it was simply because her hips and shoulders were wider and had nothing to do with her weight, but Kaelyn wished someone had told her that when she was younger.

Grandma had long, silvery hair wound in a tight, grandmotherly bun and a welcoming smile that set Kaelyn at ease.

Kaelyn drank in the sight of her, still wondering if she had slipped into a deep sleep and dreamed up the whole thing. "How was your flight? Here, I'll take your bags."

Kaelyn couldn't stop smiling as she maintained eye contact with her grandma—*her grandma!*—and placed her luggage in the trunk of her hybrid SUV.

"It was the most freeing experience of my life. I never dreamed I was missing out on so much."

Kaelyn couldn't imagine making it into her seventies without ever getting on an airplane.

She was so glad her existence and her grandmother's desire to meet had inspired Daisy to have that experience.

"Were you afraid of flying? Is that why this was your first time?"

"No," Grandma hesitated to continue. "It was never an option. When your grandfather and I moved from my home in Kentucky to Virginia, we drove. We never ventured far in all the years we lived there. Harold—your grandfather—felt we had everything we needed right where we were."

"It's an interesting perspective," Kaelyn remarked, trying to be gentle and to respect that previous generations viewed things differently. She didn't know anyone her age who hadn't flown anywhere.

The entire ride home, through the busy Los Angeles traffic and along the coastline, they talked nonstop. There was so much to share, so many details of life they were eager to impart to one another. They didn't delve into any deep issues or controversial topics, but they shared all the minutiae. Favorite colors, music they liked to listen to, experiences with cooking, and more.

"I know this is ridiculous because I'm a grown woman and I'm having a baby of my own, but is there any way that while you're here, you can show me how to make those biscuits we used to make together?" Kaelyn asked.

"That's not ridiculous at all."

Her grandmother brushed a tear from the side of her face. Oh no, had Kaelyn made a mistake bringing up something so sentimental? She certainly hadn't meant to make her cry.

"Oh, Kaelyn, there's so much I want to do with you. I know I'm only here for two days, but I hope there's a way for us to squeeze in two decades of grandmotherly spoiling."

"I'm game for that." Kaelyn laughed. "In all seriousness, I cannot *tell* you how excited I am that you're here. And you know you're welcome to stay longer if you decide to."

"You don't have to tell me, because there's nothing that makes me happier than knowing I'm in the same vicinity as my granddaughter."

Her grandmother's voice cracked, but her smile brightened the car. "And while I appreciate the offer, I don't want to put you and your husband out for longer than a weekend."

Grandma dug in her purse and pulled out a butterscotch candy, and a memory of her doing the same when they were younger popped into Kaelyn's memory as if it had happened yesterday.

They had been sitting on the front porch of Grandma's home, playing "I Spy With My Little Eye" until Kaelyn got distracted and started chasing squirrels. Grandma had teased that they didn't need a pet hound when they had a feral grandchild to do the chasing.

The sun had been warm, and the grass smelled fresh, and Kaelyn spun and spun and spun until she collapsed on the ground, where she spread her arms and pretended she was flying up to the tops of the trees that decorated the skyline.

Her mother and father had pulled up in the car, and her mom slammed the car door and screamed at Kaelyn's daddy. Her mom wiped something from her face. At first, Kaelyn thought it was blood, but then she realized it was probably ketchup because her mom could be a sloppy eater sometimes. It made more sense than having blood on her.

Kaelyn's mother practically ran across the front yard and yanked Kaelyn off the ground, dragging her screaming into the house. Grandma hurried along behind them, telling Khrista she was over-reacting and needed to go talk to Kaelyn's father and work things out.

"Like you always worked things out with Dad?" Khrista spat out.

It made sense to Kaelyn. Her preschool teachers told her she should always say sorry and tell someone if they hurt her feelings or made her mad.

Kaelyn's dad battered at the door, which must have been locked by accident when they went into the house.

Suddenly a shadow loomed in the doorway of the kitchen, right near the stairs Kaelyn's mom was trying to drag her up.

Her grandfather.

"You let that child go, and get out there and make things good with your man. You have no right to lock him away from his kid like that.”

“No right?” Khrista shouted. “Sure, you think there's nothing wrong with your daughter coming home with a face like this because it reminds you of the good old days when it was you doing the hurtin'. Well, you can say what you want, but *my* daughter won't ever live the way you made me live.”

That was all of the memory, and Kaelyn felt the overwhelming urge to vomit. She pulled over, waving her apologies to her grandmother as she barely opened the door in time to release the contents of her stomach onto the roadway.

She didn't have many memories of her father and grandfather, so why did this one come to her as clear as a movie?

Her grandmother's aged voice brought her back to the present day. “You okay, child?”

Kaelyn felt Grandma's hand land on her shoulder blade with a gentle pat.

She heaved more.

Grandma handed her a tissue and shared stories of her sickness when she was pregnant.

“Means you're having a girl.”

People had told Kaelyn that, but she'd spoken to plenty of people who had been sick during their pregnancies with boys. But she wasn't about to argue with the perceived wisdom of the grandma she had only just reunited with an hour ago.

She wiped her mouth and took a swig of her water, then gratefully accepted the butterscotch her grandmother had tried to hand her before.

Only this time, the candy tasted sour.

By the time Oliver returned home from his Saturday morning visit with his mother—where Kaelyn knew he was doing all the chores Ruby had on her list for him—and then his weekly run on the beach with his buddy, he walked into a house that smelled of freshly baked chicken pot pie, garlic cheddar biscuits, buttered green beans, and the peanut butter cookies Grandma insisted on making, even though Kaelyn had told her she and Oliver were trying to eat healthy.

Grandma had chuckled and said life was too short to deprive oneself of delicious foods.

Kaelyn was beginning to agree, especially after snatching one of the biscuits fresh from the oven.

"This tastes exactly the way I remember it." She closed her eyes and sighed at the pleasure of the garlicky butter melting into her tongue. "I don't remember a lot from my early childhood, but these biscuits have taunted me for so long. Anytime I asked my mother about them, she claimed you'd never teach her how to make them."

Grandma laughed as pressed her fork into the peanut butter dough, the sound more midnight than dawn. It was the darkest tone Kaelyn had heard from her.

"More like your mother refused to spend any time in the kitchen with me. She had strong opinions about cooking and cleaning being women's work. I didn't really understand her point of view on that, since she was a girl and would grow into a woman one day."

Kaelyn snickered.

"That explains a lot about my childhood."

"I'm sure your mother got used to the womanly arts."

"I wish I could say so, but my mother was not one to cook and she most certainly did not clean. I found a bazillion excuses for not having friends over throughout my entire childhood because I didn't want to be embarrassed by her and our falling apart, messy home."

Daisy dropped the fork on the counter. She rubbed her lower back as she stared at Kaelyn. "I'm so sorry, darling. I should have been more on top of things and made sure she learned. I under-stand why she rebelled. She didn't want to be like me or to end up in the situation I ended up in. I used to be offended by that, but I grew to understand her point of view. Actually, if I could go back, I wouldn't want to be me or end up in the situation I ended up in either."

"Let's not talk about her. I don't want her ruining the time we have together."

Kaelyn had watched her grandmother slip off into another world numerous times. Everything would be fine one minute and then something would come up that would trigger this haunted look in her grandmother's eyes.

Kaelyn hadn't been able to figure out a pattern for it yet. It didn't all have to do with her mother, and it didn't all have to do with missing out on Kaelyn's childhood. Sometimes it was just stuff about life and plans and desires for the future.

Kaelyn tried not to think too much about it.

When they sat at the dinner table, the first time Oliver and Kaelyn had used their new dining set since its arrival a week after moving day, Oliver praised the delectable goodness of the food and ate so much his belly bloated. They decided to make a cup of tea and go for a walk around the neighborhood to help them digest. When they returned from their walk, Grandma couldn't stop raving about the beautiful neighborhood and marveling that at their age, they could afford to live in such a luxurious area.

Normally, talking about money would embarrass Kaelyn, but when her grandmother raved, Kaelyn's pride grew.

She and Oliver had worked hard to get where they were, and she was not ashamed. They both had great jobs and excellent credit, and they had saved up for a down payment for the nicest home they could afford. Ruby had insisted they invest Oliver's inheritance from his father in the house, right after paying off student loans.

She couldn't wait until they became even more established and could purchase a property on the other side of the street, where the houses had full and direct access to the beaches.

Sitting around the family room after dinner, they nibbled on cookies, and Kaelyn wished her grandmother could stay and cook for them every day. Kaelyn leaned forward and reached for another cookie, sniffing it before taking a giant bite. "You mentioned something about plans with friends next week? "

"Oh yes, I've reconnected with an old childhood friend, and I'm going to continue my tour of the United States by stopping in to see her once I leave here."

"That's exciting! How did you find her if you haven't been in touch?"

"That Facebook, I tell you, it's a blessing. They have groups dedicated to people from my graduating class. It's quite astounding."

Kaelyn had noticed a shift in older people being on Facebook, so while she stayed on there to post the occasional update for Oliver's family and to keep up with trends in graphic design, she had moved on to other social media for more personal things. She had deactivated for a while so no one from her past would share information about her life with her mother, but since so much time had passed with no contact from Khrista, she had felt safe to reactivate in order to share the pregnancy announcement. For the most part, the years had distanced her from anyone on the island, so other than some likes and some sweet comments on the announcement, no harm had come of sharing.

"But I sure wouldn't mind cooking for you every day. I'm sure it's difficult for two career-minded people to find time for this kind of thing."

Kaelyn responded, "We do like to cook together when we can. Oliver's better than me."

"Nonsense, love," Oliver said. "You boil water better than anyone I know."

Grandma looked like she wanted to say something, but she held back. Kaelyn reached for another cookie, swearing it would be her last, and Oliver remarked that he wouldn't mind her getting big and round and soft and squishy. She smacked him on the arm, and once again, Grandma slipped off into that dazed look.

Minutes later, Grandma got up from her space on the loveseat and said, "Oh, I just remembered I brought something to show you."

Excitement grew in Kaelyn. Perhaps her grandmother had saved something from Kaelyn's childhood. A special doll, the teddy bear book her mother had never replaced, or maybe a cute little outfit her own baby could wear. Her mother had kept none of those sentimental things. She had practically been a hoarder with too much to carry in her vehicle, so when they moved she had left behind a whole bunch of stuff in a storage unit she had failed to pay, so they lost everything. Her mother had packed things that were important to her and left behind things Kaelyn would have wanted. Typical.

Kaelyn stiffened when she saw her grandmother approaching with a photo album. She hoped in her heart of hopes it would be wedding photos from Grandma's marriage to Grandpa or something, but as soon as Grandma sat beside her and flipped open to the first page, Kaelyn knew her worst fears were about to be realized.

She had wanted to avoid any walks down memory lane—or any lane her mother would be on.

She didn't want to offend her grandmother by complaining, so she focused on the lines in her grandmother's hands and the slight tremble as Daisy turned the pages and told stories about Khrista's early life.

The photos only went through Khrista's early teen years, and then they shifted to some loose photos of Kaelyn with her mother, revealing big smiles and lots of hugs on the glossy paper.

Kaelyn couldn't handle seeing the phoniness of their smiles, so she stood up abruptly, almost knocking the photo album out of her grandmother's hand when her thigh caught on the edge of the book.

"Is everything okay, darling?"

"Yes, I'm fine. I just have no interest in seeing that woman's face."

Kaelyn wished she hadn't noticed the tears blurring her grandmother's eyes before she spun away. She stormed off to the kitchen and poured herself a fresh cup of tea from the teapot, then belatedly remembered to offer Grandma a cup as well. Grandma shook her head, and Kaelyn felt like the worst person in the universe for having upset her grandmother when she was just excited to share a mutual part of their lives.

"I'm sorry, Grandma. I wish those memories brought me some kind of joy, but I haven't told you everything about how Khrista ruined my childhood."

Grandma sighed deeply. "I've spent years imagining that after

Khrista and you left, you had a glorious life with all the sweetness a childhood away from your grandparents would provide. Khrista had always been so set on making sure she didn't raise you the way I raised her. Maybe it's time for us to talk, and you can tell me the truth about things that happened."

Oliver stood up and kissed Kaelyn on the side of her forehead, right on the temple where her head throbbed.

"I have some things I have to do for work, but if you need me, I'll be upstairs. Thank you, Daisy, for the most delicious meal. My favorite chicken pot pie had been from a diner near Santa Monica, but I'll simply never be able to enjoy it again. You have spoiled me for other biscuits and chicken."

Daisy blushed demurely, but she seemed pleased with his doting.

Kaelyn looked at him with gratitude, because even though she didn't want to have the conversation with her grandmother, she especially didn't want to have it with him there.

He had heard it before—the parts she would share with her grandmother—but he tended to grow protective of her, and having an extra set of ears was always a little awkward, anyway.

Kaelyn sat next to Daisy, deposited her teacup next to the plate of cookies, and clasped Daisy's hand in hers. Her grandmother's hand was icy, so Kaelyn asked if she wanted the air conditioning turned down.

"Oh no, I'm perfectly fine. My circulation isn't what it used to be. I wouldn't mind if you handed me my sweater, though."

Kaelyn rushed to do her bidding, helping her position the garment around her shoulders before settling in and picking up her cup of tea once more.

"Grandma, I don't know how much you want to know, and it's not something I like to talk about a lot. I just want you to know I didn't cut things off with my mother over something petty. It's not because she wouldn't let me paint my bedroom walls a certain color or stay out past curfew. She had a pattern of consistently doing things to ruin my life and to threaten my future."

Grandma's eyes grew wider, and she picked at the skin of her knuckles.

"Can we please make an agreement that after I share a few examples of things I cannot forgive my mother for, that we not talk about her anymore? We can talk about *anything* else, but I want to get to know you without feeling angry about my mother constantly."

"If this conversation makes you uncomfortable, we don't have to have it."

Kaelyn shook her head, rushing to reassure her grandmother. "It's okay with me. I want you to have a clearer picture."

Grandma waited in silence as Kaelyn struggled to narrow her life story down to a poignant example or two.

She faked a smile, hoping to set Grandma at ease.

"It might all sound silly to you, but when I was a teenager, I went away to an overnight summer camp where I had my first paid job as a counselor and swim instructor. When she picked me up at the end of the eight weeks, she gleefully blurted out that she had a big surprise for me. I had visions of a freshly cleaned house, brand new clothes, or maybe a vacation together. All things I had never had and desperately dreamed of. But nope..."

Kaelyn felt the familiar tension of anger stiffening her muscles.

"The back seat of the car was packed full of garbage bags and boxes my mother had haphazardly thrown a bunch of my stuff into, not even taking care to wrap delicate things or to separate garbage from what I perceived to be my valuables. She had loaded the car with as much as she could fit, including all of our pet cats, which was a lot. Not that we could afford them... Anyway, I could tell she had been crying and she wouldn't answer any of my questions. She told me nothing. She drove us to the middle of New Hampshire, about two hours from our home in Old Castle, away from the shoreline I so desperately loved, and told me we could get our things out at this really crappy apartment building somewhere in the center of the state."

Would Kaelyn ever get to the point where she could discuss this without feeling as if she were reliving the experience?

"She said this was our new home. It was so different from what I was used to. In Old Castle, we lived in a cute little cottage we had rented since I was five. True, the inside wasn't the best because of her lack of housekeeping skills, but since I had become older, I had started trying to keep up with the cleaning, especially so we could let the maintenance people in to fix things that had been long neglected due to her not letting anyone in. She was too embarrassed by the state of the house to let anyone see it, yet not enough to be motivated to do something about it. Sure, she worked a lot at the restaurant and on whatever side jobs she could pick up, but other parents managed to work and clean their houses, you know?"

Kaelyn's neck itched as she shared her story. If she wasn't careful, she'd tear a hole through her skin.

"This house she had moved us to was a multi-family, and there was trash all over the yard. It was near train tracks and a smelly river, and there were toddlers running around outside in just their diapers."

Kaelyn shivered at the memory of all the neglect she had witnessed. Somehow, it had seemed worse than what her mother put her through.

"I assumed she had cruelly moved us there so we could be around other people who were just as horrible as her, but she never gave me an explanation. I was never given an opportunity to say goodbye in person to my best friend, and I had to start a new school my junior year when everything they were learning was just a little bit different from what I had been learning and everyone was already established in their own friendship circles. It set me back tremendously because between the different curriculum and standards, lack of a swim team for me to compete on, and because I had slipped into a deep depression because of the abruptness of the move, there was little chance for me to succeed."

Kaelyn sniffled, shocked that telling the story hurt just as much as it had when it all happened.

"Mom only got worse after the move. I had always suspected she was drinking in Old Castle, but she didn't even try to hide it once we moved. In Old Castle, I'd find the occasional nip bottle hidden in the house or catch her walking unsteadily from time to time, but mostly we kept our distance and I didn't question her. At the new place, we started fighting all the time until I stopped talking to her altogether. She didn't even try, Grandma. Aren't parents supposed to try when their kids give up? It was terrible. I wouldn't wish that life on anyone."

Daisy's tears fell over her craggy face. She wiped her nose with the cuff of her sweater.

"I'm sorry, Kaelyn. I wish I had been the mother yours needed so she could have been a better mother to you."

"Don't you be sorry. There's no excuse. She could have tried. I wasn't asking for a perfect mother, but she was unpredictable and didn't even try to pretend she cared about me. Besides, when I was in my senior year, she took classes at a nearby college. Get this, she went into child development and became a preschool teacher. When she realized all the things she had done wrong, she suddenly wanted to parent me the way she should have from the beginning. Problem was, I was already halfway out the door and I didn't need her to parent me any longer. That only made it worse. And seeing her get a job where everybody gushed about how great she was with kids felt like a knife in my back."

"I never saw my mother after I got married," Daisy said. "My father wouldn't allow us to have a relationship because I ran away to get married, even though we married in the church the way he would want us to. He said maybe if the Lord blessed me with a child, a little boy, I could prove myself worthy of being in the family again, but since I no longer bore his last name, he bore no responsibility for me. I understand the difficulty of being estranged from your parents, and I wish things had been different for you."

Things grew awkward after that conversation, and the next day they spent most of their time touring the area and not talking about anything too deep, especially the past. When it was time to say goodbye at the airport, sadness hit Kaelyn like a storm cloud opening up over her head after following her around for days.

Grandma hugged her tight, and their bond felt solid and unbreakable.

"If it's okay with you, I'd like to visit you again soon. I'm living the life of a nomad right now, with no home base, and I'm really excited about it, but I feel like I've only scratched the surface of a relationship with you."

"You're welcome anytime, Grandma. I love having you here. Thank you for teaching me how to make the biscuits. Next time you see me, I'll probably be twenty pounds fatter, and none of it will be baby weight. All biscuit weight."

"You have to use real butter. That's what gives it the rich taste."

"Noted."

They laughed together outside the airport, and Kaelyn stood watching her grandmother through a sheen of tears as she wheeled her purple suitcase away with her.

Despite the pain of sharing some of the past with her grandmother, the hurt of watching her go brought her back to being that five-year-old child again.

The goodbye cut just as deep.

## 12

# DAISY

Daisy's second journey on the plane went even smoother than the first. Whether it was the experience of having done it once already, the slightly shorter flight, or the natural high after reuniting with her granddaughter and meeting her handsome, unbelievably sweet grandson-in-law, Daisy didn't know. What she did know was she could finally blossom, and whatever life she had left to live would be richer and fuller because of her newfound freedom.

And yet she couldn't shake the sadness of what her daughter's life had become. How Khrista had squandered her shot at happiness and had alienated her daughter as surely as Daisy had alienated Khrista.

And drinking? Like her father? That was the last thing Daisy expected to hear. Oh, how difficult it had been to hide her reaction from Kaelyn. That poor child. Growing up the way she had.

Daisy hadn't excelled at mothering, but she had given her daughter a clean home and a sober mother.

She banished those thoughts to the back of her mind, remembering what Margaret had taught her about compartmentalizing. She was about to reunite with her good childhood friend and didn't want to spoil the reunion with hauntings of things she couldn't change.

Her friend Edith picked her up outside the airport and they laughed and joked as if they were still sixteen years old. On the drive to Edith's house, they reminisced about the days when they would spend their pin money at the soda fountains and how fun it had been to watch the older boys come in and check them out.

Edith had stayed in their hometown after high school and ended up married to a college professor from a few towns away. They settled down in Edith's family home and raised five children there, all of whom still lived in the area.

To Daisy, this life sounded idyllic and almost like it had to be fictional. Where was Edith's family drama? Where was all the angst?

Surely there had to be some skeletons to shake out. But for now, she would be happy her friend had led such a happy life.

Even though Edith's husband was twenty years older than her, he was still alive and kicking. He required a great deal of care, so Edith had invited Daisy to stay at the house with her so she would never have to be gone for too long.

"I should have learned to drive. Then I could have rented a car and not put you out like this."

Edith turned onto a tree-lined residential street Daisy still recognized after all these years. How they had loved playing together on these streets, riding their bikes and roller skating down the center. A lot had changed–the houses looked different, the tree canopies had grown thicker, but the nostalgic feeling was strong.

Edith's response pulled Daisy back. "Nonsense. I enjoy getting out for a little while. I like to listen to my rock music on the drive. Peter has never liked it, and since he's always home, I never get a chance to play it unless I'm in the car. Driving forty-five minutes to get to the airport was the respite I needed. My oldest boy is spending time with his dad today and mowing our lawn while he's there, so it all worked out great."

"How outstanding that all of your children still live nearby. Do you all get along?"

"Oh yes. They are the lights of my life, and though they're all busy, I'm lucky they still make the effort to spend time with their dad and me. Wait until you meet my grandchildren. Two of them will probably be there when we arrive. The four-year-old and six-year-old are little freshies, but in the best way possible."

Daisy leaned back slightly in her seat, mesmerized by the way Edith spoke of her family. She loved hearing the antics of Edith's young grandchildren and hoped she would play as big a part in her new great-grandchild's life as she hadn't been able to in her grand-daughter's. Edith had started her family much later than Daisy had, so though they were the same age, they were at vastly different stages of life.

"You were almost forty when you had your youngest?" Daisy asked, still shocked.

"I was indeed. They called it a geriatric pregnancy. Nice, huh? Did you feel 'geriatric' at forty?"

Daisy didn't respond, because if she were honest, she probably had. Life with Harold had aged her, no doubt about it.

The afternoon played out exactly as Edith had said. By the end of the day, Daisy was exhausted from watching the young ones running all around the house, climbing on every surface they could, and mouthing off now and then to their sweet but exhausted-looking mother.

In her day, the kids would have been slapped and sent out to do chores. These days, apparently, they were using something called positive discipline and redirection, as Edith's daughter-in-law felt the need to explain.

Didn't seem to be working, as far as Daisy could tell.

Edith had noticed the doubtful look on Daisy's face and told her it was a process, that respectful parenting was all about giving kids time to learn rather than ruling through fear.

Sounded like fiddlesticks, but what did Daisy know?

She tried to soften her thinking. The children were adorable, if rambunctious.

But all she could focus on was Khrista missing out on this kind of life with her grandchild. And all Daisy had missed out on, too.

"Now that the children are gone for the day, I have a little surprise for you."

Daisy's eyes widened. She had assumed they would go to bed after the family left, considering the long day.

"Okay, I'll just come right out and tell you. Alice and Florence are coming here." Edith clasped her hands in front of her chest and beamed. "They'll be here in minutes."

Daisy couldn't hide her surprise. "*What?* Our school friends?"

"Yes. Remember when we were known as 'The Quad'? It delighted them to find out you were coming here after all these years."

Memories of her girlfriends filled Daisy's mind and made her feel as if no time had passed at all. For not the first time in the last several months, tears sprung easily to Daisy's eyes.

Her hands covered her mouth, keeping her surprised sobs and gasps contained.

Edith giggled like a young girl.

"I hope that's a pleasant surprise."

"Oh yes, it sure is. But I have to ask you. The last time I spoke to Florence, she was upset I was running away with Harold. I know it's been fifty-some-odd years, but do you think she's forgotten?"

Edith shook her head slowly, her thin lips forming into a straight line.

"She hasn't forgotten. She held a grudge for quite some time. And she didn't have an easy life."

"She's not the only one," Daisy said, mumbling under her breath.

"She's excited to see you. Florence has regrets about how she handled things back then. She had reasons for her feelings that she never shared with you, but is hoping to leave it all in the past. Florence jumped at the opportunity to see you again after all these years."

If Daisy's heart kept growing at the rate it had since Harold's death, she wouldn't need sickness to kill her. Her heart would explode and the confetti of her happiness would flood her bloodstream and clog her brain.

And she was okay with that. Seemed like a pretty good way to go. Especially after a lifetime of misery.

And yet, coupled with all that happiness was the lingering sadness of too many unhealed wounds. Wounds she hoped to find the cure for.

When the door opened to reveal Alice and Florence standing on the other side, a hug fest, as Kaelyn would refer to it, ensued. There was no indication of any hard feelings between them or that they had felt abandoned by Daisy's departure.

As if they were teenagers again, they spent the next few hours, interspersed with Edith having to check on her husband, talking over each other, treating themselves to homemade ice cream Edith's daughter-in-law had delivered, and filling each other in on their lives.

Florence held back some of her story, just as Daisy did. Daisy had a sense of these things. Her social worker said it was common for people to develop what she called "hypervigilance" after experiencing trauma, and Daisy had certainly noticed the same thing with Kaelyn.

If Florence wasn't ready to tell all, Daisy would respect her need to keep it to herself. The same was true of Kaelyn, though Daisy wanted both her granddaughter and her old friend to feel free to speak the truth to her.

Daisy continued to hold back with her friends, too. She didn't want them to know what a mistake she had made by leaving with Harold. She didn't want to admit her life had been a shambles, that the starry-eyed girl who had been so excited to catch the eye of the man in uniform they all lusted over had ended up in a prison of her own making, abused, and had caused an estrangement in her own family.

A light in Florence's eyes dimmed when they asked her detailed questions about her life. She waved them off and said she'd had the time of her life traveling and appreciated that she had no entanglements to keep her confined.

"You would get along well with my friend Margaret. She's a world traveler as well, and we're planning a trip to Italy together." Daisy didn't share that she had been a friend for such a short time. The embarrassment of having no friends for fifty years stung, and like a sniper, the shame could shoot her in the heart before she knew the threat was imminent.

"Italy is to die for." Florence dug in her purse for her cell phone. A few moments later, she pulled up some pictures and passed the phone around to the group.

All the women were jealous as they scrolled through the photos. Though Alice and Edith had done some traveling in their youth, neither of them had gone anywhere in years. And even in their heydays, they hadn't gone far, other than Alice traveling to Canada every four or five years to her old family homestead.

"Wouldn't it be phenomenal if we could plan a trip together? All of us? Like we planned when we were thirteen?" Daisy proposed.

They all gushed about the possibility, but one by one, they gave excuses why they couldn't go. Edith had her husband, of course. Alice was getting a double hip replacement in a few months.

Florence, however, seemed all for it.

They stayed up late, almost until eleven o'clock, and before Alice and Florence departed, they made plans to get together for brunch the following day.

For the next week, The Quad was inseparable, just like old times.

Edith's pregnant daughter, the youngest of the five children, stopped by the day before Daisy was scheduled to leave.

They sat around the table and discussed ideas for her upcoming baby shower, showing Daisy all the cute little favors they had planned and talking about how they found so many ideas for games to play.

Daisy had never had a baby shower because she didn't have any family to speak of after she left home. She had never wanted a shower anyway because all her pregnancies had been cursed and she feared jinxing them.

But seeing the tiny baby bottles filled with mints made her determined to plan Kaelyn's baby shower. She had money to burn between her husband's life insurance policy and the sale of her house which had been paid in full decades ago, and since she had missed all of Kaelyn's birthdays, Christmases, graduations, her wedding, and a multitude of other holidays, she was determined to give Kaelyn a baby shower her friends would envy. Even living in that fancy neighborhood of hers.

Oliver and Kaelyn were probably up to their chins in debt anyway, as seemed to be the trend these days.

"Where are you planting your roots next?" Edith asked. "Have you thought about staying in Kentucky?"

Daisy shook her head. "Being back with you ladies has been a dream. But this hasn't been my home for a long time. I'm ready to try something new."

"Understandable. I hope you'll stay in touch, though."

"Now that I know how to use this little gadget..." She waved her phone in the space between them. "It will be impossible for you to avoid me."

Since Peter had appointments the following day, Florence offered to drive Daisy to the airport. Daisy had purchased a flight to California and had put some feelers out with a realtor in Kaelyn's area. She wouldn't buy a house—she wasn't sure she'd ever want to settle in one place again—but she didn't want to be a nuisance to Kaelyn and her husband as they began growing their family.

When she told Florence about her plan to rent a short-term apartment, Florence sat up straighter and a mischievous glint sparkled in her eyes.

"It sounds to me as if you could use a roommate. Living in California is expensive, and you're not used to being alone. I'm looking for an adventure, and I'd be more than happy to be your travel buddy for a while."

"Truly? I'd love that!"

Florence dropped her off at the airport, promising to make arrangements and to meet her in California in a few days. Daisy had texted Kaelyn, telling her she was coming back, but not to worry about putting her up. Kaelyn insisted she wanted her grandmother to stay with her, but Daisy told her she needed her own space to grow.

She texted Kaelyn, saying, "I've long thought it an irony they named me for a wildflower, and yet I've been confined for so long. A wildflower who has always lacked the freedom to grow in places I wanted to. Now is my time to grow through all the hardship and to figure out how tall I can be. Also, I'm bringing a friend and we're giving you a baby shower. Don't argue with me, young lady."

Kaelyn responded with a wide variety of heart emojis in various colors and said she would not disrespect her grandmother by arguing. She said she was honored by the offer and looked forward to whatever her grandmother had planned.

Daisy's third flight seemed to be the lucky one. The flight attendants upgraded her to first class, gave her complimentary alcoholic beverages, and they had Daisy feeling a little tipsy by the time she landed. Maybe this light-headed, carefree feeling was what Khrista sought?

A gracious woman at the airline's customer service desk helped her figure out how to get a shuttle into the city, where Daisy would find a hotel until she could get settled.

She had never acted with such impulse in her life, and it felt good. Perhaps feeling good would lead to taking more risks, like trying harder to find her daughter.

Shifting winds of the past had always left her feeling drowned and despairing, but these days the wind carried the soft tune of a gentle lullaby of hope.

# 13

## KHRISTA

K hrista added another bag to the top of the pile of garbage bags stacked by the door, then rubbed her hands together and smiled a satisfied smile.

"There we go, Bess. Once Matt gets these out to the dumpster, we'll have a celebratory dance."

"I don't know how you have the energy to dance." Bess leaned back against the couch, brushing away one of her cats, who bumped her furry forehead against her human friend's cheek. "I'm exhausted after watching you all day."

"I hope you're liking the way things turned out."

"I can't thank you enough, Khrista. You had me a little nervous when you said you were getting a dumpster because I wasn't so sure about throwing my things away. But I appreciate your insight and I'm grateful to be able to spend more quality time with the things that truly matter to me." Bess's lips turned upward in a sunny smile. "I think the cats are excited, too. Look how they run around and chase each other more enthusiastically now."

Khrista bent down to scoop her favorite of Bess's cats into her arms. The cat appeared to liquefy, and Khrista petted its belly as its tiger-striped limbs oozed toward the floor. Matt opened the door and grabbed two trash bags in each hand, winking at Khrista as the screen door banged behind him.

It had taken weeks to get Bess's apartment in order, but Matt contributed more than she had anticipated, especially in using his soothing powers to convince Bess it was okay to let go of her things.

That psychological hurdle had been the hardest to clear. Khrista was proud of Bess for overcoming that difficulty, though she struggled with every decision.

Had Daisy gone through Harold's things? Was she sitting there now, wondering how to put one foot in front of the other? Struggling to survive in a world without her husband?

She had reached out to Khrista, but had she expected a response? Her message had been so brief. Reconciliatory, but she hadn't asked for contact.

Should Khrista have responded? What was the right thing to do? When she read the email, she had been too shocked over the news of her father to consider her course of action.

And now weeks had passed. Months since the date Daisy had sent the email.

She couldn't imagine reaching out to Kaelyn and not hearing back for so long, but that was part of the reason she didn't reach out. Her communication wasn't wanted.

And Daisy hadn't said anything to make Khrista think she wanted contact.

Khrista didn't want that, either.

Right?

"Okay, Bess. Now that we have your house looking like it belongs in a country home magazine," Khrista teased, knowing its appearance was far from that nice, but she and Bess had developed an inside joke about their lack of design and organizational skills. "Time to go to Happil-TEA Ever After for celebratory tea."

"If you insist."

"I do."

Khrista waited while Bess changed out of her work clothes and into an outfit she had planned for this occasion. Matt reentered the house and kissed Khrista on the cheek. His brown eyes sparkled.

"I just got a call from my daughter, Nia. She's available last minute and asked if we could meet her for dinner. Please come."

The pleading and his longing expression nearly did her in. A bubble burst inside her, and the energy drained from her legs.

She owed him this much. She owed him a simple family dinner after he had, without a single complaint, devoted all of his free time to helping her help Bess. Her spirits had been brighter, and she had been doing better the last several weeks with all the distraction of helping Bess, but the idea of meeting his daughter when Khrista was out of touch with her own caused physical hurt. Her head pounded, and the sharp, stinging pain in her gut had to be an ulcer.

"I really wish I could, Matt, but I'm needed at the tearoom."

He reeled her in for a hug and kissed her lips. She blushed a little at the idea of Bess coming out and seeing them. Not that their relationship was a secret, but she had never been in a functional relationship before meeting Matt and she was never into public displays of affection.

"We can have a light dinner at the tearoom." He tapped his expanding gut. "I'm trying to eat lighter, anyway. Not getting any younger or fitter."

Panic set in, and she felt nauseated.

"That wouldn't be a bad idea, but we're having an impromptu knitting circle and I don't want you to see what I'm making for you." The lie rolled off her tongue too easily, and shame burned her cheeks.

"You're making something for me?"

Darn it.

What kind of hole was she digging herself?

Khrista forced a smile onto her tired cheeks. His smile was reminiscent of a kid who woke up to find every item from his wish list under the Christmas tree.

"It was supposed to be a surprise. I don't want to ruin the surprise even more by having you see it before it's done."

Now she would need to figure out something to make for him as soon as she finished making the blanket for her grandbaby. Khrista had been watching one of her knitting club mates working on socks, but that was far too difficult for her to attempt.

Maybe a scarf. That was sort of like a blanket, and though her workmanship was still terrible and he would never want to wear it, at least he wouldn't know she had lied.

Then again, what was one more lie on top of the heaps she had been telling him all along?

Bess saved her by coming out carrying her knitting bag. Bess had not only joined the social club with her peers, but she had become motivated to go back to knitting the way she had before. She had tremendous skill, and she shared stories of knitting sweaters for her children for Christmas every year.

As they were cleaning out the house, they had found old photo albums with yellow-around-the-edges photos of her children wearing the sweaters.

"Impressive," Khrista had said. And she meant it. She envied that level of skill. But although she was no good at knitting and probably never would be, she was proud of the blanket she had poured so much time and love into. She still needed help from her knitting club friends now and then, but the thing looked almost square when she held it up to study it, and Khrista could barely see the flaws anymore.

She hoped the baby would love it despite its imperfections, assuming the blanket actually made it to the baby.

# 14

## KAELYN

Having Grandma in town proved to be everything Kaelyn had hoped for. Her grandmother had been great about respecting her space and time, although Kaelyn wouldn't have minded if she had infringed a little.

Kaelyn watched as her grandmother shed the tentative skin she had worn upon arrival, displaying a fresh attitude and youthful enthusiasm. Rather than growing older, she seemed to go back in time. It was amazing to see, and Kaelyn imagined the reconnection had been good for both of them.

Oliver snuggled up to her on the couch as she focused on a work project on her laptop. Her boss had been giving her more responsibility, which was awesome since she often heard horror stories of workplaces treating pregnant employees terribly. She was lucky to work for a progressive company and a boss who believed in equality when it came to parents raising children—he was frequently leaving the office early to take turns shuffling his kids to their after-school activities or working from home when one of his kids was sick. He didn't think she was less capable of working hard simply because a baby grew inside her, even though sometimes Kaelyn swore her brain had grown squishy since the moment of conception.

Oliver's large hand splayed across her rapidly growing belly. The second trimester had been a gift to her. No more morning sickness, a healthy libido, which Oliver appreciated even if she tired him out, and she could understand why people said pregnant women glowed because her skin and hair and nails had never been healthier.

One of her coworkers, who was a couple of months further along, had suffered from acne and nausea throughout her entire pregnancy and couldn't wait for it to be over.

Kaelyn didn't mind being the lucky one for a change.

"You're getting huge." Oliver added a second hand, cradling her stomach and framing her popped-out belly button.

"Just the thing a woman wants to hear." She batted her eyes, and Oliver captured her lips with his.

"You know there's nothing you could do to be less sexy. As a matter of fact, since we're alone for the first time in quite a few evenings, I wouldn't mind proving that theory before dinner."

She kissed him back before brushing his hands away as he roamed.

"You, my darling, are a distraction I can't afford right now. I need to get this work done."

"Okay," Oliver said, hesitating as if there was more he wanted to say. He planted a chaste but romantic kiss on her shoulder and then shifted the focus of the conversation. "I completely understand you've been crazy with work. But have you had a second to decide between woodland creatures or an ocean theme?"

Irritation grew inside Kaelyn. She wanted to scream that she had more important things to do than worry about the nursery when the baby wasn't due for another three months.

But even she could tell her thoughts crossed the line into unreasonable territory.

Still, she couldn't seem to reel in her irritation.

"I don't care either way." Kaelyn snapped her laptop shut, then caught herself. Her normally calm, understanding husband looked ready to lash out right back.

"When do you expect to start caring? When we bring the baby

home and have nowhere for her to sleep? Forgive me for wanting to make things perfect. That's usually your area of expertise."

His tone was more caustic than she had ever heard it, shocking her into silence. He got up and stormed into the kitchen, leaving her with her mouth gaping. She couldn't recall a time when he had snapped at her. Nor had he thrown her need for perfection in her face before.

But he was right. For someone so committed to perfection, she sure was messing this nursery thing up.

"I'm sorry, Oliver. I haven't been sleeping well with the baby moving around constantly. I swear if he's not a kickboxer, I'll be shocked. Can we please talk about it over the weekend? This project will be done and I'll have time to go over the fabric samples with you."

Not waiting for his response, Kaelyn gathered her laptop and notebooks and brought them upstairs.

Oliver left her alone for the rest of the night.

GRANDMA ASKED if she could stop by Saturday morning, and Kaelyn told her she was welcome anytime, which she had also told her about three thousand times before. She had been really sweet about seeking Kaelyn's opinion on baby shower ideas without giving away all the plans.

Daisy strolled into the living room, arms loaded with folders and a canvas grocery bag on her shoulder. She dropped the items on the coffee table. "I'll be sending out invitations soon. I originally wanted everything to be a surprise for you, but since we're still getting to know each other better and I've been out of your life for so long, I don't know how to plan around your schedule and who to invite. I hope you're not disappointed."

Kaelyn wrapped her arms around her grandmother, laughing when the baby started kicking.

"Did you feel that? Your great-grandchild is brutal."

Grandma laughed, then reached down to wrap her hands around Kaelyn's burgeoning belly.

"Don't talk badly about my little great-grandchild monster."

"It must be crazy to think about being a great-grandma. I hope I am one day."

"It's true—it's the craziest thing. The greatest love of my life, aside from his mother, that is."

"Grandma, I could never be disappointed with anything you're doing. I think it's amazing you moved out here so you could get to know me better after all these years. So incredibly brave. Having you here is a dream come true, even if it's temporary. I don't like surprises, and it's actually killing me a little to not be in charge of everything, so knowing you're seeking my input on stuff is really helpful to me. Thank you for all you're doing."

"I wouldn't miss this opportunity for the world. But anytime you want me to back off, you only have to say so."

"Don't hold your breath. 'Cause that's not gonna happen."

Grandma shifted her eyes away from Kaelyn's face and started picking at the cuff of her sweater.

"What's wrong?" Kaelyn waved her hands in front of her grandmother. "Where'd you go there, Daisy Duke?"

"I wanted to broach a subject with you that I know will make you unhappy, but I feel it's important."

"If it's about the cloth diapers again, I'm sorry. I'm super environmentally conscious, and there are some things I like about the old ways, but I don't see it happening."

Grandma grinned, showing a dimple that matched Kaelyn's.

"It's not that at all. I don't blame you, actually." She paused. "It's about your mother."

Kaelyn's brain shut down as soon as her grandmother uttered the words.

Her grandmother had done a decent job of respecting Kaelyn's boundaries about Khrista, so her motive for bringing her up when speaking about the baby shower frightened Kaelyn. She hated disappointing her grandmother, but she wasn't in a phase where she was trying to make reparations for the past like her grandmother was.

She never would be.

"Grandma, please."

"I'm not saying I think you have to forgive your mother. But don't you think you'll feel better if you give her a chance? See if she's changed? See if your feelings have changed?"

"No."

End of discussion.

Grandma apparently didn't get the mental memo.

"Kaelyn, I'm trying to go easy with this topic. I know it's a sore subject."

"Yes, it is. And as much as I love you and respect you, I don't want to have any conversations that have to do with Khrista."

Kaelyn managed not to stomp on her way to the kitchen. She started loading the dishwasher from dinner the night before, placing each item with care and trying desperately to not act out in front of her grandmother. She and Oliver had been growing more tired every night and had struggled to keep up with some of the more basic household tasks. The realization that she was already slacking on keeping her home perfect worried Kaelyn.

What kind of mother would she be if fatigue and stress were changing her already?

"Leave those, darling. I'll do them after I cook you breakfast."

Kaelyn laughed softly.

"You don't have to make us breakfast every weekend, Grandma. Not that I'm complaining, but I don't want you to feel obligated or taken for granted."

Grandma *tsked* as she pulled flour, eggs, and chocolate chips out of the shopping bag she had carried in. "I don't feel obligated. I adore doing this for you and Oliver."

They worked in tandem for the next few minutes, the silence between them growing more and more uncomfortable.

Kaelyn paused, resting her potato cutting knife on the cutting board and waiting for her grandmother to look up at her. "Grandma, I don't think you understand how hurt I was by my upbringing."

"There is where you're wrong, my darling. I don't know all the details, of course, but I understand being hurt by a parent. I also understand being hurt by a child. I'm trying to look out for you in this situation. Of course, my dream would be for all of us to reunite and for everyone to be happy, but I know there's so much beyond my wishing. I simply worry about the price you're paying by holding onto this grudge. And I worry you'll somehow regret your decisions."

Kaelyn rolled her eyes. "You sound like Oliver."

"Oliver is a wise man. I've thought that since I first met him. Handsome, too."

"You're sounding a little cheeky there, Grandma." Kaelyn gently bumped her hip against her grandmother's.

"I love you, Kaelyn Fox. I only want what's best for you."

"Then please stop trying to fix something that is so irrevocably broken. Besides, you don't see my mother busting down my door trying to make amends, do you? Don't you think after five years, if she wanted to work things out, she'd be trying?"

Like a high-humidity island afternoon, Grandma's silence hung heavily in the room. Tears pricked Kaelyn's eyes, and her nose ran.

When would this stop hurting so badly? When would she actually move past everything and not have to pretend that she had?

Stupid hormones. They had to be to blame. What Kaelyn thought had scabbed over now felt as sharp and raw as a fresh wound. And every time Grandma or Oliver suggested a potential treatment, the wound festered and stung.

Perhaps when Oliver and Grandma stopped bringing it up, she'd feel healed. The past was perfectly fine when it remained buried. She didn't need the constant reminders, especially when she was dealing with extreme emotions from hormonal changes.

"How's the nursery design coming along?"

Kaelyn groaned. Grandma and Oliver definitely played for the same team.

"That good? I'd have thought with the way you want everything so perfect you would have been much more eager to get it done."

"Does Oliver pay you to say this stuff?" Kaelyn only half-teased.

"Wouldn't you like to know?"

Her cheeky grandmother gave a wink before flipping the pancakes.

## 15

## DAISY

Daisy's hands shook as she swept her kitchen floor for the third time that day. Her stomach had been bothering her, but she hadn't wanted to worry Florence, and she most especially did not want to worry her precious Kaelyn.

She was sure it was nerves.

The closer she grew to Kaelyn, the heavier the guilt became, sometimes rendering her unable to breathe. She wanted to reach out to Khrista so badly. To tell her she was taking care of Kaelyn in her absence. To encourage her to swallow her pride and make things better so she wouldn't miss out on everything happening.

But was it the right thing to do?

Kaelyn had made her views on inviting her mother clear. And Daisy had no faith that if Daisy turned up on Khrista's front step she'd be welcomed.

Why did she allow fear to torment her so? She had learned to be brave in so many ways. But when it came to her daughter, she remained a coward.

More than anything, Daisy wanted to mother her own daughter in a way she hadn't known back when she'd had the chance. The way she was sure she still didn't understand, but hindsight had taught her valuable lessons. Mainly, what not to do.

Something was bothering her granddaughter lately, and though Daisy couldn't push herself into Kaelyn's subconscious, and certainly couldn't pretend to read her mind, Daisy sensed it had something to do with missing her mother. Too often, the girl's smile didn't glow the same as it once had. Daisy often caught her staring longingly toward the ocean, a haunted expression on a face she normally kept neutral.

Sure, the child put up a brick wall around her heart and acted so tough about her mother's absence. But hatred that strong was too often rooted in love, and the lack of a connection pained the girl, regardless of whether she admitted it outright or not. Her emotions protruded from her skin, stark and angry. If she didn't actually miss her mother, would she still carry so much fury?

A spider dangled in front of Daisy, so she swung the broom at it and shrieked. In trying to save herself—the one good thing about having Harold around had been his spider-hunting skills—she knocked a glass off the counter.

The shattering glass jerked her back in time. An old country farmhouse. Seven children sharing hand-me-downs. A beleaguered mother who was always too exhausted. A father who didn't care if they had shoes, so long as they did their farm chores anyway.

"Mother, you can't stop me from going with him! My future isn't here on this farm! I don't want to spend my life looking after my siblings. You and Daddy don't understand a thing!"

The hurt in her mother's eyes cut Daisy deep, but she didn't back down. Harold would be waiting for her by the edge of the field in only a few hours, and though she had hoped to gain her mother's blessing, she had no desire to heed her mother's advice.

"You're young still, Daisy girl. You have so much to learn before you run off to get married."

"You've taught me well, Mother. I can cook, clean, mend—"

Something dark crossed her mother's face just before a scowl formed.

"That's not all there is to marriage, you little fool. You're seventeen. Sure, you're a woman now, but there's so much you don't know." Her mother's face turned harder and her nostrils flared. "I'm telling you right now, if you sneak off like this, you'll never see us again."

The rage that had simmered in Daisy surged forth, consuming her. Fire lit her neck and throat, and if she could turn into a dragon and burn the whole shack down, she would.

She never *wanted* to see any of them again. She didn't want to see the holes in the floorboards or the broken windows. She didn't want to wash dirty faces and listen to moans of pain after their father beat them. Daisy didn't want to spend all her time scrubbing clothes that should have been thrown out, mending spirits that were beyond full repair, or see her mother succumb to the horror Daisy's father inflicted on her daily.

She wanted everything Harold promised—a lifetime of love, a cute house with a sunny kitchen, a family they'd take good care of together, and nights of Harold stoking the passion he stirred so easily.

Daisy whirled to storm out, but her mother's bony fingertips grabbed her and dug into the soft flesh above her elbow.

"Don't do this, Daisy. I don't trust Harold at all. He's a sweet talker, I'm sure, but give yourself time to find the right one. Your father was a sweet talker in the beginning, too. And look where that led me."

Daisy tried to jerk away, but her mother's strength appeared to have grown in her desperation to control her daughter.

"Don't you dare compare my life to yours," Daisy spat out. "You never even stand up to your husband. I'd sooner *die* than let a man treat me the way he treats you! You don't even try to protect your own children."

Daisy's mother's eyes widened, and a vein threatened to burst near her forehead. Her nostrils flared and her grip on Daisy tightened. Without warning, her mother started hitting, kicking, and spitting on Daisy. She yanked at her hair, scratched the parts of her face Daisy couldn't protect, and kicked Daisy in the shin.

Trapped between the kitchen sink and the workstation, Daisy struggled to escape, screaming for help, all the while knowing there wasn't a darned person in that town capable of saving her at that moment.

Her mother had lost her mind that day. And Daisy, the young fool she had been, had used her mother's behavior as further justification for following through on the plan she intended to follow, regardless.

Daisy swept the broken pieces of the glass she had knocked over into the dustpan, her knees trembling as she tried to stand again.

It had taken years to learn the lesson, but she now knew that's what happened when a mother lost the last bit of control over her life and her children.

Something snapped.

Daisy prepared the slow cooker with a roast for her and Florence to enjoy later that evening. Florence had spent most of her days out exploring, spending a lot of time at a beach—not the one closest to their rental, but one a short drive away where all the young people went to exercise on sandy-floored equipment.

Things had been going pretty well with Florence, surprisingly, but Daisy sensed there were also things left unsaid there.

Harold hung between the two women like a long-dormant volcano ready to spread its lava and ash. The tension was sometimes so thick that one or the other would have to break it up by suggesting a funny movie or show on the TV.

Daisy had never been much of a TV watcher, but it sure provided a pleasant distraction when issues were hanging around that felt like ghosts in need of an exorcism. Unsettled, unwanted, and unable to be solved unless she and Florence became brave enough to address them.

Daisy wiped down the counters, and then, as she swept the floor one more time to make sure she got all the tiny shards of glass and all the crumbs from her dinner preparation, Florence breezed in and shouted, "Helloooo!"

Daisy gasped when she spun around to see Florence clinging to the arm of a man with broad shoulders and only the slightest bit of gray at the edges of his dark hair. He stood at least a foot taller than Florence, who was pretty tall herself.

"Do you ever stop cleaning?" Florence gestured with her free hand to the broom Daisy still held in hers. "Daisy, meet Manuel. I hope you don't mind if he joins us for dinner."

Florence gazed up at Manuel with admiration in her eyes. Manuel poked Florence's nose with a finger and wrinkled his own nose before turning back to Daisy.

Manuel extended his hand to shake Daisy's, thanking her for her hospitality in a thick Spanish accent. Daisy glanced from Manuel to Florence, trying to connect the dots. True, there were a lot of things they didn't speak about, but Daisy thought she and Florence had shared their daily events with one another.

Florence could apparently decipher Daisy's expression.

"We met at the beach. You should see him doing chin-ups on the bars at the beach." Florence fanned herself and winked at Daisy.

Daisy gulped, imagining the muscles this man must hide beneath his shirt despite his age.

Daisy tried to assess him. He didn't seem to be as old as Florence and Daisy, but he was no spring chicken either. Maybe mid-to-late sixties, yet his skin held only a hint of a weathered past.

Determined not to be rude, Daisy blinked and said, "Of course you're welcome. Do you like pot roast?"

"Sure do." He rubbed his belly and licked his lips appreciatively.

Daisy fumbled for words. "It won't be ready for several hours, but I have some cheese and crackers I can put out."

"Don't trouble yourself, Daisy dear," Florence said, staring up at Manuel and batting her lashes. "We'll occupy ourselves until dinner."

Dinner could have been more awkward, but luckily Manuel was a talker. He regaled them with tales of moving to California a decade ago, being a personal trainer for most of his adult life, and helping to raise six children with his ex-wife. He made sure to point out he and his ex had divorced many years prior and that he was interested in having fun but not forming attachments.

Daisy raised her eyebrows at Florence. Was she on board with this?

Florence smiled broadly. "Attachments are the worst. We're on Earth for so short a time. Why cut off any avenues that lead to fun?"

Daisy didn't know about all that, but she couldn't deny feeling a bit of envy when Florence disappeared with Manuel, leaving Daisy to eat dessert by herself while she tried to ignore the noises coming from Florence's room.

Surely they were too old for all that!

Daisy slept fitfully all night. When she tossed, she reflected on how she needed to honor Kaelyn's wishes and drop all thoughts of inviting Khrista to the shower.

When she turned, the brilliance of the idea she kept toying with struck her—to send an invitation and see if Khrista would come. If Khrista showed up—and knowing what a grudge-holder Khrista was, it was a big "if"—they could surprise Kaelyn and all would be right in the world.

Yet when she tossed the other way again, her legs more restless than usual and her belly aching, she went back to thinking she could do irreparable harm to her budding relationship with Kaelyn. Hadn't she already missed out on enough time?

The next day, Florence emerged from her bedroom alone, looking rumpled but happy. She asked Daisy if everything was okay, and Daisy shared her thoughts about the shower invitation.

"No," Florence said emphatically. "Absolutely, positively, no. You don't meddle in the affairs of a mother and daughter."

"This is about my relationship with my daughter, too. Doesn't that count for something?"

"Sure. But that's on you. Don't bring it to Kaelyn. You want to mess up the thing you were so eager to repair?"

Daisy hung her head. "Of course not. I just don't think—"

"I'm telling you, Daisy. Don't do it. If you want to call up your daughter and try to work things out for yourself, I'll help you rehearse what to say and support you all the way. But don't go behind Kaelyn's back with this terrible attempt at reunification. It's a horrible idea and you'll regret it."

Florence removed herself and her cup of coffee from the table, her level of irritation not matching the conversation.

What was she so up in arms about? Why did she care so much? She wasn't even a mother. What did she know about any of it?

The conversation continued to sting all morning.

Florence didn't understand. She *couldn't* understand the pain of estrangement between a mother and daughter. And from Daisy's way of thinking, she could bring rainbows to Kaelyn's darkened skies. If Daisy could pull off the reunification, everyone would be happy.

There was no downside.

If Daisy could get to the point, at her advanced age, of wanting to repair the damage in their family tree, Khrista would want to, too.

Daisy remembered how protective Khrista had been of Kaelyn. How she had refused to leave her alone with Harold or the child's own father. How she had held Kaelyn's hand and taught her to dance.

Khrista had to be hurting from this estrangement with her daughter. And it was clear to Daisy that Kaelyn was hurting, too.

What better opportunity to heal than at a baby shower? They'd be surrounded by people, so would all need to be on their best behavior.

By the end of the day, Daisy had made up her mind.

She'd send the invitation.

Even if Kaelyn was angry about it at first, she'd come around. She was a sweet thing, full of heart, and softened by becoming a mother herself. She wouldn't cast her grandmother away over something so small.

Yet she had hardened her heart against her mother...so there was that chance.

A chance worth taking. Losing Kaelyn after all this time would send Daisy into the grave, but she couldn't live a full life if her happiness came at the expense of Khrista's. And if Kaelyn were to cast her aside, Daisy would always carry the memories of these past months with her. They had been the best part of her life.

Daisy had never been allowed to see her own mother after that fateful day and the physical attack. She had run off with Harold as planned, and he had comforted her after seeing the evidence of her mother's insanity.

He kissed her and made love to her and told her he'd never let anyone hurt her again.

He had promised.

Harold had kept none of his vows—not a one—but he had kept her from ever seeing her mother again, even when she wanted to make amends.

Daisy supposed the old adage about marrying a man like your father was true, even if the daughter thought she was marrying the complete opposite.

Both men had refused to let her see her mother again, even after her death.

Daisy wouldn't let that happen for Khrista and Kaelyn.

# 16

## KHRISTA

When Khrista arrived home at the end of a wonderfully fun school day, she ran into Rafael downstairs by the mailboxes.

"I was hoping to see you," he said.

He held a cotton candy pink and blue-colored envelope out in front of her. Though blurry from this distance, she could see a California return address.

Her mouth went dry, and her mind turned to the bottle of rum sitting upstairs.

Though she had emptied her original collection after getting the news of her father's death, Khrista had told herself that if she just bought small bottles, she would limit herself to the kind of "drinking to relax" that normal people did. Just a little nip to get herself through the night and help her relax. That was a normal thing to do. She wasn't a wine person, but wine was socially acceptable, according to every woman she knew. So if wine was alcohol and rum was alcohol, maybe it had more to do with the quantity than the drinking itself...

"This was in my box, but it has your name on it. It looks like some sort of invitation. Wanted to make sure you got it."

"Thank you, Raf. I appreciate you keeping it safe."

She distracted herself by checking her mailbox and pulling out the stack of coupon inserts, car warranty solicitations, and an old payment demand from a debt collector.

"I wish I could stay and chat, but it's been a long week, and I'm beat."

She reached up on tiptoe to kiss his rough cheek, said good night, and ran up to her apartment, the cotton candy envelope clutched to her chest.

Could it truly be a baby shower invitation?

By her calculations, Kaelyn would be approaching the sixth month of pregnancy. Seemed like a time when her friends would send out invitations.

Khrista had always wondered if Kaelyn would follow her dream of living on the opposite coast. She had, after all, threatened to go as far from her as possible. The West Coast was a good start. And it fit with the story Khrista fabricated.

She knew for certain her daughter would want to find her way toward a shoreline.

Khrista set the envelope on the coffee table, propped up against the small liquor bottle that lured her and tormented her and teased her and enticed her and bedeviled her.

What to open first?

The bottle won. She twisted off the cap and downed the nip in one swallow. When her nerves settled a bit, Khrista was ready.

She lifted the envelope and brought it to her nose, sniffing to see if her daughter's favorite Amber Blush scent clung to the paper. Foolish, yes, but Khrista had never pretended to be anything less than foolish or desperate.

Memories of playful fights in the fragrance store where they would squirt each other with samples of body spray played like old movies across Khrista's memory.

She usually tried not to think about the good times for too long, because they were long ago and adorned with a magical quality that Khrista was pretty sure she dreamed up for her own self-protection.

Ever the coward, Khrista clutched the envelope close to her chest once again and sought her stash of nip bottles. She lifted another that she would have saved for the next day, but she desperately needed to consume it immediately. Khrista swallowed that one down faster than the first and then, a crazed woman needing to end the torture, she tore into the envelope and read it carefully.

As predicted, it was a baby shower invitation.

Kaelyn had invited her.

At the very least, Kaelyn had told whatever friend was organizing the baby shower her mother's name so *they* could invite her.

What did this mean?

Khrista collapsed onto the couch. Tears clogged her throat but remained at bay.

Was that sensation deep in her chest...*happiness?* The tiniest bud of fresh growth in an otherwise dark ice age?

Did pregnancy soften Kaelyn? Make her want to reconnect?

Whatever the reason, Khrista would not mess up.

Not this time.

Before she tucked herself in for the night, she dug underneath her bed until she found the special sealed bag holding Kaelyn's favorite doll from childhood—a raggedy quilted toy they had picked up at a craft show at the tearoom many years ago. With yarn hair and a sewn-on smile, this doll had replaced her favorite panda from early childhood when she started feeling too grown-up for a stuffed animal.

Khrista crawled into bed with a different attitude.

She hugged the doll tight, allowing herself to believe for the first time in too many years to count that she might actually be on the right road to redemption.

KHRISTA PICKED up her order at Happil-TEA Ever After, a little bummed Clarice was so busy and unable to chat. Elanna had been busy, too, and Khrista was practically bursting with the need to tell someone about the invitation. She held off telling Matt until making a decision, because he'd ask more questions than she could answer.

She took her drink and her chocolate croissant and was grateful to discover that her favorite seat was available by the fireplace. Even though summer approached and the fire no longer ran consistently, there was a comfort that came from the stone hearth and the distant, lingering smell of burnt wood.

As reliable as ever, Mr. Ed jumped onto her lap before she could add the honey to her cup of lavender earl grey. Khrista gave him the ear scratches he demanded. His purr vibrated across her lap, setting her at ease and filling her with a sense of joy that had felt more natural these days.

"Khrista!"

Khrista's head jerked up to see Elanna sailing toward her, her green and white polka dot dress swirling around her legs like a fashion model. They hadn't been in touch as much lately, and Khrista had missed her. Her friend had three teenage children and an important role in the community, thus limiting the time she had for casual conversations with old friends.

Come to think of it, Khrista hadn't seen her much since the fundraiser they had worked together on months back.

They had grown up in the same town in Virginia and had been best friends since fourth grade. They knew things about each other's lives nobody else did, or probably ever would.

Elanna had come to Old Castle to visit after Khrista settled there, and her blonde Barbie doll beauty had won over one of the town's most eligible bachelors, spearing his heart and reeling him in for a fast engagement.

Khrista was grateful to have her around, even if there had been times when they had grown apart or simply hadn't been able to connect the way they used to because of life's responsibilities. Elanna didn't overtly judge Khrista for the public image she had built, even if she had built the foundation on swampy land.

Sometimes Khrista got the feeling Elanna's public image wasn't as genuine, either.

Though Elanna was the only person Khrista had trusted with the knowledge of her estrangement with Kaelyn, Khrista knew Elanna would hold her secrets, just as they had held each other's secrets when they were kids.

"Khrista, I've been wanting to call you forever. Things have been so insane with Charlotte's dance program and Seth's sports and Hailey's social life. I'm telling you—these kids are trying to kill me."

Elanna pulled out the chair next to Khrista and settled herself into position, shaking a packet of Splenda before pouring it into her tea.

She stared longingly at Khrista's untouched croissant.

"How do you stay so thin when you eat such yummy things? I swear I have to live on water and celery and work out every single day and I still gain weight."

"You look great, as always, Elanna. You're too hard on yourself."

"There's a reason you're my best friend." Elanna smiled as she sipped her tea. "Anyway, I probably shouldn't even say this to you, but you and I have always had an agreement about not keeping these kinds of secrets."

She suppressed a squeal and practically bounced in her seat.

"I'm just gonna say it. I saw Matt leaving the jewelry store the other day, and it got me thinking that I don't even know what's going on in your life. Did he propose? Is he about to propose?"

Something fluttered in Khrista's chest. Proposal? She hadn't considered that would ever be an option.

"You look terrified. I'm so sorry, I did *not* mean to put scary thoughts in your head. Forget I said anything. But the intent of my mentioning this to you remains the same. We need to catch up."

"I have so much to tell you. It's actually been killing me to keep it all inside." Khrista looked around to see if there were any prying ears paying attention when they shouldn't be. The last thing she needed was for her private business to end up on the community's anonymous Spill the Tea forum.

Elanna's eyes grew wide. "Has she made contact?"

Elanna had been there trying to pick up the pieces when Kaelyn left, leaving Khrista a shattered mess on the floor. Khrista had gone into a two-week-long binge, nearly destroying her life and not even caring.

Khrista's smile crept onto her face, and she nodded slightly.

"My goodness, Khrista. This is amazing news. How did it happen? Did she call you?"

Khrista shook her head. "I got a baby shower invitation in the mail. I can't believe it."

"That's so great. You know I've been upset with Kaelyn for a while over the way she's treated you," Elanna said, "but this is great that she's finally smartening up."

"I'm still so nervous about the whole thing. I don't know how to go there and reunite with her after so long and after so much hurt and pain. I wish we could connect ahead of time, but I don't dare to push things. If this is her comfort level and this is how she wants to do things, I should just go along with it, right?"

"I would. She might even want to pretend none of it ever happened. You have to figure out if you're willing and able to do that."

"I would do anything. But I do want to apologize to her. If it has to be done in front of a group, I owe her at least that."

"Khrista, you're not going to apologize in front of everyone at the shower. Besides, it wasn't all your fault. It wasn't all Kaelyn's fault either. You guys had a difficult life, and nobody's perfect. If you'd been able to talk it out back then, that would have been great. But that wasn't where each of you were at that time in your life. There's nothing you can do about that. You can't turn back time, you can't read her mind, you can't dissect what she needed or wanted or how she perceived things. And the same for her. If this is an opportunity to start fresh, you need to take it. Where's she living?"

"California. Not far from LA."

Elanna's perfectly trimmed eyebrows rose.

"Nice. She did what she set out to do."

Khrista nodded again, picking at the edges of her croissant, unable to consume it.

"So just go there and what? Pretend we've been living across the country from one another as a matter of geography, and everything has been fine?"

"Yes, if that's how she wants to play it. What choice do you really have?"

"It feels so strange to me. Like it goes against everything I thought I understood about relationships and conflict resolution. Not that I understood any of that back then, but am I doing us any favors if I ignore the alarm going off in my head?"

Elanna reached out and set a hand on top of Khrista's wrist.

"You don't have to figure it all out ahead of time. It's quite all right to follow your heart and let your mind catch up later. Get yourself dressed up, treat yourself to new makeup and a haircut, splurge on a really cool grandmotherly gift, and go out there and show Kaelyn how much you love her and miss her and how devoted you are to making things better with her and this baby." Elanna's pearly teeth sparkled, and empathy oozed from her expression and her touch. "I'm so excited for you, my friend."

Khrista absorbed everything Elanna said. She almost brought up her conflicted feelings about hearing from Daisy, but she wasn't ready to voice that. Besides, why burst this rare bubble of happiness and hope?

She could do this. She had always sworn she would do whatever it took to make things right with her daughter. Khrista couldn't throw away this opportunity just because it felt funny.

She had promised herself she would walk through fire to make things right with Kaelyn. She couldn't decline the opportunity to attend the party and see her daughter's face.

The cuff of Elanna's sleeve slid up as she reached across the table, revealing a fading purple bruise around her wrist.

Khrista reached out and placed a finger on it, concern sending more alarm bells, but for Elanna this time.

Elanna snapped her hand away and buried it on her lap beneath the table. An unasked question hung in the air between them.

"I've been so clumsy lately. It's crazy, the kids are always making fun of me. Cam says I really should have some tests done to see why my balance is so off." She laughed, once again showing her perfectly straight, bleached white teeth and the lack of laugh lines on her face.

Khrista didn't buy it. The bruise looked like someone had gripped her wrist and squeezed too tight. Khrista was familiar with that kind of bruise.

"Is there anything you'd like to talk about? This is a no-judgment zone. And you sure have had to listen to a lot of my stuff over the years."

"Don't be silly. I'm really okay. I appreciate your concern, but I think I just need to get lower heels. Maybe add some electrolytes to my water. Cam's up for a promotion, isn't that great? Can you imagine me being married to the chief of police? Crazy to imagine how you and I used to sneak out at night and do all sorts of illegal things, and now I'm married to the law."

Her laugh seemed disingenuous, but Khrista couldn't force her friend to admit or confront the truth they both knew she hid.

"Yeah, that sure is something."

Elanna spent the next few minutes recounting a funny story about her middle child and then abruptly excused herself, saying she had a PTA meeting to attend.

"I hope everything goes well for you, Khrista. Please call me and let me know how it works out."

"I will. And don't forget, I'm here if you want to talk about anything. Anything at all."

KNOTS IN STOMACH and lies told, Khrista couldn't deny the feeling of excitement as she boarded the plane. She had spent the last several weeks finishing the blanket for the baby, which she poured all of her love and affection into. Love for Kaelyn, love for the new baby, and she even tried to weave in a little love for herself.

Self-love was a novel feeling, but one she vowed to continue to work on.

From the time she had made the decision to attend the shower, she had wrapped herself in all of Kaelyn's teenaged interests, like she should have done when Kaelyn was still around. After spending time binge-watching shows she remembered Kaelyn loving, listening to music that used to annoy her when Kaelyn would play the same songs and artists over and over and *over*, and really considering what had drawn Kaelyn to the art she had chosen, Khrista felt more prepared than ever to meet Kaelyn on even ground.

Khrista desperately wanted to connect through time and space and correct the past in any way she could.

Sure, doing good deeds on the island had helped Khrista to start feeling better about herself, but no good deed could wash away all she had done in the past. Digging deeper and analyzing all the ways she had gone wrong hurt but she knew she could do more to fix the past.

She *had* to do more.

The lady next to her on the plane tried chatting her up, so Khrista pretended to be asleep when the woman returned from the bathroom. Her nerves were too on edge, and everything in her trembled. When the flight attendant came around offering drinks and her neighbor asked for wine, the urge to break her own vow and have a drink to settle her nerves was strong.

Khrista had to be stronger. Alcohol had not been her friend, no matter what mental hoops she tried to leap through.

When the urge grew stronger and stronger and the plane grew closer and closer to California, Khrista dug the photo album out of the carry-on bag she had nestled under the seat in front of her. She had painstakingly spent her spare time making a scrapbook for the baby. Before losing Kaelyn, Khrista would have cried over the photos, but since crying was not something she'd done since that day, she internalized the pain instead. Achy limbs and digestive problems weren't exactly new to her, but receiving the invitation had certainly exacerbated those issues.

Khrista had wondered if she could go through with it. But there she was. On a plane. Her heart may be in her throat, but it was Kaelyn's if Kaelyn would take it back.

"Oh, is that your daughter?" The woman next to her didn't seem to understand personal space. Her shoulder bumped against Khrista's as she leaned forward to study the scrapbook pages, not picking up on Khrista's attempts to turn herself invisible.

"Yes. I'm giving this to her for her baby shower."

"What a dear she is. You must be so proud."

Even without knowing anything about what twists and turns Kaelyn's life had taken, Khrista was indeed filled with pride. She knew her daughter would be the mother Khrista had never been.

Each page of the scrapbook represented specific stages of Kaelyn's life. Khrista had devoted a full page to each of Kaelyn's first months, then did her best to select photos that represented Kaelyn for all the other years of her life, right up until she was eighteen.

Rifling through the photos on her bedroom floor, and sticking to her one drink per night rule, Khrista had come across quite a few photos of her and Kaelyn laughing and playing together. They were all from Kaelyn's first ten years. After that, Khrista had only found one of the two of them together, and they had taken it when Kaelyn was thirteen.

Khrista remembered the day clearly. Nothing special had happened, and it wasn't a holiday or anything. Kaelyn had come home from school and had been excited because Khrista had managed to find some energy that day. She had straightened out the living room, cleaned the kitchen, and even had time enough to bake cookies before Kaelyn arrived home.

"Smells so good in here. What happened? Is someone coming? Is the landlord doing an inspection?"

Khrista laughed.

"No, it's just so warm and sunny out today, and I thought it'd be nice to open the windows. The litter boxes needed changing, and one thing led to another. If you're looking for anything of yours from the living room, I left it in a basket by your bedroom door."

"Thanks, Mom." Kaelyn, too cool for hugs and kisses, surprised Khrista by hugging her tight.

Khrista had cried, and Kaelyn called her weird.

They ate cookies and drank tea together from a ceramic tea set Khrista had given her daughter when she turned ten. Kaelyn had been eager to celebrate "double digits."

After their impromptu tea party, Kaelyn suggested going for a walk along the beach. They danced and dug in the sand and stayed out to watch the sunset on the harbor, perched on rocks with their feet dangling in the cold water.

Khrista snapped a million pictures, and then Kaelyn snatched the phone out of her mom's hand and showed Khrista how to take a selfie of the two of them.

When Khrista turned to the last page of the scrapbook, she pulled out the loose photos she had tucked into a pocket on the back cover. She flipped through them, mesmerized by the happiness on the glossy paper. She hadn't wanted to include the photos of mom and daughter in the scrapbook because she didn't want to ruin it for Kaelyn if Kaelyn hadn't reached that point of healing yet.

And even if things didn't go well at the reunion, she wanted her daughter's baby to have this photo album of her mother's life. Since Kaelyn had left with no warning, she likely hadn't brought any of her childhood photos along with her.

Khrista had been in that position herself, and she always regretted not having her own childhood photos to share with her daughter as she grew.

Familiar pangs struck a melody in Khrista's heart. Maybe they could have bonded more. Maybe Khrista could have opened up and shared some of her own stories.

Maybe not keeping it in would have prevented the festering that had turned to decay. Maybe the rot wouldn't have spread to her relationship with Kaelyn.

Soon after hitting the ground, Khrista settled into the hotel and took a bubble bath in the large Jacuzzi-jetted tub. Desperate to settle her nerves and keep herself busy, she texted back and forth with Elanna, who gave her the pep talk she needed.

She then sent a borderline risqué selfie to Matt, laughing maniacally at his surprised (and intrigued) reaction.

They always said laughter was the best medicine, and she was desperate for anything that would help this heartache cease. Whatever Khrista had to do to keep from falling into her old patterns was what she would do.

Matt called her and asked if she was meeting up with Kaelyn before the baby shower. Of course, he had no way of knowing this was the first time they'd be seeing each other after five years and that it had been because of choice and not because of busy lives as she had led him to believe, so she brushed off his question and asked him about his daughter who was staying with him over the weekend while her apartment was being fumigated.

Khrista took an Uber to the restaurant where the shower was being held. The California sunshine wasn't as intense as she had thought it would be midsummer. It warmed her without scorching her, and the warmth radiated throughout her body and gave her strength to carry herself out of the vehicle, clutching the gift bag she had brought like a lifesaving raft.

Though her hands shook, she channeled Elanna and her advice and straightened her shoulders while lifting her chin. She was the guest-of-honor's mother, and she had as much right to be there as anyone else.

She was not a fraud.

Not really.

She had been invited. Kaelyn wanted her there, for whatever reason.

Khrista was only doing what any mother would and should do.

She was about to see her baby.

Love would fill the emptiness inside her. The sorrow and pain would be behind them. A new path forward would emerge.

Khrista also knew, deep in her soul, that if all went well, she wouldn't need to drink anymore. Her years of hiding would be over. The curse would end.

All would be right.

She followed the sign in the restaurant's foyer, directing her to the function room where Kaelyn's shower was being held. Green and yellow balloons decorated the corridor, and pictures of the happy parents-to-be decorated the wall. An enormous banner saying "Love Planted a Seed" hung over wedding photos of Kaelyn with a handsome, tall, thin man.

Not the jerk Kaelyn had been with when she left home, but a man who looked at her daughter with the adoration Kaelyn deserved.

Though relief at Kaelyn's apparent happiness opened Khrista's airways and allowed her to breathe easier, seeing the wedding photos tore at Khrista's heart.

She should have expected it. Kaelyn had wanted this sort of life. She was traditional in all the ways Khrista hadn't been—marriage, family, love, stability.

Missing out on those precious moments with Kaelyn would be one of Khrista's greatest regrets. But seeing the love in this man's eyes for her daughter made everything okay, and she needed to move forward.

They would all be okay.

As soon as she entered the room, Khrista noticed a pile of beautifully wrapped gifts on and around a large oak table, all different sizes, towering over one another.

Kaelyn had become quite popular here in her new life.

Khrista frowned at her own wrapped gift. She should have gone for something more extravagant. She simply hadn't known what they'd need. Would they need a crib? A high chair? They hadn't included registry information in the invitation, asking instead for favorite children's books, so Khrista hoped the love she had put into her handmade gifts would be enough. She also had the savings account going, but surveying the room, Khrista wondered whether the paltry amount was even worth mentioning. And, of course, she had included a small board book version of a story Kaelyn had loved.

Though she had been proud of the blanket, she suddenly feared the lopsided square of knit yarn that was full of errors wouldn't be good enough for a daughter whose life had become fancier than anything Khrista could have dreamed for her.

She banished that thought from her head, focusing instead on the image of her precious, innocent newborn grandchild-to-be all wrapped up in the blanket Khrista had spent so many hours creating. Learning stitch by stitch, handpicking the colors, overcoming the frustration. Tearing out row after row and learning to accept the flaws.

Anyone could buy something from a store.

This was from the heart.

So much learning had gone into the creation of the gift. So many stories shared by her knitting club friends. So much hope for a better future. All woven into each and every stitch.

She imagined Kaelyn browsing through the photo album with her new husband and admitting to him that perhaps her perception of her childhood hadn't been entirely accurate.

There *had* been love. She *had* had a bond with her mother. And though her mother hadn't been perfect, she had always loved Kaelyn, no matter how Kaelyn felt on that one fateful day. No matter what Khrista had done to lead to Kaelyn's emotional breakdown.

The crowd cleared slightly, revealing an older woman, a few younger women who appeared to be in their twenties, and then, finally, Kaelyn.

Tears, actual tears, stung Khrista's eyes.

*Don't let this be the day I cry.*

Her daughter looked ethereal, even from across the room. The light glinted off her hair and made her coppery curls glow. She almost looked like she had a halo. She wore a floor-length floral gown that showed off her round belly.

Kaelyn clutched her belly gently, cradling her baby as if it were the most precious thing in the world to her. Like Khrista had when she had been pregnant with Kaelyn. When motherhood was nothing but a confection of dreams and promises, and none of the pain or challenges reality brought.

Kaelyn's smile brightened the room, just as it always had before her terrible teenage years. The dark days, when everything Khrista had done had been wrong. The days when Khrista thought she had been looking out for her daughter, but her daughter pointed out that everything Khrista had done had been the worst of the worst.

Khrista hadn't had a choice in all of it, but she understood the perspective now.

Banishing the past and the guilt she carried to the back of her mind—for the moment, at least—she took another step into the room. No sense loitering at the entryway like an outsider, no matter how well the title fit.

Just as everything started feeling okay, and confidence surged through Khrista, one of the older women moved, revealing a blast from her past that had Khrista paralyzed, her feet anchored to the floor.

Her mother?

This couldn't be happening. This was not a twist she could have seen coming. There was no way her mother, a woman she hadn't laid eyes on in twenty years, a woman her daughter had no way of knowing, could be here.

Khrista felt a bubble of laughter rising in her chest.

Of course.

*Of course* her mother could've tracked down her daughter just the way she had tracked down Khrista to send her the message about dear old Harold dying.

Why wouldn't she insert herself into Kaelyn's life as well? Why wouldn't she beat Khrista to the punch, probably rushing out here to tell Kaelyn that as bad a mother as Khrista had been, she had been an even worse daughter?

Her mother spotted her and her face lit up as if seeing someone she had looked forward to seeing her whole life.

No. This couldn't be happening.

Her mother rushed over, barely hobbling despite her age. In fact, she seemed like she hadn't aged over the last twenty years. Like time had frozen and preserved her in the precise moment Khrista had left behind. She had a certain youthful vigor she hadn't possessed when Khrista last saw her. When the weight of Harold had pulled her down.

Arms open as she approached Khrista, the woman had the audacity to believe Khrista would welcome a hug.

Was she mad?

Or was Khrista the one who had lost her mind? Was this all one ridiculous hallucination? A product of her own fear and anxiety about reuniting with her daughter?

Had she gone on a bender and passed out in the tub? Was this all a dream-sequence-turned-nightmare?

"Khrista!" Tears filled her mother's eyes, and her cheeks reddened as she came within a foot of Khrista.

The spicy perfume her mother had always favored stung the insides of Khrista's nostrils. Her head throbbed. Her muscles tensed.

This was all too real. It was happening.

Khrista, her arms pinned to her side, refused to pretend—no matter who might be watching—that she could let this woman put her arms around her.

"Khrista, my darling girl. It's been too long."

Not long enough. But words wouldn't come.

Daisy halted steps away from Khrista, dropping her arms and fiddling with a tissue that peeked out from the cuff of her sweater.

"I hoped you'd accept the invitation. Kaelyn will be so happy when she sees you here. Please don't let it bother you if she doesn't seem too happy at first. I took my chances on inviting you, but I know in my gut and in my heart, it was the right thing to do."

Khrista's blood clotted in her veins.

What was the sign of a stroke?

She was pretty sure she was about to have one.

Nothing made sense. Had Daisy just said…

"She doesn't know?"

The words sounded mousey.

Khrista didn't recognize her own voice.

Her mother had the nerve to laugh.

She sounded nervous, but not ashamed.

"I thought it best to be a surprise. I didn't want to get her hopes up in case you decided not to come. And if you did come, which of course you did, she'd see how much she means to you and she'd realize forgiveness is what's in everyone's best interest, which is what I'm trying to earn from you."

Vomit gathered in Khrista's esophagus. Darkness swam in front of her eyes, and if she didn't get out of this room, which was suddenly too hot to breathe, she would pass out in front of everyone. It wouldn't look right if the mother of the guest-of-honor died on the floor at the baby shower.

She had done enough to Kaelyn. She couldn't die before her daughter even got to open her presents.

"You did this."

The horrible woman who had birthed her stood there gloating. Pride in finally doing Khrista in made her eyes brighter.

How long had she plotted this revenge? What steps had she taken to fulfill her wish to prove to Khrista that no matter what, she'd never escape her past?

"Yes, honey. For you. And for my granddaughter. I finally understand how to make things right."

"You don't know *anything* about what's right," Khrista snapped. The pressure in the back of her eyes threatened to give way. She would cry for the first time in five years, and the tears would be blood.

"My darling..."

Khrista stepped back, away from her mother's poisonous touch.

"Don't call me that."

Daisy cocked her head to the side, her fake look of concern as chintzy as the green velvet curtains that had once adorned the tacky living room of Khrista's childhood home long after they had gone out of fashion.

"I know I've done my share of harm."

A bubble of hysterical laughter, tangled up with the web of a broken child's lost dreams, balled up in her throat. Khrista couldn't hold back the caged animal that begged to be allowed the freedom to roam.

"Your share of harm? Understatement of the year." *Do not cry. This woman doesn't deserve your tears.*

Khrista leaned forward slightly, surprised she didn't topple over as the world spun around her.

"You're right, *Daisy.* You have. If there's one thing you know how to do, it's mess things up. And you sure as hell managed to mess this one up. Congratulations."

Khrista placed her gift on the table—praying Kaelyn hadn't laid eyes on her—and rushed away.

She could hear the *click-tap-click-tap-click* of her mother's wide-heeled shoes as she tried to keep up, but Khrista increased her pace and by the time she stepped out to the sidewalk, her mother had stopped chasing.

How typical of her to give up so easily.

Khrista ordered an Uber and started walking down the street. She couldn't stay there any longer. She couldn't be so close to her daughter, so close to the foolishness and the false hope and the pain and the torment of having shared the same air with her beloved daughter after so many years and after so much heartache. After getting so close to believing she could actually have a chance at being a mother again.

A real mother with her real daughter solving real problems and living a real happily-ever-after. No longer estranged, but fully settled into one another's hearts.

Khrista should have fought harder back then. She knew that now. But pride and lack of understanding had destroyed the fragile bond.

She searched the app to see how close the Uber driver was. She needed to get out of there. She couldn't stand being so near the woman who made her feel murderous. The woman who had been an undying presence in her soul, if not her mind, and had refused to be drowned out no matter the time and distance and constant, aching pain.

She didn't know how the relationship between Kaelyn and Daisy had formed, but it was clear Daisy was a welcome part of her life.

And she had not asked for Khrista to be present at her baby shower.

Khrista saw clearly where she stood.

Contrary to what Daisy spouted, Kaelyn would not be happy to find out Khrista had dropped in. She would not be happy to see her there. It would ruin Kaelyn's day, just like Khrista had always ruined her life.

Whatever hope Khrista had for reconciliation was gone.

It had died the day Kaelyn blamed her mother for everything else that had gone wrong.

And there would be no resurrection.

This trip to California had served one purpose—it had convinced Khrista of what she had known all along.

There were no second chances.

The Uber dropped Khrista off at the airport as she had requested, and Khrista didn't even care when she realized she had left her luggage back at the hotel she had checked into.

There was nothing she needed, anyway.

Sitting outside the airport, she searched her phone for the first flight home and paid an exorbitant amount for it. Bye-bye, rainy day savings. It didn't matter. What was she saving for when life had aborted all her hopes?

With her boarding pass downloaded onto her phone, she whipped through security with just her purse in hand. When Khrista made it to her gate, she still had six hours before boarding. She used that time as wisely as she could.

By sidling up to the bar and getting wasted.

Alcohol was her only friend. It was her only medicine. It was her only hope.

Why had she ever thought she should let it go?

Drunk and out of her mind, she sent a text to Matt telling him she was on her way home and asking if he could pick her up at the airport.

He had questions. Lots of questions.

Khrista turned off her phone.

# 17

## KAELYN

Good thing Kaelyn's mother had prepared her how to smile through the tears and how to fake joy when you wanted to hurt yourself and everyone around you.

That lesson came in handy as Kaelyn stood there surrounded by friends and a family of her choosing, pretending her mother hadn't emerged from her own personal hellscape and fled like the demon ghost she had become in Kaelyn's memory.

A cramp struck Kaelyn's midsection, and she winced a little.

"Are you okay, love?" Oliver's mother reached out and rubbed Kaelyn's lower back. The woman was incredibly tuned into other people's feelings. Kaelyn could definitely see where Oliver developed his kindness and empathy.

"I'm great." The forced smile almost felt natural.

She *was* great. This was her shower. A celebration of the new life she would soon hold in her arms.

A new life she wouldn't ruin as her mother had ruined hers.

"You need water." Before Kaelyn could tell her it wasn't necessary, Oliver's mom rushed off to fetch the liquid.

Kaelyn tried to stay tuned into whatever her friends were

discussing, but her gaze searched the room for a sign that her mother had returned.

When the door swung open, only Daisy emerged.

Grandma's face was beet red, and even from across the room Kaelyn could see the path her flowing tears had left.

"Will you excuse me, please? This baby loves to jump on my bladder like it's a trampoline."

Her friends laughed and let her pass by. Kaelyn locked herself in a stall in the women's room and allowed herself to sob ferociously, grateful she'd had the foresight to wear waterproof makeup since she figured she'd be crying happy tears.

How wrong she had been.

A gentle tap on the stall had her frantically grabbing toilet paper to wipe her tears and blow her nose.

"Just a minute," she called out in her cheeriest voice.

Why the heck didn't they use one of the empty stalls?

"You don't have to use that fake voice with me."

Oliver.

"What are you doing in the women's bathroom?"

He ignored her question. "Daisy told me what happened with your mother. She's very sorry and realizes now she should have listened to your request."

Kaelyn laughed, but there was no humor in the sound.

"Lovely time for her to think about it." She blew her nose noisily, irritation and anger replacing the sadness and hurt.

"This feels exactly like my fifteenth birthday when my mother promised me this big party and then got wasted before my friends showed up. Oh, and did I mention she also promised she would get the house under control so the smell and the mess wouldn't humiliate me? Instead, I had friends show up thinking they were gonna get to come into my house for the first time ever, and I had to improvise by hosting them in an old kiddie pool in my backyard. They pretended to buy the lie about how our plumbing was broken and that's why they couldn't go in to use the bathroom. They all ended up going to Sarah's house while I stayed home, hating my mother for the rest of my life."

"We all have tragic birthday party stories to tell. I'm not making light of your pain, but I don't think your mother was trying to humiliate you today. Daisy told me your mother thought you invited her."

Kaelyn whipped the stall door open, calming down slightly at Oliver's kind, quirkily handsome face. He was her antidepressant and anti-anxiety medication all rolled up in one, but right now she needed a direct shot of him in her veins.

"There's no excuse. Why would she think I wanted her here?"

Oliver shrugged. "I don't think it's such a bad idea. In fact, I think we should go after her."

"Are you insane? I thought you were on my side."

"I am. I am firmly entrenched in your camp. Look, my feet are frozen to the ground. That's why I'm suggesting going after your mother. I've been trying to be as understanding as possible as you struggled over these last many months, but it's painfully obvious to me you need to fix what's broken. Your mother showed up here. Obviously, that means she wants to fix things too."

He stepped into her space, wrapping his arms around her hips and drawing their baby into his circle of protection. For the first time, she had to resist the urge to pull away.

"I love you, Kaelyn, but you're not a child anymore. You can't go into new motherhood carrying this burden. This pain is too much for you to bear, and now is your chance to step a little out of your comfort zone and see if there's a way to repair what was broken. It's time."

She searched his face, certain he had been drinking. Or someone had drugged him. Or he had morphed into someone completely foreign to her.

"I have a party to attend, if you don't mind."

Kaelyn slammed out of the bathroom, leaving Oliver behind.

Despite feeling betrayed by both Oliver and her grandmother, Kaelyn managed to *ooh* and *ahh* over adorable little outfits—gender-neutral since they chose not to find out what sex they were having—

really cool, modern pieces of baby furniture, various things she couldn't figure out what purpose they served, and stacks and stacks of diapers and bibs and bath supplies, and tons of books–the only things they had asked for. People apparently loved buying baby gifts even if there was no registry.

Oliver stayed by her side, rubbing her shoulder and doing the obligatory, "Oh, how cute" over and over. As if they hadn't almost had their first real fight.

Her grandma had outdone herself in planning activities. Kaelyn's favorite had been the onesies each group had to design. Some were hilarious, some inappropriate, and some downright adorable and tailored to what her friends knew of Kaelyn and Oliver's personalities.

She stared at the table where one small gift bag, very wrinkled and looking as if it had traveled across the country, remained on the table, drooping with no support from the other gifts. The bag looked as heartbroken and torn as she felt.

She wanted to look away. Kaelyn wanted somebody to recognize a train wreck was about to occur, take the gift, and hurtle it out of the room. Heck, she wanted somebody to drive it up the coast all the way to the Golden Gate Bridge and throw it off so she would never have to see it or think about it again.

No one took that kind of pity on her. In fact, it was her grandmother, the one already walking on thin ice, who delivered the gift.

"Your mother left this."

Kaelyn closed her eyes and fought the tears. As if being handed the gift wasn't bad enough, she had to point out the obvious? Brutal.

"Okay, what's next?" Kaelyn leaned forward, wincing a bit at the pressure in her belly. "Is it cake time? My little watermelon is telling me it's cake time."

A coworker she didn't even like but had invited out of guilt pointed out the truth that she was trying to avoid.

"You have one more present to open. We want to see what's in there."

Oliver scraped his chair closer and curved an arm around her shoulders. She knew he was infusing her with strength, and she greedily soaked it all in. All that he could offer. She had become a vampire, but he was her willing victim, and though Kaelyn usually tried to protect him from her voracious need, today there was no choice. She had to get through this.

Kaelyn knew her coworker enough to know how relentless she could be, and if she didn't open the stupid gift, the woman would make a big deal of it and everyone would start asking questions Kaelyn wouldn't know how to answer.

She opened the bag, inhaling and exhaling slowly and deliberately as she did so.

The first thing she extracted was a small cranberry and navy blue hand-knit afghan. Kaelyn thought back to a time when she had begged her mother to paint her room in those colors and to let her buy a matching country quilt from the annual craft fair held at Happil-TEA Ever After Tea Room, Kaelyn's second home. Her mother had drunkenly told her they couldn't afford nice things like that, and if she wanted a quilt she'd have to learn to make one herself.

Of course, her mother always said she didn't have a crafting bone in her body, so she couldn't teach Kaelyn, but this little blanket had a "handmade by Khrista" tag attached.

Kaelyn gripped her belly as a wave of pain shot across her lower gut and up behind her breastbone. She gasped at the sharpness of the pain, causing people around her to stop their quiet conversations and to tune in to the show Kaelyn was putting on. Fear gripped her and twisted her heart.

Not again.

Not when she was this far along.

As Oliver dropped to his knees in front of her, encouraging her to make eye contact with him so he could decipher what was wrong, she jolted back in time, seeing her mother in front of her rather than the love of her life.

*"You're making the same mistakes I made!"*

"I'm nothing like you! Stop trying to compare your bad life decisions with mine."

Kaelyn started out the front door of the apartment she despised, but Khrista followed like an ankle-nipping puppy.

"Oh, we're more alike than you even know. I thought you were smarter, but you sure are showing me, aren't you?"

Kaelyn whipped around, glaring at the woman she hated more than anything else on the planet. She had no words for this pathetic excuse for a mother.

Kaelyn had just told her she was going to be a grandmother, and she had the nerve to lecture her about it? What did she think would happen—she'd give away her baby because her loser mom was unhappy about it?

Shouldn't her mother have been excited for an opportunity to show off her new early childhood skills with a new kid in the family?

"Kaelyn, you're a junior in college. You're so close to finishing. Why would you want to have a baby now?"

"Obviously I didn't plan it, but unlike you, I don't regret that the love I feel for Ryan led to a little blessing."

Khrista looked as if Kaelyn had slapped her. What a coincidence, since Kaelyn desperately wanted to do just that.

"I never regretted you, Kaelyn. Your father was—"

"Don't say anything about my father. You ripped me away from him and it's your fault he died."

The scarlet on Khrista's face deepened, and she took a step forward as if she wanted to attack right back.

"You don't know what you're talking about, *baby girl!*" She said the words with menace, her intoxicated eyes narrowing into slits. "You want to know the truth? I tried to protect you from your father and from the truth of how he was. Obviously, I did you a disservice because you weren't able to learn from my mistakes. Your father was all sweetness and affection in the beginning, much like your Ryan is, but like Ryan, he slowly infiltrated all of my relationships. He made it impossible to do anything with anyone but him. And I thought it was *oh so* romantic because we were in love. *Love,*" Khrista spat. "Love is nothing if the man mistreats you. And when he has you turning your back on your friends and your family and stuck at home playing house with the new baby and no support system, let me tell you, darling, that's when the beatings start."

Kaelyn gasped, her famous redheaded temper rising.

"How dare you make up lies about my father to try to get your way? What exactly in my life makes you think I'm going to believe you or that I think for *one second* Ryan could be like that, even if your story was true?"

Her voice grew shrill and her head felt like it was about to pop off in rage.

"And if you think I'm going to believe your lies about my father when I remember so clearly how he cried because you took me away, you're insane. But I think that's the problem. You've been insane all along—it just took me a while to realize it. That's why I'm pulling away, *Khrista*. Not because Ryan is making me. Not because this delusional fantasy of yours is anything close to being real. But because you're nuts. You're insane and *you* are the abuser and *you* are the neglectful one and it's *your* fault I don't have a support system. You took me away from Grandma and Grandpa, you took me away from my dad. And now you think when I'm twenty years old that you still have the power or credibility to take me away from my boyfriend? Correction, my fiancé. Because we're gonna get married and do this the right way. I'll raise this baby with all the love you were incapable of giving me. Since I couldn't learn from you, I learned from my friends and their happy families. Something you know nothing about."

"I know you're trying to hurt me. But you need to listen."

"No, *Khrista*, that's not what this is about. Not everything is about you. I'm trying to have a *life*. A happy life. I'm building a family, and no, I'm not too young. Living with you helped me mature faster than I should have had to. I *know* I'll be a good mother to this baby."

Kaelyn placed her hand over her belly, feeling her child as if it were already in her arms.

A sharp cramp stabbed into her gut, like a period cramp. Fear washed through her, but she was sure it was normal. It had to be normal.

"Kaelyn, please come and sit and talk to me. I didn't tell you about your father because I was trying to protect you. I was trying to give you a happy childhood. Clearly, I failed. And I'm sorry. But you haven't made it easy. When I took you away from your father and we went to stay in a women's shelter, it was because he had beaten me so bad that I almost couldn't see to drive us there. I wasn't afraid for myself. I was afraid he would get angry with you and lose his temper. I couldn't stand the thought of him hurting you."

"That's *bull.*" Kaelyn's screech hurt her own ears, but she couldn't stop herself from screaming louder. "He loved me. He was always nice to me."

"You really think I would've left behind the nice house we had and what I had always perceived to be a good life? For what? Why would I have gone to a battered women's shelter with my little girl if I wasn't desperate? If I had any other safe place to go?"

"I don't know, maybe because you're crazy? You took me away from a loving father and a nice house and moved us from place to place for what seemed like forever. You think I'm too young to remember it, but even high school psychology teaches about trauma responses."

Khrista closed her eyes, and Kaelyn wondered if she had gone too far.

"When he died of an overdose, I wasn't happy about it because I had loved him once, but I was happy that it meant we could settle down in one place and not have to move around so much. He was no longer a threat. Settling into Old Castle was supposed to give you a good life. Stability. I'm sorry if you feel I didn't do enough."

Her mother's voice took on that martyr tone Kaelyn hated so much. Always the victim, and never afraid to use her supposed pain to keep Kaelyn in line.

"Yeah, and it wasn't so bad aside from having you for a mother. But then what did you do? Oh yeah, you moved us to another part of the state. Without even telling me. Without even giving me the opportunity to say goodbye to my friends in person. You know what that does to a teenage girl?"

Khrista stopped responding, hugging herself and emotionally withdrawing like she always did.

"Oh, this is just perfect. Here goes poor little Khrista. Are you gonna hide in your room for three days and pretend you have a migraine? Are you gonna make me fend for myself out here, thinking you're gonna kill yourself? Well, guess what, *Khrista*? Little girl Kaelyn cared about that. Worried about that. Freaking *cried* about that! The adult, the future mother, no longer concerns herself with whatever you decide to do. You have no power over me. And just because you're upset that I don't need you and that you'll be alone, that doesn't give you the right to tell lies about my father and to try to convince me this baby is a mistake."

Kaelyn stormed out of the house, running down the stairs until she could exit the apartment building.

Her mother apparently snapped out of her mental state in time to run after her. As Kaelyn climbed into her vehicle, her mother screamed, making a scene in front of all the other losers in the neighborhood.

"You're being a stupid fool! I was trying to save you from yourself, but go ahead and make your own stupid decisions and see where they lead you!"

Later that night, in Ryan's parent's basement where they had their own little apartment of sorts, Kaelyn woke up to extreme cramping. She cuddled up to her pillow, afraid to move. Afraid of what the crippling pain meant. Afraid if she voiced her concerns, she'd manifest them into reality.

The numbers on her bedside clock hypnotized her. She watched them change, one minute at a time. As if the world would continue moving on, no matter what happened there in her bed. In her body. To her dreams.

At 3:36 a.m., she found the courage to peek beneath the sheet, where she already knew what she'd find.

A bloody puddle between her legs.

She had lost the baby.

Kaelyn didn't wake Ryan up. She hated him for sleeping peacefully through the death of her child. She hated him for not knowing she needed him without her having to call out. She hated him for not holding her tight and kissing away her tears and helping her to clean up the mess.

Ryan had the nerve to seem happy about it when he woke up to find her practically comatose, still lying in the splotches of drying blood.

He said he wasn't really ready, but that he loved her anyway and they would make a good life for themselves. That he would make a good life for her. That they only needed each other. And maybe someday they would have real babies. Babies that wouldn't evacuate from the womb so easily.

She hated the smarmy tone of his voice. The taunting look in his eyes. Had her mother been right about him? Why was she suddenly feeling like everything she had thought she understood about him was wrong? How could he be so insensitive when their baby had just died?

Kaelyn wanted to deliver the news to her mother in person. She wanted her mother to see the agony on Kaelyn's face at the loss of her hopes and dreams.

As expected, Khrista was in bed, the whole dirty apartment reeking of alcohol.

After throwing a few of her things in a bag to take with her, Kaelyn whipped her mother's bedroom door open, screaming inside and startling her mother awake.

"Well, Mother Dearest. Never let it be said that your wishes don't come true. I miscarried last night."

Kaelyn amazed herself with how calm she stayed. How even though a spiky ball formed in her throat and the words were slaughtered as they squeezed past the lump, the words emerged matter-of-factly. No tears flowed. Only anger resided in her heart.

Khrista, wearing only a long T-shirt and her panties, wrestled with the blanket, trying to untangle her legs as she left her bed.

Arms outstretched, she said, "Oh, baby girl. I'm so sorry. I do think it's for the best, but I can't imagine how much it hurts."

Kaelyn took a step back.

"Of course you think it's for the best. The all-knowing mother-of-the-year, who gives such good advice. You think it's for the best. I think it has destroyed me, but since you think it's for the best, it must be okay."

Kaelyn turned away from her mother before she could say another thing. Hurt pummeled through her limbs, weighing her down and making her feel as though she were no longer human. The absence of life inside her went beyond her womb. She was no longer among the living herself.

"Kaelyn, I hurt for you. Let me offer you comfort."

Kaelyn whipped around, one hundred percent certain that fire flew out of her eyes like a laser pointed at her target.

"Comfort me? This is your fault. It's your fault I miscarried."

Khrista winced and looked as if Kaelyn had slammed her in the face with an iron.

She stammered, "Kaelyn, these things happen. A lot of pregnancies don't survive the first few months. I am truly sorry, and I know your hormones are all over the place, making you think and say things you may not otherwise think and say."

"Don't mistake what I'm saying for hormones. I hate you, Khrista. This isn't new. I tried to be a good daughter. I thought if I could just move out when I finished school, then eventually time and distance would make me forget the horror show of my childhood and my experiences with you and maybe we could have some sort of relationship. But you killed my baby. You killed my hopes. You killed my dreams. And I won't stick around so you can kill anything else in my life."

Kaelyn grabbed the bag she had packed before storming in on her mother, prepared to leave for good.

This was it.

"I never, ever, *ever* want to see you again."

Oliver's pleading voice cut through the fog of Kaelyn's memories.

"Kaelyn, love, talk to me. Are you okay?"

Kaelyn pressed her palm into her side, unable to believe she would undergo this experience at her own baby shower, surrounded by her friends. She closed her eyes against the memories. As bad as it had been to miscarry the first time, this would be worse. This baby had a list of potential names carefully cultivated. This baby almost had a nursery. This baby had loving parents and a future.

And it would be all Khrista's fault again. Khrista brought stress anywhere she went, and though Kaelyn thought she had put enough distance between them, she had been wrong.

Kaelyn had known over the years that her younger self had been a little on the cruel side. She never regretted leaving her mother, but she had regretted some of the crueler words she had used. Kaelyn had even, on occasion, reconsidered whether her mother had truly been at fault.

But this proved her theory correct.

This proved her mother was a poison. That no new life could grow around her fetid soil.

It must have looked bad, because Oliver's face registered a level of concern she rarely saw from him.

Tears spilled over her bottom eyelids, and she shook her head. She wasn't okay.

He pulled his phone out and dialed 911. People gathered around her and murmured words of concern, offering advice she couldn't even hear.

*Please, not my baby. Please. Take my life if you must, but please, not my baby.*

By the time the ambulance arrived, the only thing keeping her from full-blown panic was Oliver's calm reminders for her to breathe. He told her everything would be fine, and she believed him. The paramedics asked her questions she couldn't answer, but thankfully Oliver was there to be her voice.

After a whole bunch of testing, and the reassurance of the baby moving inside her, the doctor told her everything looked good and it was more or less likely to be a stress reaction coupled with a slightly low-lying placenta. The baby was fine, Kaelyn was fine, and the only prescription she needed was for some rest and relaxation.

Oliver kissed her soundly and told her he was signing her up for a weekend at the spa.

When she and Oliver were alone in the room and the panic had died down, Kaelyn made a face at his attempts to coax a smile.

"Still think it's a good idea to have my mother involved in my life?"

It was catty and a cheap shot, and she cried a little inside when Oliver winced, but he kissed her belly and she rubbed his head, and they put their disagreement behind them.

She was a grown woman and wouldn't let a miserable childhood destroy her happy adulthood.

## 18

# DAISY

Daisy fought to maintain control over her anxiety. Watching her sweet granddaughter being wheeled out of her party and into an ambulance, knowing full well she was responsible for it, brought a wall of despair tumbling down on Daisy.

What had she done?

Daisy empathized with the pain of losing a baby. She prayed hard Kaelyn wouldn't have to discover this for herself.

Oliver's mother kindly drove Daisy back to her apartment, offering to stay with her.

Daisy declined the offer, needing to be alone and figuring Ruby probably wanted the freedom to check in with her son and daughter-in-law. She was a stable and wanted branch of their family tree. Not the shaky overhanging branch that had been rotting for years and eventually crashed on the neighbor's barbecue buffet. Daisy held that distinction.

Daisy collapsed at the kitchen table, burying her head in her arms and sobbing.

Once she had cleared her tear ducts and regained control of her emotions, she made herself a cup of tea and sat in a chair by a window overlooking the backyard. She watched birds flit about, free from human emotions and worries.

She checked her phone, hoping for an update. Still nothing.

Florence flounced in as Daisy's cup grew cold on the table next to her. Daisy dreaded confessing that she had gone against Florence's advice. She had managed to avoid the topic over the last several weeks.

Florence gushed about something Daisy couldn't register as she set her purse and keys on the table by the door and stopped short at Daisy's lack of reaction. She halted her pacing and stared at Daisy.

"Why the tears, *Mamacita?*"

Daisy couldn't speak. She didn't want to break down again.

"How was the baby shower? Are you feeling overwhelmed by all the cuteness?"

Daisy swallowed the last of her tea, not caring that it had turned cold or that some of the leaves had sunk to the bottom of the mug.

"Not good, huh? Talk to me, Daisy. I'm here for you."

"It was a d-disaster."

"I'm sure it wasn't that bad. Did they not like the cake? I thought that whole fake pregnant belly cake was kind of weird myself, but I figured it must be the thing people are doing these days. Was cutting it open really gross? Please tell me they didn't have strawberry syrup or something equally creepy oozing out of it."

Daisy shook her head, not wanting Florence's opinions.

"Everybody thought the cake was well done and adorable. It's very Pinterest trendy. But we didn't make it to the cake."

"What? A baby shower with no cake? That's half the point."

Tears gathered in Daisy's eyes once again, and a sciatica pain shot through her thigh. It always seemed to do that when something triggered her emotions.

"Something happened, and I'm afraid it was all my f-fault."

"I'm sure it was fine."

Daisy shook her head. "No, I went against my better judgment and your advice. Kaelyn was ta-taken out in an ambulance. Something was wrong with her baby. I think it was the st-stress of seeing her mother show up. That was all my f-fault."

Florence slammed a hand on the kitchen table.

"You invited her mother, didn't you?"

Daisy didn't know what she had expected as a reaction from Florence, but she certainly hadn't anticipated the anger that rolled out in waves. She blinked, taken aback by the ire in Florence's voice and her expression.

"*Daisy*. Have you learned nothing over the years?"

"What do you mean? I made a mistake. I admitted it. It's not like I can take it back, though I would if I could."

"You're always making these kinds of mistakes, Daisy. Don't act innocent. I told you straight out what would happen if you interfered. Now yes, if she loses that baby or suffers any health difficulties because of the stress you brought on her, it will in fact be, at least somewhat, your fault."

Daisy's mouth dropped open, and her insides ached. Her hands shook and her heart thudded. Cold sweat gathered on her lower back.

"I can't believe you would say that to me. I already feel t-terrible."

"But not terrible enough to not make the same mistake again next time. You've learned nothing in over fifty years. I suspect you'll never learn."

Florence stomped off into her room, slamming the door behind her and muttering loudly enough for Daisy to hear her voice but not to make out the words.

The last thing Daisy wanted to do was deal with Florence's baggage, but clearly Florence held something against her, and she wanted answers.

Daisy opened Florence's door without knocking and entered, only to find her friend packing a bag.

"What are you doing?" Daisy didn't like the trembling in her voice.

"I'm leaving. This," she sputtered, waving her hands in the air, "was a mistake. I thought I could get past the hell you put me through fifty years ago, but seeing you as the same old Daisy you were back then has proven me wrong."

"What are you talking about, Florence? I haven't done anything like this before. And don't my motivations count for something? I was trying to repair a rift between my daughter and my granddaughter. Is it so wrong to want to find harmony and to repair a generation of brokenness before I leave this Earth?"

Florence threw her hands up in the air again and exhaled loudly.

"You asked my advice about whether to send that invitation. You asked Kaelyn if she wanted you to. We both were adamant in our response. Yet you did it anyway. Why? Because Daisy does what Daisy wants to do. Daisy doesn't think about other people's feelings or their desires before she takes it upon herself to take what she wants in this world."

Florence flung open another drawer, withdrawing her socks and underwear and tossing them haphazardly into her suitcase.

"You did it because you wanted to look like the hero. You want to say you did something great. Well, guess what, Daisy? Nobody is going to see it that way."

"What is this really about? You keep bringing up fifty years ago." Daisy stuck close to Florence as she turned and marched toward the bed. "I know it upset you when Harold chose me, but I didn't know your feelings were that strong for him. I thought it was the same crush we all had on him when he started showing up."

"Ha!"

"And besides, it's not as though I ended up with a happily-ever-after. You've had a much better life than I did. You had freedom, you've traveled, you have a whimsicalness to you I can only dream of. If you had ended up with Harold, believe me, you wouldn't have any of that."

"You don't know what happened to me after you left. Yes, I learned to accept my life the way it is, but it was a long, painful process."

Daisy covered her ears and strode out of the room, wishing she hadn't followed Florence in the first place. She couldn't take hearing anymore. The breakdown of their friendship had happened a long time ago, and Daisy had naïvely believed fifty-three years would separate them from that.

"Oh go ahead, Daisy. Just walk away. Pretend you don't hear what I'm telling you, just like you pretended you didn't hear years ago."

Daisy retreated into the kitchen, wishing their apartment was bigger and she could put more distance between them.

Florence followed her. "Remember when I told you I had a thing for Harold? Yeah, if you remember correctly, it was before you and he became involved. And you know what? The day you left is also the day I told him I was pregnant. Yeah, wipe that shocked look off your face. You know what it was like to be seventeen and pregnant by a man who was leaving with another woman? In my family, there was no greater sin. You want to know what happened to me? Take your hands away from your ears and look at me."

Daisy's knees threatened to give out on her. She didn't want to do this.

Why couldn't she just live the rest of her life not hearing it spelled out this way?

"Yes, you left. You married Harold. You had what you say was a horrible life. Well, guess what I was doing while you were there? While you had a husband who bought you a home and put food on your table. Know what I was doing? I was disowned by my family. I didn't get to finish school. I had to seek an illegal abortion that almost killed me. It rendered me infertile, so I was no good to *anybody* anymore. You know why I became a traveler and a free spirit? Because that was the only option for a woman like me. I lived a nomadic life because I had *no choice*. And those early days were *hard*. It wasn't as fanciful and free as you like to imagine. I was abused on the streets. I was mistreated. I got myself into dangerous situations because I had no other options."

Florence's body shook with her anger. She balled her hands into fists, looking for all the world like she wanted to pummel Daisy.

Daisy couldn't blame her. How could one event have triggered such an avalanche of catastrophe?

"But over time, I learned to see myself beyond shame. I wasn't the person my family had condemned me to be. I wasn't the person who had done the wrong. And after fifty-three years, when you came back and seemed so contrite, I actually convinced myself you had been a victim and you hadn't done anything wrong, either. But, once again, I was mistaken."

Florence shrugged. Her tone took on a singsong quality that made Daisy want to stuff rocks in her ears. Anything to drown the sound.

"Daisy never does anything wrong, does she? She is the victim in every way."

"You don't understand!" Daisy lashed out right back, shocked at the ferocity of her anger as it grew inside her. "Yes, I took Harold up on his offer to rescue me and to whisk me away. But if you think I didn't suffer as a result of my decision, you are *wrong*. However bad your life may have been, I can guarantee mine was worse."

"Of course you can, dearest Daisy. Because you're the only one who has ever suffered. What kind of mother were you? Did you make sure your daughter was fed and clothed nicely? Did you make sure she was educated and nurtured? Did you protect her from the brutality of your husband? Oh, wait a second. She cut you out of her life. Why is that, Daisy? It had to have been something your young daughter did and not something you did, right? You know, because you're the victim and all."

"Just leave. I don't need you here. You invited yourself anyway."

"You're right, I did. I thought we could put the past behind us and move forward, knowing we were both hurt by a world that not only pits women against each other but also sacrifices us for the good of a bad man. But that's not what happened here. Instead, I got a glimpse into the selfish life of a selfish woman who is trying to claim that her selfish decisions are an effort to make someone else's life better when in reality it's just to try to make herself look and feel better."

Daisy watched as Florence stormed out of the house, hurt through to her bones over what had transpired. She had thought she would get support from her old friend. That even if Florence didn't agree with her method, she would understand she was hurting, see the motivating factors, and offer her the consolation a friend should offer.

Daisy sat huddled at her kitchen table for a long, long time, hands folded. Wondering if prayer could bring her salvation. Wondering if she deserved another chance.

By the time she received a text from Oliver letting her know Kaelyn was okay but would be kept in the hospital for observation, Daisy felt a tightness in her chest and nausea that wouldn't subside.

Her hands wouldn't stop shaking as she dressed for bed and climbed between her cold sheets. She woke up in the middle of the night bathed in sweat, her heart hammering and sending a piercing sensation through her sternum and up her spine, between her shoulder blades. An ominous feeling rippled through her. She could smell the bleach on the sheets and the distant scent of someone's cigarette smoke. She squinted to see in the dark, terrified of what was happening in her body. She had the presence of mind to call 911. Would this be how she went out?

Alone and remorseful, with no one left to apologize to.

# 19

## KHRISTA

The flight back to Boston was a blur. Khrista had become so inebriated before getting on the plane that airport security nearly kept her grounded. Luckily, after sharing her sob story with a sympathetic young man standing in the boarding line, he helped cover for her as she stumbled and gave her a handful of Altoids to shield the stench of the alcohol while she boarded the plane.

She slept most of the flight, but when she awoke upon landing, her skin tightened and a sour taste rose in her throat as the realization that the entire day hadn't been a drunken nightmare hit.

Khrista slouched in a hard plastic seat in the passenger pickup area, hugging her purse to her chest and doing her best to look like a functioning human.

When she turned her phone on, there were a million texts from Matt. Her eyes welled when she tried reading them, so she skipped ahead to the last one, where he gave her his expected arrival time.

Khrista had sobered up enough to remember she had driven herself to the airport and parked her car. That was probably one of his many questions. She didn't want to think about what assumptions he made about her request for him to drive all the way to Boston to retrieve her when he knew she had taken her car.

She watched happy families reunite with hugs and greetings. Those scenes would never play out for her.

Yes, Matt would be happy to see her. That is, if she sobered up enough before he got there. He had dismissed her drunkenness before. This was different.

Why had she contacted him?

Struggling to type on the tiny screen, she sent off a text telling him he didn't have to pick her up after all, but he said he was only half an hour away and to sit tight.

A woman around her age wheeled a suitcase behind her and carried a drink tray with two hot cups nestled in the holder. She sat beside Khrista and wiggled one cup out of the cardboard carrier.

"Here you go." The woman handed the cup to Khrista. "You look like you could use one of these."

"Are you serious? That's so kind of you. Thank you." Khrista accepted the cup with two grateful hands, pleasantly surprised that her words didn't slur. "You are absolutely right. I could use some caffeine."

The woman passed her a bag that held packets of sugar and cream. Khrista mixed some into her coffee and sipped it gratefully.

"I'm Anna. You look like you have a story you want to tell a stranger."

"Khrista. And I appreciate your kindness, but trust me when I tell you, you do *not* want to hear my story. *I* don't even want to hear my story."

"Okay, let's play a guessing game. I say, you sold everything and moved across the country to meet a guy you met online and he turned out to be a scam artist so now you escaped back here with nothing but your purse and a teensy bit of pride to show for your adventures?"

Khrista burst into laughter and shook her head.

"Oh." Anna raised her slim eyebrows. "I guess that was just me."

Khrista whipped her head around to face the well-dressed Anna.

"Really? Oh, please do tell me the story. It would make me feel so much better about my experience of trying to reunite with an estranged daughter who is now pregnant and had a baby shower and who didn't want to invite me but my estranged mother, who I haven't seen for twenty years did invite me, and I showed up to a great big disaster and fled back here maxing out my credit cards and leaving my luggage behind because I am an *actual* disaster and can't make a good choice to save my life."

Anna fanned herself. "Whoa, girl. I knew my senses were correct when I saw you had a story to tell."

"I'm so sorry. I got drunk before the flight and my inhibitions are still non-existent. Remember when we were in our twenties and we'd make best friends with the girl in the bathroom when we were all drunk? Apparently, I haven't grown out of that stage of life. Almost none of my friends know this stuff, but now you, dear Anna, stranger at the airport, are privy to my deepest, darkest thoughts."

In a fake southern accent, Anna replied, "Oh gosh, darlin', I'm beyond honored."

Together, they sipped their coffees and watched the people rush by.

Anna placed her coffee cup on the seat beside her and turned her body to face Khrista the best she could, keeping her oversized purse on the floor between her feet.

"This is crazy, and you definitely don't have to listen to me. But since I've spent thousands of dollars on therapy to deal with these issues, I sort of want to share what I've learned."

Khrista laughed again, not feeling any joy, but marveling at the irony of this life she lived.

Anna pressed on. "I was estranged from my mother for many years. We had a big falling out when I got a divorce and my kids were teenagers and, well, it was a mess. We never spoke again, and just a few months ago, I discovered she had died. No one even told me. I didn't know she was sick. I don't know if that would have changed anything because I was *really* mad at her. But losing your mother before you make amends does a number on you. I won't say anymore, but I wanted you to know that. From someone who understands what you're going through, and can give you a wee bit of insight into what you may go through in the future."

Khrista didn't respond. She couldn't imagine any greater agony than what she felt now. Making up with her mother wasn't at the top of her to-do list. Not when she had her own daughter's estrangement to worry about.

"Oh, there's my ride. How humiliating to be fifty-four years old and have to call your little brother to pick you up after you swore you were starting a new life somewhere else. I swear, if he lectures me the whole way home, you might end up seeing my face on the evening news."

Anna gathered her things and told Khrista it was nice chatting with her. She wished her well and went on her way.

Khrista stewed in the memory of that odd experience with Anna. Why did everybody always think it was so important to make amends? Why did everybody think trying to heal a toxic family was so important? Wasn't it better to close the book on people who couldn't treat you well?

She dozed in her seat until she was startled awake by the deep tone of Matt calling her name.

She sat up and wiped around her mouth, trying to smile.

"I've been worried sick about you." He held his arms out to her, and she allowed him to give her the comfort she desperately needed but didn't know how to ask for.

"Khrista, you've been drinking?"

As if it was actually a surprise.

"Gosh, the smell is strong." He closed his eyes as if resetting the mood. "Whatever happened, I'm sure this will all make sense once you tell me the story. It's just a little awkward because my daughter came along for the ride and this is how she's going to meet you."

He shrugged. "It's okay though. Maybe she won't notice."

His daughter? His daughter came with him for the ride?

She had dodged his requests to meet his children for three full years. And now he sprung this on her with no warning? No consent?

How could he do this to her?

"Actually, Matt, I'm sorry I messaged you. I was a little buzzed after the shower, you know how those things are, and I ran into an old family friend at the airport and we shared a few drinks." She laughed like a proper ditz, shocked at how easily the lies continued to roll off her tongue. "I forgot I actually have my car here, and I had planned on spending a few days in Boston since I'm here, anyway. So you just go ahead home. I'm sorry I wasted your time. I'll give you gas money. Promise."

"I'm not leaving you here. Something is obviously wrong, and what kind of dirt bag do you think I am that I'd leave you, vulnerable, in the city?"

"Believe it or not, Matt, I'm capable of taking care of myself."

He studied her for a heartbeat too long. Her skin itched and pulled, and she wished she could peel it off and slither away.

Matt cleared his throat. "Is this because my daughter came along? I know you've been weird about meeting my girls, but I didn't think it would be such a big deal. She was worried because I had to leave before sunrise to get here on time and she knows I've been having a hard time driving at night. I wasn't trying to make you angry."

She didn't have a way to answer that question. Fuming that he put her in this uncomfortable position, Khrista left her coffee on the little table beside her seat and walked away. But mostly, she fumed at herself for being so selfish, so self-indulgent. So scared.

That's where she was in her life. Walking away from anything good, anything bad, and anything that could possibly be good in the future.

"Khrista!" Matt reached for her arm, and Khrista jerked away.

Matt put his arms up in the air when a security guard took interest in their interaction. Khrista felt terrible for putting Matt in that position. A large black man reaching out for a small white woman who was trying to escape was terrible optics and could endanger him. She didn't want anything more to happen to him than what she had already put him through, so Khrista froze in her tracks, looked him deep in the eyes, and begged him to please go, lowering her voice so as not to raise alarm.

He shoved his hands in his pockets. She hated how his shoulders slumped. She had done that to him. She caused this kind, vibrant, confident man to doubt himself. To doubt her.

"I can physically feel your pain right now, Khrista. I won't leave you."

"It's for the best. This was going to end eventually, anyway. Now is as good a time as any. I'm damaged goods, Matt. You're far too good for me. Too kind for me." Why did her voice have to sound so darned strangled? Why did her throat close around the words? "Please go. I can't handle this anymore."

Leaving him in shock, she darted away, dodging a group of passengers who trudged through the terminal, heading toward the exit. She ducked into a ladies' room, knowing he couldn't follow her in there.

She locked herself in the stall, and for the first time in longer than she wanted to think about, she cried.

Khrista sobbed so hard she vomited. Her head throbbed, her joints burned, and the "good" parts of her she had worked so hard to build over the years screamed in agony as she killed off every fake piece of positivity.

When she thought enough time had passed that it would be safe to emerge, Khrista washed her hands and face, rinsed out her mouth, applied some lip gloss, and left the bathroom.

Matt waited outside the door. Waiting patiently, his beautiful, soulful eyes filled with sadness.

Sadness she had put there.

Even through the haze of her developing hangover, her aching heart, and her feelings of unworthiness, the truth blasted itself as blatantly as a neon sign lighting up Times Square. She had been unfair to Matt.

Matt who had never uttered a word of anger anywhere near her.

Matt who had always been willing to welcome her into his heart and his home and his family, even when she had been at her lowest points.

Matt, whose warm eyes beseeched her to open up to him, whose gentle kindness promised he would protect her and keep her safe—warts and wounds and worries and all.

She had been unfair. She knew it.

Khrista walked sheepishly toward him, ashamed of what she had done and who she had become. Who she always had been, she supposed, but who she had just now allowed him to see.

In reality, he had fallen in love with the bubbly preschool teacher who parents adored and requested as their children's teacher.

He hadn't signed up for *this*.

But he had stuck around through it all.

And he was still there.

"Matt…"

What could she say?

Khrista reached up to wrap her arms around his neck. He stopped her, grabbing her hands and holding them down between them.

His eyes grew wet.

She honed in on his quivering chin. At the way he struggled to tame his breathing. The way he avoided making eye contact with her even as she desperately sought the connection they had always had.

She had hurt him. Irreversibly. She sensed finality. Knew the acrid scent of it.

Yet another casualty of her dysfunction.

"I'm tired of being pushed away, Khrista."

His deep voice squeaked and his emotion killed her a little bit more inside.

"I love you. I've loved you since that very first day you asked all those brilliant questions at the diversity training. I could see beyond just your physical beauty and into the beauty of your heart. The way you nurture children and worry about people who don't have the privileges you have. The way you have always made me feel, day in and day out, whether we were together or apart."

He choked on his words again.

"Matt…"

What was there to say?

He didn't let her speak. He shook his head gently, reverently, the authority figure in this scene.

"I'm going to give you what you want. What I sense you have wanted for a while now. You've been pulling away for a long time, maybe even our whole relationship. I didn't want to believe it, but I see it clearly now. I can't keep waiting for you to self-destruct. I can't keep waiting for you to be lost to me for good. I can't tell you how desperately I've wanted to protect you from yourself, but I'm only a man, Khrista. I thought I was strong enough to see you through all of your low points and to help you feel comfortable enough to join me in this relationship. I'm not."

"You are, Matt. You are *everything*. I've never deserved you, but I haven't wanted to lose you. I *don't* want to lose you."

He raised the hands he held so tightly to his mouth, holding her knuckles to his lips and letting his tears fall onto her skin.

"Goodbye, Khrista. I wish you well and I will always hope for good things for you."

His lips, his soft, loving, kind lips, planted themselves on her forehead, searing her. Burning her. Destroying the last remnant of hope inside her.

She wanted to beg him to stay. To throw herself on the ground and clutch his ankles and not let him walk away from her.

For the first time in her life, a man was walking away when she so desperately wanted him to stay.

For the first time, a man had seen something in her she could have never seen for herself.

And she ruined it all.

Khrista took his love greedily, never gave enough in return, and broke his heart in the process of breaking her own.

She watched him leave, hoping he would turn around and witness the tears streaming down her face. Hoping he would reconsider; that he would realize she didn't want to self-destruct.

And she certainly didn't want to bring him down with her.

Khrista didn't know how to be better. To do better. She only knew how to fake her way through a world that constantly threw sticks and stones her way. Bricks she once thought she could use to build walls around herself only weighed her down. If she tumbled into the Charles River, they'd carry her to the bottom where she'd finish the drowning process she had started on dry land.

But even now, as she felt more alone than Khrista had in her entire miserable life, she knew she had stacked and secured the bricks herself. She had brought on so much of her own misery and pain.

And now it was too late to do better.

Too exhausted and probably still too inebriated to leave the airport on her own, Khrista found a corner seat where she could shrink into herself and mourn the loss of any semblance of stability she had known.

# 20

## KAELYN

Waiting for discharge from the hospital took forever.

Kaelyn sat on the edge of the hospital bed, needing to escape the sterile environment and get back into the sunshine. She couldn't wait to reconnect with the beach, absorb the healing properties of the salt air, and soak her feet in the water.

This place she had settled in was so similar to Old Castle, the home of her heart. But without all the haunting memories.

Well, until recently.

Kaelyn sent a text to her grandmother, compelled to reach out to see why she hadn't texted or called. She sensed her grandmother blamed herself for what happened at the shower, and rightfully so. But Kaelyn couldn't stay angry with her.

Mostly, she was angry with herself. She was angry with the entire stupid situation, but right now the one suffering was her baby. How was it possible for her to already start failing at this parenting thing? She had been so determined to do everything right and never risk the health of her baby.

She closed her eyes and took a deep breath.

Didn't work. Still angry.

Oliver, usually her peace of mind and her conscience, had become the greatest source of annoyance.

He rested a warm hand on her bouncing leg, applying pressure that fueled her irritation. "Love, you need to quit fidgeting. I can tell you're thinking about things you shouldn't be worrying about right now. You have no control over anything outside of this room right now, so please stop stressing. Remember what the doctor said. Happy thoughts, cheerful movies, and smiling at your husband."

"He most certainly didn't say that last part."

"True, true. But I like that addendum. And as much as I love your face, it's looking quite grumpy."

Why was she feeling like a petulant child? The rage building and swirling inside her was so foreign to the adult she had become. The last thing she wanted to do was unearth her damage and allow it to prey on Oliver, and yet no amount of internal self-talk could stop the landslide from crushing him.

"Get out." She pointed to the door, heat infusing her cheeks. She was certain she would find hives rising on her chest if she checked.

He laughed in response.

"I mean it, Oliver. You're making me so mad and I'm trying to settle my thoughts. I want you to leave."

He still thought she was joking. Oliver quirked half a smile and muttered something about hormones and then tried to wrap his arms around her shoulders while she sat upright in the stupid bed waiting for the stupid nurse to bring the stupid discharge papers.

Kaelyn didn't know where it came from, but fury like she hadn't known in years washed through her and tore out of her mouth before she had a second to think about it.

"Get. Out. *Now!*"

Mortification colored his face as Oliver finally took her seriously. He looked around to see if anyone else had heard, and judging by the expression of the nurse at the nurse's station across the corridor from her room, they had.

What did Kaelyn care, anyway? Let them think she was the worst person in the world. Maybe she was. But right now she wanted solitude so she could calm down and figure out a way to get her body to cooperate with keeping the baby safe. She needed room to breathe.

Oliver stepped closer to the bed, lowering his voice so the conversation stayed between the two of them.

"I've never done anything but love and support you, even when you're moody. I'm trying to be bloody patient because I know you're going through a lot, but you're not playing fair keeping things from me." He ran a hand through his hair and his jaw hardened. "You're not the only one who needs space. I'm out."

Oliver ducked out of the room, grabbing his keys off the rolling tray on the way out.

As soon as he was out the door, she broke down in tears.

Why was she pushing him away? He hadn't even done anything. If she was honest, all the stress had more to do with secrets she kept and lies she told by virtue of withholding information. If Kaelyn had confided about her previous miscarriage, he would have given her the comfort no one else had. He would bend over backwards to reassure her that things would be different this time. And he would move mountains to be sure she didn't suffer in any way whatsoever.

And she had kicked him out of her room.

She had no right to do so. This baby was his.

*She* was his. And he was hers. And of all the things she could mess up in her life, she never wanted it to be their relationship.

It wasn't like him to actually leave her. Yet Oliver hadn't hesitated when he grabbed his keys, and she had heard his footsteps pounding down the hallway. The resounding echo planted firmly in her heart, breaking it.

But it wasn't him who had done the breaking.

She waited ten minutes for him to come back.

He didn't.

She waited another five minutes.

He didn't.

Kaelyn picked up her phone and typed out a text.

"I'm sorry. I'm the worst. You're the best. Please come back."

He was back in less than two minutes.

His bashful smile repaired her heart as quickly as it had broken. He helped her lean back in the bed and pulled her feet into his hands, massaging every toe, every inch of her tired feet, and up into the sore muscles of her swollen ankles and calves.

He was literally a saint on earth, and though Kaelyn tried to be good, seeing her mother had brought out the worst. All the work she had done over the years to make herself a better person had eroded in a flash.

She hated that. She would do better.

Oliver didn't question her about her sour mood, for which she was grateful. She didn't want to brush it under the rug, but she didn't know how to explain either.

Neither of them mentioned his angry response. Though it was uncharacteristic, it wasn't undeserved.

The nurse came in moments later with discharge papers, acting cold toward Kaelyn. She didn't blame her. She had been a shrew.

As they left the hospital, Kaelyn poked Oliver in the side.

"That nurse who discharged me was definitely team Oliver."

He chuckled and put his arm around her, and then planted a kiss on the top of her head.

"Can't say I blame her. I don't know who that crabby patient was in that room, but even though she was kind of mean, she was rather hot."

Kaelyn tickled his ribs and they walked step by step, their hearts beating together in this one love they had created.

Halfway home, he drove the car into the lot of a roadside ice cream stand by a small beach tourists rarely knew about. This ice cream shop had the best banana caramel fudge ice cream she had ever tasted, and she salivated as soon as he pulled into a parking spot.

"I had a feeling you might be okay with a minor detour on the way home."

She sighed and closed her eyes; her smile cutting into the sides of her face.

"You are a god among men."

They carried their ice cream back to the car so they could sit in the air conditioning. The heat had been making her cranky, and every crevice of her expanding body was sweaty and uncomfortable.

"You know, Kaelyn. At the risk of your wrath, I have a challenge for you. Don't hurt me, but I wanted to hear a wee bit about your childhood. Don't panic, I don't want to talk about anything that will upset you. I want to hear a few good things about your mother."

"That will be a quick conversation." She pretended to think. "Oh, here's one. Nothing. Done."

Kaelyn took a large bite of her ice cream, wiping her lips with a napkin as she allowed her tastebuds to differentiate between the individual flavors.

"Everyone has something good. Certainly, you have good memories."

Kaelyn shook her head. "Nothing I want to think about. I don't know what your angle is here, but can we please not do this?"

"I'm on your side, Kaelyn. But your mother raised you to become my favorite person in the world, not even just on this continent, but on all the continents. You can't convince me she's all bad."

She sat in silence, hoping he'd drop the subject.

He didn't.

"Come on," he urged. "Tell me one thing."

"Okay, and then can we drop this?"

"Absolutely. Just tell me one good thing about your mother. It can be a personality trait, it can be a memory. Go."

Kaelyn made him wait in silence as she licked the edges of her ice cream where it started melting over the sides of the cone.

"Okay, fine. But only 'cause I love you and was awful to you earlier and owe you now."

She breathed deeply, allowing her mind to drift to a different time in life. A time she typically kept locked away.

"In the early days of living in Old Castle—I was probably about six years old—she used to take me out by the beach, a particular beach that was very dark. It was on the opposite side of the island from where most people lived. She would lay this blue and white checkered blanket out on the sand, and we would lie on our backs and watch the stars. We would make up stories about the stars and their families and their relationships. The stories could get quite imaginative. I thought that was pretty cool, and as I grew up and made some friends, I found out not everyone did this with their moms. So that was one of the few things that made me feel special as a kid."

Sharp tears gathered behind her eyelids, and a sharp pain stabbed her in the chest. She hated thinking of the happy memories she had with her mother. She had walked away for good reason, and it did no good to think back on good times. Releasing the memories caused too much pain. Much better to focus on the bad. She could protect herself that way.

But Oliver wanted her to share memories, and now that the door was open, she couldn't stop herself from walking through.

"That's a nice memory," he agreed.

"We used to make these little jars, well, we didn't make the jars, but we decorated them. Whenever a condiment or sauce jar emptied in the summertime, we'd clean it out and decoupage things on the outside. They had to be semi-transparent though, like tissue paper or other light-weight materials, because the goal was to catch fireflies and be able to watch them in the jar. I was convinced they were fairies, and my mother did nothing to dissuade me of that notion. We didn't catch many, but on occasion, I would catch a dragonfly or ladybug and let it live in the jar for a few minutes before setting it free. I guess the one good thing about my mother was she taught me about respecting all living creatures."

Oliver nodded. "That is an important thing. Definitely one of the many things I adore about you."

He reached over and bopped her nose with his index finger. Kaelyn rubbed her nose with her wrist and made a face at him, then bit into her ice cream cone.

"Don't start romanticizing my childhood, though. My mother also thought there was nothing wrong with me having chips and cookies for dinner. I'm not talking about one time being all cool like, 'hey we're having an Upside Down day and having ice cream for dinner.'

I'm talking, like, she'd just have these snack foods available and then withdraw to her room and not make dinner. Or when I would ask her what we were having, she'd say, 'Oh, you can have those cinnamon rolls or whatever. You're a smart girl. Figure something out.' Wouldn't exactly call that top-notch parenting."

"Maybe she thought she was creating fun memories for you."

Kaelyn glared at him and then rolled her eyes before looking out the car window and focusing on the waves lapping the shore.

"No, she'd withdraw into her own world and couldn't be bothered to do something as annoying as taking care of her young child. Eventually, I developed so many stomach problems and I noticed when I ate at my friend's house and they had actual proper meals, my stomach felt a lot better. So I started learning to cook a little bit at a time, but when you're twelve and your mother doesn't do the grocery shopping regularly or correctly, it's a challenge. Sometimes she'd bring home food from Raf's restaurant, but she didn't like people to think she couldn't provide for herself."

Oliver reached over and placed his hand over hers on her thigh.

"I think it's hard when we're young to understand our parents are human, too."

"Yeah, but you can be human and still make a good decision every once in a while."

"No parent is perfect."

"Yours is."

He laughed at that. "You keep saying that. And I love my mum dearly. But I promise you she is far from perfect, though she likes to pretend she has always been the way she is now. Which is still not perfect, by the way."

She smiled at him, grateful he was trying to make her feel better —even though she didn't believe him.

"Give me one bad thing your mother ever did. And it can't be something stupid."

"Oh, where to begin? We had some rocky times when I was a teenager."

"I'm pretty sure all mothers and their children have some rocky times as teenagers."

Oliver nodded. "That's true. And I want you to remember you said that."

He smiled.

"Okay, one time I wouldn't put the trash in the bin exactly when she wanted me to because I was playing video games with my mates and we hadn't quite reached a pausing point. I said I would do it in a little while, and I admit I was not polite in the way I said it. Mum came in, grabbed the controller from my hands, and threw it across the room, then grabbed me by the hair and dragged me up out of my seat. She screamed at me in front of my friends, which was the worst part, and kicked me out of the house. She'll tell you a different version of the story, but I ended up staying at a friend's house for three days before both of us were willing to talk it out. Not exactly the image you have of her now, is it?"

Kaelyn gaped at him. Was he teasing? "I can't believe that. I mean, I believe you, but it's so hard to imagine your mom being like that. She's such a... perfect mom."

"Yes, she is. But that doesn't mean we didn't do things to get on each other's nerves and to hurt each other. Sometimes relationships go through tough times, and the only way to heal them is to acknowledge that our versions may not be the same version the other person sees."

Kaelyn took the last bite of her cone and savored it, trying to block out the message he was sending her. She turned toward the window, desperate to quell her rising irritation.

He didn't understand.

"You don't know everything about my relationship with my mother."

"Then tell me. I can only know what you tell me."

She fought the urge to yell, to scream, to cry. She fought the urge to throw away all the good things in her life. She fought the urge to run away, to take her baby away into another dimension where fairies *did* exist and people didn't question things she didn't want them to question.

Kaelyn knew keeping her secret was stupid and wrong, but she couldn't tell him.

She couldn't express what had created the huge void that he didn't even suspect existed.

She couldn't bring herself to talk about the baby who never was.

Especially because if she spoke the truth, all her feelings would rush out.

And the guilt of feeling grateful this baby she carried would be her first would crush her if ever spoken aloud.

# 21

# DAISY

A panic attack.

Daisy had heard of such things, of course, but she never imagined one could make her feel as if she were dying.

When the paramedics let themselves into her apartment after her call, they found her collapsed on the floor. Her heart was pounding, she was sweating all over, and her mind wouldn't stop spinning with all of her wrongs circling round and round in her head like a too-fast merry-go-round going rogue.

One of the paramedics, a young, friendly man, checked her out thoroughly. He reassured her that one of his most frequent calls to respond to included panic attacks—that people experiencing them for the first time often mistook them for heart attacks. He asked her about her day and if there had been any stressors. She nodded, not wanting to go into detail, but suddenly unable to hold it in any longer. The poor boy sat and listened attentively as she recounted all the happenings of the day.

His radio buzzed with another call, so he told her he regretted not being able to stay and listen longer, but recommended she seek therapy.

So that's why as soon as the morning light lit up her apartment, she showered, made tea and an English muffin, and set off to the bookstore to buy some of those self-help books they talked about on her daytime talk shows.

It couldn't be too late for her to be a better person. Daisy hadn't thought she was *terrible*, but given the reactions of people around her recently, she may have been wrong.

When she arrived at her destination, shelves and shelves and shelves of books proclaiming they would help the reader turn their life around taunted Daisy. How could she choose one when she didn't know what was actually wrong with her?

She could ask one of the booksellers, but stopped short. Wasn't it enough she had unloaded everything onto one poor unsuspecting fool? Daisy had been lucky the paramedic had given her his ear for so long while his partner paced in the kitchen. She couldn't expect the same of a bookseller, especially with the store being so busy.

Her heart started racing again, just as it had done the night before when she thought she had been dying. Daisy did as the paramedic suggested and told herself everything was okay. She did her best to breathe, worrying about making a fool of herself in the middle of the bookstore.

Just as she could see properly again, and the sweating abated, her phone chimed to notify her of an incoming text.

"Hey Grandma, wanted to let you know I'm out of the hospital. Doctor said it was really nothing, and I just need to think happy thoughts. I know you probably think I'm mad at you, but I'm not. I love you. Stop by later if you'd like. Oliver and I are spending the day on the couch, eating ice cream and chips and watching sappy movies. Doctor's orders, so Oliver isn't allowed to tell me no. xoxo"

Daisy smiled, looking like a goof in the self-help section of the bookstore, but not caring. She admired the relationship her granddaughter had built with Oliver.

If only all men could be so fearless in their functionality.

Daisy's thoughts drifted back to her own marriage, then went deeper into areas she rarely liked to explore.

Her motherhood.

In the early days, things had been good. As Khrista got older, Daisy spent a great deal of time trying to keep her young daughter from annoying her father so Daisy wouldn't have to suffer the consequences. Of course, Daisy worried about him lashing out at Khrista as well, but she hadn't believed he would actually do it.

Until he did.

Once he realized he could have power over both of them, the mistreatment escalated. Daisy grew more frightened of him and Khrista outright defied him, challenging him to hurt her.

He was never one to back down from that sort of challenge.

At first, Daisy intervened as a mother should. She'd get in between them and catch the whipping of the belt on her own arm. But that was never enough for Harold. Her interference in his discipline enraged him. He would lash out in front of Khrista, then take Daisy privately into their room to make sure she'd never want to interfere in his parenting again.

It had been so common for her to have bruised ribs, thighs, and even black eyes that when one faded, she knew it wouldn't be long before another took its place.

Some part of her had experienced the strangeness of finding artistic merit in the layout and coloring of her bruising. Maybe other women saw the damaged areas of their abused skin in the same light, but she doubted it.

Not that she'd ever had anyone to ask.

Not that she would have asked if she could.

As Khrista approached eight years old, she had already become rebellious and stubborn and didn't seem to care that her actions caused beatings for both of them.

It was around that time when Daisy started feeling less sorry for Khrista and more sorry for herself. Daisy had done her best to keep her head low, to keep Harold's beer cold, and to keep him well fed to stay on his good side.

But Khrista...*Khrista.* She couldn't keep her head down if her life depended on it. She knew how to get under Harold's skin like it was an Olympic sport. She knew how to agitate him seconds after walking through the door. Sure, she may have been a young girl, but she had the mind and the spirit of a much older child. She taunted him until he would drag his drunken behind off his chair to chase her down. Khrista would maintain eye contact while he meted out his punishments.

Daisy couldn't remember when Khrista stopped crying at the beatings. At some point, she started laughing just to get a bigger rise out of her father.

Oh, how that enraged Harold. He'd hit Khrista until his arm grew sore.

Daisy tried to go the protective route. But then it struck her that she had probably been too soft on her daughter. She had enabled Khrista to grow into this beast of a child who didn't know her place and didn't know how to not bring pain upon herself and her mother.

One day, when Khrista was a young teenager, Harold beat Khrista so badly she couldn't get out of bed for days. He had gone too far, and Daisy had to find the nerve to tell him.

She was a mother, after all, and even if she didn't particularly like her child with her raging temper that matched her father's and her inability to use the common sense the Lord had given her, she was still Daisy's only child. And if this kept escalating, Harold would kill her.

The conversation with Harold hadn't gone well. He gave Daisy a beating nearly to the same level as the one he had given Khrista.

And then he killed their cat.

Daisy spent that night in bed, unable to make him the dinner he wanted because every part of her hurt. He came in to teach her a lesson about being lazy, but took pity on her battered body that she couldn't lift off the bed.

That was the first time, and the last, he had ever taken pity on her.

But he still hadn't said he was sorry.

Khrista recovered quicker than Daisy, as young people do, and before Daisy could even walk without hobbling again, her daughter was poking the bear.

While Daisy had spent all those hours in bed willing herself to get up so Harold wouldn't get infuriated again, she made a plan to get away. To take Khrista somewhere, anywhere, where they would be safe.

She was willing to risk her life to save her daughter.

And yet her daughter was out there making him angry again.

At that moment, Daisy realized she hated her daughter.

Hated. Her.

If she hadn't been born, Daisy's body wouldn't have changed. She wouldn't have been forced into menopause at only twenty-one years old. She would've been able to have other children and they may have made Harold happy. Maybe one of their children would have loved her, too.

If Khrista didn't have her wild attitude and her stubborn, fierce ways, she wouldn't get beaten so much and Daisy could have lived a mild life tiptoeing around the cruelty of a man she was bound to until death did them part.

Harold would kill Daisy. He would try to kill Khrista. She knew this in her bones. In every nerve ending. Every hair follicle. With every breath.

But Khrista by then was a young teenager. She could run away from Harold, who was drunk half the time, and worn out from work the other half. She could evade his evil grip.

Daisy had to sleep beside the man every night, always on guard for when he would decide she had done something poorly or tried to intentionally, according to him, offend him.

After another sleepless night, Daisy knew what she had to do.

The next day, when Daisy was able to lift a small bag, she made her getaway.

She had nowhere to go, no ability to drive herself, and no one to take her in.

As she struggled to walk down the rural road they lived on, a man in a pickup truck took pity on her and offered her a ride. He was gentlemanly and kind, and that frightened Daisy more than anything. If a cruel man could hurt her in the way Harold had, what would this man who pretended to be kind do?

But she had no choice. She needed to get somewhere far away. Harold would come home for lunch like he did every day, expecting to see her there. When he found her gone, he would drive his truck all around looking for her. And then there would be hell to pay.

She asked the man to drop her off in any town he passed through, as long as it was a good ways out of the town she left behind. They drove for an hour in companionable silence. The man sang along to country music on his radio. He had a nice voice. A little off-key, but he didn't seem to notice, and she didn't mind a bit. The minor flaw was sort of endearing.

"You sure you're okay out 'ere?"

Daisy nodded, feigning confidence. She had two hundred dollars squirreled away, unbeknownst to Harold. It wouldn't be enough, but she hoped she'd be able to find a job as a domestic worker in someone's home. She had cleaning and cooking skills, could do laundry, and could maybe even take care of a child or two.

Her heart ached at the thought of the child she had left behind.

But Khrista was no longer a child. If she was old enough to trigger her father every single day, she could be old enough to fend for herself.

Daisy tried her hardest to make a new life away from home, but eventually, she acknowledged she couldn't be on her own. No one would hire her, especially when she approached them in dirty clothes and with bruises all over her face and not a reference to speak of.

People couldn't distance themselves fast enough.

On the third day, she was forced to call Harold and beg for his forgiveness.

He drove out to pick her up, acting like the besotted, remorseful husband for the first time.

Yet beneath his public charm, she felt his seething anger.

She'd pay for her actions. She knew it.

But her decision had been made.

When Daisy returned home, Khrista was uncharacteristically silent. Harold waited several days before punishing Daisy, crying and vowing he would never make her want to leave again, only to get drunk and angry and accuse her of leaving him for another man. His punishment had been so severe that Daisy blocked it out and still had lapses in her memory from that terrible time.

But still, Khrista hadn't said a word.

Khrista stopped taunting her father. She basically became invisible. And when Daisy tried to bond with her in any way, Khrista would pull away and give Daisy the most horrified, shell-shocked looks.

Daisy knew she shouldn't have left her daughter behind, but obviously it had been for the best. The Khrista she returned home to was more docile, more compliant like a teenager should be, if not respectful, and obeyed rules.

But then she started sneaking out.

And then she started getting involved with boys.

Harold didn't like that.

Not one bit.

And Daisy hated the idea that her daughter would end up with the same life she had been tricked into.

Daisy had known even way back then that she hadn't actually hated her daughter. She wanted the best for her, even if she never knew how to express that desire.

They had both been wounded bits of driftwood, discarded and washed up and forever changed by the virulent nature of a wild sea.

She never found the nerve to ask Khrista what had happened to her over those days when Daisy had run off. What had caused her to change so much.

She didn't want to know.

Whatever it had been, Daisy could never repair the damage.

But now, standing in the bookstore, Daisy realized she didn't need a self-help book to tell her what to do.

She needed to pack her things and go to her daughter.

She hadn't been there for Khrista back then. But Daisy could be there for her now.

Whether her daughter thought she needed her or not.

# 22

## KHRISTA

Khrista had no idea how much time had passed.

Since returning home from her ill-fated attempt at reunification, she had barely sobered up enough to drive herself home from the airport, and hadn't had a sober moment since. She started drinking as soon as she woke up in the morning, unable to stand her own stench. She found dried vomit in her bathroom but had no recollection of putting it there.

She poured herself a Bloody Mary for breakfast and finally forced herself to listen to the messages on her phone.

She listened to the last one first.

The director at her preschool. Her boss.

"Khrista, we expected you back two days ago. We've been strapped and trying to find coverage, but we're worried about you and need you to get in touch so we know what's going on. Have you made it back from California? Give me a call or text as soon as you get a chance. Hope all went well."

Shame and horror burned through Khrista's veins.

She scrolled through numerous texts from Danielle, who begged her to come in because the substitute teacher was driving her bananas and there was no way they could find anyone to replace

Danielle once the baby came, which would be soon. *Any day now soon.*

Khrista would fix this. It would be okay. They would understand. She'd tell them her flight got delayed. Maybe there had been a storm out in the Midwest somewhere. She'd tell them she had been so wrapped up in the joy of seeing her daughter that she lost track of time and missed her flight and she was really sorry.

She hated herself even more for having those thoughts.

So she drank more.

The next morning, the blaring of her alarm jolted her out of bed, and though Khrista wanted to smash her phone, she was grateful she had remembered to set it.

Unable to walk straight, she forced herself into the shower and gave herself a full shampoo and conditioner treatment and scrubbed all the smell off of her unwashed body. Memories of her father sitting in his chair in his own stench made her even more disgusted with herself.

Khrista got to work on time, and when she couldn't take off her sunglasses, she told everybody she had a terrible migraine, but she'd be okay. Once all the parents had departed, leaving her classroom filled with smiling, if loud, children, and Khrista had done her very best to present her sunny, cheerful preschool teacher alter-ego, her director called her into her office.

What had she decided her excuse would be for missing work? Her mind went blank.

Susan closed the door behind Khrista and sat at her desk. The director usually took a more casual approach and generally didn't believe in barriers during informal meetings, so Khrista sensed trouble brewing. She remained standing closer to the door, praying the alcohol stench had worn off.

"Khrista, you can't wear those glasses in the classroom. It doesn't look professional."

She was calling her unprofessional? Khrista had never been called unprofessional at any job, but especially in this field. Quite the contrary, actually. She was a highly sought-out teacher. And she told Susan so.

"Khrista, I need you to be honest with me right now. Are you drunk? Several of the parents stopped by my office to complain after they dropped off. They said they could smell alcohol on you and you weren't acting like yourself. Two of the parents reported their children wouldn't let you hold them when they usually run to you for hugs. Is this true?"

Khrista froze in place. Parents were tattling on her? The very parents who constantly praised her and asked for favors?

Anger replaced her trepidation.

"What exactly are you accusing me of?"

She whipped off her sunglasses and glared at Susan, allowing the director a good glimpse into the depths of Khrista's irritation.

"Khrista, I don't know what's going on with you, but I'm your friend. I care about you *so* much, and anything I can do to help you, I'll do. But I'm also your boss, and I know you're drunk right now. I can't have you in the classroom. I know you wouldn't try to hurt the children or anything, but having you here is a liability. Go home."

Khrista turned on her heel and pushed the door open, knocking a taped, hand-drawn picture off the back. She didn't bend to pick it up, but instead whirled back around and glared at Susan.

"I can't believe you're doing this to me."

"I'll be in touch, Khrista, but I suggest you take some time off to figure out what's going on here. I'll bring in a teacher to take your classroom while you're figuring stuff out."

"You're firing me?"

Susan shook her head too quickly, then paused and tilted it to the side, pinching the bridge of her nose.

"I have to look out for the students here, before anything else. And the reputation of the school matters. I also care about you, and as soon as you're back on your feet, you can come back."

"Don't count on it. I'll go somewhere I'm wanted and appreciated."

Khrista didn't wait for Susan's response. She stormed out of the school, got in her car, and didn't make it to the end of the street before a police car pulled up behind her with lights and sirens blazing.

That woman Khrista had looked up to for several years and had worked her tail off to help make her school the most in-demand preschool on the island, had set her up to drive away knowing she had been drinking and had a police car waiting to capture her.

She knew the trick. She had witnessed Susan employ that very tactic when a parent once dropped their child off mid-afternoon and they could smell the booze on him.

Fantastic.

Khrista slunk down in her driver's seat as people she knew strolled by, watching with great interest as the officer escorted her out and put her in the backseat of his police car.

Just her luck that the officer was Elanna's husband.

He kept his lips pressed in a tight line and he said little until dropping her off at her door and informing her that a tow truck would retrieve the car and she could pick it up once she sobered up.

She didn't like his tone.

Inhibitions vanished, Khrista got out of his car and leaned down to speak to him through the open window. He probably expected her to thank him, but instead, all she could say was, "Have you been hurting my best friend?"

Cameron didn't bat an eye, and he didn't break eye contact. Several heartbeats later, as the ground beneath her turned wobbly and she desperately needed a drink, he said in his very firm police officer voice, "I suggest you go in your house, make yourself some coffee, and keep your doors locked until you smarten up."

And then he drove off.

When Khrista got into her apartment, her cell phone started going crazy. Though she couldn't bring herself to answer the calls, once the ringing settled down, she listened to every message and read through all the texts she had been ignoring—the current ones and the older ones from days past.

Bess texted, asking if she was okay because Khrista hadn't

picked her up to bring her to the tearoom when she was supposed to. Danielle left a whispered voicemail, telling Khrista she'd call as soon as she got off work but swearing up and down she had tried to cover for her. Winnie from knitting club left a message asking what was going on because she had read on the Spill the Tea neighborhood forum that people had witnessed Khrista getting pulled over and escorted into the police car. Clarice left several messages asking if she'd be coming to work on the project Khrista had promised to chair when Elanna was spread too thin to take on one more thing.

A different Khrista had made that promise.

A Khrista who had some hope.

A Khrista who believed there was a slight possibility that even if she didn't get her happily-ever-after, she might get a happy moment.

A Khrista who had knit a freaking baby blanket because she had been so certain she could be the kind of person who did such things.

A few minutes later, Elanna called. Then called again when Khrista didn't answer. Then called again. She didn't leave a message. Eventually, Elanna sent a text saying, "WTF?"

Khrista buried her fingers in her hair, her forehead resting against her palm, and sobbed.

But she didn't get a drink.

What had she done?

She curled up on her living room floor, hating that her sanctuary had become her gallows. Everyone had turned against her, and it was her own doing. She had no one to blame. Khrista couldn't blame her mother, her father, or Kaelyn. She couldn't blame Matt for her heartbreak, because even though technically he had caused it, she had been the one to bring it on. All she could do was lay in the fetal position and wish she had never been born.

After a nap on the floor, and realizing she had truly hit rock bottom, Khrista knew if she wanted to break this pattern of pain and self-induced torment, she had to make changes.

It was time to clean up her act.

She wanted to live.

At least long enough to repair all the damage she had inflicted upon people who had done nothing but love her.

Khrista would never regain the image people had of her before this breakdown, but she could show them something else. She could let them see the real her. Not the cheerful, fake persona she had put on display.

She could do better. She could *be* better.

Khrista dumped her alcohol—for good this time. She would give herself three days to detox, and if she made it through those full three days without taking even one sip of alcohol, Khrista would follow through on the rest of her plans.

Three days would seem an eternity. Khrista couldn't remember the last time she had gone that long without at least a nip.

But she had to have the strength to make it three days.

If she could do that, she could do anything.

But first she had to make it three days.

THREE DAYS OF TORTURE LATER, after many moments of not feeling she would come out on the other side alive, Khrista pulled at the front hem of her shirt and knocked on the front door of Matt's colonial home, nicely situated near one of the prettiest beaches on the island.

His plastered-on smile faded when he registered that it was her at the door.

"You seem shocked to see me."

He raised his bushy eyebrows and smirked.

"Have to admit, I am. I've heard things weren't going too well for you, and I figured you'd be disappearing. Don't get me wrong, I'm glad you're here. I wanted to reach out, but you made your feelings clear."

"Can I come in for just a minute?"

He opened the door wider. She stepped in, appreciating the warmth of his bright, clean home in contrast to the dreary day outside. She was careful not to brush against him, though she wanted his comforting touch more than anything.

"It's been three days."

He wrinkled his forehead and looked at her skeptically.

"I don't mean three days since I last saw you. I mean three days since my last drink of alcohol. I know you were suspicious of my drinking, and you were right. A few days ago, I would have lied to you and told you I didn't have a problem. But I know now that I did. I mean, I guess I *do*. I'm ready to make changes, but the first person I needed to reach out to was you."

Matt stood in silence, assessing her or trying to figure out a way to get her out of his house, she couldn't tell.

"I'm proud of you for realizing it if you have a problem. You don't owe me any explanations."

"But I do. I've been lying to you for a long time. It's not anything to do with you, and it wasn't your fault. It was all about me. I want to tell you the truth now."

She sucked in the sides of her cheeks and wrapped her arms around her body, suddenly cold.

"I never felt I deserved love, any love, really, and you tried so hard to help me feel that I did. I will forever be thankful for my time with you. I'm sorry I hurt you, and I'm sorry I built our entire relationship on lies. I'm working on myself, so maybe one day I'll be worthy of you."

Khrista held her hands up in front of her as he took a step forward.

"I'm not asking you to take me back. Even if you would, it's not the right time. I'm trying to do better and I hope you'll find your way back to me, but I want it to be a new relationship when and if I'm fortunate enough for that to happen."

Tears slipped down her cheeks, and she didn't brush them away. They were almost a relief to her, a rainfall over a desert that had been dry too long.

"I've been lying to you all this time about my daughter. We haven't spoken in five years, and I was so hurt and ashamed of how I pushed her away and how poorly I parented her that I made up this lie about her living across the country. I mean, she does live across the country, but I'm not part of her life. I sent myself flowers. I made up a profession for her." She laughed. "I still don't even know what she does for a living. But now I know she's happily married, having a baby, seems to be doing really well for herself, and still wants nothing to do with me."

Saying those words out loud hurt something awful. Her throat grew raspy and her toes dug into her shoes so tightly she was sure she'd wear a hole in the bottom.

Matt reached out, all empathy and strength, and tried to comfort her the way he always had, even when he didn't know he was doing it. Khrista wanted desperately to take his comfort, but it wasn't hers to accept and she couldn't hurt him anymore by letting him give of himself.

She had known enough toxic vampires to know she didn't want to be one. Not anymore.

Khrista stepped back, smiling at him through her tears.

"I want your comfort so badly, but this is a process I need to go through on my own. I know you're going to want to try to fix me. That's not what I'm here for. You can't fix me; only I can do that. Nobody else can clear my path, my past, or my future, and it has taken me this long to actually figure that out."

Matt shoved his hands into his pockets and looked for all the world like an uncertain teenage boy.

His gruff voice dripped with emotion as he said, "It's hard not to hug you. As you're finding your way, please know you already have my forgiveness. You had it before I knew you needed it. Before I knew anything was wrong. And when you're ready, I'll be here."

The urge to kiss him burned through her, but Khrista fought it as strongly as she would need to fight her urge to have a drink.

She denied herself the hug he offered, giving him a shy smile and a shrug as she slipped out of his home. Khrista tried to visualize a future where she would present her real self to him and he would love her with all her flaws and see her strengths beyond them. A future where she would come to terms with her past and her relationships and meet his grown children and offer them all the love she hadn't been able to offer herself.

She needed to stay focused. Not get too far ahead of herself. One day at a time. One decision at a time.

One breath at a time.

Khrista's next task after leaving Matt's house was to swing by Old Castle Gifts. The tiny gift shop, nestled alongside the shoreline in the street-level basement of an old colonial home, sold homemade paper and old-fashioned quill pens for what Kaelyn used to call "fancy writing."

She selected several glass tubs of ink, the kind Kaelyn used when she was thirteen and so desperately wanted to write and mail letters written in calligraphy to everyone she knew. People in town, penpals in other states, and the President of the United States. Khrista hadn't made the time to take part in that activity that had meant so much to Kaelyn back then, but she was ready to make that time now.

Even if it was too late, Khrista owed it to Kaelyn to show her that her mother, with all her flaws and all her pride and all her lack of self-worth and her inability to show love the appropriate way, really, truly loved Kaelyn. That even though she had so often checked out of parenting when battling her own personal demons, she had observed, even if from a distance, the details of Kaelyn's life.

She had noticed.

She had cared.

She had loved. Nothing would ever change that.

If Khrista intended to heal all of her wounds, that meant reaching out to her mother, too. Because if Khrista had embodied this much pain after five years of her daughter's absence, she could only imagine what her own mother had suffered.

After spending the rest of the day watching YouTube videos and learning to form the fancy lettering, and then writing the letters to both Kaelyn and to her mother, she felt lighter. As if letting her heart bleed onto the paper had started a healing process Khrista hadn't realized she needed or deserved.

She sat back in her seat, staring at her sloppily scrawled handwriting and the smudges that gave her away as a calligraphy amateur. Though she normally would beat herself up over her lack of talent or perfection, her pride at having taken this initial step toward redemption instead filled her with a sense of freedom. And, dare she say, happiness.

*Happiness.*

The word sounded foreign as it bounced around inside her mind. Khrista had never believed she could be truly happy, and maybe it wasn't meant to last.

But for now, she'd revel in it.

And hopefully, with all her life lessons learned, she would allow happiness to become a permanent part of her life.

# 23

## KAELYN

With the nursery still in disarray and Kaelyn feeling the weight of her hesitation crushing her, she clocked out of work early and planned to surprise Oliver by organizing the nursery while he was at work.

He had given up pressuring her into completing the all-important room. He hadn't said anything about her lack of interest lately, and she knew he was giving her the space to sort through whatever she needed to sort through so she could find joy in the planning. They still had a couple of months before they needed the room to be complete, and though Kaelyn couldn't pinpoint what caused her hesitation, she had to overcome the reluctance.

She opened the door to where their new baby would sleep soon. Oliver had painted the room sage green, but they hadn't decided officially on a theme and so the walls remained bare other than one framed photo near the crib he had set up.

She stepped closer to the photo, loving the comforting feel of the plush carpet beneath her bare feet. The photo was a picture of her and Oliver on their honeymoon in Anguilla. They had stopped to snuggle a goat that had run up to them on the beach. A passerby had taken the photo, and it captured the joy they were feeling at that moment. All the love, all the hope, all the promises they had made one another for an amazing future. The passerby asked Oliver for his phone number so she could text it to him because she said such a magical, candid moment should be preserved.

Her heart swelled that Oliver had chosen that picture for their baby. Not one of the expensive photos they had purchased from the wedding photographer, not the fancy photo shoot from their engagement, but this unscripted moment on a beach on a tropical island where the only thing that mattered was love.

Their love.

She rubbed her belly, laughing when her sweet baby kicked her hand as if to remind her that he or she would be the best extension and proof of the love that bloomed so beautifully in this sunlit home.

Kaelyn scoured the room, searching for something helpful she could do.

She started by sifting through the pile of adorable infant clothes they had received at their shower, along with the items they had ordered online months ago. She opened each of the boxes and neatly folded every item before placing them lovingly into the dressers. They seemed impossibly small.

How would a baby so vulnerable, so tiny and helpless, thrive in this world?

Easy. She and Oliver would guide and protect.

For the first time in her pregnancy, she allowed herself to imagine what raising the child would be like. She had, of course, teased Oliver about it being a little boy like him, but she almost knew it would be a girl. It was crazy, but she felt as though the child already communicated with her.

Kaelyn felt the sort of connection she had wanted to feel the first time around, but she hadn't been pregnant long enough to have anything resembling this.

Here, though, kneeling on the floor in a room where a baby would learn to crawl, learn to walk, and cement her and Oliver together more firmly than even their wedding vows had, she finally knew she was ready to let go of her pregnancy loss.

To let the tragedy leave all the cells she had stored the pain in for so long.

She stood up and stretched, easing the aches out of her lower back. She then gave her belly a nice rub, resulting in a massive gymnastics show inside.

"Okay, baby. I'm not usually one for using tools, as you'll discover, but I'm gonna put this cradle together for you. That's me, an involved mom."

The baby kicked her in the rib, seemingly lodging her little foot in the tender spot. Kaelyn contorted her body to open up that space and gently pushed the foot back down.

"I'm signing you up for gymnastics the second you're born."

She picked up the screwdriver Oliver had left on the floor near the crib and got to work on assembling the wooden cradle.

Would she be a good mom?

Kaelyn thought she would be, but her mother had probably thought she would have been as well. Did anyone go into parenting thinking they'd be a terrible parent? Or were all babies born into a world of hopes and dreams and happy wishes, topped off with good intentions?

What if she failed as miserably as her mother had?

No. She wouldn't.

The fact that she questioned it told her she wouldn't.

Kaelyn was quite certain her mother had never second-guessed herself.

As she went to attach the legs to the cradle, Kaelyn realized she had put one side on wrong and now it wouldn't line up with the end piece.

"Are you kidding me?"

Exasperation set her temper afire, and she pushed the cradle, knocking it over.

Tears shot to her eyes, and shame sent the icy chills down her spine.

Did she seriously knock over her baby's cradle because she got a little frustrated?

What if she became that way after her baby was born? What if she couldn't handle the stress of new motherhood? What if Kaelyn was only one birth away from becoming exactly like her mother?

She wouldn't allow it. There was no way she would allow that.

She left the house, needing fresh air and sunshine to reset her mood. Kaelyn drove up and down the streets, tears blurring her vision. To the beach. No, to the forest. Where should she go? She had no clue and was incapable of deciding. The beach. Definitely the beach. That had always been her happy spot, her place where she could easily reset her mood.

Tears continued to stream down her face and her nose ran profusely. Kaelyn had to get control of this sense of self-doubt sooner than later.

She also had to release the guilt of keeping a secret from Oliver. He deserved to know everything about her, the good and the bad, and she needed to tell him before this baby was born. She would tell him tonight. She would tell him everything. And then maybe he would understand why she hadn't been able to share.

A sharp kick from the baby startled Kaelyn, sending her swerving into oncoming traffic. In an attempt to get back in her lane, she must've over-corrected because her car spun out of control, crashing into a tree. Her head slammed against the steering wheel, and blood ran from her mouth.

Of all the ways she had thought her day would go, this had not been one of the idealized versions.

OLIVER BURST into the curtained emergency room cubicle, frantic and practically shoving the doctor out of his way.

"What happened? Love, are you okay?"

He brushed the hair away from her forehead, gently fingering the area they had stitched up.

Through her swollen lips, she tried to smile,

"I'm okay. Just a chipped tooth and a concussion. Baby is totally fine, though."

He lifted her hands to his lips, closing his eyes tightly as he breathed on her knuckles.

"Thank God, Kaelyn. I was terrified when I got the call saying you crashed."

"I'm really sorry about the car. I hope it's not totaled."

"I don't care one bit about the car. All I care about is right here in my arms."

He held her tight, and she winced a little.

"Could you hand me some water, please?"

Oliver rushed to do her bidding, bringing her ice from the nurse's station and then Jell-O and then pudding. She suddenly felt ravenous and wondered if stress had brought on that hunger.

"They want to keep you for a few days."

"Why? They said everything was fine."

Oliver shrugged, but he avoided her eyes.

"Oliver, is there something you aren't telling me? This is my baby, too. My body. I deserve to know if they're telling you something different than they're telling me."

Her voice grew shrill and shrieky and she couldn't keep it down.

"Tell me, Oliver."

When he looked up at her, there was something in his eyes she didn't recognize.

He cleared his throat and rolled the doctor's stool closer to the bed, where he reached again for her shaking hands. Kaelyn snapped them away from him, needing to hear whatever it was he had to say.

"Did you do it on purpose, Kaelyn? Did you mean to crash the car?"

She pulled away as far as she could from him in the bed, hoping her expression told him everything he needed to know about how crazy his question was.

"Of course not! Why would I do that?"

Kaelyn was tiring of his familiar shrug.

"You haven't been yourself. I hoped not, but if there's more going on that you're not telling me, I don't want to regret not helping you get through it."

"I didn't do it on purpose. I wouldn't do that. I love you, I love this baby, and I love my life."

A fresh wave of tears cascaded down her face. Oliver rushed to kiss them away, but before he stepped away from her, she felt his tears mingling with hers.

"You weren't wearing shoes, Kaelyn. I'm trying to understand the scene they painted for me, but so much doesn't make sense. None of it sounds like you."

"I ran out without thinking. I promise I didn't think I'd be crashing and having to explain myself. You know I never wear shoes when I don't have to. I just forgot to put them on for the drive."

He climbed into bed beside her, pressing her head to his heart.

"I can't lose you."

"You won't."

She sobbed into his arms, desperate to merge into one being with him.

"I know I've been a bit messed up emotionally. It's this whole thing with my mother. I thought I was long past it." Kaelyn choked on her words and studied her hands as she twisted the hospital gown. "It's hard to go into motherhood with such an unhealed wound, you know?"

He studied her face, searching for truth. Searching for connection.

"Maybe it's time to heal it." Once she had spoken the statement aloud, the strength of her conviction convinced her she was finally on the right path.

Oliver, the compassionate heart and mind of the relationship, didn't take advantage of the opportunity to say "I told you so." He just let her realization roll forward like a rising tide, called forth by the feminine energy of a full moon.

"I love you."

Before he could respond, the nurse came in and ushered him out. When the nurse finished checking on the baby and Kaelyn's vitals,

Oliver told her he would go home and get some things to make her more comfortable for her hospital stay.

He swore there was nothing wrong, and that she didn't have to go to the psych ward or anything. Oliver reassured her they wanted to keep her for observation to make sure her head wound wasn't worse than it appeared and that she didn't start bleeding or anything, especially with the low lying placenta. He told her they'd be monitoring the baby's heart rate.

She relaxed at his reassurance. She could live with that.

The next day, Oliver relented and went to work as Kaelyn asked him to do. There was no point in both of them missing work, and there was nothing he could do for her there.

She tried catching up on sleep, but couldn't get comfortable.

Eventually, Kaelyn must have drifted off into a deep dreamland, because when she startled awake there was a familiar woman from her past sitting beside her bed.

"Elanna! So strange to see you here. How did you even know where to find me?"

She shifted to sit upright in her bed, embarrassed at seeing her mother's best friend—Kaelyn's godmother—under these circumstances.

"Sweetheart, it's so good to see you. I'm sorry to barge in like this, but I flew out to see you so I could talk to you about your mom, and your neighbor told me you were in the hospital after a crash, so I came to find out. I had to see you for myself."

They chatted for a few minutes, but Kaelyn's curiosity finally overcame her social finesse.

"Why did you want to fly out here to talk to me about my mother? I mean, *Khrista*."

Elanna's beautiful face contorted in a pained expression.

"Sweetie, I know things have been hard. And I haven't wanted to intervene. But, well, your mom is hurting. And as her best friend, and as one of your biggest fans, I couldn't stay out of it any longer."

Kaelyn's heart thudded so hard in her chest, she was surprised alarms didn't go off.

She shook her head. She didn't want to hear of her mom's pain. It was too close to her own. And yet, all this time she had told herself her mother didn't care about her at all. That all of the choices she had made had been direct attacks against Kaelyn.

Her heart and her mind warred with one another.

"I know things weren't good between you and your momma for some time. But she's trying, sweetie. She's fighting her way toward sobriety. She's gone quite a few days without drinking, has joined Alcoholics Anonymous, and is being honest with people in our community for the first time. She has a good, strong support network, but the one person in the world she'd want to be cheering her on is you."

"I've never been a cheerleader," Kaelyn snapped, the irrational urge to scream and cry and kick Elanna out of her room conflicting with her desire to have the comfort of home and the kind attention of a woman she considered an auntie.

Elanna's lips pouted and she cocked her head to the side.

"That's your pain talking, Kaelyn. And I don't expect all your pain to go away overnight. I just wanted to come out here and see you in person. To let you know that while everything bad you and your mom went through is valid, there's also a lot of good in her. She's changed. I've seen it with my own eyes."

Kaelyn fought the urge to cover her ears like a child who didn't want to be told it was bedtime.

"She's a respected member of the community. Active in helping others, has a top-notch reputation in her school, and her insight has helped me realize I need to look out for me and my children."

Elanna's gaze dropped to her delicate hands, placed properly in her lap, fingers intertwined.

Kaelyn waited to hear more, as it seemed Elanna was mentally preparing herself to share something intimate.

"Your mom helped me to see the way Cam treats me when we're alone... It's not okay. I don't deserve to be hurt. No one does. And there are no marital vows strong enough to permit someone to treat the person they're supposed to love like... well, I didn't come here to talk about me."

Kaelyn drew in a breath but tried not to react. Elanna and Cam were fairytale material. They had the perfect mansion home with a circular drive, courtesy of Cam's inheritance, perfect children, and they always took the perfect vacations. Seriously, like, social media influencer level.

Elanna sat up straight, adjusting her earring and looking toward the hospital window.

"I know your mom did a lot of things wrong. But despite it all, she has *always* loved you, and at least she's woman enough to try to change so she doesn't continue to do you wrong in the future. No one can change anything that happened in your childhood, but having known your mom when we were kids, I promise you don't know a tiny bit of what she went through. She protected you from that knowledge. She did the best she could with what she knew at the time. Now she knows more, so she's doing better. But I've gotta tell ya, a mother without her child is a dried-out stump, no matter how hard she tries to grow branches."

Kaelyn didn't get the chance to respond, not that she could have if she wanted to, as Oliver entered at the same time as the doctor came in, doing rounds with med students.

Everything became busy in the room, and Kaelyn lost track of what was going on. She sort of remembered introducing Oliver to Elanna, but all her thoughts were caught up in the wheel of time.

Elanna had flown all the way here to push Kaelyn toward forgiveness? Kaelyn couldn't make sense of it.

Oliver attributed her spaciness to fatigue, so he leaned back in the chair beside her bed and dozed off after Elanna said her goodbyes, encouraging her to sleep as well.

Kaelyn dozed off for a bit, but sleeping in the hospital with all the beeping machinery and the constant flow of nurses entering to check on things prevented her from resting.

Early in the morning, Oliver ran home to shower and get the

shoes he had forgotten to bring the first time since the doctor had said last night she should be all set to go home in the morning.

She checked her phone, but there were no new messages.

Anxious and restless, Kaelyn scrolled through her social media feeds, then did something she had resisted doing for so long.

She googled her mother's name.

Kaelyn clicked on the first search result, which brought her to the preschool her mother worked at in Old Castle. She zoomed in on the unmistakable image of her mother, smiling for a professional headshot.

She took a screenshot of the image and, tears streaming down her face, clicked on several more links. Article after article from the Old Castle news site highlighted acts of kindness her mother had performed. Kaelyn studied a photo of a smiling Khrista surrounded by a dozen preschoolers, each of whom held up colorfully painted canvases on the town square. Another article had a picture of Elanna and Khrista snuggling with cats and urging community members to donate toward an important surgery one of the kittens needed. There was an image of her serving packed picnic lunches to children at the beachfront park.

Kaelyn set the phone down and allowed herself to get lost in memories. Times when her mother had given her rubber gloves and taken her for walks along the beach to clean up trash. Summer nights spent collecting shells and fashioning them into jewelry. Sandcastle contests and splashing wars and learning how to float amongst the waves.

All the things Kaelyn had secured in a locked part of her mind.

She had told herself it was better to maintain a grudge than to risk being hurt by her mom again. But what if she had been using her mother as a scapegoat all along?

Oliver returned to the hospital, carrying her small flowery tote bag stuffed with her sneakers, her favorite breakfast bars, her prenatal vitamins, and a sealed letter.

"What's this?"

"It's for you."

She studied the handwritten address on the front of the envelope. Her name written in careful loops and lines, in navy blue ink. The return address in the same careful handwriting in cranberry.

She gulped. A letter from her mother. The last thing she had expected.

"I'm going to run down to the cafeteria because I heard they have legendary key lime pie and I'm hankering for some. Want me to get you a slice?"

Kaelyn nodded, struggling to staunch the flow of tears. She appreciated what he was doing... Leaving her alone to read this letter that was sure to bring about the most powerful of emotions.

The letter smelled the way she remembered her mother smelling. On her good days, anyway. The floral scent lured memories out of Kaelyn's mind that she had desperately kept hidden with the skeletons in the closet.

Somewhere along the line, her mother had learned calligraphy. Kaelyn had gone through a phase of wanting to write all of her letters in calligraphy with fancy pens, and her mother had never joined her the way she had wanted her to do.

Until now.

The importance of that gesture didn't escape Kaelyn.

Wiping tears away from her eyes so she could see, she began to read.


*My dearest Kaelyn, the one true and real love of my life,*

*I remember the moment they handed you to me after you were born. You didn't look as if you had been through the rough ordeal of birth. No, your eyes looked up at me, so wide and open and clear and beautiful, as if you could see right through me.*

*They say babies don't smile socially so young, but the smile you gave me told a different truth. You were meant to heal, to repair a broken soul.*

*But even then, I knew it wasn't your job to heal me.*

*Though I hadn't been sure about becoming a mother, the moment I held you so close to my heart, I knew I'd die for you.*

*I failed as a mother. I see it now. For so long, I blamed you for being who you were—strong, matter of fact, intelligent enough to see through the games people played. You were naïve, true, but so was I.*

*I don't know what I'm trying to say, other than I'm sorry.*

*I'm sorry I couldn't be the mother you needed. The mother you deserved. I'm sorry I didn't listen to you when you told me you needed me to stop checking out emotionally and physically. I'm sorry I left you to fend for yourself so often, and I wasn't there when you were vulnerable and needed the guidance of a mentally strong parent.*

*My weakness for my personal demons was stronger than the strength of my love for you, and because of that, I failed to give you the life you deserved.*

*I have a million excuses I could offer, and some of them are valid reasons for my behavior.*

*But none of them was your fault, and you deserved better.*

*You've always been the one to try to get me to talk things out, to listen to you, and to work harder to do better. Your strength made me feel weaker, and that weakness made me more susceptible to the demons.*

*Yet at the same time, I've always admired your strength and your spirit. I've always been proud of you, even when we conflicted.*

*After you left after our big fight, I went to Boston to see you at your school when you wouldn't answer my calls. Your roommate told me you dropped out and moved, and she said she didn't know where you had gone. The school refused to give me any information without a signed waiver from you.*

*My heart stayed in Boston that day.*

*I said a lot of bad things when we fought. I didn't mean them. I was hurt. Again, not your fault, but I couldn't see the truth of that back then. All I could see was that you were hurting me and I wanted to hurt you back. This sounds childish and foolish to me now, but I suppose I never grew much beyond my own childhood trauma. Unlike you, I didn't put the work in that I needed to in order to heal and to ensure that my daughter wouldn't suffer the way I had.*

*I tried to protect you from the world, but I failed to protect you from me.*

*I hope this letter doesn't upset you or cause you stress. That's not my intent.*

*While I know you have ended the generational trauma that has plagued this family tree, I want you to know that your strength has also begun the healing of some of the roots.*

*I love you, Kaelyn.*

*Whenever you're ready, I would welcome contact. I'll do whatever you want me to do to prove that I'm trying to be better.*

*I know I can't change the past, but I hope to change the future.*

*Love,*

*Mom*


WHEN OLIVER RETURNED to the room, it was to find a new woman. Tears dried, conviction set, sneakers on.

Still the woman he loved and married, she hoped, but one who was ready to break the curse of the past and to propel their family into a happier, brighter future.

"How quickly do you think you can pack for a getaway? We're going to Old Castle."

# 24

# DAISY

Daisy had to hand it to herself. She had never been good at very much outside of the home, and more specifically outside of the kitchen and laundry room, but she had become quite adept at picking up everything and moving across the country on a dime.

She hadn't exactly made plans for what to do once she arrived in Old Castle, but she should be able to find a hotel room until she figured it out.

Heck, if she had to sleep on the streets, at least she would be close to her daughter.

Maybe if Khrista saw the lengths Daisy would go to make amends, she'd be more likely to lean into forgiveness.

Regardless, Daisy didn't plan to leave until Khrista at least had a conversation with her.

After that, Daisy had no plan and no destination in mind. She'd figure it out as she went along.

Getting from Boston where her plane landed up to the little island of Old Castle, connected to New Hampshire by a bridge but otherwise fairly remote, proved to be a challenge. She'd had to hire a driver from the airport who she was pretty sure was ripping her off.

She gasped at the price he quoted her. Highway robbery. But she could either pay it or be stranded in the city, and Daisy had never been much of a city person. Not that she'd had experience with cities.

Besides, she didn't want to waste any more time. She needed to be close to her daughter. Even if the closer she got, the more uncertainty plagued Daisy.

What if Khrista turned her away?

What if Daisy's presence infuriated Khrista more?

What if Khrista accused Daisy of infringing on her space and doubled down on her hatred?

Daisy squared her jaw and held her head high. She was a mother.

A mother who needed her daughter.

And this mother had given up far too many times. She wouldn't do it again. She was no longer a puppet on a string, and no one controlled her movements but her.

The driver dropped her off in a populated area of the town, full of colorful homes that seemed to double as art galleries, gift shops, candy shops, and other specialty shops, but she couldn't read the signs from afar.

Since Daisy hadn't known where to go, she directed him to drop her off at the rambling Victorian house that had a little sign saying Happil-TEA Ever After Tea Room. It appeared like the sort of place that might rent out rooms, and it was the only prospect she could see that looked like it might fit her needs.

She took her small bag out of the driver's hands and thanked him. Despite him ripping her off, he had been good company for the ride, distracting her with tales of the Red Sox/Yankees rivalry and other things she hadn't cared about, but that kept her mind off her more pressing problems. He had been passionate about the topic, so she kept him talking and appreciated the time away from her thoughts. His Boston accent had intrigued her.

Daisy entered the tearoom, hoping her heart had led her to this spot because she would walk in and find Khrista sitting at a table, sipping tea and pondering how she wanted to reunite with her mother.

All fantasies, of course, but from what Daisy could tell, this was a small town and Khrista had always liked tea, so it was a possibility.

The tearoom was abuzz with chatter and various groups of people. A woman nearly Daisy's age glanced up from the counter and greeted her with an extra-large smile. Her eyes were friendly and her energy positive. Daisy had never really thought about someone's energy all that much before, but Florence had rubbed off on her. Florence had insisted you needed to get to know somebody's energy so you could sense if they could be trusted and if they were likely to hurt you or scam you.

"Welcome to Happil-TEA Ever After. I don't remember seeing you before. Are you new to town? Visiting one of our fine residents?"

Daisy wasn't ready to spill everything, even to this friendly person. She didn't know who knew who and who would run to warn Khrista. Better for her not to get a heads up that Daisy was looking for her, if at all possible.

"I'm passing through. Embarking on an impromptu tour of the country now that I'm newly widowed."

The woman behind the counter frowned, and her expression oozed sympathy.

"I'm so sorry to hear that. But are you enjoying your travels? I so admire a woman who can turn her grief into an adventure."

Daisy's smile rose from deep within. She nodded, and she didn't mind if this woman, with all her empathy and kindness, could see how *not* unhappy Daisy was at the reality of being a widow.

"I'm enjoying it very much. I wouldn't mind a tea if you don't mind."

"You're in the right place. What can I get you?"

Daisy hesitated. She loved tea, but the long list of options written on the board behind the woman was overwhelming.

"I don't want to come off too strong, but maybe I can help," the woman said. "I'm Clarice, by the way. Owner of the tearoom. I have what some say is a sort of tea ESP. ESTea?"

She laughed at her own joke, which usually annoyed Daisy but had the opposite effect on her this time. She found Clarice's laughter rather endearing. If circumstances were different, they could be friends.

"I sense you could use a lavender chamomile with some lemon, blended with green tea for a touch of caffeine without overdoing it."

"I don't know how you got these powers, and I never would have dreamed up that blend on my own, but I think your ESTea is on the mark because that sounds delightful."

The women laughed together, a welcome release for all the tension that had been building inside Daisy. Clarice turned to scoop tea from little tins on the counter behind her, then brewed them and poured the liquid into a dainty teacup.

"Do you know if there's a place nearby that rents rooms?"

"Oh my, you breezed into town and don't have a place to stay?"

Clarice's shrewd eyes studied Daisy, who had the disconcerting feeling she could see more than Daisy had anticipated.

"It's your lucky day. I don't typically rent out rooms anymore, but just recently I opened up a section upstairs for my goddaughter to stay before she took off for the UK again. She just left a few days ago, so it will be easy for me to throw on some new sheets and freshen up that room."

"As long as it doesn't put you out at all."

"Not at all. We're all about the hospitality here. Please appreciate that I'm resisting the urge to insert another tea pun."

Daisy smiled as she brought the cup to her nose and inhaled the sweet scent.

"I have to admit, this smells quite *taste-tea.*"

Clarice laughed and wagged a finger at Daisy. "I'm gonna like you."

Daisy excused herself and found a lovely seat tucked away in a corner by a fireplace that wasn't running but still had an ambient glow. As soon as she sat, a cat jumped onto her lap. How had she not noticed there were cats here when she first came in?

This cat was all white with one tiny black mark on the top of its right ear. Its unique appearance sent Daisy back in time to the cat her husband had killed. That cat had looked almost exactly like this one, but it had been the left ear with the black spot.

"Are you here to give me a message, little kitty?" She stroked the cat from the tip of his head to the tip of his tail, earning a rumbling of purrs and gentle kneading on her lap.

She had missed having pets but hadn't dared get attached to another living thing.

"Maybe one day I'll settle in one spot again. And then I'll take you home with me."

The cat nudged his nose against Daisy's ear, chewing on her dangling earring. Daisy chuckled, feeling genuine joy for the first time since before the baby shower.

Kaelyn, her sweet granddaughter, had become so busy with the baby preparations and her marriage and her job that Daisy had backed off considerably, especially since they had only exchanged a few brief texts about the incident at the shower.

Kaelyn had sworn she didn't hold anything against Daisy, but Daisy sensed there was something going on. Best to get things figured out here and then she'd go back to work everything out with Kaelyn. The poor girl needed time to adjust to all the changes in her life. She sure as heck didn't need an old lady putting more pressure on her.

She scratched the cat's neck and reveled in its purr. "You're a feisty thing, aren't you? Now, now, settle in right here while I sip this heavenly smelling tea."

The cat did as she requested, and Daisy had to admit that Clarice's tea instincts were spot on.

The tea was delicious, and the room Clarice later led her to was even better.

THE ISLAND WAS small and the area surrounding the tearoom seemed walkable. The tearoom overlooked the ocean from the rear and side of the house. Daisy could stand on the back deck and have an unobstructed view of a gentle cove complete with brown sand her toes itched to sink into and white seabirds dipping into the waves to find dinner. She sat on the porch swing and rocked with her tea as she breathed in the fresh, salty air. Something about the island already had her feeling recharged. No wonder Khrista had made this her home.

When Khrista moved Kaelyn away, there must have been desperate circumstances that Kaelyn hadn't understood. No way would anyone voluntarily leave this place.

Daisy tried to remember what her social worker Merigold had taught her about searching for people, and then she pieced it together with Florence's lessons about using the map function on her phone. This technological world was a strange one, but it sure was convenient.

On her own, without having to ask one of the people downstairs for help, she found directions to the address where she had sent the shower invitation.

Daisy didn't hesitate, after another cup of Clarice's hand blended tea, to set out on a walk to find her daughter.

She arrived at 10 Ladyslipper Lane, knowing exactly why Khrista had chosen that spot to live. Standing at the front door of the small apartment building, Daisy breathed salt air from a nearby beach, not within sight, but certainly close. Khrista had always loved the water, so it didn't surprise Daisy that she had ended up in a place surrounded by it.

She stood on the front step for quite a while, unsure how to proceed if nobody came to the door. The locked door prevented her from entering the building, and there were only two cars in the small gravel parking lot.

Just as Daisy was almost ready to give up for the day, the door swung open and a very tall, very muscular gentleman stepped out.

"Hey there. Can I help you with something?"

"Yes, thank you. I'm looking for Khrista O'Donnell."

He crossed his arms over his chest and studied her.

"Is Khrista expecting you?"

Why did she feel like she was under investigation? Did Khrista have personal security?

"Well, um, no. But I need to see her."

"Who are you? If you don't mind me asking." The man relaxed his posture but kept up his guard.

"If you could just let me pass, I'll go to Khrista's door."

"No can do." The man lowered his chin toward his chest and studied her. "Are you a relative? I don't recall seeing you around here in all the years I've known Khrista, but you look like her."

Daisy didn't respond. Would he chase her off if he knew? Had he heard horror stories of Khrista's terrible mother?

"She never told me she had a sister."

"A sister!" Daisy exclaimed. "Do I look young enough to be Khrista's sister?"

She had meant to point out his nonsense, but he nodded and continued to study her.

"Pretty enough, too."

A flush rose within her. An uncomfortable feeling stirred in her belly, and it horrified Daisy to realize it might be *attraction*.

She hadn't felt anything like that for longer than she cared to admit.

Daisy couldn't deny, however, that this man who seemed close to her age, if not a little older, with his big hands and his dark complexion and his gap-toothed smile and his kind ways, from what she could tell, stirred something within her.

"I can assure you I'm not her sister." Her voice sounded flirty to her, and she wondered where the real Daisy had gone. "I can also assure you I mean her no harm."

He studied her quizzically. "If you're not her sister, what's your relation to Khrista, and why are you looking for her?"

He looked her up and down as if assessing her. Could he see how she and Khrista shared a body type? Could he tell through the filter of her years that their eyes and cheekbones were the same?

Daisy breathed deeply, a sharp pain striking her in the side.

"I'm her mother."

He nodded as if predicting such news.

"I'm not going to ask for any history or any stories. I'm just going to tell you that if you're here to hurt her in any way, I won't allow it."

She bristled. Who was he to tell *her* how to treat her daughter? "What's your relationship to my daughter?"

"I've been looking out for that girl since she rolled up here with her little one, gosh, I don't know how many years ago."

"Twenty," Daisy interjected.

"Sounds about right. My wife and I took her in under our wings and patched her up after whatever she had been through." He held his hands up in front of her as if warding off the offense his frank talk may have induced. "Now I'm not judging nothing, but that girl is like a daughter to me. My wife passed on many years ago, but if she thought for a second I wasn't looking out for Khrista, she'd send a lightning bolt down to strike me right in the gonads."

He blushed as if catching himself.

"My apologies, miss. I get a little worked up when I think about anything happening to Khrista. She's got her problems, I'll give you that. But she's got a solid heart of gold, too."

Daisy nodded solemnly. Why had it taken her so long to realize that about her own flesh and blood?

Tears gathered in the corners of her worn-out eyes, and her nose ran. She fumbled through her purse to pull out a tissue and dabbed at the sides of her eyes before wiping her nose.

"Thank you for looking after my daughter when I couldn't. When I *didn't*."

He watched her for several long minutes, and she just knew he was going to send her away.

"Okay, here's the deal. Khrista's not home right now. I don't see an unfamiliar car here, so I assume you're walking. You can hang out in my place until she gets home, or I can give you a ride back into town. Whatever you want."

The man, who soon introduced himself as Rafael, owner of the building and a local restaurant in town, told Daisy that Khrista had been on a bit of a self-improvement kick, working her way through the town to make all the amends she felt she needed to make.

She accepted his invitation into his first-floor apartment, admiring his abundance of houseplants as he led her to the kitchen table.

"Tea or coffee? On this island, it's mostly always tea, but I like to ask."

Daisy grew uncomfortably warm. "I just had tea in the tearoom. Thank you, though. If I could trouble you for some water…"

He filled a glass and handed it to her, and when their fingers brushed she nearly dropped the glass. She fought the embarrassment and focused on the rainbow of light that streaked through a prism on his kitchen window.

"As you've probably guessed," Daisy began, not sure why she felt compelled to open up to the stranger, this man who loved her daughter and treated her better than Daisy ever had.

She cleared her throat and began again.

"As you may have guessed, I haven't treated Khrista the way she deserved to be treated throughout her life. We haven't spoken in over twenty years, and it was my fault things ended the way they did."

There was something freeing about confessing her sins out loud. She had carried them so close to her broken heart for too many years, making excuses and digging up justifications. Admitting to what she had always known, on some level, felt more empowering than she had imagined.

"I want to see her desperately. I want to hold her hand, rest her head on my lap, and smooth her hair away from her face like I did when she was a young child before everything went sour between us. But you can probably guess that my wishes may not align with hers. I need to see her, though, which is why I came all the way here. My greatest hope is that she'll hear me out before booting me off the island. And if I'm lucky, one day she'll want me by her side."

## 25

---

# KHRISTA

Khrista checked her list to see who was next on her Make Amends Tour. Though this was only the first step of many she'd need to take to ensure she moved forward and never slipped backward, she felt confident that her eyes were now opened to the truth of what she had become.

And who she wanted to be.

She had written the letters to the most important people–Kaelyn and Daisy. She hoped they received them and could read the sincerity, which would hopefully lead to the opportunity to have those conversations in person one day.

There was so much more she needed to say to Matt, but at least she had started the process. When she had last spoken to him, she was still at the rawest point of her new journey. Since that day, she had done a lot of reflecting and had started jotting down notes about all the things she wanted to say and apologize for if given the opportunity.

This morning she had visited with Danielle, who gave birth to her son less than a week ago and was out on maternity leave.

Danielle had forgiven her with no reservation, and asked if she could join the Knot-TEA Knitters so she could learn to make a blanket for her baby. Khrista agreed they'd have a great time together and assured her there were no age restrictions.

Holding the newborn healed something deep inside Khrista and filled her with hope that one day she'd hold her own grandchild close to her chest, too.

"Danielle, I'm truly sorry I put you in that position. You were already having contractions and I left you hanging. I will never, ever behave that way again."

"You are more than forgiven, Khrista. You're amazing. It's not often that people do dumb stuff and then realize they did it. You're good. I promise. But if you want to make it up to me with an offer for free babysitting, I'm not gonna talk you out of it…"

"That should be a given," Khrista said. "I will babysit this precious creature anytime. Anytime at all."

As the baby began to demand a feeding, Khrista handed him back and said her goodbyes.

After leaving Danielle's home, Khrista headed straight to Bess's, relieved and ashamed when Bess so willingly opened her door and let her join her at her table.

"Bess, I know I left you hanging and didn't follow through on my commitment to you. It breaks my heart to think of you waiting for me to show up, and then having to miss out on the tearoom event because of me. I'm so sorry, and I want you to know I'm going to do better." Khrista appreciated the purr of the kitty on her lap as she poured out her heart and the kitty refilled it.

Bess assured her no apology was necessary, but she listened patiently and lovingly as Khrista told her the truth of her estrangement with her mother and daughter, some of what had led to those estrangements, and how she had self-medicated.

When she was done sharing, Bess wiped tears from her own eyes.

"Sweetheart, if there's one thing I can understand, it's grief. And you've been carrying it around all alone. Listening to your story, I think that perhaps grieving for those still living is a worse kind of grief than the sort we go through when someone passes."

Hearing that the complex feelings she had experienced had been grief was a revelation.

"Thank you, Bess. For your understanding, your forgiveness, and your friendship."

Bess thanked her back. "You're inspiring me to fix some things with my children, too."

They made plans to get together later in the week.

Every stop along her Make Amends Tour eased a portion of her anxious burden, yet her nerves lit as she climbed into her car after saying goodbye to Bess. Next on her list was Clarice, and that meant sharing more soul-deep parts of her story than she'd shared thus far.

Khrista arrived at three as Clarice requested. She opened the front door slowly, shocked to see the handwritten sign on the door saying the tearoom would be closed until three-thirty. Clarice never closed in the middle of the day.

Clarice had a steaming pot of mango green tea waiting for Khrista. Khrista thanked her but shook her head as she looked around at the empty tearoom.

"You didn't have to close the shop for me!" Guilt coursed through Khrista. She had thought she'd pull Clarice aside for a few moments during a slow moment.

"Your tone of voice on the phone hinted that you may need some uninterrupted time and an uplifting flavor of tea." Clarice placed two teacups and the small kettle on a table in the center of the room and gestured for Khrista to join. "What's going on with you, hon?"

Khrista inhaled deeply, trying to remember what her sponsor told her about staying calm and centered during these conversations.

"I know you've heard the rumors about my behavior recently."

"You know I pay no mind to rumors. They're a dime a dozen on the island. Don't get me started on that ridiculous Spill The Tea forum online–those people need to learn a thing or two about community. And dragging tea into it like that..." Clarice exhaled forcefully. "Well look at me getting myself going. But I know you. And whatever you've been going through doesn't change where you stand with me."

Khrista stared at the tabletop, mesmerized by the lace doilies under the glass surface.

Clarice deserved eye-to-eye contact, so Khrista fought her way through her cloud of shame and looked her good friend in the eye.

"I kept secrets from you over the years. I didn't want you to see me as a pathetic mother who chased her only daughter away. It was easier to construct a story. To make excuses. To pretend it was Kaelyn's busy life keeping her away." Khrista scratched the back of her neck and hesitated a moment before Clarice's sympathetic listening led the way for Khrista to tell her everything. All the mistakes and heartache. And when she stumbled over the most uncomfortable parts, Clarice soothed her with her compassionate murmurs of understanding.

When she finished unloading, Khrista relaxed into her seat. Clarice might never trust her again. She may never look at her the same way.

But at least she'd know the truth.

"I'm sorry. I shouldn't have lied. And if I hadn't let my drinking get out of control, I wouldn't have flaked on the things I told you I'd do."

Clarice poured herself another cup of tea from the kettle and sat back in her seat. She studied Khrista from across the table.

Khrista fought the urge to squirm.

"You've been carrying around a huge burden. The last thing you should worry about is me." Clarice sipped her tea and kept her focus on Khrista. "We all have our secrets, my friend. And no one is entitled to your truth unless you want to share it."

Khrista released a breath. "You've always been so good to me."

"That's because you deserve to be treated with kindness simply because you exist, not because I expect anything in return. And you've always been equally good to me and everyone else here."

"Not my daughter." Khrista's face blazed. She hadn't expected Clarice's quick redemption, and she certainly didn't deserve to be praised.

"We all make mistakes. Have you ever met a perfect person? I sure as sunrise haven't." A cat Khrista didn't recognize meowed at Clarice's feet, so Clarice bent down to lift the calico kitty onto her lap. "Have you reached out to Kaelyn?"

Khrista picked at her fingernail. "I wrote her a letter, but I don't know if she received it. I'm trying to decide on my next move. All I know is I won't give up this time. I can't expect her to welcome me back into her life, but I need to make sure she knows I realize the mistakes I made and I'm willing to do whatever it takes to make it up to her. And to be a better mom."

"I appreciate your openness now, and I wish you well on your healing journey." Clarice continued stroking the cat in her lap. "But now I owe you an apology. I had no idea you struggled so much when Kaelyn was a little one. Sure, I knew things weren't great for you financially and all, but I wish I had asked you. I could have done more."

"No! I hid the truth from everyone. It would have killed me for people to know how I was living. I couldn't admit I was letting down Kaelyn at that time, anyway. It's taken me a lot of years of reflection to get to this point. Trust me, if you had tried, I would have pushed you away. Believe it or not, I thought I was doing a good job at parenting at the time. All I knew was that I was doing better than my parents did." Khrista's tears flowed. No use trying to stop them at that point. "Clarice, you welcomed me when I got to this island and you've been a great friend since."

"Correction. *Family.* We've been a great family. And I've long believed the family we're born into isn't always the one we're meant to grow with. And relationships don't always mend, but we can always heal."

Khrista surrendered to the sobs that threatened, allowing them to wash away the anguish she had kept to herself for too long. Oh, how she wanted her family to be whole again. She appreciated her found family and the way so many people on the island had wrapped her in their warmth for all these years, but she couldn't quit until she had Kaelyn back in her life. And, as she struggled to be honest with herself, a huge part of her hoped her letter to her mother would begin the path of healing.

"Khrista, I admire the work you're doing. And I know it's going to be a hard road for you. But I'm here. You can trust me to always be here for you." Clarice refilled Khrista's teacup. "And while I can't do the hard work for you, I sure can make you tea."

Khrista burst into a fit of crazed laughter, scaring the cats who lingered in the area into running into one of the side rooms.

Drying her eyes and calming the rush of emotions that had cascaded out of her, Khrista excused herself to head off to check off another box and hopefully repair another relationship, but Clarice stopped her at the door.

"Just remember, Khrista. Forgiveness–for yourself and for others who harmed you–doesn't mean accepting behavior–yours or theirs. It just means accepting that there may have been a reason for their treatment of you that had nothing to do with you. Forgiveness doesn't even have to mean fixing or repairing. It's simply a way of accepting and letting go and moving forward. And if that means building new relationships with the people you love, then that's the mindset you need to hold onto."

KHRISTA PAUSED outside the preschool building, struggling to compose herself. Her heart threatened to leap out of her chest, and though she knew a drink would take the edge off the anxiety, she replaced the image of drinking with the promise of a walk on the beach after her meeting.

Fear crept in. What if she went through all the effort of sobering up and making amends and it turned out the drinking wasn't the actual problem and didn't fix everything?

Khrista closed her eyes and envisioned a giant stop sign–the signal she had agreed she'd picture when changing the direction of her self-sabotaging thoughts. Her sponsor made Khrista write in a journal all the ways she had been working to clean up her life. Quitting the booze was only one of them.

She didn't know if she'd have a job waiting for her or not, but regardless, Susan had been a mentor to Khrista and provided her a job she loved in a place she felt comfortable. She couldn't let the last encounter they'd had be the one Susan thought of most when she thought of Khrista.

Susan greeted her with a warmer than expected smile and a tight hug.

"You're looking so good. How have you been?"

"A lot better, thank you. Certainly better than the last time I saw you."

Susan invited Khrista to sit as she took her seat on the other side of her desk.

"Thank you for making time to meet with me today, Susan. I wanted to clear the air."

Susan didn't respond.

"I need to apologize for my behavior. As you may have guessed, I've been struggling with alcoholism for some time. For a long time, I was able to control it enough so most people didn't suspect anything, and I never came to school drunk. Well, until I did." Khrista paused and thought back to the speech she had carefully rehearsed in front of her bathroom mirror. "I know I lashed out at you, and I'm sorry for that. I'm not here to make excuses. I want you to know I'm undergoing treatment and I have a sponsor and I'm attending meetings every day. I never want to get to that point again."

"Your apology and willingness to hold yourself accountable means a lot to me. That's the Khrista I know and love."

Khrista's limbs relaxed at the gentle acceptance her director offered.

"I'm embarrassed that some of the parents witnessed my condition. I'll do whatever you think would be best to make it up to them."

"Most parents have simply been concerned about you. They want you to come back to work, especially with Danielle out on maternity leave. They want stability for their kids." Susan clasped her hands together and leaned forward on her desk. "*I* want you to come back to work. When you're ready, of course."

That familiar hot ball of emotion clogged her throat. She hadn't expected to be welcomed back so soon–if at all.

She remained in the office for another twenty minutes as they ironed out the details of Khrista's return to work.

On the way out, Susan hugged Khrista again and told her she was glad she'd be back, and assured her she'd handle things on her end and Khrista could focus on being in her teacher state of mind.

Khrista took herself for the walk she had promised herself on a more remote beach on another part of the island–a place most people didn't go even though it provided the best view of the old castle ruins that had given the island its name. She needed time to herself after the emotional onslaught of the day.

After walking the length of the beach and climbing a rocky embankment, she sat on the rocks and watched the boats drift by as people spent their July evening making happy family memories.

Memories she hoped to have the chance to make, too.

**26**

—————

# KAELYN

Kaelyn leaned against Oliver's shoulder as he drove the rental car across the bridge. It was uncomfortable, and the baby didn't seem to appreciate the position, but she wanted to be as close to him as possible as they entered the town that had built her.

"I can see why you loved it here. We haven't even made it onto the island yet, but this view is outstanding."

"The town is an amazing place. I don't think I've ever been anywhere that had the warmth of the island. Even though in the winter months it can be pretty brutal being on the water like that, the warmth of the people more than made up for it."

She sat up in her seat, and Oliver's hand found her knee.

"I have to say, Kaelyn, I'm impressed you wanted to do this. I didn't think flying out here when you're seven months pregnant was exactly the strategy we'd take—I think I pictured more of maybe a Zoom call or maybe even a call on that thing they call a phone?"

He quirked his familiar smile at her, setting the butterflies in her chest to rest.

"But I have to admit, I love seeing the heart you're showing."

Pain shot through her chest. Now that she had allowed herself to feel for her mother again, she couldn't stop beating herself up emotionally for building such an impenetrable wall around her heart. "I can't believe I wasted so many years."

She burst into tears, not for the first time during this pregnancy, but it was probably the strongest flow.

"Oh, love. I can't pull over on the bridge, but I so badly want to hold you."

She gasped for breath amid her sobs and struggled to regain control.

"I'm okay. Keep driving. We just have to make it to Happil-TEA Ever After to get our room before they close up for the night. Clarice offered to stay open in case the traffic was bad leaving Boston, but I don't want to put her out like that."

She took several deep breaths, releasing the strain of the days and the buildup of tears.

"Oliver, I have to tell you something."

"I'm listening, love."

"This isn't my first pregnancy." She blurted out the words, half relieved they no longer belonged to her only and half regretting the risk she took by releasing them from her prison.

He didn't say anything. Oliver didn't give any clue that what she said surprised him or shocked him. He simply listened. He held space for her to unload all she had carried with her for the last five years. All the feelings she hadn't wanted to admit. All the hopes and fears she had kept inside.

"The worst part, the part that's unfurling itself from memories that were either repressed or hidden behind the lies I told myself..."

"Go on." He held her hand tight with his free hand, rubbing the skin on her thumb.

"The night I slammed out of the house, I think I knew she was right about my choices. And especially about Ryan. Like she saw something in him that I couldn't see at that point. I wanted to believe I was in love, but he had been getting dismissive with me and got a bit rough when we fought. I had a temper, so I blamed myself when he'd shove me or whatever. But that night I felt hopeless. Like I had no one and was getting into this enormous responsibility. I couldn't see it then, but Ryan had isolated me from anyone remotely close to me. I wanted to believe I'd get the fairytale ending I longed for, but a voice in my head wondered if my mother was right. But mostly I was just sad. Sad and tired."

Oliver pulled over as soon as they entered the town. The spot overlooked a rocky bluff, and the waves crashing against the shore were reminiscent of the waves crashing over her. Would they consume her and sweep her away, or would they offer healing and restoration?

He shifted the car into park and positioned himself to face her.

He brought his hand to the side of his face, cupping her cheek in his palm and infusing her with his love.

Kaelyn continued to unload the burdens she had carried for too long. "I had a colossal headache and was feeling sore all over, and I wasn't really thinking. I took a few ibuprofen and then took a few more. When Ryan got home we got in a huge screaming match—I'm talking, neighbors called the cops to check on us kind of fight. I was so mad that he didn't try to understand anything about the fight I'd had with my mom, and I took more pain meds, trying to feel better. To numb the pain. I guess I expected him to be more sensitive, and he expected me to not be such a crybaby."

Numbness washed over Kaelyn as she remembered that day. The dark feeling of hopelessness. The desperation to feel better. The need to get out of the hole she had dug for herself.

"I spent so many years blaming my mother for the miscarriage, when in reality I could have been the reason. And if all the meds I took didn't cause it, it could have been the stress I put on myself. Or that Ryan caused. Or maybe it was just nature's way of correcting a mistake I hadn't fully admitted I was making. I'll never know. But it was easier and so convenient to place the blame at my mother's feet."

Things Kaelyn hadn't even known she felt flowed out of her and into Oliver's willing ears. He took his time to process all she was saying, nodding and whispering words of reassurance as she unloaded.

"Kaelyn, you've kept all of that from me for so long. It makes sense now why you haven't been yourself. I can't pretend to understand how pregnancies work or how they feel, but I wish you'd come to me sooner. We are a *team*. We're meant to help one another. When you withhold this kind of information from me, you're not giving me a chance to do my job. To live up to my role or expectations for myself in this relationship."

She nodded. This would be it. Oliver was all about trust and open communication. He wouldn't like that she had kept the secret. What might not have been a big deal if she had shared it all along could be what led to her having to share her child every other weekend. Or maybe he would get full custody and she would go off being the crazed wannabe mother she never dreamed she'd be.

"Stop thinking those negative thoughts," he said, tilting her chin upward, forcing her to meet his eyes. "Yes, I wish you told me, love. I don't want secrets between us."

"I know..."

He interrupted. "The only thing that changes is that it brings me closer to you. You made a mistake. Even if the miscarriage was your responsibility, it's not unusual for something like that to happen. You were young, upset, distracted. Maybe part of you knew you weren't ready to be a mother. And that's okay."

Oliver shifted once again in his seat, turning to face her more. "Now, blaming your mother all these years... that must be a hard one for you to have been living with. But all of that is in the past. You were barely a woman at that time, but you are a fully functioning, compassionate, driven woman now and there is not a single doubt in my mind that I chose the right woman to be my life partner. I don't think there's a single thing you could tell me that would make me want to leave you or would make me think less of you."

She hiccuped and prayed he was being honest. That he didn't blame her. That he didn't hate her. That he wouldn't change his mind.

"This baby, our baby, will have two imperfect, loving parents. We will help balance each other out. We will point out when the other one is messing things up and will do our best to fix it. We will learn from the mistakes we've made and the mistakes our parents have made, and someday our children will learn from our mistakes and make different mistakes with their children. Kaelyn, I love you. I love our baby. And nothing will change that."

Heart restored and shield down, she couldn't stop all of her truths from rolling out. "I don't want to keep working. After the baby's born, I mean. I want to be a stay-at-home mom, at least for the baby's first year. I haven't wanted to tell you because we just bought the new house and you've always said you admired my work ethic, but I can't stand the thought of anyone else spending more time with my baby than I do."

No more filters existed between them, and everything poured out of her, but it felt good. Like a healthy cleanse.

He laughed and shook his head. "I admire everything about you. If you want to stay home with our baby, I'd love it. If you want to keep your job, I'd love it. If you want me to take time off and be a stay-at-home dad, we'll figure it out and I'm sure I'd love it, too. I don't think you're understanding the depth of my love and adoration for you."

"We can't afford the house if I quit."

He shrugged.

"It's just a house. And it's the house you wanted. I'd be content living in a tent with you."

The amount of love she felt for this man overwhelmed her. She had lucked out, and she thanked her lucky stars for transferring to the college in California. Even though the circumstances that had led her to run away had been dire and Kaelyn hadn't thought positively about them even once, she knew now that if things hadn't gone that way, she never would have met the love of her life.

He smacked her lightly and playfully on the thigh.

"Now let's go get settled so we can go see your mom and make up for lost time."

He kissed her so tenderly, with so much love, that even the baby settled down inside her womb for a peaceful nap.

RIGHT AS THEY pulled up in front of the Happil-TEA Ever After Tea Room, Kaelyn's phone buzzed. Clarice called to tell her that her mother had just arrived for her evening tea, and that Clarice had encouraged her to sit in the library room since it was empty. If Kaelyn hurried in, they'd have the whole room to themselves and Clarice would close it off to other patrons.

"You want me to go in with you or wait out here?" Oliver's hand on her lower back steadied her, and his soothing voice did the same. She grabbed his hand and pulled him in with her, the heat of his body sending signals to remind her to walk and not fall over on her face. She didn't need another incident.

Kaelyn paused in the doorway, unable to breathe as she watched her mother from across the room. She studied the lines around her mom's eyes as the lanterns above her head cast shadows. Lines that hadn't been there five years ago. Her mother had always looked young for her age, but now she looked like the world had crushed her.

Kaelyn stepped back and hid on the other side of the wall as a sob tore out of her. She bit her knuckles to keep it contained.

Why had she waited so long to figure things out? To realize what was important?

"Go on, love," Oliver urged.

Clarice rushed over as soon as she finished serving the customers who had lined up at the counter. She wrapped Kaelyn in a hug and gushed about how much she had missed seeing her and how happy she had been to get her call.

"You look absolutely stunning. Here, drink up." Clarice handed her a small water bottle. "You look just like her. Even more so than you did as a teen."

"I'm not sure I can do this."

Oliver rubbed her back, but Clarice filled her with the courage she needed.

"Your mother has been doing a lot of work to make things right in her world and in yours. But it's been a trying day for her. Seeing you is going to help her stay strong."

Kaelyn sipped the water Clarice had so kindly given her, then held it out for Oliver to have a sip.

"Go ahead," he urged. "Say what you need to say."

Tears trickled down her cheeks. She let them sit there, itching her skin and reminding her of the complicated path that had led to this moment.

She stepped into the room. Her mother continued staring down at the cat in her lap, seemingly tuned out of the world around her.

"Mama." Kaelyn's voice sounded childlike to her own ears. Her inhibitions melted away as her mother looked up.

Kaelyn walked closer, stronger and more sure than ever.

"Mama, I got your letter. Your calligraphy was beautiful. Way better than mine. You wrote much longer letters than I used to, too. I'm so impressed."

Kaelyn hesitated, having no idea how to fill the silence as her thoughts whirled in a tornado formation in her scattered mind.

"Kaelyn..." Khrista looked as if a ghost had turned up to haunt the library room. Her eyes widened and she didn't blink. Her mouth gaped, and she looked alarmed.

Kaelyn rubbed her growing baby bump and walked closer. *Just keep talking.* "I love the blanket you made for our little nugget. It will be the one blanket we wrap her in the most, and she'll always know her grandmother made it with love."

Kaelyn's shoulders shook with unspent sobs as she struggled to maintain her composure.

Her mom remained seated. Kaelyn didn't know what she had expected, but she hadn't imagined she'd send her mother into shocked silence.

She took another step closer.

"Mama, I remember all the good times we had when I was little. Remember how you used to let me run into the tide and jump over the incoming waves, even on warm days in the winter? Nobody else's parents let them do that, but I loved it. And remember when you dragged our TV out to the yard to have a drive-in movie with my friends? Even though we couldn't afford to go to the real drive-in, you made that day special. My friends loved the little boxes you decorated to look like cars and the homemade popcorn you brought out. I still don't know what your secret ingredient was in the sweet popcorn you made, but I'm gonna need you to tell it to me so I can have some cool mama moments, too."

Tears streamed down Khrista's face, but she remained frozen in her spot.

"It's okay if you don't want to say anything yet. You said so much in your letter. Now I want to tell you what's been on my mind."

Kaelyn kept talking, all the positive memories breaking free from the chains of the negative memories she had allowed herself to dwell on for so many years. She felt the weight of the angsty, mean teenager who was full of grudges leaving her body as the little girl clung onto the happy memories and the good times her mother had tried so hard to give her. The memories Kaelyn had fought so hard to suppress so she wouldn't hurt so much at the loss of her mom.

The more she talked, the brighter the light around her mother seemed to be. What Kaelyn had so easily dismissed as bad parenting now seemed like the actions of a desperate mother who originated from a difficult childhood and struggled to overcome things no child should have to overcome.

"Grandma told me about your childhood, and about how badly she and Grandpa treated you. I didn't know things were so bad. I only saw things through my own lens, and I had no heart for forgiveness when I felt you had hurt me so badly. But all along, you were the one hurting deep inside, by things I can't even fathom. I turned into a spoiled brat, and though I know you know you made mistakes, you also protected me from so many of the things you had to endure. I resented you for taking me away from Grandpa and Grandma and Daddy, but you never betrayed my positive memories of them by filling me in on the truth. What an act of love that was, and how hard that must have been for you to carry around, knowing I was judging you for things I was wrong about."

Kaelyn got close enough to reach out and touch her mom. She hesitated.

And then she watched as something shifted in Khrista's eyes and she came to life. A bright light shone in the loving depths, and she gently placed the cat to the side and jumped out of her seat. A tiny gasp escaped Khrista's throat and she pulled Kaelyn as close as the baby bump would allow. Her mother's thin arms practically strangled Kaelyn as she tightened them around her neck, but Kaelyn wouldn't pull away for anything.

Kaelyn lost it then. She no longer had any semblance of control over her emotions, and let them all pour out onto her mother's shoulder.

"Mama, I'm sorry I hurt you. I'm sorry I made things hard, and I'm sorry I didn't understand. No matter what happens, I hope you can know I forgive you. I forgive you for every mistake and every way you hurt me, whether you meant to or not. And even more importantly..." She choked on a sob, struggling to get the words out that were so very hard to say. "I hope you'll be able to forgive *me*."

The baby kicked furiously as if all the pain washing through Kaelyn caused a disruption.

Khrista must have felt it, because she pulled away and cradled Kaelyn's belly in her hands, staring at it as if it was the most magical thing she'd ever seen. She reached up and wiped tears off Kaelyn's cheeks and then planted a delicate kiss there.

"Oh, my sweet baby girl. There's nothing for me to forgive. I love you more than you could ever know, and I'm sorry you ever had to doubt that." Khrista placed her hands on Kaelyn's dampened cheeks, and Kaelyn covered her mom's hands with her own. "I want us to get to know each other again. We can start fresh and look forward, not back."

Kaelyn nodded as a fresh wave of tears erupted. "I'd like that."

They clung to each other for several moments, and the longer their hearts beat next to one another, the more certain Kaelyn was that this time things would be the way she had always dreamed they'd be.

# DAISY

Daisy sat in Rafael's living room, waiting for him to get back with the pizza he had picked up from his restaurant. He told her all about the special brick oven he had imported from Italy and insisted she try the pizza. She had tried to tell him she'd head back into town earlier, but he had insisted she stay and wait for Khrista to return home. As the hours ticked by and she and Rafael didn't run out of conversation, she grew more and more comfortable in his presence.

Just as her stomach started growling, he strolled in. He held a letter in his hands and handed it to her.

"This was left by Khrista's box. It appears to be addressed to you, but was returned to sender, which appeared to have been Khrista."

Daisy stared at the envelope, unable to believe Khrista had actually written to her. Her heart thumped faster in her chest, and she wondered about the health of that organ.

She tore the letter open, forgetting Rafael was there. Forgetting where she was. Sliding back in time or an alternate universe, perhaps.

. . .

DEAR MOTHER,

I didn't know I would ever write this letter, but I think at fifty years old I'm finally maturing. Losing my daughter to estrangement has taught me a lot of lessons about life.

I didn't think I'd ever be able to forgive you for hurting me. I blamed you for a long time for not protecting me from Harold, and there are still things we haven't talked about and probably never will about the time you made your getaway and left me behind with an angry man who would punish me in any way he knew how. Turns out he knew how in many ways I had never even considered.

I don't say this to hurt you more. I think you've paid your penance. I think I've learned as I've grown older and as I've studied parenting and child development that the hurt you endured influenced how much you were capable of protecting me, and you were hurt long before I was. I'm sure you know all the things you did wrong, and we don't need to rehash those. I hurt my daughter, too. Not in all the same ways, but it had the same effect. She left me just as I left you.

The last day I saw you way back then, I've come to realize you probably did believe that inviting Kaelyn's father to your house when I had been trying to get away from him was for the best. All you had ever known was abuse from the men in your life, but you also knew stability from having a man who paid the mortgage and kept food on the table. Maybe you thought you could help us get back together. I'm trying to believe you had my best interests at heart, even if they were misguided.

I'm sure it hurt you to see me struggling while trying to raise a young girl. I didn't love living out of shelters for those times when I had to move around to hide from him after that incident, but at least we were safe. You broke my trust that day when you encouraged us to visit, and I knew if I didn't get away, the cycle would continue and Kaelyn would be the next victim.

For that, I don't regret leaving. You never would have developed the strength to stand up to Harold, and I don't even think you would have encouraged me to have the strength to stand up to my abuser.

But I know you're now free. I think when someone is free from the prison of an abusive lifestyle, they can change. You can't undo what was *done, and maybe you don't even know enough to regret it yet, but I do believe you have all of our best interests in mind by trying to make amends and reconnect. I'm sure you didn't know how much it would hurt me to get to the baby shower and learn that it wasn't Kaelyn who wanted me there. Looking back, I feel like you were trying to do something good.*

*I realize now as I heal my inner wounds and fight to find a way to stop the flow of self-destruction that if I want a relationship with my daughter and if I hope for her to forgive me for my transgressions and my weaknesses that I need to forgive you as well.*

*None of us asked for this lot in life, but it is what we were given. And I hope we can do our best to appreciate the tide that flows onto the sandy beach of our lives. A beach filled with debris and danger, but also with beauty.*

*I forgive you, Mom. I hope you can forgive me, too.*

*With love,*

*Khrista*

DAISY'S HANDS shook as she placed the letter on her lap, unable to take her eyes off of it.

"Everything okay over there?"

Rafael's concerned words and tone delivered comfort she hadn't known she needed. She shook her head, then nodded, then shook her head and nodded again. She couldn't make up her mind.

Would her daughter accept Daisy's presence there on her island, where she had nestled in to find safety all those years ago?

What if her daughter extended this olive branch, but she never intended to have Daisy grasp the other end?

What if the time had finally come where they could put their past behind and forge a new future built on the foundation of love and healing, and Daisy messed it up by going there without asking first?

Daisy sobbed, sure she would float away on a river of her misery. Her sadness overwhelmed her and her hopes slipped.

Rafael rushed over and sat on the edge of the couch and pulled her into his arms. She took his comfort, cocooned in the strength of his arms. She should have been afraid of him, this large man who could snap her in half, but something told her he would never do such a thing.

"I don't know what that letter said, but I know Khrista's heart. She's a fighter. She's fierce and strong and scrappy. I could tell you stories about how she handled college boys who came to the island on breaks and tried to get fresh with the waitstaff, but I don't want to shock your ears. But she was also the first one to pay for someone's meal if she thought they were having a tough day. Right out of her own paycheck, even as a struggling single mother. And she was the first one to volunteer to come in earlier if I needed her. That girl you raised has a heart of gold, and no matter what came between the two of you, she'll want to make it better. I know it."

She felt the warmth of his lips pressing on the top of her head.

She should tell him that wasn't appropriate, but she didn't care. Daisy appreciated his warmth, his kind spirit, and the fact that even though he probably knew more about her than she wished he did, he found it in his heart to comfort her anyway.

A text notification buzzed on Daisy's phone, and she held it up to read it.

"It's a text from Kaelyn. She's here on the island and made peace with her mom. She wants me to come to the island–she doesn't know I'm already here. Says Khrista mentioned wanting to work things out with me, too."

Shock froze Daisy in her seat. Her limbs grew heavy and immovable. A roaring in her ears picked up tempo, drowning out whatever Rafael was saying.

Without thinking, she reached her shaking hands up, grabbed the sides of Rafael's face, and dragged his head down to kiss his lips in gratitude for giving her the letter and offering her such kind words at her emotional moment.

And then she collapsed on the floor.

# 28

## KHRISTA

The process of making amends hadn't been the most pleasant. But she would do it over a thousand times if it meant that each time she would end her day with the surprise of having her daughter sitting by her side.

The days that followed were ones Khrista would keep etched in her mind for the rest of her life. Days spent getting to know her Kaelyn all over again. And though she hadn't slept well since Kaelyn surprised her with her arrival, she had never been happier, even if the happiness was tinged with concern for Daisy.

"Any word from the hospital?" Kaelyn asked right after greeting Khrista.

"She's doing great! They wouldn't give me any information other than to say she's out of the ICU, but they also said we can go see her today."

"Oh, yay! She'll be so happy." Kaelyn stood by the table and pushed her burgeoning belly toward Khrista. "Baby wants you to say hello. She's jumping all over the place."

Khrista reached out eagerly, closing her eyes to the sensation of the rolling movements beneath her palm.

"It's a girl?"

Khrista felt more awake than ever.

Kaelyn grinned and sent a knowing smile in the direction of her husband, Oliver, who stayed quietly and happily by Kaelyn's side, consistently rubbing Kaelyn's back or shoulders or holding her hand as he asked polite questions and seemed to accept Khrista as an instant family member. He seemed like a nice guy, and obviously madly in love with Khrista's daughter. Khrista had never been the best judge of character, but she liked to believe that since she had chosen Matt for herself and he had turned out to be the cream of the crop, that perhaps her instincts were getting better.

"Well, Oliver thought from the beginning it would be a girl. And I've come to realize that Oliver is always right."

Oliver pulled his phone out of his pocket with a stunned look on his face.

"Hold on. I need you to say that again so I can record it for posterity."

Laughing hurt Khrista's lack-of-sleep headache, but it sure healed her heart.

THE NURSE at the hospital greeted Khrista, Kaelyn, and Oliver with the best news—not only could they go into the room to visit Daisy, but she'd also be released later that day.

"You're sure you're ready for this?" Kaelyn asked, a look of concern warring with excitement.

Khrista nodded. She was ready. She wanted to complete the circle of healing so they could welcome Kaelyn's baby into the warm folds of a matriarchal line where love was the energy that kept things running.

"But I think I should go in alone. You and Oliver can go grab a slice of pie from the cafeteria. They always have the best pies in hospital cafeterias."

Kaelyn eventually relented, especially with Oliver practically drooling over the mention of pie.

Khrista watched them as they strolled away. They couldn't stop touching one another, and Khrista loved how playful they were together.

She hadn't had the urge to drink for days. She never wanted to try to escape this reality again. It was too beautiful.

"You can come in now." The nurse opened the door and stepped aside so Khrista could enter.

Khrista willed her frozen legs to carry her in.

For several days, she had waited for this moment. She couldn't run from this necessary step in her healing process now.

She didn't plan to rehash the past—their letters to one another had served that purpose—but she wanted to begin their new relationship on solid ground and positive footing.

When Khrista first glimpsed her mother sitting in the hospital bed, she felt transported back in time. Yes, her mother had aged, but more than anything, Khrista noticed the absence of anger and cruelty etched in the lines of her face. This was not a woman who looked like she'd lash out in anger at her child. She didn't look like the kind of woman who would turn a blind eye when her husband was abusing a little girl.

Remorse was written on her face like graffiti under a bridge. Loud, vibrant, and slightly artistic and beautiful if you could see past the surface or the stereotypical expectations.

Khrista had long outgrown the need for someone to parent her. But knowing that a thread that had been severed so brutally now grew stronger gave Khrista hope that the quilt of their family, with all the repaired threads interwoven into a patchwork of recovered beauty, would allow them to create family traditions and stop the cycle of family harm.

Of all the things Khrista had lost, hope had been the hardest to exist without.

Her mother stared at her, and Khrista sensed she felt the same uncertainty and insecurity Khrista felt about how to bridge the gap of time and pain.

"Mom, how are you feeling?"

Her mom sniffled and swiped at a tissue she had balled up in her hand.

"Hearing you call me Mom makes me feel brand new. I never thought I'd hear that word again."

"I don't want to make you cry."

Daisy waved her hand in the air dismissively, sending the IV connected to her arm flailing.

"Let's not go there. The past is in the past, and this is a blank slate, but we're bound to have emotions creep in. We both know what we've done and we both know we don't want to pay the price any longer. Let's just move forward. New day, new smile."

And then Daisy did as she said they should, and her smile warmed Khrista as deeply as a child sitting in front of a plate of warm chocolate chip cookies, their ooey-gooey centers baked by a loving mom.

"You got my letter? Raf said he found it by my mailbox."

Daisy inhaled deeply, then fiddled with her hospital bracelet.

"I did. And it was the most beautiful thing I've ever read." She stifled a high-pitched inhalation. "Khrista, I was so wrong to allow you to be hurt so much. To hurt you so much. If I could turn back time, I'd do it all over again. I didn't know anything about being a good mother, and I–"

"Shh, Mom, it's okay. I understand now. It took me longer than I wish it had, but I understand. We were both victims of Harold's." Khrista moved to the edge of the bed so she could place a hand on her mother's. "Tell me what's going on with your health."

"Before I left Virginia, right before I sold the family home, though I should've just burned it down and charcoaled those memories— anyway, that's neither here nor there—before I sold the house, I got news from my doctor that I had some heart troubles."

"Mom!"

The despair that emerged from Khrista's throat sent tremors of fear down her own spine. Had she regained her mother's love in her life only to lose it again?

"It's rather treatable. I had declined treatment before because I didn't want to waste time in hospitals when I could focus on fixing relationships, but now that I know the fragility of life and now that I have you and Kaelyn to live for, I agreed to the surgery and treatments."

She suddenly looked bashful, staring at her lap before looking up through her lowered head.

"I don't want to waste any more moments with you, Khrista. I was thinking maybe I could settle down in Old Castle. I'll get my own place of course. I have plenty of money because of the life insurance and the sale of the home, and of course, I plan to set some aside for you and Kaelyn and the new baby, but I'd like to buy a little place near the beach. Knowing how much you loved the ocean, I always wanted to go there, but he-who-shall-never-be-named-again refused to take me, or would promise to take me and then back out at the last minute. Anyway, this place you've chosen as home already feels like home to me. Would you mind terribly if I stayed?"

Khrista didn't have to think twice. "I'd mind terribly if you left. I think it's a brilliant idea for you to stay."

The nurse knocked on the door before entering. "Sorry to cut this short, but I have some discharge papers."

The doctor wanted to meet with Daisy one more time to go over some things, so the nurse asked Khrista to step out. She reluctantly retreated to the waiting room down the hall. Khrista sent a quick text to Kaelyn letting her know she'd be bringing her grandma down to see her in a moment.

Khrista paced the small waiting room and was startled by a familiar voice behind her.

She turned to face Matt, who handed her an iced chai latte from Happil-TEA Ever After.

"Now that you seem like you're fully in your own mind, we have things to talk about."

"Oh, Matt. I've been wanting to see you, but haven't wanted to bother you. How did you find me here?"

"I have my sources." He winked, melting any ice that flowed in her veins. "I met your daughter, by the way. Nice girl. And never let it be said that Clarice doesn't excel in her matchmaking skills."

So many questions filled Khrista's mind, but more than anything she couldn't stop staring at the love on his handsome face.

"Matt, I swear things are different now–that I'm different now–but I meant what I said when I set you free. I hope to deserve you one day, but I won't force it or make you feel bad."

"That's a relief," Matt said.

That was an odd response. Khrista had to admit, she had hoped for a big romantic gesture and that he would pull her into his arms and tell her he couldn't live without her and that he could see the good in her even when she couldn't see it herself.

Instead, he sat in the chair on the opposite side of the room, tapping his hand frantically against his bouncing leg.

"Are you okay? You seem super antsy."

"I've never been better. Just a little anxious about what I'm about to ask you."

Khrista sat on a chair across from him.

"I told you, Matt. I'll tell you the truth about whatever you want to know. I'm never lying to you or anyone else again. I'm never going back to the person I had made myself into. Not really for you, not for anyone. But for me. Because I feel now that I deserve health and happiness. I've never felt that way before, so it's a little strange for me to say it. But I promise I will *never* lie to you again. I regret it more than the harm I did to myself."

He slipped off his chair and onto his knees, grabbing her hand between his two.

"I'm delighted to hear you say that because I've always felt the same. About you deserving all the good things, that is. And married couples shouldn't have secrets or lies between them, do you agree?"

She attempted to swallow past her dry throat, and the sting of tears pricked at her eyes.

"Married couples?"

Matt nodded and removed a ring box from his pocket.

He flipped it open, revealing a gorgeous ring with an aquamarine stone riding on a wave-shaped setting. Every curvature of the wave possessed a tiny diamond, giving the illusion of water shimmering in the sunlight.

"Will you make my life complete and spend your life working with me to always better ourselves and each other? Will you be my wife?"

Khrista couldn't answer with words, but her head nodded enthusiastically. He let out an uncharacteristic whoop, and several nurses, accompanied by Kaelyn and Oliver, rushed in holding flowers and a bejeweled tiara. They laughed and teased as they called themselves bridesmaids, and with a tiara on her head and the beautiful scent of flowers promising a new life, she couldn't take her eyes off the man whose light shone brightly on her.

He slipped the ring on her finger as their audience clapped.

Khrista's life had changed so drastically over the last few weeks, and she wanted to keep the momentum going. "I want to meet your children. As soon as possible. I'm done with waiting for the good things in life for when everything is perfect on my end. I will never be perfect, and circumstances will never be ideal, but life's too short to live for perfection."

"I was also hoping you'd say that. They couldn't make it for a spontaneous engagement party tonight, but Nia has already started the planning process for later in the week."

She burst into a grin.

"Feeling pretty confident about my answer, were you?"

"A man can have hopes. And you have always been mine."

The nurse who had been with her mother wheeled Daisy in.

Daisy's face lit up as she greeted Khrista. "Did I overhear something about an engagement?"

"Good thing you're planning to stay close by, Mom, because it seems as though I'll need you to give me away."

Khrista held up her hands to flash the beautiful ring at her mom, who clucked her tongue against the roof of her mouth and held her hand out, demanding to see the ring on Khrista's finger up close. Daisy raved about Matt's exquisite taste, and then they both did something neither had ever done with the other.

They cried.

And then they talked about their visions of an ideal wedding.

Oh, how her life had changed overnight.

Though even as she had the thought, she knew it wasn't true. It hadn't changed overnight. It had changed as the product of three strong women who didn't know they were strong, analyzing their own lives and reflecting on the past in new and fresh ways. And then realizing that no amount of strife could make them unwilling to put in the work to repair relationships. As long as they were all putting in the work, there was no way they would fail.

As they wheeled Daisy through the hospital, Khrista filled Kaelyn in on Daisy's plan to stay on the island.

"I know," Kaelyn said, a mysterious grin on her lips as she looked over at Khrista. "We talked about it in-depth while you and Matt were getting the rundown from the doctor. We kind of had to coordinate, because we're both going to be in the market to buy a new place, and we wanted to make sure we didn't fight over the same property. Not to mention Oliver's mom, who we are *pretty* sure agreed to relocate as well."

Khrista couldn't have heard right. She paused in the lobby, and everyone stopped in their tracks and watched her.

"I'm sure I'm dreaming right now."

Kaelyn laughed and pinched her mom's arm.

"Nope. Not a dream. Hopefully, it won't turn into your worst nightmare to all of a sudden have four generations of us here in the same town."

"Are you kidding?" Khrista couldn't see through her tears. "I am the luckiest person on the planet, and I'm trying hard to believe I deserve to be this happy."

"Mama, we've already wasted too much time, and I want all of us here together so we can do the work we need to do. It'll take us a little time for Oliver to transfer his job to the East Coast, or to find a new one if they won't allow him to transfer, and we have to sell the house we just bought. But I only bought that house, I realize now, because it reminded me of Old Castle. And though I never would have admitted this a few months ago, it reminded me of you. It made me feel like I was closer to you, even though I truly believed I would never have you in my life again."

Khrista watched with gratitude and admiration as Oliver comforted Kaelyn. She reached out and grasped Kaelyn's hand, and together they cried it out, and then they hugged it out, and then they climbed into their cars to head straight to Happil-TEA Ever After to celebrate their full reunification in the heart of the island. Khrista made a quick detour to her apartment, but they all arrived at the tearoom within minutes of one another.

Clarice beamed as they entered the tearoom. Her knowing smile filled Khrista's mind with words she could hear as clearly as if Clarice were speaking them. Words Clarice had once uttered, long before Khrista had been ready to fully receive them.

*We only get one life to live. Might as well fill it with love.*

And though the struggle to get to this moment–this beautiful moment in this beautiful place surrounded by beautiful people who filled her heart with more joy than she ever imagined she'd deserve– had been arduous, she would go through every moment of the painful process again if it led her this far.

Once Khrista got everyone seated in her favorite area, all of them gushing over the cats that swarmed them, she privately conferred with Clarice, who didn't ask any questions before fulfilling Khrista's whispered request.

While waiting for Clarice to pull it all together, Khrista surprised her daughter with a gift she hoped would warm her heart.

"What's this?" Kaelyn asked as she took the grocery bag from Khrista–she hadn't had time to do any fancy wrapping.

"Open it." Khrista couldn't hide her grin.

Kaelyn pulled the raggedy doll out of the bag and squealed so loud, Oliver jumped. "Priscilla! I didn't know you still had her!"

Kaelyn hugged the falling-apart doll close to her chest and sobbed into her frayed yarn hair.

"I can't believe you kept her all this time. I didn't think I had anything sentimental anymore. Thank you, Mama. You have no idea what this means to me."

"Of course I kept her. You said you didn't want her once it became uncool to have a doll, but I couldn't bring myself to let her get thrown away. I hoped that one day you'd love her again."

Khrista's heart nearly imploded as she watched the faces of her daughter and her mother as Clarice carried the tray of baked goodies with the lit birthday candles to the table.

And though she could barely squeeze any sound out of her emotion-clogged throat, and though tears streamed down her cheeks and she couldn't stop blubbering, Khrista sang the "happy birthday" song with all the off-key gusto she could summon.

She had missed far too many birthdays. They all had. And yet, the birth of every one of the people surrounding the table had been the moment that had cemented their places in her world. They had a lot of missed time to make up for. They'd have challenges as they continued working to correct the past.

And yet today was the birth of a new life.

Their new life together.

The matching tears and bright smiles that greeted her as she encouraged each of her loved ones to blow out the candles helped Khrista to know that the life they all forged together would be as smooth as a perfectly steeped cup of tea.

*TURN the page to read the epilogue :)*

*Visit Amanda's website for more information about the Old Castle world: AmandaDaire.com*

*Return to Old Castle and follow the O'Donnell women along their journey toward reconnection in* Old Castle Sparkle.

*For exclusive content and to stay up-to-date, sign up for Amanda's newsletter on her website: amandadaire.com*

# EPILOGUE

A fall wedding.

Could anything be more perfect?

Well, yes. A fall *beach* wedding. A fall beach wedding right outside Khrista's second home–Happil-TEA Ever After Tea Room.

The moments leading up to the event both cruised and dragged.

Khrista stared at her phone and fought the temptation to call Matt. She longed to hear his voice. To video chat so she could see his face. To let his calm manner soothe her frayed nerves and help her believe this fairytale ending was actually in the cards for her.

"Stop looking at that phone like you're hoping your knight in shining armor will burst out of it," Daisy chastised. "Get over here and sit yourself down. The manicurist is all set up, and Nia has a question about the polish you prefer."

Khrista grinned. She'd been doing a lot of that over the past couple of months, but having this special time with Matt's girls and her mother made her cheeks hurt more than she imagined they could. They had insisted on having a bachelorette evening of sorts, and Matt's girls had been adamant that Khrista and Matt not see each other for a full twenty-four hours before the wedding. Since Kaelyn was still recovering from a difficult birth six weeks prior, Khrista had insisted she stay home and rest so she'd be ready for the big day. Kaelyn had been uncharacteristically quiet about Khrista's insistence, but Daisy assured Khrista that she had spoken to Kaelyn and she was fine with it.

And though Khrista missed having Kaelyn there with her, she cherished the time she got to spend with Gabby, Aliyah, and Nia.

Finally meeting Matt's children shortly after the engagement had healed the last cracks in Khrista's previously shattered heart. From hearing Matt's stories over the years, Khrista had known she would adore his adult kids, but seeing them make quick friends with Kaelyn and Oliver and the genuine kindness they each displayed to Khrista had settled Khrista's anxiety immediately. After three years of avoiding them because she missed her estranged daughter so much, she had worried they'd somehow see through her and hate her for the avoidance. But they didn't. Each of his daughters had not only hugged her tight but had smiled brightly and opened the doors to their lives wide enough for her to walk in with all of her baggage.

Baggage she worked every day to declutter.

"Khrista. Stop that daydreaming. They're waiting," Daisy admonished once again.

Though there would have been a time when the idea of her mother ordering her around would have triggered her and had her digging her feet in and refusing to budge, now the lighthearted urgency brought joy. After so many years of motherlessness, and too many years of life with a mother who hadn't been equipped to parent, Khrista allowed herself to relax under the glow of a woman who now wanted to be the mother she had never been.

Khrista understood her mother's position so much better now. Losing Kaelyn for all those years had been the deepest pain Khrista had ever endured. Missing her daughter had cut deeper than any of the abuse Khrista's father had dished out, so she intended to revel in the comfort of both mothering and daughtering for as long as she could.

"I'm coming, I'm *coming!*" Khrista fiddled with the cuff of the plush robe Gabby had gifted her, trying to decide between rolling up the sleeves and keeping them down. When she finally looked up, the first person her gaze landed on was Kaelyn.

Khrista opened her arms and folded Kaelyn into her embrace. "Kaelyn! What are you doing here? I thought you were going to rest up?"

Kaelyn squeezed her mom. "No way would I miss your last night as a single woman. I can't stay long because I left Poppy with her daddy, but I was definitely not about to miss this. No matter what you said." Kaelyn stuck her tongue out at her mother, as saucy as she had always been.

Nia, Aliyah, Gabby, and Daisy gathered around, questioning Kaelyn on everything from how she was feeling to how the baby was eating and sleeping.

"I'm still sore at times, and I'm eager to fit into my old clothes again, but she's perfect. Last night she actually slept three hours in a row. Of course, I kept waking up to check her breathing, but it's nice to imagine that Oliver and I will start getting some sleep sometime soon."

"Well, you look fantastic," Gabby complimented, looking every bit like the doting sister she had become since the girls met.

Nia excused herself to check in with the manicurist in the adjoining room and then ushered them all in. She paused at the door to ask Khrista, "Matching polish for everyone, or individual choice?"

"Definitely individual choice. We're not doing anything formal or overly traditional."

"Maybe we should all stick with an ocean color scheme?" Gabby offered.

"I'll leave it up to all of you," Khrista said. "Whatever gets your wave rolling."

The four young women groaned in unison.

"Mom, are we to expect corny ocean references all the way until you say 'I do'?"

"Do you mean until I've *tide* the knot?" Khrista put her arm around her daughter's shoulder and pulled her in so she could kiss the top of Kaelyn's head. "*Shell*, yeah. 'Tis appropriate for the *sea*-son, amiright?"

The woman enjoyed laughs as they took turns having their nails done. Khrista couldn't remember the last time she'd been pampered like this. It felt strange, and she wasn't sure it was quite her cup of tea, but she went along with it since it seemed so important to the family for her to be as put together as possible. She certainly didn't want to embarrass any of them. But if it had been left up to her, she would have married Matt in a potato sack in the middle of a muddy field. Didn't matter. What mattered was anchoring their hearts and preparing for the next chapter.

"Hey, Kaelyn," Aliyah began, handing cold bottles of seltzer water to each of the attendees as they settled into the couches with their freshly done nails. "You've probably answered this a million times, but I'm curious about the name you chose for your little angel. I love it, by the way. It's just not one I've heard much."

"Oh, don't worry. There's nothing I like to talk about as much as my baby girl." Kaelyn sipped her water and sighed. "Oliver and I had several names picked out, but after the long and harder-than-antici-pated labor—who knew there was such a thing as a baby coming out sunny-side up?—I took one look at her and knew she would be as strong and resilient as a wildflower, and whenever I think of poppies I think *peace*. Her existence in the world not only brought me a sense of peace and comfort, but I also believe she changed me. Made it easier for me to seek peace within my family. And so Poppy became Poppy, and luckily Oliver agreed. I honestly don't think I could have called her anything else."

All the women in the room sighed collectively, including the manicurist who was packing up her things. Kaelyn laughed at their reaction.

"It's also sort of a tribute to another special wildflower." Kaelyn reached over to grab Daisy's hand as Daisy walked by on her way back to the kitchen after placing a tray of vegetables and dip on the coffee table. "A subtle way of naming my girl after a special grandma."

Khrista clapped her hands over her mouth as she watched Daisy's face alight with surprise and then dissolve into a puddle of emotion.

"Grandma, don't you dare cry. You'll get me going, and it's not fair because my hormones are still all over the place. I meant for you to smile."

Khrista jumped in to rescue her loved ones from washing away in a flood of tears. She hugged her mother from behind and smiled at Kaelyn as tears streamed down Kaelyn's face.

Kaelyn sniffled and straightened in her seat. "You think you can remain so stoic, Mother Dearest," Kaelyn teased. "Just wait until..."

Khrista held her breath as Kaelyn leaned down to retrieve a small pouch from her purse. Daisy shuffled to the other side of the room in search of a tissue, and Khrista appreciated how Nia and Aliyah both offered comfort to Daisy.

"What's this?" Khrista stared at the pouch in Kaelyn's hands. Her hands shook as she accepted the black velvet. The slight weight of the contents in her palm and the softness of the velvet jolted her back in time to when Kaelyn had first handed a pouch just like this to her mother.

"Remember when we did that Secret Santa thing in third grade and I was allowed to buy something for you from the little shop the PTA set up?"

Khrista nodded, too choked up to respond.

"And then do you remember when I was a raging brat and took it back because I was mad at you?"

"You weren't a raging brat, baby girl. I let you down, and you didn't know how to express your feelings."

Kaelyn made a face. "I was a brat. Yes, I was mad at you, but when I took it back, it was because I wanted to hurt you."

"You were a powerless child trying to—"

Kaelyn laughed. "I don't need you to make excuses for me, Mom. Open it up."

Khrista hesitated. All the memories of Kaelyn's sad and angry face tore at Khrista's insides. Khrista had promised Kaelyn she could have friends over, but when the time came, Khrista hadn't been able to muster the energy to clean up the house like she had promised she would. With a sick cat and months of Khrista not having the energy to clean, she'd had to tell Kaelyn that they'd reschedule the playdate. In retrospect, Khrista could understand perfectly why Kaelyn had stormed into Khrista's room and snatched the gift off Khrista's bureau. She had then bolted down the street, and when she returned, she told Khrista she had tossed the necklace into the sea.

That night, Khrista paced along the shore and waded into the waves, hoping to recover the precious gift and thinking Kaelyn wouldn't have been able to throw it too far in with her tiny arms.

She'd gone home empty-handed and distraught, with yet another negative mark to add to her parenting profile.

But she had never blamed Kaelyn. And now hearing Kaelyn blame herself after all these years pained Khrista.

"Mom, stop. You're agonizing when you're supposed to be celebrating. Open it up!"

Khrista fought off the tsunami of tears that threatened and did as told. She uncinched the ribbon and slipped her fingers into the pouch, gulping when she made contact with the familiar beads.

"Oh, Kaelyn. I don't even know what to say."

"Pull it out."

By now everyone had gathered around, eager to see what Khrista was blubbering over. She smiled at her soon-to-be stepdaughters and hoped they wouldn't deem her crazy after this night together.

But when Khrista finally pulled the necklace out of the bag, she couldn't hold back her tears anymore.

"Kaelyn!" Khrista gasped. "How did you? It's so—"

"You like it?"

Khrista studied the piece. It looked just the same as it had all those years ago, yet Kaelyn had made a modification that amplified the specialness factor. The seashells and the blue beads were the same, but she replaced the stretchy string that had once threaded them together with a strong silver chain. And hanging in the middle was a gorgeous pendant that matched the engagement ring

Matt had given her. The rolling wave with the glittery gemstones washed away any lingering pain and amplified the love in Khrista's heart.

She hugged it to her chest and studied her daughter's excited face.

"It's the most precious possession I'll ever own." She meant it, too. Khrista had never been big on jewels and material things. Until now.

"I thought maybe you'd want to wear it during your wedding. You don't have to, though!"

Khrista set the pouch down on the arm of the chair Kaelyn sat on and opened the clasp. "Help me put it on?"

Kaelyn assisted, and everyone gathered around to ooh and ahh over the masterpiece, and then the four daughters stumbled over themselves telling stories from their youth. Khrista was shocked by some of the antics Matt's girls confessed to. She had always assumed they'd been as flawless and patient and sweet as kids as they were as adults.

As the evening drew to an end and they all prepared to head out, Gabby cleared her throat and sat up straight. Aliyah and Nia ducked out of the room and came back with their hands behind their backs.

"Since Kaelyn's gift could be considered both something old *and* something new, we wanted to make sure you had something borrowed and something blue..."

"Open mine first," Nia rushed forward and withdrew a gift bag from behind her back.

"Oh, honey. You didn't have to!"

"We wanted to. Open it up."

Khrista did as told and found a small jewelry box. Through watery eyes, she looked at her new daughters and cocked her head. "You're all spoiling me."

The expectant and emotional looks on their faces had her wondering what she'd find. She opened the box and gasped at the gorgeous earrings. Glittery and glamorous and vintage.

"They're absolutely gorgeous!"

"We hope you don't feel offended, but they were our mother's. But first they were our paternal grandmother's. She gave them to our mother on her wedding day. They were our mom's favorite earrings in the world." Nia struggled to compose herself.

Aliyah rubbed her sister's back and added, "We know how much our mom would approve of you for our dad. We sort of feel like she found you and led you to him. So many things about you remind us of our mother. Maybe that's why we've adored you since before we met you in person."

Gabby's bright, bouncy energy entered the circle. "We've all said it from the minute we met you. How much our mom would love you. And how much it would mean to all of us to have you wear our mother's earrings as you marry our dad."

"We tried to decide if that was too weird," Nia said. "But we decided it wasn't weird for us, and we hope it won't be weird for you."

"But we totally understand if you don't want to. Honest," Aliyah said. "We just thought that since you're so full of sparkle, the earrings would be a natural extension."

"Girls," Khrista's words squeaked through a tightening throat, and she had to focus on her breathing to gather her wits. "I have never been more honored in my life. Not only to wear these earrings and to carry a bit of your mother with me—a woman who must have been amazing considering the family she raised—but also to have the three of you in my life and my heart."

Gabby jumped forward to hug Khrista, but before Khrista could hug the other girls, Aliyah lifted the bag she held up for Khrista's perusal.

"Before we dissolve into mushies, it's time for your 'something blue.'"

Khrista wasn't sure what the glint in Aliyah's eyes hinted at, but as soon as she pulled the piece of cloth out of the bag, it all became clear.

"Oh my word. How on Earth did you pull this one off?"

Khrista unfolded the muslin shawl and marveled at all the blue-painted handprints.

"They're the handprints of your preschoolers. It took some coordination, but we were finally able to get them all. I'm surprised none of them told you." Aliyah smirked as she told Khrista all about sneaking in during Khrista's lunch breaks for several days and how great Danielle was at helping them to coordinate. "I told one of the kids we had to keep it a secret, and he told me, 'Miss Khrista says we don't keep secrets, but it's okay to keep a surprise.' Schooled by a preschooler!"

Khrista threw her head back and guffawed. "I'm glad my teaching is sinking in. And apparently they're better at keeping quiet about a surprise than I would have given them credit for."

Khrista draped the shawl around her shoulders and wrapped it around her like a hug.

"This is so special. I was a bit worried about wearing my dress on the beach in the fall air, so this will help me stay a little warmer."

"That's what we thought, too. Your dress is gorgeous, but those short sleeves might make you too cold," Kaelyn said, hugging Khrista and then saying her goodbyes.

"Wait, do you have time for one more thing before you go?" Gabby asked.

Kaelyn nodded, though Khrista thought she looked a little too tired around the eyes.

Gabby ushered all the robed women out into the brisk night and down onto the beach. She instructed them to stand with their backs to the water as she set her camera up on a tripod she had carried out with them. Moments later she jumped into the group, remote in hand, and they giggled and played as if they were all young kids again while the camera's flash lit up the night and the girls lit up Khrista's life.

KHRISTA STOOD on the pavilion that would lead her to the sandy aisle and to the man waiting by the shore. The man who had helped her to grow and heal even when he didn't know she needed to do either. The man who had treated her with kindness, patience, and compassion. The man who opened his home and his heart and his family to welcome her in.

She intended to stay forever.

Khrista closed her eyes and lifted her face to the sun, absorbing the energy and letting it wash over her. Though she'd worried about being cold, Mother Nature had gifted her with a perfect, warm day.

"Everything okay, Mom?"

Khrista snapped her eyes open and watched as Kaelyn approached with baby Poppy in her arms. Kaelyn's green and blue plaid wool dress accentuated her bright red hair, slightly ruffled from the breeze.

"Of course, sweetie. I'm just waiting for your Grandma to get back. She had to use the bathroom again. Why don't you go on and sit down with Poppy? But first I need to see my little angel."

Khrista bent down to kiss the sleeping baby on the forehead.

"Just look at her bright hair. Same exact color as yours."

"I have to admit," Kaelyn began, stroking her daughter's hair with her free hand. "Even though I hated being a redhead, it's super beautiful on her."

"It's super beautiful on you, too. Always was."

"Eh, I don't know about that. But I do know that *you* look outstanding, Mom. Matt is going to *faint* when he sees you."

"Really? It's not too much? I feel overdressed."

Khrista ran a hand over the form-fitting gauzy material that covered the satin bodice. The flouncy sleeves and applique floral design made her feel fancy, but now that she was about to let everyone see her in something other than her usual jeans and t-shirt, she was practically paralyzed with doubt.

"Um, Mom? You're getting married. I think it's one of those times when it's actually impossible to be overdressed. But seriously, this dress is the perfect beach wedding gown. I wasn't sure about that shawl, to be honest, but the little handprints are so you, and it sort of pulls everything together." Kaelyn glanced over Khrista's shoulder. "Oh, there's Grandma. Guess it's time to get this show rolling."

"I'm too nervous to even think up a stupid ocean pun," Khrista lamented, her voice shaking and her palms sweating.

Kaelyn inhaled visibly and then, rolling her eyes, said, "Don't be so salty, Mom. You look *fin*-tastic. So-*fish*-ticated, even. Do I need to go on?"

Khrista snorted in laughter, which made Kaelyn erupt, too. The abruptness of their laughter startled Poppy awake, and she let out a loud cry to express her dissatisfaction.

"Yup, she's got the redheaded temper, just like her mom," Khrista teased. "Go sit, Kaelyn. I'll see you on my way across the beach."

Kaelyn wrinkled her forehead and scrunched her nose. "Um, no. You didn't think I was going to let you walk down the aisle without me, did you?"

Daisy fussed over Khrista's appearance, straightening a tendril of hair, adjusting the seashell necklace, and then repositioning the shawl.

"Yes, we know you didn't want to plan too much for your wedding, so we took it upon ourselves to add some special touches," Daisy said, her face serious but serene.

"What... kind of... special touches?"

"For one, I dressed Poppy in a floral gown and you're going to carry her down the aisle. She'll be your bouquet since you didn't want to order flowers."

Daisy nodded at Kaelyn's explanation. "Right. And though we know you and Matt opted not to have bridesmaids and groomsmen, we honored some requests..."

Before she could finish, four of Khrista's preschoolers bounded down the pavilion, each carrying baskets of seashells.

"Seashell children—you know, in place of flower girls. They came up with the idea themselves," Daisy insisted. "They're going to scatter shells along the way."

Khrista was once again rendered speechless. Too much love. Too much happiness. Too much wonderfulness.

She bent down and embraced all four children in a group hug, and then waved to the children's parents who stood a few yards away, smiling and taking pictures with their phones and blowing kisses her way.

"This will be the most magical wedding ever," Khrista said through her tears. "Shall we begin?"

Daisy and Kaelyn each looped an arm through Khrista's, and Khrista held Poppy facing outward. The baby stopped fussing, seemingly enjoying the pressure of Khrista's forearms on her belly.

"I know she can't see far yet, but it seems like she's happy to have a view of the beach," Kaelyn said. "At least she stopped crying. For the moment."

"Maybe she likes the ocean air on her cheeks. I know I do!" Khrista said.

"I wasn't sure about a wedding on the beach," Daisy quipped, "but you've got me convinced. Look how beautiful everyone and everything is. I love the tents Clarice set up over there."

"Yes, she insisted on a tea booth. Said we couldn't start off a marriage without tea."

"Sounds like Clarice," Kaelyn said, giggling.

"Okay, young ones," Daisy called out. "Time to lead the way."

The kids reached into their baskets and started half skipping, nearly running, and pausing sporadically to pick up things that caught their interest. Khrista laughed at their typical preschool behavior, though Daisy didn't seem amused at their lack of conformity to wedding etiquette. Of course, there had been no rehearsal and only simple explanations about what was expected of them, so Khrista thought they did amazingly well, considering.

Besides, she had never lived a life anyone would deem perfect. Or flawless. No, she was riddled with flaws and always would be. But Matt had worked hard to show her the beauty of imperfection.

As they got closer to the end of the aisle, everything else faded away and all she could do was lock eyes with her soon-to-be husband. The man she hadn't even known to dream about.

His eyes watered as she approached, so Khrista's did, too. She didn't wipe away the tears and didn't care if her mascara washed away. She wasn't one to wear makeup, anyway, but Kaelyn had suggested wearing a bit for photos.

Matt's daughters stood beside him, holding hands in solidarity and offering welcoming, loving, joyful smiles. Though Khrista and Matt had decided against having a wedding party, the girls had very much wanted to stand up with him and to show unity as they joined their families together.

When they made it to the front, Khrista kissed the top of Poppy's soft, sweet-smelling, peach-fuzzed head and handed her to her mama. Kaelyn brushed her own tears away and mouthed, "You are beautiful," and then leaned up to kiss Khrista on the cheek. She then stepped back with Poppy and took a spot next to where Khrista would soon stand.

Daisy gripped both of Khrista's hands, and Khrista leaned down slightly to rest her forehead against her mother's. They breathed the same air for a heartbeat of time, and then Daisy squeezed Khrista's hands before dropping one. "I'm so happy to witness you achieving your happy ending."

And then Daisy placed one of Khrista's hands into Matt's and officially gave her blessing.

Rafael rushed over as Daisy swayed, putting a hand around her shoulder and leading her to a seat in the front row.

All of Khrista's attention turned to her groom.

"Ready to get this show on the road?" Gerard's grumpy voice demanded attention. He'd been the only person they could get to marry them on short notice after the person they had scheduled canceled because of a family emergency. Khrista turned toward Gerard and prayed she hadn't made a mistake in enlisting his help. He had held onto his Justice of the Peace certification, and though he hadn't performed a ceremony for years, he had obliged after Nia had a talk with him. Nia never confided what her tactic had been and how she got Mr. McGrumpster to relent to their request, but in the end, it wouldn't matter. As long as the union was legal by the end of the afternoon.

"You opted to keep it short and sweet, so let's get to it."

There was nothing special about the vows—they hadn't written their own and Khrista barely registered what she was saying, simply reciting them and memorizing the pride and love in every line on Matt's face. She, of course, knew she'd promised fidelity, loyalty, and honor, but those things had always belonged to Matt. She'd never betray him. She'd never give him a reason to doubt her or their love. She'd never be the reason he walked away.

And she'd never be tempted to shut him out. Not ever again.

They had come too far.

When Gerard begrudgingly mumbled that Matt could kiss the bride, Khrista tilted her head upward with an eagerness she'd never known. They'd kissed thousands of times, and each time had been special. But this was a kiss meant to seal their lives and their fate together.

She couldn't wait.

And yet, Matt hesitated.

A low murmur rumbled through the audience. What was the problem?

Was he...

*Changing his mind?*

"Khrista, don't look so alarmed," Matt said, and his voice was gruff and embarrassed. "I'm fumbling this badly, aren't I? It's just... one second, please."

He turned away from her.

He turned.

Away.

From her.

She stood there, feeling like someone had switched a spotlight on and pointed at her so no one would miss the confusion and terror that must have played across her face.

Khrista fiddled with the fabric near her thigh. What was he doing? He had turned toward Aliyah and there was some movement, but her eyes refused to focus. She was too scared to look at anyone or to see anything.

When he turned back, he held a furry surprise in his arms. Definitely not what she had expected.

"My wedding gift to you, my love. I figured it wouldn't be right to start our marriage and our lives together without your other man."

Khrista's mouth dropped open. Was this real life?

"Mr. Ed!"

Mr. Ed let out a loud yowl and fought to get out of Matt's uncertain grip. Khrista reached out to accept him, hugging him to her and feeling her heart expand, even though she had already thought it had reached capacity.

"Did you..."

"Adopt him? Yes. He's all yours. Ours. Gabby picked up everything we'll need to help him get settled into the house."

"This is the greatest surprise! Thank you so much, Matthew."

"I'll give you anything you ever want. There will never be a day when I won't want to elicit that smile from you. There will never be a day when you won't fill me with everything I'll ever need."

"Oh, Matt." She couldn't form words. Definitely none as beautiful as his.

He rescued her by swooping in to claim the "husband and wife" kiss, and everyone around them applauded.

For the next hour, the celebration was in full force. They all kicked off their shoes and danced in the sand. Children built sandcastles and no one worried about their nice clothes getting messy. Aliyah put Mr. Ed back into his carrier and brought him up to the tearoom because he continuously expressed his displeasure at being outside.

As they prepared to serve the platter of wedding scones Clarice had made, loud bleating interrupted the festivities.

They all turned to see what was going on.

Sure enough, several goats descended upon the group, running and jumping and chewing anything they could get their mouths on, including the hem of Geraldines's hot pink polka-dot dress.

Chaos erupted as two of the goats climbed onto the table and started devouring all the scones. Khrista laughed and turned to ask

Matt where the heck goats came from. Everyone around her speculated. The only goats on the small island belonged to the MacKenzie farm, and since the woman who owned the goats was in attendance because she was the mother of one of the seashell children, she quickly assured everyone that these particular goats didn't belong to her.

A brown and white goat slammed his front hooves on the table next to where Gerard sat. The animal pulled at Gerard's sleeve, earning scathing looks and threats of making the goat dinner from the old man.

Clarice, uncharacteristically still and ashen, as if she had seen a ghost, quickly sprung into action when she heard Gerard's threat.

"You'll do no such thing," she snapped, and Khrista twisted her brain in knots, trying to remember a time when Clarice had ever snapped at anyone.

Clarice shooed the goats away from the food, bending down to pet a small one with the tiniest features. The goat nuzzled against Clarice as if loving the attention. While the little guy transfixed Clarice, several people chased the goats off, and they disappeared as quickly as they had appeared.

As if just noticing that his brethren had made their getaway, the little goat pulled away from Clarice's tender touch and bolted away.

"I hope he catches up to them," Khrista said, offering a hand to help Clarice up.

Clarice ignored the proffered hand and continued to look like she had seen a ghost.

"Are you okay, Clarice?"

She shook her head slightly. A tear gathered in the corner of her eye. Clarice closed her eyes and turned away slightly, pressing three fingers to the spot between her eyes.

When she turned back to Khrista, she looked like herself again. But there was something there, curtained behind her calmness.

"I've seen a lot of weird stuff on this island," Khrista said, smiling as Matt came back to her side after helping to clean up the mess the goats had left. "But that takes the cake. Or the scones, as you have it."

Clarice didn't laugh. Didn't insert a tea pun. She slipped back into that withdrawn mood and gazed off in the distance as if searching for the goats or a long-lost part of herself.

"I'm sure there's a reasonable explanation for their sudden appearance." Khrista winced as she tried to fill in the strange silence. She shrugged at Matt's questioning gaze.

"I'm sure there is," Clarice said, still looking away and with the voice of a confused woman. "In fact, I know there is."

After the goat incident, they moved the party into the tearoom, where Clarice compiled an array of whatever baked goods she had on hand to replace the ones the goats had ruined. And though she smiled and seemed to engage in the festivities, Khrista sensed that something was still off with her.

She'd talk with her later. For now, it was time to say goodbye to everyone and allow her husband—*her husband!*—to whisk her away to their home. The home they'd now share.

That night, as Khrista realized the light of the full moon streamed into her new bedroom, she knew she'd never felt more at home.

***For insight into Clarice's weird goat reaction, sign up for Amanda's newsletter so you can be one of the first to hear when Clarice's story is released. (A prequel to this book.)

***To read an excerpt of the next book in the series, Old Castle Sparkle, turn the page :)

Thank you so much for reading. <3

**30**

_______

# OLD CASTLE SPARKLE EXCERPT

The manifestation of all Khrista's hopes and dreams, and the culmination of her hard work to overcome her emotional hurdles, clustered around a group of tables pushed together in the Happil-TEA Ever After Tea Room. Sunday morning brunches had cemented themselves as tradition, and Clarice, the owner of the tearoom and motherly friend to all in town, had been generous in reserving the library room for the gathering each week.

"I saved you both seats over here," Khrista's mother, Daisy, declared, gesturing wildly for Khrista to come and sit.

Still holding hands, the newlyweds accepted the invitation, stopping to kiss each of their girls on the way over.

Matt's daughters had welcomed Khrista into their family and expressed gratitude over finally getting to meet her after three years of hearing their father gush about how wonderful she was. Aliyah, Nia, and Gabby, ages thirty, thirty-two, and twenty-six, quickly nestled their way into Khrista's soul. Though they were all full-grown women, whenever their father spoke of them—which was often—his eyes lit up as any outstanding father's should. Those girls had him wrapped around their proverbial fingers, and it made Khrista proud to have won the love of a man so devoted to his daughters.

Matt had welcomed Kaelyn, Khrista's only child, as freely as Khrista had his daughters. And now that Kaelyn had made Khrista and Matt grandparents, the amount of love filling Khrista threatened to suffocate her. But she'd go down smiling.

Khrista bent to kiss Kaelyn on the cheek, telling her to stay seated as she nursed her newborn.

"Sorry, we were running a little late. I accept full responsibility," Khrista said.

"Don't worry, we all know Matt would never be late without your influence." Kaelyn winked to soften the blow, and they all burst into laughter at the idea of Matt willingly being tardy.

"Sit. Try this special blend Clarice brought over." Rafael, Khrista's surrogate father figure and landlord before her marriage, and now companion to Khrista's mother, Daisy, reached forward to grab the teakettle. He poured a cup for Khrista and then for Matt.

Khrista brought the steaming cup to her nose to inhale the sweet scent. "Mint? And chocolate?"

Daisy sipped hers with an exaggerated look of ecstasy on her lined face. "It's a mint chocolate chai. You won't believe how delicious it is."

"Oh, I'll believe it. Remember, Clarice's tea has spoiled me for over twenty years. Nothing compares."

Aliyah leaned forward as she joined the conversation. "I wish my new hometown wasn't so far away. I miss having Ms. Clarice's tea every day. Maybe we can talk her into moving the shop over to my area. I think she'd love starting over in Massachusetts."

In unison, her stunned tablemates turned toward her with mouths agape and shouted, "No!"

Clarice entered and raised her eyebrows at the sudden objections. Carrying a tray of pastries, she looked from face-to-face as if trying to piece together the source of the argument.

"What on earth is going on in here?" she demanded.

Khrista struggled to suppress her urge to giggle. "Aliyah just had the crazy notion of trying to steal you from us. She wants you to open a tearoom in her town, but I think a better option would be for her to just move right back here to Old Castle."

"I concur," Matt interjected

"Believe me," Aliyah replied, "if I could have stayed on the island, I would've. The housing market here is terrible."

"I've always said you were welcome to live at home for as long as you wanted to." Matt placed an arm around his daughter's shoulders.

"Daddy, I'm thirty years old. It was time for me to go out on my own. How am I ever going to find a man if I'm living with the most perfect one already?"

"Good one!" Khrista said. "But you know he had a plan to make a row of tiny cottages on his property for all of his girls to live with him forevermore."

"I don't see any problem with that plan." Matt shrugged and reached for his tea.

"There should be a rule that our favorite people aren't allowed to leave the island." Clarice lowered the tray of pastries in the center of the table for everyone to serve themselves. "I'll leave this right here. You all let me know if you need anything else. How's the chai?"

Nia raised her mug and grinned. She had such a glowing smile, and Khrista couldn't keep herself from grinning as she watched her stepdaughter. "Exquisite. Perhaps your best ever."

Murmurs of agreement followed Nia's declaration, and Clarice bowed her head and accepted the praise. She then left the room, and the group members conversed with those sitting near them.

"Is it me or does Clarice not seem herself today?" Khrista asked Daisy and Matt. "She's her usual cheerful self, but she seems, I don't know, maybe more tired than usual? Maybe a little blue?"

Matt reached for the creamer. "Seemed fine to me."

Soon Matt and Raf were talking about the Jeep Raf was rebuilding in his downtime. Daisy tapped Khrista on the arm and leaned closer, turning her body slightly as if about to confide a deep secret.

Would her mother finally confess that something was going on—

something more than friendship—between her and Rafael? They were always together, making eyes at one another. Daisy had taken to bursting into random bouts of youthful giggles every time Raf said something even remotely humorous, and though Khrista had never seen Raf blush in all the years she had known him, his red cheeks had become a common occurrence whenever he was around Khrista's mom.

It thrilled Khrista that, after decades of abuse in a horrible marriage, Daisy would have a second chance at finding love. And though Raf was a widower who had adored his wife, he deserved another chance, too.

"I've been wanting to talk to you about Clarice."

Alarm gathered in a spiky ball in Khrista's gut. Definitely not the secretive topic she had expected. Was her mother about to put Khrista in a precarious middle-man position?

Her mother had been working in the tearoom to thank Clarice for letting her stay in a room upstairs, since finding an apartment had become so challenging. Raf offered to set her up in the apartment Khrista had vacated, but Daisy didn't want to rely on a man again. Due to her arrangement, Daisy had better access to anything happening in Clarice's life than Khrista did, though Clarice had been a close friend for years. Family, really. She'd been a maternal figure during all the years of Khrista's estrangement from her mother.

"I overheard something..."

Khrista held up a hand. "Wait, Mom. We don't do rumors here. Anything you heard about Clarice is her story to share. She'll tell me when she's ready."

Khrista reached for a muffin and picked up her butter knife to slice it in half so she could apply Clarice's legendary brown sugar butter.

"It's nothing like that. I'm not being a busybody."

Daisy's hushed tone told a different story. Khrista resisted the urge to roll her eyes, but it was a struggle.

"I wandered into a part of the house I shouldn't have—I was looking for where she keeps the towels. The third floor had a door that was ajar, so I opened it and noticed buckets catching water. She has a leaky roof, and it looks like it's been that way for a while."

Khrista frowned. "Did you ask her about it?"

"I did. I asked her right away, and she got embarrassed and seemed troubled that I knew. Every time I bring it up, she changes the subject. I overheard her talking on the phone to one of the rescues she works with and telling them she may have to turn away some new litters of kittens they planned to send her. I'm sure it's because she's saving to fix the roof. I know she's trying to handle things on her own, but there must be something we can do."

Khrista munched on her muffin, no longer tasting the sugar.

Daisy sighed and twisted a napkin in her hand. "I've been racking my brain trying to think of something we could do. Do you think she'd be offended if I offered her money? She does so much for all of us, and—"

"No, don't offer her money. I guarantee she wouldn't like that."

Clarice had been there for Khrista in every way possible, and if there was trouble now, Khrista needed to help her. She'd have to tread lightly, though, as Clarice prided herself on her self-sufficiency.

The rising tone of the conversations at the table drowned out Khrista and Daisy's attempts at quiet contemplation. Oliver, Khrista's son-in-law, had the table in an uproar of hilarity with what he called "anti-jokes." Khrista didn't quite get what they were about, but the laughter at the table helped set her at ease and reminded her that this was a strong community, and Clarice was the matriarch of it all.

When Matt turned his attention back to Khrista, she told him what Daisy had confided.

Concerned, Matt folded his napkin and tucked it under his plate as he pushed his chair back and stood. "I'll take a look. I can probably patch it up temporarily, at least."

Khrista tugged on his sleeve. "No, sit back down. We can't let her know we know. That would shatter her pride. We need to think this through."

As Khrista's gaze drifted across the faces of the people she loved most in the world, an idea struck her.

Khrista could throw together a fundraiser. A tea cocktail extravaganza right there in the tearoom. The beach would have been an ideal setting, but Khrista didn't dare push it off until spring or summer, and though the winter had been mild so far, it was hard to trust a New England winter.

Unable to keep her excitement at bay, Khrista turned to Daisy. Her flash of brilliance tumbled off her tongue almost as fast as the thoughts formed.

Daisy hesitated, her eyes darting around the room as she averted Khrista's gaze.

Matt put a hand on Khrista's upper back between her shoulder blades and stroked. She sensed his hesitation, and Khrista knew what he was thinking without him having to say a word.

Khrista shifted in her seat so she could face her husband—how strange that sounded in her head still—and let the joy of her idea show on her face. He'd see it. He'd get it. He'd support her once he knew she could handle the exposure to alcohol, despite her history.

Alcohol wasn't even tempting anymore.

Matt rubbed his eyebrow as he stared at her, and she assumed the gentle way he cupped her shoulder was meant to reassure her.

"Honey, it will be fine. I obviously won't drink any of the alcohol, but I'm best qualified to determine what alcohol would go with what tea, am I not? I'll put together a committee for taste testing, and I'll take the notes. You know the people on the island love a good cocktail, and Clarice has talked for years about creating cocktail blends with her tea. We can make a big event of it. A band on the beach, a great seafood buffet, and we can charge admission. All proceeds will go to Clarice's cat rescue—she can spend it in whatever way she deems most appropriate. It's a cause the entire island will gather around to support. I'm sure people will come from off-island to support it if we market it correctly." Khrista lowered her voice. "And we won't mention the roof thing, but with an infusion of cash, she can shift things in her budget to take care of it."

Kaelyn tuned into the conversation and bounced in her chair at the mention of a fundraiser. "I can help with the marketing. I can do the graphic design work and advertising."

"Perfect." Khrista clapped her hands. "See? It's already coming along perfectly."

The idea developed as word buzzed around the table. Soon enough, everyone took part in the brainstorming session.

Gabby smiled big and leaned forward to offer her input. "I'll volunteer my time to sing. Dad, you can play guitar. I might be able to get my band members to volunteer, too, but even if it's just the two of us, I think we could pull off something pretty special."

"Wonderful, Gabby. Thank you!" Khrista's entire body tingled with excitement and gratitude. How lucky was she to be surrounded by so many kind, generous souls? Though almost no one knew why Khrista suddenly started planning a fundraiser, they all dove in without question and with zero hesitation.

And though her family was right to worry about Khrista as she continued to recover from her deep dive into the bottle, there was no temptation strong enough to make her mess this up.

Her world had flipped into constant sunshine and rainbows, and though she loved a magnificent storm, Khrista had no desire to cause one.

***

Continue the journey with Old Castle Sparkle <3

# ACKNOWLEDGMENTS

Writing this book in this genre has been a dream come true for me. Thank you to you, the reader, for allowing these characters and this story to live a life outside of my imagination.

I have so many people to thank for helping me to bring this baby to the world.

To Stacy Juba—thank you for the invaluable editorial feedback. You helped me shape the story into something shinier. (And saved poor Khrista from more mayhem than she needed!)

To my talented cover designer, Jaycee DeLorenzo of Sweet 'N Spicy Designs—thank you for bringing my series visions to life and for giving me gorgeous covers I can show off!

To my amazing beta readers—Kari Fitzmaurice, Karen Desmarais, Stacy Christopher, and Kathy DiSanto—THANK YOU for helping me to pick up on those pesky errors that slip through and for the fantastic feedback, most of which was, thankfully, positive. :) You gave me the confidence to move forward with this story, and I appreciate your time and interest more than I can say here.

To my wonderful friends, especially Alison Konicki, Vicki Mazzola, Maureen Ostrowski, and Jena Root, who put up with me going into hermit mode even more than normal to get this series done. I appreciate your love and support so much. I also appreciate all the encouragement and the laughter (and from Jena, the TikToks!)

To my fabulous MDGAs—Melissa Chambers, Christine DePetrillo, and Amy Knupp—you three are truly my author besties, the three women who have been my fiercest supporters over the past year—I am so thankful for you! I love that we can be there for one another during the highs and the lows of this crazy author life. Counting down the days until our next retreat, even though it's not even booked yet! Love your energy, ladies. Love YOU! Green hearts all around.

And of course, I'm forever grateful to my family for all the love and drama-free living. You all believe in me even when I struggle to believe in myself, and any success I achieve will always be because of and for you. I love you.

# AFTERWORD

If you or anyone you know struggles with alcohol consumption, please reach out for help. One good resource is SAMHSA. Always know you're not alone.

# ABOUT THE AUTHOR

Amanda Daire loves spending time with her adult children and her real-life hero. If she had to pick a few of her favorite things, they'd be trees, elephants, castles, tea, and traveling.

Amanda loves to write about complicated family dynamics, flawed characters who could be your friends, and healing hearts. But no matter how emotional the story may be, she prides herself on ending in the most uplifting way possible and maintaining hope through any hardship. She is a USA Today Best-selling author of romance under a different name.

Know what else she loves? Connecting with readers! So please sign up for her newsletter and find her on social media to stay in touch!

facebook.com/amandadairebooks
instagram.com/amandadairebooks
tiktok.com/@amandadaire
goodreads.com/amandadaire

# ALSO BY AMANDA DAIRE

Old Castle Secrets

Old Castle Sparkle

Old Castle Road Trip

Old Castle Rumors

Old Castle Courage